Emails from Jennifer Cooper

Robert Scott

To Tammi —
I hope you Enjoy Jennifer's
Tale.
R

Tammi —
You have wonderful
taste in books!
Joan :)

Rob Scott Books

www.robscottbooks.com

ISBN - 13: 978-0692387559

ISBN - 10: 0692387552

www.robscottbooks.com

Cover & web design by Kyle Pratt at www.tubbypratt.com.

Author photo by Sam Scott.

Lyrics from "Here Comes My Man" used courtesy of Universal Music Group.

For Peg Race, Virginia Noble, and Joan Vohl-Hamilton
with all the gratitude I can muster,
however late.

'How much time do you think that we have?
If I wanted to, I could start over again.'

--The Gaslight Anthem

'As for you, my galvanized friend, you want a heart. You don't know
how lucky you are not to have one. Hearts will never be practical until
they can be made unbreakable.'
'But I still want one.'

--*The Wizard of Oz*

Introduction

'Okay, William . . . Don't foul this up.'

Here's how I remember it . . .

April 7, 1991 – Day 1

William Klein, Billy to his friends and teammates, tucked the paperback into the side pocket of his cargo khakis. He'd finish the paper later, assuming he failed to make a connection with the redhead from the bleachers. If they surprised one another and discovered they had some chemistry, the night might get downright productive. If so, he'd worry about Ernest Hemingway and fly fishing and indecipherable naps and half-fallen-cedar-tree metaphors later, tomorrow, or never.

Screw Hemingway, anyway.

If the old bastard had gotten his act together, he'd never have shot himself. Besides, with the weekend road trip to Syracuse on the schedule, Billy would have ample time to work through Papa's 'iceberg theory' on the bus.

He fixed his hair in the mirror beside the bouncers' worn rostrum, leaned in and grinned to check for bits of leftover lunch. He'd brushed his teeth and gargled with a mouthful of Pete's Listerine, but one couldn't be too sure when dealing with the resilient string beans served cafeteria style in Monmouth Hall. Those suckers could hold the space shuttle together. Perhaps they did.

Billy descended dilapidated wooden stairs to the Ratskeller's mezzanine. *Every step's a gamble*, Pete's voice reminded him. *Don't fall and break your ass, especially if she's already there, dipshit.*

He paused three steps from the bottom, surveyed the early crowd of twenty-five or so Rutgers University students, didn't see her. Maybe she wouldn't show up. Maybe she'd misunderstood his non-verbal invitation, mouthed awkwardly from the patch of worn dirt near second base: *Ratskeller later?*

Nah, she'd understood. She nodded, even mouthed back: *Okay, bye.*

She'd be here.

In a red hat.

'Hey Billy!' Sondra Whatshername, Joey Carlton's girlfriend, waved from the bar. 'Congratulations on the win today!'

'Thanks,' he called back, 'but I didn't do anything.'

Sondra shrugged, didn't give a damn.

'I'll try harder this weekend,' he descended the steps, started for the bar. Billy wanted to ask if Sondra'd seen a tall, skinny redhead in a tired RU baseball hat with *#27* scrawled in indelible ink beneath the brim, then thought better of it. While only a thin crowd of drinkers hung around the Ratskeller now, it would thicken to human paste before too many songs played on the jukebox. There was no sense having every teammate, booster, girlfriend, and cleat chaser in the place knowing he'd been stood up by a girl who'd stolen his hat.

Woman. Sorry.

Instead, Billy grabbed a handful of Chex Mix from a bowl on the bar. 'Hey, Sondra . . . where's Joey?'

'Hey, baby,' she hugged him. 'He'll be here . . . had to get a paper handed in to Professor Howard before you guys take off for the weekend, something about Hemingway. He's on his way over. You wanna beer?'

'Um . . . yeah, no . . . well, maybe,' he looked around again, didn't find her. 'Just gimme a second. I'll let you know.'

'Whatever, baby,' Sondra filled her glass from a pitcher of nearly translucent keg brew. 'We'll be right here until the paramedics arrive.'

'Thanks, I just gotta take a look downstairs for someone.'

'You got a girlfriend, Billy Klein? Finally?'

His face reddened; he was glad for the near darkness, just a splash of candlelight here and there along the bar. 'Nah . . . you know: my Aunt Mae's in from Memphis, and she's got a bit of a crush on Captain Morgan. I'm sure she's been downstairs since they opened this morning, guzzling rum. Lemme get her to the hospital; then I'll be back to dust a few off with you and Joey. I think Pete's coming over, too, with that new girl from Merrill Hall, the one from California . . . *woman*, sorry.'

Sondra didn't care, and didn't bite. 'Bullshit, William Klein. You've got a girl stashed here somewhere.'

'Nope, now, I –'

'Where is she?'

'I dunno if she's even showing up,' he admitted. 'I'm gonna run downstairs and see if maybe she's there.'

'In the dungeon?'

'Shit, I dunno,' he shrugged. 'I think Blue Planet's playing down there later. Maybe she wants a good seat.'

Tipsy, Sondra hugged him again. 'Good luck, baby. And bring her up, if she's, you know, not a howler.'

Billy shook his head; his cheeks flushed anew. 'Not a chance. See you.' He turned toward the back stairs, a violation of about thirty-seven Middlesex County fire codes. Someone in the Board of County Supervisor's Office was either an alcoholic who enjoyed drinking for free, or an extortionist with a greasy palm. Were a fire ever to break out in the Ratskeller, upwards of two hundred people might be roasted alive in the murky sub-basement known affectionately as *The Dungeon*.

Billy sidled through the crowd. He'd not accepted a beer from Sondra, didn't want his opening salvo with the redhead to smell like Busch Light. Now, descending yet another set of venerable wooden steps, he wished he'd gulped a few bracing swallows. His nerves seemed to wake as one, and he felt an unexpected need to pee. Sweat beaded on his forehead; he ducked into a convenient shadow to drag a sleeve across his face. Even his feet felt awkward, crammed into too-tight loafers. He chided himself for not wearing flip flops, but open-toed shoes in this place could result in a flesh-eating infection in a hurry.

From the mezzanine, Sondra called, 'Hey, Billy!' Backlit by track lighting, her face lay in shadow.

'What's up?' he called.

'You look yummy, just so you know.'

'Thanks. See you soon.'

'No rush.'

Again, Billy paused three steps from the mildewed concrete floor. Compared with the dungeon before him, the mezzanine bar at the Ratskeller was a brightly-lit, commodious establishment akin to a café in the Four Seasons. Down here, horny students guzzled cheap beer and Jägermeister. They groped to garage bands, sweated like farm animals, and stacked bones in charnel recesses in the wall. Legend had it that two graduates from the class of 1967 came down here for one last drink, passed away, and were buried behind the bar. No one noticed for twelve years that they'd even gone missing. Billy, like eighteen thousand of his closest friends and classmates, loved the place.

There she was.

At the far end of the bar, just off the raised stage where Blue Planet would offer up noisy grunge covers until the Middlesex County Sherriff's Office pulled the plug, the redhead sat beneath a bad portrait of either James Joyce or John Lennon. Billy hadn't realized how closely they resembled one another until just that moment. Lit only by a pair of candles in smudged highball glasses, she picked through a bowl of Chex Mix, rooting around for something specific, probably those little pretzel squares.

And she wore his hat.

'Okay, William,' he exhaled slowly, braced himself. 'Don't foul this up.'

From the stage, a lean, mop-haired rock star in a torn T-shirt and hemp necklace, watched, bored, as the good-looking student – he might have been an athlete, tall and wiry, like a baseball player – approached the cute redhead sitting alone at the bar. The rocker had noticed her when he brought the first load of amplifiers down from the van. She'd been there a while, alone and nursing beers. Sort-of sexy in that red baseball hat, she was going to be the one face he saw tonight in the mass of gyrating, incoherent, anonymous revelers. He'd play the entire show to her alone.

Maybe.

Now that Mickey Mantle'd shown up and taken the seat beside her, Richie Teasdale might decide to choose another good looking coed, another face in the crowd as tonight's lucky winner.

He watched like a voyeur as the redhead reached over and touched Mickey Mantle's forearm. She gave it a little squeeze, then tossed her head back and laughed out loud. Yeah, he'd have to find another target tonight. Too bad.

August 18, 1992 – Day 499

On the same stools, in the same corner of the same pleasantly unpleasant sub-basement of New Brunswick, New Jersey's Ratskeller, Jennifer Cooper and Billy Klein shared a pitcher of the same watery Busch Light beer. At $7.50 a half gallon, it ranked among the better deals available for miles in any direction. But it tasted like squirrel piss.

Billy grabbed a handful of Chex Mix from a wooden bowl. Somewhere, Ratskeller staff shoveled hundreds of tons of the stuff, like firemen on a steam locomotive.

Jennifer picked through the same bowl, hunting for miniature pretzels. She grabbed his wrist playfully, forced his fingers open. 'Gimme those,' she stole two from his stash.

'Hey, I like 'em, too.'

'My needs first, big guy,' she sipped beer. 'You wanna stay for Blue Planet? I like their singer, whatshisname, Teasdale, Taserdole, something like that. He's good.'

'Yeah.' Distracted, Billy didn't care. 'They're all right. I saw them at the Deke semi-formal last month. They've been together for a coupla years, pretty tight.'

'Let's stay.' Jennifer sensed his discomfort. 'We'll just park ourselves here forever. These two candles will never die, like that, you know –'

'Hanukah –'

'That's it! The Maccabees or whoever. Right? We'll live by the light of our Maccabean candles –'

Billy tilted the bowl, checked their supply lines. 'And we'll live on dry, salty cereal, which will never run out.'

'Loaves and fishes,' she said.

'Old *and* New Testament miracles reminding us we need to stay together,' Billy said. 'It's a sign from above.'

'We'll just stay here and talk and . . .' she frowned at the floor, '. . . make love . . . somewhere . . . and grow old and only ever be together and die at ninety-two on this spot –'

'Like those two guys from the class of '67.'

'Yes!' she laughed. 'They'll bury us here, and we'll become the stuff of Rutgers University legend!'

Billy traced silk-thin lines tugging at the corner of her eye. 'I love you.'

'But . . .' Dense, unspoken tension nestled between them.

'But . . .' Billy hesitated, considered his options. 'But I'm going to Chicago, and you're staying here. And I'll be working sixteen-hour days, and you've got senior year to look forward to. And I love you, and I'm coming back here next May, before your graduation, and I'm going to ask you to marry me –'

'Ask me now.' She cut him off.

'What?' he started. 'Wait . . . what?'

'Ask me now, knucklehead.' She cocked an eyebrow, 'I double-dog dare you.'

'No . . . I can't . . . Jen, I'm not . . . no.'

'Why not?' she pressed. 'You wanna go to Chicago and fall in love with some skirt?'

'Jesus, no.'

'So what's the problem?' She gulped beer, snorted indecorously, then wiped her chin on her shirtsleeve. Belching open-mouthed, she asked again, 'Huh? What's the problem?'

'Pig.'

'That's sexy, irresistible, pig to you, Mr. Klein.'

'Yeah, still a pig,' he tried kicking the conversation someplace safe.

'Marry me,' she stopped, realized that she meant it, then stared at him in stunned silence. Her hands shook. 'Yes, Billy Klein, marry me.'

'In ten months,' he said. 'Enjoy yourself. Have the senior year you dreamed about. Go away for spring break. Drink in the Deke basement. Party with the Scoutmaster. Live loud and reckless; then sober up sometime around May. I'll be back for you.'

'No, Billy,' she said, 'I'm not going to . . . any of that. C'mon, you know me better.'

On the Ratskeller's small stage, Richie Teasdale, lead singer for Blue Planet, placed two guitar cases behind a stack of ominous-looking amplifiers. He glanced at Jennifer, made eye contact for just a second, then looked away.

'Promise me,' Billy pressed, 'that you'll have fun. Enjoy your year. Don't wait around for me while everyone else parties.'

'No.'

'Promise.'

'You promise that you'll be back?'

'Yes,' Billy sighed. 'Where else am I gonna go?'

'With a ring?'

'Sure,' he said, then added, 'unless you wanna pick it out. Then we'll go right after graduation. You don't even have to take off your robe.'

Jennifer leaned close, kissed him. 'You better come back.'

'I will,' he returned the kiss. 'You better be here.'

'I will.'

Yeah, that's about right.

Inbox

letterstobillyk@gmail.com

August

He drank that Piels with a cigarette, a Pall Mall or a Lucky Strike, and never knew that his future could be told in the ashes he flicked between his loafers, or the sudsy aftermath he let backwash into the bottom of the bottle.

August 25

Dear William Klein,

I'm writing in hopes of locating the William A. Klein (Billy to me) who graduated from Rutgers in 1992. If this isn't you, Billy, I apologize. Feel free to delete this.

    If this is you (and I think it is) . . . hello. It's Jennifer Teasdale. You knew me as Cooper way back when.

    I've been trying to find you. The alumni office won't release contact info, and our class page only has your mom's old address at her place by the lake. I heard she passed away a few years ago. I'm sorry. I wish I could have been there with you, but I didn't know. Kelly Brisbane (you'd remember her as Scoutmaster Kelly from Monmouth Hall) sent me a note about it, but I didn't get it until a couple of weeks after the funeral.

    Is this you, Billy? You don't have a Twitter account (that I can find), and you're not on Facebook. I don't know how that's possible today, but maybe you enjoy your privacy, or you're tired of hearing about other people's weight loss, paths to Jesus, vacations in Orlando, or frustrations with their job. Sorry, rambling a bit.

    Do you mind if I write from time to time? I've only been to Albany once, for a long weekend when my principal had some money to send me to a conference. I teach now, fourth grade. Well, off and on. If I'd known that's where you lived, I might've looked you up. But you're hard to find, if this is you. Sorry, I'll stop saying that. And I'll stop apologizing. And I'll try to avoid beginning my sentences with a conjunction, but some habits die harder than others.

    And I'm rambling again. See? Another one.

    Write back when you can. Let me know how you're doing and what you're up to. I'm married . . . was married . . . for eighteen years. I suppose I still am married. We have some paperwork to sign before we can get this thing into its coffin and buried face down with a stake through its heart.

    I'm not writing because I'm getting divorced. God, imagine that: *Hi, how've you been? Great. I'm divorced and desperate now; how about I come find you! Albany's only three hours up the road.* Please don't worry. I just have a few things on my mind, bits and pieces that have bubbled to the surface in the past two years that I wish I'd known when we were in school.

And I swear I'm not always this awkward; I'm just nervous.

I'll shut up now. But I hope I've found you, Billy (thanks to Google). Please let me know how you're doing.

Sincerely,

Jennifer (Cooper) Teasdale

Oh, and feel free to dispense with the pleasantries. I will too. We knew one another a while back, even in dog years, but we knew one another well.

I'm good with that.

Jennifer

Oh, also . . .

My dad asks about you. He does it on the sly, when Richard, my husband, isn't around. It's amusing that the man I'm leaving because of stunts he pulls on the sly reminds me so much of my father, who invented doing shit on the sly and only asks about you on the sly. And that's the last time I'll use that phrase, ever.

I swear I'm signing off now. If this gets any more awkward, I'll have to kill myself, and you won't have a chance to reconnect with a forty-three-year-old, nearly-divorced, post-traumatic, mother of three who teaches school, cuts her own lawn, and jogs four times a week to burn calories in Cabernet Sauvignon. Who wouldn't want that?

But I love watching my sons play baseball. That's got to count for something.

Bye,

Jennifer (In case you missed the last two.)

Oh, and yes: I married a man named Dick. It's just more evidence that God hates me.

August 28

Dear Billy,

I'm going to dive in. There's no point mitigating the experience. Right?
I want to start with my father. Much of what makes sense, now that life
has dragged me over a few miles of dirt road, relates to Dad. Stick with
me; this'll come into focus soon. Yet please don't think I have 'Daddy'
issues . . . unless periodically getting angry enough to kick the shit out
of him counts. If so, then I have at least one 'Daddy' issue.

Keep in mind that my grandmother, Dad's mother, drank. I don't
know why, didn't know her.

    My grandfather left, broke her heart. So my grandmother drank
and smoked Chesterfields with the silver hairs from St. Christopher's as
if Sir Walter Raleigh had her on his delivery manifest.

    My father didn't stand a chance.

    I'll write *that* again, because that bit feels crucial: My father
didn't stand a chance.

    He worked at a grocery store, nights, and slept through high
school classes during the day. They needed the money, had to make
rent.

    It got him an eight percent in Geometry and a GED two years
later.

    Dad had his first beer, a Piels, on a June afternoon in 1956,
used the fender of a friend's '49 Ford to open the bottle. He fumbled it
a couple of times, didn't want the others to see him awkward, or to
realize it was his first.

    Beer Number One had its own personality. It made an
impression on my father. Little else had prior to June, 1956. He'd never
heard of General Ho Chi Minh, couldn't find Korea on a map with
both hands, hadn't seen a marijuana joint, heard a Langston Hughes
poem, or read any Allen Ginsburg. China and Japan were the same;
blacks were coloreds or moulignons. Italians were dagoes, wops, or
guineas. Puerto Ricans were spics, and the Irish were mics who went to
Mass, drank water with their Scotch, and communicated better with
their fists than with their feelings. General Eisenhower told the truth.
The news media would never spin a story, and Mickey Mantle and Joe
DiMaggio's reign as childhood heroes could only be threatened by a

skinny, white singer from northern Mississippi who represented all that could come to those who worked, prayed, respected their elders, and banged waitresses, cheerleaders, and office girls with abandon - in exactly that order.

Planet Earth ran from the juncture of Broadway and Water Streets, on the river, out 52 to Orange Lake and down 9W to Storm King Mountain.

That's it.

There was no East Germany, no Czechoslovakia, no Cuba - outside the deli on Third Street - no Chairman Mao, no *Dien Bien Phu*, no hippies, no LSD, and no knowledge of American soldiers headed anywhere near that flyspeck of jungle on the South China Sea.

Beer Number One represented a significant first step on a blue collar kid's path toward the American Dream depicted in majestic images by John Ford and pursued by Gary Cooper, John Wayne, and Jimmy Stewart. Tyrone Power was a pussy; Rita Hayworth and Ingrid Bergman were prettier than Marilyn Monroe, and the Dodgers-Giants rivalry was the greatest conflict the United States had mustered since the Battle of Gettysburg.

He drank that Piels with a cigarette, a Pall Mall or a Lucky Strike, and never knew that his future could be told in the ashes he flicked between his loafers, or the sudsy aftermath he let backwash into the bottom of the bottle.

My father, a poorly educated, dropout, knucklehead, unsupervised teenager had no idea of the ghosts sneaking up on him that June afternoon as the waning sun painted the Hudson the color of autumn in Hell, and lightning bugs appeared in the shadows beneath the cottonwoods and the willows down where Broad Street spilled into the river.

He wasn't aware, hadn't been warned. But he was smart - smart enough to multiply three-digit numbers in his head, even after a few of those beers. (They got easier to crack open after two or three.) Yet he never had a prayer against the burgeoning reality that, even then, the booze would get its hooks into him.

And my grandmother drank.

My grandmother drank.

No one waited at home to caution my father that the nails and the beers would fasten their talons around his good Irish heart.

He didn't stand a chance.

He was a kid, nowhere near as prepared a kid, as protected a kid as I was thirty years later. It's not surprising that he fell.

And yet I blamed him.

And then I got hooked, too.

My grandmother drank; she probably blamed my grandfather.

I blame her for Dad.

I blame me for me, and in a roundabout way, for us, Billy.

I hope you're well. I think about you often, especially these past couple of years. I'll be back in touch soon.

Jennifer

Oh, and PS: I don't normally go around using foul language. With three sons, I try not to swear at all, actually made it a few days with a No Cursing resolution last January. But I need to be honest with you, and if that means ripping the Band-Aids off and taking a good long look at the scabby bits beneath, then I'm in. I'm too old to play make-believe with myself, so I won't play it with you either. I hope you'll forgive me a curse word here and there and maybe see the threads holding all of this together. They're hidden beneath the Band-Aids I've plastered on the last eighteen years of my life. Let's peel a few of them off.

September

Weekends meant roasting a pig, swilling keg beer, making out to Bruce Springsteen, and walking in uncut grass in Kmart flip flops and a bikini top.

September 2

Dear Billy,

This isn't going to work unless I tell you the truth. I'm sorry, but I've already lied to you. And I've got to clear it out of my head before I go on: I knew your mom had been sick, and I should've made it to the funeral. I didn't go, because my life had been in the toilet at the time, and I didn't want you to see me such a wreck. That's the level of selfish I'm trying to flush out of my bloodstream these days. Your mom (who was always great to me) passed away, and I skipped the funeral, because I was afraid you might find me fat, depressed, and ugly.

But I'm done lying to you. I promise.

Jennifer

September 3

Dear Billy,

I was offered a job today, a first grade class in a Title I school down in Freehold. I'm a teacher; I think I told you that.

Granted, with school starting this week, it's bad timing, but I want to accept it.

It's been three years since Homer was born and I left my job at Marlboro Elementary. I'd planned to go back sooner, with just one year away, but then the wheels came off my marriage, and now I'm trapped.

I sent a note to Richard yesterday, told him the news, and asked that we split the cost of Homer's daycare, so I can go back to teaching. I figured he'd be all for it. It's a chance for him to see me get back on my feet, make some money, maybe reduce the amount in alimony he's got to pay after the judge reviews our tax returns next April.

Nope. He won't give me another cent.

He's Homer's father. He was there the night Homer was conceived at our beach house down in Avalon. It's actually a good (albeit depressing) story; I might write it out for you one of these nights. But he won't help me get Homer into daycare, because that would mean giving in to me, agreeing to something I've requested.

Can't do that.

I'm going to wait to hear from my lawyer, the judge, Richard's lawyer, then my lawyer again. It'll take weeks. I'll have to turn down the job.

I hate this.

Jennifer

September 9

Dear Billy,

In 1986, I fell in love with the varsity quarterback, because I believed in Hollywood and Tom Cruise and happily ever after and sweat and muscles and honest dirt beneath fingernails and being swept off my feet.

If Marty McFly had found a way to transport us back to 1956, my quarterback would have dressed, acted, worked, fought, drank, defied authority, and chased women exactly like my father. His aspirations were for a newsprint-flat stomach, enviable biceps, perfect hair, a truck, a loyal dog in a red bandanna, and a Mastercraft speedboat to take me waterskiing on Shark River for the next twenty-five years. Weekends meant roasting a pig, swilling keg beer, making out to Bruce Springsteen, and walking in uncut grass in Kmart flip flops and a bikini top.

No one had a library card; no one dreamed of medical school.

My father hated every minute I spent down there with the river rats. You'll soon realize that his hypocrisy can be detected by satellites orbiting twenty miles up.

Dad would sit at home, smoking cigarettes and drinking Michelob. We didn't have air conditioning; New Jersey summers dripped polluted humidity as if the entire place had been draped with a wet comforter. He drank and sweat, filled my mother's kitchen with smoke and roasted peanut shells, and waited.

When I got home, we'd fight viciously until Mom leaned in to take a bullet for me. I'd go to bed after promising my empty room, the muggy night, even the lightning bugs just visible in the dark spaces beneath the dogwoods that I was getting out of there. And I'd never drink and I'd never say an unkind word to my mother, but I'd never come back, even if it meant living in a tarpaper cabin on Shark River with a varsity quarterback who might have been my father's twin in 1956.

Fourteen years later, my husband, Richard, masturbated to images of Brad Pitt in *Fight Club*. I don't hold that against him; half the planet masturbated to the same photos. What troubled me was his singular determination to become that character. Whether it was Brad or Edward Norton's horny, stoned, abundantly sexy ID, personified by those emaciated, 8-pack abdominal muscles, Richard decided to make that physical and emotional transformation his fundamental goal in life. If the number of discontent, disenfranchised, suburban mothers he was able to seduce is any indication, my husband succeeded handsomely in his efforts at change. His chrysalis was an ever-growing clutch of opulent homes, diaper-polished sports cars, and boats that would make the varsity quarterback's Mastercraft look like a birch bark canoe.

In 2007, he actually spent $150,000 on a forty-foot Chaparral he used to Vegas one of my girlfriends. Christ, how could she say 'no?'

It knocked her senseless.

Here came Brad: wiry, muscular, blonde, wash-and-wear hair, in cargo shorts dangling on the perky shelf of his chew-toy ass and a pack of Marlboro Lights dangerous in his shirt pocket. Hillary Clinton, Barbara Bush, hell, the Queen of England would have slept with him. My friend, Debbie, folded like a dishrag.

Mike, her husband, worked seventy hours a week in a dead-end sales job. He'd gained forty pounds since their wedding night, and while he promised her a magical life in a McMansion twice the size of her parents' house, the days alone, the wifing and mothering, the boredom, and the rich kids across the street – Richard & me – conspired against her. And Debbie crumbled.

She'd majored in something she'd never do for a living. Her college boyfriends, the ones who respected her intelligence, studied with her, even asked her opinion while wearing a dress shirt tucked into gabardine pants, those boys were gone. They'd taken seventy-hour-a-week jobs of their own, had gained forty pounds of their own, and had disappointed, discontent wives in McMansions of their own – feeling like failures as they baked multi-colored cupcakes for birthday parties at the daycare center.

Then Brad Pitt moved in.

Debbie loved boating.

With a forty-foot yacht in a slip down the shore, Richard claimed to love boating as well, but generally claimed it to the swell of Debbie's ass or the cleft between her tits ($6,200 at CentraState Hospital, not a bad deal).

He nailed her on the deck above the cabin.

I wonder how long he let her lay there, naked, sunbathing, waiting for him while he steered forty feet of penis metaphor and injured a shoulder patting himself on the back. I'm sure she was out of her bikini before they cleared the last of the channel buoys. She would have greased up with half a bottle of coconut oil, then lay back on one of *my* beach towels and enjoyed Barnegat Bay, the sun, the glorious reprieve from a life that hadn't turned out the way Jon Bon Jovi promised in all those songs she and Mike had groped to in the fraternity basement.

Nope, Debbie was in no hurry.

And Richard . . . he could have waited all afternoon, just letting the mental images flood his mind with the sun-streaked glory of another conquest, another boat, another shiny car, another motorcycle, another horny housewife on the run from her family for a few stolen hours of play pretend.

When he finally dropped the anchor, far enough offshore to preserve some privacy but close enough to feel indecent, old Debbie was just about ready to shed her skin in a noisy, sloppy orgasm that she had no idea already heralded the end of their relationship. She'd gone two days without eating, practiced sexy, come-hither poses, even used a mirror to work out the perfect degree of downturned, doe-eyed innocence, right before sucking him off like a clarinetist auditioning for the community orchestra.

Poor, stupid, sorry woman.

She's divorced now, living alone in a one-bedroom apartment out in Morristown. Alienated from her ex-husband and her kids, she's packed on twenty pounds of self-loathing in the process.

I want to call her, but I don't. I want to ask if that one afternoon, those few purloined hours were worth losing all of it, everything she had.

If so, that must have been one brain-melting, slam-bang squadron of orgasms.

But I doubt it.

And Jon Bon Jovi is a shameless liar, always has been.

Keep well,

Jennifer

September 10

Hi Billy,

I found a house that I love and can afford. I'll keep you posted.

Fingers crossed!

Shithead found one, too. It's a bachelor pad. We've spent the past few weeks amicably dividing up everything we own. It's been friendly, because he doesn't want anything more than a few of the paintings, his computer, and the office furniture.

Why?

Because he's going to fill his place with new stuff. New house, new girlfriends, new car . . . gotta have new stuff.

There are about sixty framed photos of our family on one wall in the living room. It's a large, open space that spans two floors (we only have upstairs rooms on one side of the house). I love that wall, all those photos like a living history of our time together as friends, lovers, and parents.

On his list of 'must haves,' Richard's asked for only two of them, pictures of him and the boys. I imagine he'll want to be able to put them away quickly in the event that *company* comes over in the evenings.

I don't mind. I've just got to find a house with room for fifty-eight framed photos, minus the shots with Richard. Those we'll hang in the bathroom . . . one good shit deserves another and all that!

Jennifer

September 12

Hey Billy,

I'm no angel.

I'll bitch and complain like an Olympic medalist, but I don't deserve more than a pinch or so of pity. This isn't about pity or shame or embarrassment or any of those sliding-continuum emotions that redline when I get frothed up over what someone else might think.

Nope. This is my story, such as it is, told in a scattering of snapshots, many of them with colors fading to black and white. Years boil down to phases, months to a few days, and days to a few seconds of moving picture memories embellished with all the lies I might tell myself to deaden the humiliation or the editorial license I might take to straighten my hair, fix the hole in my socks, or wipe the smeary shine off my forehead.

What the hell, everyone does it.

Except maybe Buddhists, but we don't see many of them at happy hour.

I drink too.

And smoke sometimes. Sorry, yes, I know they'll kill me.

I surprise myself, because I've had twenty thousand formative experiences that have left scars up and down my body, mind, and worldview.

Alcohol has buggered my life, my marriage, my wedding day, my high school and college graduations, forty-three years of vacations, birthday parties, first dates, second dates, last dates, Friday nights, Sunday afternoons, Thanksgiving dinners, Christmas Eves, Easter brunches, cross-country flights, even a few mundane trips to the grocery store. I've been embarrassed at school concerts, church picnics, graduation parties, work socials, job sites, community pools, movie theaters, airports, hotel lobbies, toy stores, clothing stores, book stores, and even the garage where old Mr. Carmen used to fix my car. I've been asked to escort my father from bars, restaurants, churches, amusement parks, college residence halls, tailgate parties, even Giants Stadium.

Giants Stadium, for Christ's sake!

I've seen him wreck his car, ride his snowmobile into a partially-frozen lake, punch a stranger, kiss a woman who looked like my sixth grade teacher and another who looked like that actor from

Young Frankenstein. I've seen him fire his service weapon at street lights, street signs, billboards, stray cats, stray deer, and even a family of wild turkeys too goddamned stupid to move away from the road – where he'd been operating a police cruiser under the influence of about $49 worth of Michelob.

One night in Spring Lake, he taught me how to vomit on demand – I am not making this up – a useful skill for those troublesome moments when you've just got to make room for more booze.

Fun, right?

Just a night out with Dad; what eleven-year-old daughter wouldn't enjoy that?

The trouble was that he conducted this lesson just off the wide portico steps of the old Essex & Sussex Hotel with a posh, summer cocktail party going on. Lovely.

I've seen him escorted home by a half-dozen police cars. President Bush came through the county once, en route to a golf outing in Short Hills, and even he didn't have a half-dozen police cars leading the way.

He spent fifty-five years of his life hovering around a .08 blood-alcohol level, and he was never, not once, ever held accountable for his behavior.

So anyway, who lives through that kind of shit and still drinks? How goddamned stupid can I be?

Apparently, fairly stupid.

I didn't drink much in high school, just a few of those river rat drafts my quarterback's older brothers and father slugged every weekend from Palm Sunday to the Super Bowl. I'd sip and burp and marvel at how much peeing I'd do after just a couple, but I didn't earn my first Beer Funnel merit badge until I moved into Monmouth Hall at Rutgers University in New Brunswick, NJ, home of the slate-gray cloud, the traffic jam, and the middle finger.

Most college students arrive on campus hoping to navigate life's pathway to a promising future. For those who arrived on the main campus in late-August, 1989, the only path out of that place lay along Route 18 or Interstate 287 – both of them diabolical arteries to nowhere fast.

But matriculate I did, and quite soon after unpacking my bags, I met the scoutmaster who would lead me through the harrowing requirements for my Beer Funnel merit badge. Scoutmaster Kelly, *Cappa di Tutti Cappi* of inebriate, North Jersey debutantes, had planned on following in her mother's footsteps and attending that snooty, Ivy League kindergarten just down the block. Her father, some investment banker or bond salesman, had an office on Wall Street, a seat on the Stock Exchange, and a British racing green, Jaguar convertible. What he didn't have was quite enough clout to convince the Board of Trustees at Princeton to pressure the Dean of Admissions to overlook Scoutmaster Kelly's 1.42 GPA at Bergen County's venerable, Sisters of the Perpetual Clitoris, or some New Testament thing.

In return, Scoutmaster Kelly turned down offers from Wellesley, Bucknell, Bowdoin, even Simmons, and signed on to slum for four years with New Jersey's great unwashed at Rutgers University. I think she arrived on campus about two hours before I did, but by the time I drove up, Scoutmaster Kelly had established the fact that she was in charge of the harrowing, daredevil stunts required to earn the Beer Funnel merit badge.

Now you might laugh at my use of 'harrowing' as an adjective, but when one of the tickets freshmen had to punch was to shotgun a beer on the fifty-yard line of the football stadium and cross into the end zone – all in fifteen seconds or less (guys had to do it in under twelve, the sexist bastards) – well, you might still laugh and accuse me of trying too hard to scaffold my memories into something special. Suppose I added that every time we failed to reach the end zone in less than fifteen seconds, we forfeited an article of clothing and a second *and* had to go back for another round, and another, and another until we were too drunk to run, too naked to care, or too busy vomiting to do much of either?

Harrowing. Perfect adjective.

Without boring you with war stories, those can come later, I'll try to impart just the facts.

Over four years (that's 208 weeks) at Rutgers, I consumed 2,496 twelve-ounce beers for a grand total of 299,520 calories of unnecessary carbohydrates and alcohol that I, in turn, burned off playing Frisbee football, alcoholic Twister, co-ed naked wrestling, and a game many of my sisters in Kappa Delta enjoyed, called 'Holocaust Dieting.'

Any nutritionist or exercise therapist will counsel clients to avoid excessive alcohol, not because of the risk of addiction, but rather because every 3,500 calories of unnecessary eating results in another pound of flesh one must plunger into the pair of jeans that used to fit when all we did was sip foamy suds before waterskiing for three hours.

And how much weight would 299,520 additional calories add to my ass and thighs? Only 85 pounds.

That's not so much.

Hang in there. It gets worse.

By senior year, Scoutmaster Kelly and I had modulated over to wine. We believed we were being classy, sniffing and slurping sixteen-ounce glasses of cold Riunite Lambrusco from plastic wine goblets we'd heisted from a Deke social that winter. But honestly, we moved to wine because we were tired of starving ourselves to stay thin, tired of beer burps and farts and quarts of urine threatening to ruin our pumps as we pissed out behind some shithead's crowded apartment.

Most of all, I was tired of needing four or five beers to coax a decent buzz into my temples and the base of my skull. Wine worked faster. I bought more of it for less money – a gallon of Riunite sometimes dropped as low as $6.99 in those days. And it tasted better than the dregs of some keg that had been left in the sun all afternoon.

I can read your mind: Wasn't Scoutmaster Kelly a Quadrazillionaire? Why drink donkey piss when she could afford to have hooch imported from the Medoc Valley?

Keep in mind, Kelly was slumming. We went to Wal-Mart for wine. Granted, we went in her Audi, and she wore twelve-thousand dollars in pearls over her KD sweatshirt, but it was Wal-Mart Riunite or nothing.

I don't stay in touch with Kelly much these days. Her Facebook photos look pretty good, though, not like someone still slurping from the Costco-sized bottle of chemically-aged grape juice. If she's still high today, twenty years later, she's clearly moved on to prescription dope and Perrier, because she looks terrific: thin, big tits, professional dye job, great teeth, clear skin.

Me, on the other hand, I've never been a quitter and am a strong advocate for going with what works.

In the years between my college graduation and 2014 (let's say 1080 weeks), I took part in drinking 4,320 liters of wine, most of it red. As a social drinker, I rarely polished off the entire bottle by myself. I'm not saying that never happened, but as a rule, I drank with at least one other partner, normally my husband Richard. Assuming we shared each bottle evenly – unlike so many other variables in our dysfunctional equation – I finished 8,640 individual glasses of wine for a grand total of 1,728,000 unnecessary calories, or 493 additional pounds I had to sweat out on the treadmill like that poor Greek bastard who has to push that rock uphill, all day, for eternity.

And in case you're wondering how much wine 4,320 liters amounts to, it's a surprising and versatile bucketful. For example, if former NBA star Shaquille O'Neal happened to be peeing, standing up in my guest bathroom, 4,320 liters would be enough to drown him, even at seven feet tall.

Or to go with a fun variation on that theme, if my former husband and would-be porn star happened to be driving my Honda Odyssey mini-van (the same van he bought for me when he bought himself a BMW M-class convertible) and we dumped 4,320 liters in the window . . . yeah . . . it'd drown him, too. And I thought I'd never need Algebra.

When did I quit?

I figure you're waiting for me to get to that punch line so this letter can wrap up with a decent arc, or at least an ellipse that's been run down by a beer truck.

I didn't.

I still drink. I have about eight ounces of decent Cabernet on my desk while I'm writing these notes.

Granted, it takes me longer to swim to the bottom of the bottle today than it did fifteen years ago, but I still get there. I read somewhere that drinking alone is one of the surest signs that you're an alcoholic. I don't let it bother me, though. Nah. If 8,640 glasses of wine aren't enough to convince me that I'm an alcoholic, then I probably should look into getting myself tested for a learning disability.

From time to time I made a passing gesture at the notion of quitting. Again, this wasn't because I was concerned that I'd become an alcoholic, and it wasn't because I feared I would eventually turn into my father – I did fear that; *do* fear that. Rather, the times I tried to quit were those periods in my marriage when Richard made it clear that he wasn't interested in being married to a fat woman, and that my ass or my hips or my thighs or my endearing little roll of flesh that I got from pregnancy and which today acts as the perfect lifeguard whenever I risk the wrong jeans or a skirt that fits but maybe fits a skinnier woman better . . . that any of those moving parts had ballooned just a step or two outside the regulation field of play.

He'd not touch me for days, and when he did, it would be to take a handful of whatever part of me he wanted shrunk. And I'd grind to a stop, embarrassment paralyzing me, flushing my face and flooding my brain with so much hot blood that I couldn't think to turn around and shout, 'I'm 43, shithead! I've had 3 kids. I'm not supposed to be the same size I was at the frigging senior prom!'

But I didn't, even with him standing there in running shorts, dripping sweat from a ten-miler he just had to sneak in while I made breakfast for the kids and folded his laundry.

I didn't tell him off. Instead, I quit drinking, for a little while anyway. And I bought packs of cigarettes, so I could smoke breakfast and lunch and bring my daily caloric intake down to about 900, enough to lose three pounds a week with exercise.

See? Even the funny chapters get humiliating when I tell the truth. But you've got to imagine the embarrassment of standing naked in my own bathroom and having my husband inspect my fat, my cellulite, as if he might offer some dealer $1000 less because my mileage is showing.

My bathroom.

There aren't many places a middle-aged woman can be naked and feel entirely safe. Perhaps that's because we live among snobs and sociopaths, determined to hang on to that 27 year-old body with bloody, 45 year-old fingernails. And I don't insist on too many things. I'll get to that list later, in another email. But I do insist on feeling entirely safe in my own home, particularly in my bathroom.

I know it's not much when you consider that Syria is bombing Jordan who's bombing Israel who's bombing . . . shit, I don't know . . . Hamas or North Carolina. But to me, being touched by the man I love is supposed to be sensual, erotic, exciting, at the very least loving or protective . . . every time.

Having him grasp the bottom swell of my ass and say, 'You trying to set a record or something?' would've been funny if he'd have kissed me and bent me over the sink for a quickie. But to frown and leave me standing there to look at myself in disgust, I felt helplessness, like steam from my shower, coat all my wrinkled, dimpled, private, softening parts. I dressed in the closet and didn't eat for three days. Sheer self-loathing kept me upright.

Yet I drank wine with him that night, glass number 7,112 or thereabouts.

And when we made love later – fucked, I guess (sorry) – he insisted I turn over, I'm sure, so we wouldn't have to look at one another.

In an instant of stark realization, I understood why women get lower back tattoos. Without one, it's just a movie screen back there. He can see anyone he wants projected on that soft expanse of post-partum canvas. So I think if I ever get a tramp stamp, I'm going with a full-color image of myself and Scoutmaster Kelly, chubby in our bikinis, chugging Riunite from a gallon jug on the hood of her Audi. That ought to soften things up.

Yours (for a while anyway),

Jennifer

September 19

Hi Billy,

Like most kids from Jersey, I didn't start driving until I was seventeen. Living fifteen minutes from the beach, I used to head out there all the time. Belmar, Ocean Grove, Bradley Beach, even Asbury Park were close enough that my friends and I could hit the beach after school, prowl the boardwalks for a couple of hours, and still be home in time for dinner and homework.

Before my eighteenth birthday, I discovered a ritual I never knew I needed. Periodically, I'd sneak out of bed, drive to Ocean Grove and park just off the beach. At 2:00 or 3:00 in the morning, the Neptune Police often had their hands full with troublemakers in town. No one created much work for them on Ocean Avenue after midnight.

I'd park, listen to a couple of my favorite songs, then jog down the beach and dive into the inky water. Winter, summer, autumn, it didn't matter. Some nights I'd be in the waves for an hour. Other nights I'd only be able to stand the cold for ten or twelve seconds.

Call it self-medication; call it a dunking; call it a baptism. I don't know. I needed it, and it worked. I'd hold my breath and let the maternal embrace of the North Atlantic wash away my understanding of my sins, my regrets, my father, my boyfriends, my bad grades, anything. The planet's greatest solvent went to work on me, and I drove home with my favorite cassette in the dashboard and my dramatic renewal of hope and faith ready to usher me on to new adventures.

Self-medication. Everyone does it. For years I used the ocean. I know it sounds odd, but the ocean at night is a vastly different animal from the tourist-spattered waves at midday. It's powerful and frightening and ambiguous and exhilarating. I was a kid who needed all my teen angst washed out to sea, and those waves did the job.

What utter irretrievable horseshit.

Just for grins, I tried it again a few weeks ago. My brother crashed on my couch after drinking too much in Belmar. He didn't want to drive home, so I took advantage of having him in the house and crept out at 2:30 am for a lonesome dunk in the deep black sea.

With the windows open, I cranked up the radio and like a heroine in a Springsteen anthem, I parked behind the dunes in Bradley Beach, stripped to my undies, and threw myself in.

It didn't work.

Being eighteen and needing a fresh baptism from Mother Nature every couple of months made sense twenty-five years ago. Now it all feels contrived, as if I was trying too hard to emulate a character in a Thomas Hardy novel. There are no fresh baptisms for forty-three-year-old mothers muscling through a nasty divorce. Not even the North Atlantic can scrub that shit off.

So I drink wine, and I occasionally mix it with a diphenhydramine, or when I can score some, a half Percocet. It works. Granted, it lacks the majestic beauty of a midnight swim in the Atlantic, but it knocks me senseless and I sleep through the night.

That counts for something.

Trust me on the late-night ocean, though. It's what my principal used to call a 'powerful formative experience.'

Jennifer

September 22

Dear Billy,

At the north end of Main Street, USA in Orlando's Walt Disney World, just in the shadow of Cinderella's castle, stands an 1890s-era, upright, honky-tonk piano where a gantry-thin musician plays mildewed oldies like 'A Bicycle Built for Two' and 'Sidewalks of New York.' He's been there for decades – I am not making this up – improvising the same tired glissandi over the same disintegrating melodies. He's got to be completely smoked on anti-psychotics or ground-and-snort Demerol to sit there, every day, for multiple, four-hour sessions of Gay Nineties tunes, each more saccharine sweet than the last. I don't know who he is, but I know without hesitation that if I ever have the opportunity to kick Walt Disney in the balls, it will be that diabolical music I hum as Walt grips his stones and tumbles into that fake river coursing through *it's a small world.*

I dream about kicking Walt Disney in the nuts. I do. Call me anti-American, but if they ever thaw that sonofabitch out, I'm paying whatever the going rate is on eBay to be the first frustrated tourist to squash his little, rodent jewels.

Six dollars for a Diet Coke?

Six?

They make that shit in a chemistry lab for $ .27 a gallon, and the Mouse sells it for six bucks.

We buy it. We have to. It's 106 degrees and humid; we've got no choice. And the drinks are mostly ice, that fluoride-flavored ice they have down there to keep all the dentures cavity free.

So we pay six bucks and we get a paper cup with Mickey Mouse on the outside and eight ounces of ice over four ounces of Diet Coke on the inside. And if we didn't think to bring our own rum, we have to leave the Magic Kingdom, because the Mouse doesn't drink alcohol, the teetotaler. Yet I don't recommend leaving for booze, because anywhere on the property a cathartic blast of Captain Morgan is nine dollars (eleven for an extra shot – gotta do it).

We don't buy the bottled water.

Why not?

Because it's four dollars for sixteen ounces. That's outrageous. Most Americans won't pay it unless they're trapped in an airport during a blizzard and literally expiring from thirst. Four dollars for water!

Enough flows through the mouth of the Amazon River every day to provide drinking water for three hundred million Americans . . . for five months. And a mouse as big as a grizzly bear is hawking it for four bucks.

But you see; their bottled water is the better deal. Disney wins. When we pay six dollars for Coke, we think we're winning that one, because we get to keep the cup, but invariably Nimblefingers Nancy in airport security crushes it while checking for WMDs. When we buy the Coke we're actually paying for ice the Disney Corporation makes for free from their own tap water.

How can you tell?

Let it thaw; it's limestone gray. Call me a chemist but water isn't supposed to be gray. That's Florida water.

I have no idea what Wharton School genius comes up with the red line they use to encourage tourists to purchase one item over another, but whoever it is, that guy needs to get paid millions.

$3.98 for a cup of coffee?

Nonsense.

Buy the $14.00 mug instead and drink all the coffee you want for free. What a deal!

No one realizes that the Disney Corporation gets those mugs from a rural Pennsylvania company they've strangled into mass producing brightly-colored images of Mickey, Donald, Minnie, and Goofy for next to nothing.

Screwed. Every time I went down there I got screwed . . . in intransitive terms.

Sadly, every time I went down there (or anywhere else, come to think of it) in the past thirteen years, my husband managed a more transitive version of that happiest verb on Earth.

According to the slogan, I promised my kids that Walt Disney World would be the happiest place on Earth. Who knew that when the boys and I left for Florida and six-dollar Diet Cokes, my house, my own bedroom would take those honors?

Why do we stay with them?

I don't know.

Actually, that's a lie. I do know:

Money, security, predictability that breeds a sense of belonging, knowing I have a husband who has a job and a haircut and a work ethic when so many women don't. Or maybe it's that we'd rather stay miserable than risk the not-knowing, the waiting-for-happiness after striking out on our own and maybe failing or finding circumstances even worse in a borrowed apron with a borrowed vacuum cleaner.

Bear with me; that bit's coming up.

Perhaps we live with decades of unhappiness because we end up accepting that most everyone gets by with the illusion of contentment. Our mothers did, while our fathers drank and lost jobs and catted around the bars and gin mills of our towns. They weren't genuinely happy, but they pressed on, and they lied to us. They told us that we could be what we wanted and have what we wanted and build our own futures and bullshit, bullshit, bullshit. All of it bullshit.

Most of us chased those promises and lies right into the same glitter-glued mediocrity that found our parents back when Gerald Ford promised prosperity to women who stayed home and men who made five dollars an hour in a factory.

Women my age, from this part of the Universe, we're tightrope walkers. Half of them will call me crazy; while the other half calls me a whiner. But I'm so often discouraged when I talk with my friends – and by *friends* I mean women from this neighborhood who are nice to me and who have never been naked in front of my ex-husband. There are a few.

The cutthroat, professional hard chargers with their law or medical degrees, their MBAs framed on the office wall, when they get a glass or two of wine in their bloodstream, they complain that they never had time for kids or that they don't have time for the kids they managed to squeeze out between board meetings. On the other hand, the stay-at-home mammas in their yoga pants are the ones who page through old college yearbooks, remember studying Russian literature or music theory, and wish they had some reason to quote Chekov or Franz Schubert between episodes of SpongeBob SquarePants. At cocktail parties, they get a little high and show off, spouting nonsense they scribbled in a spiral notebook twenty years ago or some intellectual dribble they saw on the Today Show while the rest of the planet was at work.

The forty-year-old, professional woman with children, a marriage, a college degree, and a home is the most interesting creature on this planet. It can't be done, not by mere mortals and almost certainly not by men. But that's not the reason she's so compelling. That forty year old is captivating because she's all in. There's no going back. She's too far down the road to make significant changes without losing significant ground, sense of self worth, and confidence. She's got to keep all the balls in the air, keep the house nice for the local bitch squad, and keep the husband happy with periodic blow jobs or slutty PJs. She's got to stay smart, trim, with it, and on duty from dawn to dark every day.

And when the wheels come off the wagon and she discovers that her husband has been diddling every willing, warm-bodied cooze since before they were married? What does she give up?

That's the heartbreaking part.

That's why I'm writing to you, Billy, why I'm telling you this story.

My kids love Walt Disney World; they ask to go there more than anywhere we've ever been on vacation. Even my three year old –

Yeah, do the math. We'll get back to him later.

– whenever he finds a dollar or a handful of change, he'll present it to me and say, 'I have money. We go to Disney World.'

A few times, I took the boys alone. Richard stayed home to work. It made sense: he owned a business. It demanded his time and attention, and when things went well, he made stacks and stacks of money, plenty for all the six-dollar Diet Cokes I could drink.

My parents and I would load the kids into my father's truck. We'd kiss Richard good-bye and head south, bubbling over with enthusiasm for a week with the Mouse. The kids loved those trips; they still talk about them. My parents loved them, too. Traveling down there with my boys gave them an opportunity to relive those early-70s vacations when they'd cart my brother and me to Orlando in a forty-foot Winnebago complete with Cheerios, powdered milk, and Frank Sinatra on 8-Track.

But at the time, I never suspected that I had conveniently removed all of Richard's domestic responsibilities. He had a week to himself, a week to play house with Debbie or Lisa. And because he believes in unmitigated experiences, he didn't just meet these women for an afternoon at the No-Tell Motel.

Nonsense.

He invited them in for the week to play house . . . in my house, with my soap, and my dish towels, my toilet paper, and my vacuum cleaner. I imagine Lisa in my apron and nothing else, vacuuming my carpets. She and I used to play softball together, take our kids to the neighborhood playset, and make brownies for the preschool bake sale. While I stood in line behind a sweaty, obese man hoping to score a personal best on the *Buzz Lightyear Space Ranger Spin*, Lisa made omelets in my kitchen, in my t-shirt, and sucked my husband's dick while he splashed hot sauce on his eggs and got ready for another day of playing out porn fantasies with Dolly Domestic.

My father . . . God bless my father . . . but my father always complimented Richard on how clean he'd kept the house while I was away. 'She won't have to pick up or anything. This place is spotless!'

Well of course it was spotless! After kicking Debbie or Lisa out that morning, Johnny Wad tore through the house like a man on fire, scrubbing away any evidence that he'd entertained guests all week. The whole place smelled like that faux lemon they use to mask the stench of bleach in Clorox wipes. It can give you a headache when it's been slathered on 5,400 square feet of suburban McMansion.

What should have clued me in that he'd been up to no good was when I discovered that the small trash cans beside the toilets had been emptied. I'd known Richard since you graduated, back in 1992, Billy, and I'd never known him to empty those cans when I was home. I thought he'd done it to impress my father. People are always performing out-of-character circus feats to win approval from my father.

Imagine it.

Imagine how discontent my 'friends' had to be to move into my house – I admit: it was a nice place – and live as a sex toy for my husband for six days. Imagine what their lives must have been like, what unfulfilled needs they had for too long. Jesus Christ, how could they look at themselves in the mirror knowing they had slept in my bed, showered using my towels, cooked in my kitchen, and *pretended it was all really theirs*?

And I have the nerve to bitch about six-dollar sodas and fluoride-flavored ice cubes.

We're in it together now. I hope that's okay with you. But you've got to agree that I get the first go at Walt's rodent nuts.

Jennifer

September 30

Dear Billy,

I bought the house. (Insert obligatory excitement and terror here; I'm too tired to write it.)

A local bank held the note; that's why I managed to get it so quickly. And it's been empty for a while, so we can move in as soon as I get done signing my name 278 times, ensuring that I'll be in debt until my seventy-third birthday. What the hell. Right? Debt only stings when you envy the rich – I don't; trust me – or starve, and things aren't that bad. Not yet, anyway.

But I've got to tell you the truth, Billy: Buying this place, as ready as I am to move on, confirms for me that I've failed at the second most important thing I was supposed to do in life.

The good news: I'm doing okay with the boys. I think. They're Number 1. So far so good. Sure, their mother's muddying the path a little, but we're all still headed roughly north together.

I'm going to hang on to that as I pack boxes to the brim with regret and self-loathing. We're all still headed north together.

Jennifer

October

When I die, I'm going to get shitfaced with Zelda Fitzgerald in a noisy speakeasy, somewhere on the dingier side of Heaven.

October 2

Hi Billy,

When I die, I'm going to get shitfaced with Zelda Fitzgerald in a noisy speakeasy, somewhere on the dingier side of Heaven. We'll guzzle bathtub gin and bitch about our husbands. If Jay Gatsby or Hugh Jackman is there, maybe I can coerce one of them into whispering a sonnet or two my way. That'll get the engine running.

Hugh. He doesn't know it yet, but he's in love with me.

Jennifer

October 9

Dear Billy,

I'm pretty sure I shared bits and pieces of this story with you back when we were together. But truth be told, I most likely scraped off some of the scabby parts. Even after we'd been dating for a year, I can't imagine I would have wanted you to know quite every twist and turn in the road to my deflowering at the hands of my varsity quarterback.

These days, I've learned to take some of the bad with the good, and I don't mind as much if you get a chuckle out of the clumsy fumblings of my youth. Looking back on it, I'm more amused than embarrassed at the comic tragedy of my first sexual experience.

I lost my virginity on the banks of Shark River in August, 1988. Quarterback's parents threw a pre-Labor Day barbecue, complete with cheap, pop-and-fizzle fireworks someone's uncle had schlepped all the way from South Carolina. They tapped a keg of Budweiser in a truncated fifty-five-gallon drum stuffed with ice from the A&P. It stood beside the family grill upon which no farm animal, small game critter, or whitetail deer was safe. Anything slathered with a generous coating of spicy barbecue sauce was subject to dismemberment and consumption by pot-bellied cousins, wide-hipped aunts, and river rats in affordable fiberglass speedboats, Old Town canoes, even the occasional kayak. Absolutely everyone along the river had a standing invitation to eat, drink, swim, or water ski, with fireworks to follow, such as they were.

I spent most of the day on the water, either sitting beside my shirtless quarterback as he towed intrepid skiers down river, or trying my hand at staying upright, first on two skis, then on one. That late in the summer, I'd just about mastered the one-ski-tow-rope start. I'd no doubt perfected the one-ski-bikini-ripping-ass-over-handlebars dismount.

Crashing, sometimes downright gracefully, was a cinch.

By August, Shark River ran piss warm and turbid with pollution and industrial runoff. We didn't care. We skied, tubed, swam, wrestled, waded, and dunked in those waters, never thinking twice of what they carried down or washed away.

Time slowed that weekend, delaying my return to high school and Quarterback's indoctrination into the local construction union as a roofer and carpentry apprentice.

He'd already begun wearing Dickies, started up around mid July.

By 1:00, I knew I'd finally give in, let him have me. It'd been nearly two years, time to pull the trigger. My only worry was if I'd be any good at it. I wasn't concerned that it would hurt. I'd been a field hockey, basketball, and softball player, had taken my share of nasty falls, tumbles, and embarrassing collisions.

Pain didn't concern me. Sucking at it did.

By 3:30, if he'd have asked me to marry him in that Mastercraft speedboat, with his biceps flexed and his sexy abdomen putting his entire extended family to shame, I'd have said, 'yes.'

No hesitation.

I wore a shortie wet suit all day. It was about as flattering as a nun's habit, but Quarterback didn't mind. With one arm draped strategically across my thigh, his hand rested dangerously close to the Promised Land, close enough that despite my bathing suit and the Neoprene, I felt an alarmingly pleasant, hedonistic warmth awaken, ready to welcome him home. All he had to do was ask.

During Uncle Whoever's fireworks, he did.

With the sun sliding silently into Nebraska, I excused myself to change. I'd brought an old flannel shirt to wear over a camisole and a pair of cutoff jean shorts. Standing in his bathroom with shower steam enveloping me in uncertainty, I decided to forgo the flannel. Instead I tied it around my waist and wiped the mirror clean for a last unobstructed view of the braless, horny virgin looking back at me.

At the bottom of the stairs, I felt more than saw his mother in the adjacent kitchen. She draped an uncooperative layer of plastic wrap over a floral-print tray of deviled eggs. With a burning Virginia Slim dangling precipitously from the corner of her mouth and a similar flannel pulled close over forty-five years of river life, she got one look at me and smirked knowingly.

Yeah: smirked. That's about right.

I read her thoughts: *Go ahead, sweetie. I'll see you on the other side. There's plenty of room in this kitchen for two.*

She cast me a half wink, half smoke-induced wince and nodded to the porch door.

All told, the entire show – from unzipping to upzipping – took about ninety, tepid, sluggish seconds. Rufus, the dog, watched our one-act performance from his favorite spot beside the snapdragons.

It hurt more than I'd expected but not nearly as much as I'd feared. By the time I embraced the novelty of the sensation (and allowed it to distract me from the clear and uneasy migration of river mud into the crack of my ass), my young quarterback gave a sharp intake of breath, held it, spasmed like a polite epileptic, then blew catfish-and-beer-flavored breath into my face. The aroma punctuated his performance with an exclamation point that exclaimed comparatively little. Somewhere down river a boat stereo played Stevie Ray Vaughan, one of the weary tunes.

Pop! Crack! Fizzle! We've all been there, Billy: late summer picnics, burned hot dogs, tepid beer, mosquitoes, the lot of us might have fallen out of a John Mellencamp song.

Distracted and a bit embarrassed, Quarterback tossed his condom into the current, pulled on his swimsuit, and fussed with his hair. He didn't hold me, kiss me, tell me he loved me, or help me to extract the sludge from my butt. I watched the rubber until it floated out of sight, bobbing and spinning, another sin headed for the North Atlantic.

On the beach, Quarterback's family oohed and aahed at the junior varsity fireworks display. Stevie Ray soloed mournfully then wailed about floods somewhere down in Texas. Quarterback leaned close, didn't kiss me, just whispered, 'I'll see you back there.'

And he left.

I didn't know what to say. I certainly wasn't prepared for the evening's agenda to wrap up with a 'see you.' But I played along, said simply, 'okay,' and waded, naked from the waist down, to clean up in central Jersey runoff and turbid silt.

I told myself that I loved him, tried hard to convince anyone listening – just Rufus and me – that it would get better and things would be as wonderful as they had been during those delicious hours when we'd both known, with his hand dangling carelessly between my thighs.

I ignored the pesky sense of nagging dread that something had deflated between us, something I had no idea how to re-inflate, not braless in a mud-stained camisole with my shorts tossed into a stand of bulrushes, anyway.

Part of me thought it'd be best to stand there with Shark River baptizing my once-virginal Netherlands and figure this out. He'd done his business, barked a couple of spasmodic jerks, then fled. It didn't add up to what I'd been hoping for. But rather than let myself gain confidence proportional to my disappointment, I allowed the chicken-shit part of me to take the helm again, and I followed him.

Rufus stuck with me while I pulled my shorts on. I always liked that dog.

And there you have it, Billy, all the mud-splattered truth.

Jennifer

October 12

Good morning Billy,

Yesterday, I spent the afternoon volunteering for the boys' little league team over in Freehold. The City Council allowed the Mayor's Office to close streets in the center of town. Vendors, scout troops, PTA moms, community service organizations, and local dance and tae kwon do schools were encouraged to erect a canopy, decorate a table, and engage in a few hours of community outreach while a mix of bar bands from down the shore played jangly tunes from the gazebo. I think the whole works would've been a dud if it hadn't been for the beer and wine tents. Local breweries got together, staked off a rope barrier, checked IDs, and then charged a flat seven bucks for as many tastings as thirsty customers could stand. Given that the port-o-johns were over near the train station, a five-minute hike, the beer corral quickly devolved into a bunch of guys slugging as fast as they could while crossing their legs or outwardly gripping themselves to avoid wizzing in their khakis.

The wine folks had a better idea. For twelve dollars, those with a valid ID could purchase a commemorative glass, get six ounces of regional grape juice (imported from some cookie-cutter industrial vineyard in California, no doubt) and swill pleasantly while taking in the shows or rifling through dog-eared, ten-cent paperbacks outside the library. Refills were free, so while the guys chugged, jogged, and peed, the winos meandered pleasantly, enjoying whatever flavorless Malbec sloshed from the wine tent.

Because I volunteered at the little league station, I didn't have beer or fruit juice. Rather, I stopped off for a *Venti Xanax Double Vanilla Demerol* from Starbucks and spent the afternoon handing out flyers and watching the parade of people as they ate kettle corn and wandered up and down Court Street.

Have you ever lived alone, Billy?

I doubt that you have. Even that year in Chicago after graduation, I think I remember a roommate. Right?

With three boys and a dog, I can't pretend that I live alone, but you know what I mean: I'm alone from 11:00 at night until 7:00 in the morning.

That kind of alone.

And alone making dinner while the boys play outside.

Alone washing dishes while the boys do their homework or watch TV with Homer.

And alone in the bleachers during baseball games.

Alone at the grocery store when they hang out at Myrna's and I go shopping.

And alone wrapping last-minute presents at 11:45 on Christmas Eve.

That kind of alone changes you. I know I've only been at it for a short while and that some people manage it for years. But I'm a social animal first, and I'm not entirely myself without at least some close human contact.

I didn't truly realize this until recently when I stopped being a woman who worried all the time what other women might think about my hair, my make-up, my clothes, my ass, or the condition of my kitchen counters. And I didn't truly realize this until I spent a few months turning to ask someone to pass me something, hand me something, grab something from a drawer in the bathroom, and no one was there, not even Richard who I didn't want around anyway.

Say *that* two hundred times fast, and I'll meet you in therapy.

Sitting for four hours and watching ten-thousand women walk past the baseball table, an unanticipated realization bubbled over for me. It's a sad and fundamental truth that had nearly defined me for decades and one which I hope will never swallow me up again.

But I'm full of shit. We can agree on that.

I have to admit: if I ever get involved with another man, or if I ever get over the self-loathing I feel when I think about the implosion of my marriage or the ugly red welts it left up and down my self-image, I'll probably be right back on that bus with the ten-thousand sorry sonsofbitches who showcased their failings, fears, and insecurities for me yesterday.

But I'll regret it. I'm all about regrets these days.

Have you ever noticed women, Billy?

And by women, I don't mean old ladies – God bless them – on the north side of sixty five.

And I don't mean girls – God broil them – on the south side of twenty two. Young women, even teenagers, who look relatively good in their yoga pants (Jesus Christ) or their tank tops, Lycra skirts, booty shorts (yes, they should be illegal), with their hair done up just so, and their skin clear, and their boobs defying gravity in a way that none of us can truly appreciate until they've exhausted their magic and fallen limply into our lap . . . those women define what is sexual and attractive in our culture. They do. The twenty-one-year-old, size two, lanky, wiry, big-boobied woman – *girl*, let's keep that straight; we're talking about individuals who were only recently children – is the poster child for sexuality across the purple mountains majesty.

And why?

Because the rest of us allow it.

Not you guys. Nope. No one blames you for following your penis up and down Fifth Avenue. (Although we should.)

And I should stop being so damned parenthetical. Sorry.

Rather, other women, older women, women from age thirty to age fifty, who should be running the show (and who are in so many important regards), can't reclaim the minimum basic standards for sexy from the legions of air-brushed swizzle sticks.

That's wrong.

And while I don't expect you to disagree with me, Mr. Klein, I am going to take a few minutes of your time to illustrate what I think is a sad symptom of our culture's acquiescence to busty, scrawny children.

The rest of us camouflage our shortcomings.

We do. It's depressing.

I sat yesterday and watched a veritable parade of women pass by the little league booth. The overwhelming majority of them were in camouflage, some without knowing it.

Long, untucked shirts, hooded sweatshirts, big sunglasses, pony tails, large canvas bags or purses slung over hips or even dangling across a wide ass, scarves of all shapes and sizes draped here, looped there, covering small boobs, floppy boobs, fat boobs, baseball hats smothering undone hair, jackets and sweaters tied strategically over ten pounds of clingy baby weight or twenty pounds of unfriendly caboose.

What the hell is wrong with us?

We do it for the men in our lives and for the women in our neighborhoods, but most of all, Billy, I think we do it for ourselves. When we look in the mirror we lose. I get dressed every day and make the unfair comparison of the wrinkly, sagging skin around my belly button – my belly button that's been stretched and ravaged by three pregnancies – with the belly button on the twenty-year-old model from the cover of every magazine in every checkout line in every grocery store on the continent, and I lose.

I lose every day.

So I wear a long, untucked shirt or a baggy sweater or a jacket tied around my waist, even when I know it's going to be over seventy-five degrees in the afternoon.

Imagine it. Imagine if I'd stopped every woman who walked by my booth yesterday and said, 'You're attractive. Stop trying to hide your ass. Stop covering up your boobs. Stop hiding the few pounds around your middle; you've had children for Christ's sake.'

Do you think it would have made a difference?

Nah, me neither.

But it's a nice thought.

So today I'm going to wear my old jeans (they make my ass look fat), and I'm going to wear my hair in a ponytail because I don't feel like taking an hour to get it right. Then I'm going to Wegmans to push a grocery cart around the store for an hour. But most of all, I'm not going to regret how I look, and I'm not going to apologize for how I look, but I am going to start planning a web page or a blog or a social media site for women thirty to fifty called,

www.letstakeoverthemotherfuckingworld.com.

Who can stop us, really? Men? Twenty-year-old size twos?

Not a chance.

When I see you, I'm just going to be me. I'm done wearing camouflage. Will you be okay with that? I hope so.

I hope so.

Jennifer

October 14

Hey Billy,

I'm scribbling at you tonight just to say, 'thanks.' I'm glad you're hanging with me through these ramblings. And while I'm hammering away a bit at my father and my husband (and myself) I feel compelled to give you as broad and deep a perspective on this jumble of formative silliness as possible.

Why?

Jesus, Billy, I dunno. It's therapeutic?

Yeah, that's it.

I don't know if you read the *National Geographic* article; it's a few decades old now. But there was a team of researchers who conducted a study in the early 80s to determine the planet's worst softball player.

Yup, it's me: this planet's worst. Come to think of it, I might be the worst softball player on all the other planets as well.

Sure, I get in a game every now and then for Myrna and Dave's beer league. And they all pretty well suck snot. There's not much like a keg of sudsy light brew to impair even the finest of bronzen athletes. So I go and I hack and I stumble and I burp and I make errors, but no one cares. We kick the keg, eat chicken wings, and sleep the delusional sleep of those comfortable lying to themselves about their athletic prowess.

No one even knows the score as long as there's beer.

But that wasn't always the case.

When I was twelve, I tried out for the middle school softball team. Everyone did. We were all the same: small, thin, wiry, with nubby boobs, big teeth, unruly hair we hated, and the first crop of pioneer zits sprouting on our noses and foreheads. We knew which of us had started her period and which hadn't by those who lusted after boys and those who remained zealously insane, even sociopathic.

My father came to all of my games, sometimes in street clothes, but often in his Asbury Park police uniform, 'on duty' at the middle school field outside Freehold. I never asked if he got in trouble for that, wandering fifteen miles outside his jurisdiction. He never seemed nervous or in a hurry to get back on the beat, even though my friends' parents saw him, said 'hello,' or sat with him in the bleachers.

One afternoon, we played Marlboro Township. Christ, I hated those girls: rich, bitchy, country clubbers. Thirty years later, I realize they all probably grew up to marry rich, snobby, self-absorbed corporate douche bags, so the lot of them are probably as miserable as I am these days.

Heh. Never saw *that* coming!

Back then Marlboro Township was the enemy. The game was invariably a barn burner, a grudge match, a bloodbath, or whatever epic metaphor you like to capture the sheer, stupid, mundanity of clumsy adolescents grimacing with each wimpy swing, throw, or ground ball.

Late in the game, I missed an easy popup. I played second base, saw the ball coming, and promptly let it fall past my glove and dribble into shallow right field. Two runs scored; we lost.

I was as heartbroken about it as I'd ever been about anything.

Dad drove us towards Asbury Park while I sat in silence staring out the window of his police cruiser. Monmouth County smeared by as the dispatcher garbled incoherent odds and ends through the radio static. My father turned it down, too low to hear if they needed him for an emergency. 'You all right?'

'Yeah, I'm good,' I said to the window.

'If you guys hadn't left six runners on base in the first two innings, you'd've been up by four in the sixth.'

'I know.'

'Those two runs wouldn't've mattered. Moni coulda pitched you outta that mess, and we'd be goin' for ice cream right now with the team.'

'Dad . . .'

'Hmmm?'

'I'm awful.'

'You're not awful, honey,' he said. 'You're twelve. You're just gettin' started.'

'I hate softball.' Saying 'hate' in many homes was forbidden. In our house it was a useful, flexible verb with great potential.

He said, 'You shouldn't hate it. Isn't it fun playing with your friends?'

'Some days, I guess.'

'Then what's the problem?'

'I feel bad that you come to see me, and I mess up like that.'

'Like what? Missing a fly ball? Ninety out of a hundred people on the street couldn't've caught that ball, honey,' he said. 'And besides,

I don't come to see you play because I want you to win. I come to the games because I wanna see you happy.'

I didn't know what to make of this. It sounded like parenting bullshit to me. Now, three decades and three kids later, I understand him perfectly, immaculately (sorry, extra adverbs). I asked, 'really?'

He shrugged, 'Of course, honey, half the time I dunno who's winning or losing. I just like watching you have a good time. It isn't your job to make me happy.'

'I hate the way I throw . . . and run . . . and I can't hit, Dad.'

'Do you know what I would change about you, Jenny?'

This scared me. I figured he was going to tell me no matter what, so I went along with him. 'No . . . what?'

'Not a thing. I would change exactly nothing about you.' This, he said out the front window. He and I have never been able to maintain eye contact during serious conversations, unless we're drunk, of course. He turned onto Ocean Avenue just north of Sea Girt, deliberately taking the long way back to the barracks and my mother's station wagon. Dad knew that I loved this stretch of road – from Spring Lake up to Asbury – more than anyplace in the world. 'If you think that being a good softball player is going to make me happy, you couldn't be more wrong.'

'But . . .'

'Now lemme finish.' The old Essex & Sussex Hotel, as big as an ocean liner, rolled past, still towering over the dunes a hundred years later. 'The only thing I need from you is for you to come home every night, safe, healthy, and happy. That's it.'

I held my breath, didn't want to cry in front of him, and not in his police car.

He gave me a second, contentedly watched gazillion-dollar homes in Spring Lake give way to million-dollar places in Belmar, my choice for the geographical center of the Universe. (It still is, by the way.)

Finally I sucked in a pretty good breath and yanked us to safer ground. Like the eye contact thing, my father and I don't linger too long on serious subjects either. I lightened the mood. 'Dad?'

'Yes?'

'Would you swim through a school of sharks for me?'

'I already do, every time we go to the beach.'

'Dad!'

'Look over there,' he pointed out my window. 'What's that?'

'The ocean.' I said with as much *duh* as I could muster.

'You know what lives in the ocean?'

'Mom says there's no –'

'Mom says that so your brother will get in the water.' He smiled for the first time since we left the middle school. 'Sharks live in the ocean, honey. They live right out there.'

I didn't like thinking about it. (I still don't.) 'Dad?'

'Yes?'

'Would you crawl through a burning building to bring me a glass of water?'

'Of course, that's when you'd need a drink of water the most. Right?'

I laughed, my failures on the middle school softball field fading to blurry bad memories. 'Dad?'

'Yes, my winsome lass?' We passed the Tenth Avenue Freeze Out, a great local spot for ice cream until Hurricane Sandy tossed it halfway to Iceland. How Springsteen's attorneys allowed that place to exist I never understood.

'Dad, would you climb Mount Everest to bring me a sweater?'

'I did that, just last weekend.' He brandished his best sincere-bullshit look. 'Wasn't that you? Darn. I thought for sure that was you. Must've been some other twelve-year-old girl up there all chilly. That was a lotta work for one sweater.'

'Can we get pizza?'

'If you want your mother to divorce me.'

'Dad?'

'Yes, your highness?'

'Would you wrestle Lawrence Taylor for me?'

'Well, honey, I would, but Lawrence Taylor finds me attractive, so that might be a little uncomfortable for him.'

'Dad!'

And on it went.

I promise you this: every girl, young woman, mature woman, old lady, whatever, every one of us wants a bottom drawer filled with memories of her father just like this one, that drawer we all have that no one's allowed to sift through. Every woman wants at least one crisp, HD, Blu-ray memory of her dad behaving exactly as beautifully and perfectly as my father behaved that afternoon, when I flubbed an easy fly ball and lost a pointless softball game.

I don't have many of them in that drawer, Billy, but I've got that one.

About an hour later, with twilight swallowing central New Jersey whole, we stopped at the liquor store for a six pack. With the Mets game slogging into the eighth inning, Dad fell asleep in his recliner, six empty beer cans in a neat row beside the coffee table. If my father has . . . *had*, he's too old for that degree of discontentment now . . . but if my father had a tragic flaw, it was that: for every immaculate afternoon, there was a Mets game and a six pack. Whenever I hear some suburban housewife talk about her love-hate relationship with her dishwasher, her dog's groomer, or her snooty kid's Algebra teacher, I want to slap her, then slap her again. Love-hate, Billy. Think about it. It can make for a confusing and problematic trip along life's yellow brick road.

But don't worry. I'll fill you in as we go.

And the bottom drawer thing? Yeah, trust me on that.

Jennifer

October 16

Dear Billy,

Richard's argument for refusing to help me cover Homer's daycare costs could infuriate a corpse. He suggests that I should be happy just to stay home and take care of the baby . . . toddler, whatever Homer is now, bloodthirsty carnivore. He sent me a note last night saying (I'll omit the profanity) that I used to complain about being a teacher, so why would I want to go back to all that stress, frustration and emotional exhaustion?

      Here's the response I want to send Richard. I won't, because he doesn't get it. He's been making a living behind a desk, in a golf shirt, for twenty years. It'd just be more mental masturbation to send him an explanation. But I'll send it to you. Yeah, it's mostly a run-on sentence in blocky paragraphs. Ask any teacher; they'll confirm it.

I love and hate many of the same things about teaching.

      I love and hate the fact that my day starts before dawn, that I see the sunrise every day, and that I get home after dark throughout February. All teachers hate February: dark when we arrive, dark when we leave. I love the feeling of unlocking the door to my classroom, turning on the lights, and getting ready for the day. I love the coffee maker in the teachers' lounge and how it doubles as a tavern all week, until we get to the tavern together on Friday afternoons. I love those quiet minutes before the buses arrive when I am alone in the room. Everything in the world makes sense, and I know exactly what we'll be doing for every minute of the day. And then the kids arrive and my lesson plans blow up by 8:58, and I'm scrambling to find ways to help the smart ones feel challenged, while the not-so-smart ones take three, four, or eight hundred repetitions of the material and sometimes still don't get it. And I love and hate that I know in thirty seconds who the kids are whose parents read with them at night, or play those irritating math games while on road trips, and I hate that I only need those same thirty seconds to determine which kids don't have books at home or parents who read. I love and hate that I know the world isn't really split along racial or ethnic lines.

      That's bullshit.

      This world, our classroom world anyway, splits along the line of the information rich and the information poor, and that access to resources is the second most important thing we can do for kids outside of school. Because not having access to educational information at home is a felony only surpassed by refusing to read with your kids. I hate that parents respond to that accusation by saying, 'We work double shifts. We have to make ends meet. When do we have time to read with our kids?'

And I want to say, 'Yeah, I get it. I understand. But find time anyway, jackass.'

And I love and hate that I'll be teaching fractions again today and tomorrow and the day after tomorrow and on and on and on, and I could have students come back to me thirty-five years from now and still not understand fractions. I know why they're going to fail Algebra three times in high school, and it's not because they can't grasp the concept of X as a variable. Rather it's because they can't clear a fraction from an equation. Fractions are the Devil's Playground in my classroom. We've tried 861 different ways to understand fractions: baked cakes, cut up linoleum, used blocks, drawings, films, online games, old fashioned paper-and-pencil tasks, and still I have students who look at me and say, 'When's recess? Or lunch? Anything but fractions.'

I love and hate that I might be the only adult who gives a damn about some of these kids. I hate it, because I want to go to their house and kill their mother's boyfriend with a flame thrower, and I want to slap their mother and say, 'You could've gone out for Chinese food, shithead, but you stayed home to get laid. Well it's time to pay up. Get some books, and get busy reading.' Then I want to find the biological father, and I want to do unspeakable things to him with a fork and a hypodermic needle and a couple of tablespoons of broken glass, because the only reason Mom is out chasing useless boyfriends is because Dad couldn't be bothered to stick around, and because no one stops to think that their selfishness is as clearly evident as a Neon sign every single goddamned day in my classroom, in every teacher's classroom.

I love that I get to teach them that Maine is up north and Florida is down south and California is out west and that there are three in the middle that start with the letter 'I.' And they'll still surprise me with their lack of basic geographical knowledge. They'll mark that big one north of us as 'Cuba' and that big one south of us as 'China' and that clutch of small countries north of Africa as 'Asia.' But every now and then God gives me a cookie, and the one student I'd never guess would grasp a concept finally grasps a concept and takes the floor and takes the risk and speaks up and hits it out of the ballpark, and I know I'll get up before dawn again tomorrow and come in here and do it all over.

I hate that my assistant principal is an absolute boob, who ogles the young women on the staff and will grow old and die having had no impact on anyone, anywhere, with regards to anything, but that he has all sorts of look-at-me-I'm-a-middle-manager crap on his desk, like those little balls that bang and clack together until you want to duct tape him into his chair and set the charges for 3:05 pm, when all the kids will be safely on the bus.

But I love my grade level coordinator and my lead teacher, superhero geniuses who amaze me every day at their ability to manage a full teaching load and still listen to nine teachers whine (myself included) about everything from pencil sharpeners to the lunch schedule to the bus duty schedule to the Xerox machine that probably hides Jimmy Hoffa's corpse deep in its unexplored caverns to our lecherous assistant principal to the parents who email to bitch and complain to the parents who never email but should to the moronic absurd pointless ridiculous Commandments we receive from the district's central office to test and test and re-test and pre-test and post-test and gather data on every single standard (there are 9,876 for fourth graders) every ten minutes every day all year until my lesson plans look more like notes for an amphibious landing of kids who don't understand fractions than they do as a means to engage and inspire nine year olds and everything begins to blur together.

And I want to slap every single education consultant who has ever gone into a school and told third and fourth grade teachers that we're not doing enough to get these kids ready to compete in a global workforce. They're nine for Christ's sake. How about you back off for a year or two? But then they'll say that American kids can't compete with India, Germany, or Japan in Engineering or Calculus, and I say, 'Yeah, okay, fine, but we kick the holy dog snot out of those countries in Creativity, and that should count for something.'

Ever seen a great film come out of Germany? Yeah, me neither.

The bell rings, and I have twenty-seven minutes.

I have to pee, eat lunch, get another cup of coffee, make copies, check in with my grade-level team, deliver my assessment data to the office, and clean up the clutter before the kids are back from lunch. It sounds like a lot to do, but I can manage it in fourteen minutes, because I need some extra time at midday to get back to parents who've emailed in the morning and who demand a response before the end of the day.

I hate them.

Do they email their doctor or their dentist and demand a response that day? Do they show up at their doctor's office and refuse to leave until they get to see him/her?

Assholes.

When the kids are back, we go again. It's the daily Merry Chase, and I love it. Much of the afternoon is a repeat of the morning, except that after my students leave, I play a game I like to call, 'Leave Me Alone So I Can Get Stuff Together For Tomorrow.' But I lose this game almost every afternoon. My colleagues often come in to chat. In any other profession, I might be considered rude, because I chat while doing seventeen must-finish tasks. Other teachers don't help. They sit at one of the desks and chatter with me while I scurry around and pick things up, move furniture, adjust bulletin boards and calendars, prep lessons, check online links for tomorrow's notes, clean up papers from the floor, wipe dry erase boards clean, sharpen pencils, restock paper and tape and glue and staples, and organize folders and turn everyone's color back to green.

Because everyone should start the day on green.

And my colleagues don't care that I'm being rude, because somewhere down the hall their classroom waits for them to go through the same machinations I'm going through now. And I love that they can read my thoughts, because it's one thing to chatter with me while I'm hustling around the room. But the best of them understand that it's time to clear out when I finally sit down at my desk to answer email. And I love and hate that feeling of logging in to my email account at 3:37 pm, every day, and playing 'Email Roulette.'

How many will I have? Five or fifty?

Can I get out of here in thirty minutes, or will this be another two-hour session? Escaping in a half hour is usually a pipe dream, because while I often have emails I can answer in thirty seconds, I also receive messages that require twenty minutes each. My principal gets about two hundred emails a day and says she can get them all cleared out in four hours. Cyborg. I'd kill myself. Four hours? Just maybe, if they let me have a bottle of wine at my desk.

But they don't.

Some emails I don't answer, because they can wait. And some emails I don't answer because I have to call those parents. Sure, they'll have my cell number and can text me at all hours of the night, but it's a small price to pay for the time I'll save trying to get all my concerns, plans, efforts, and frustrations crammed into one email. I call them from my car, and we problem solve, commiserate, and share ideas until I get home – often wrapping up conversations while sitting in my driveway for fifteen minutes.

So yes, when I was teaching, I'd get home from work and Richard would often ask, 'How was your day?' I sometimes responded with, 'Exhausting, stressful, pointless,' or something similar. But that didn't mean I wanted to stay home.

Don't forget to read with your kids, Billy. (Do you have kids? A wife? As much as I hope you're single, I worry that you could be divorced and jaded and just as negative as I am. That might not bode well for us, my dear, because at least one of us needs to be positive about the institution of . . . that word . . . and it sure as hell isn't going to be me!)

But I'm getting ahead of myself. I don't plan to talk you into another marriage until we've both had ample time for therapy.

Just kidding,

Jennifer

November

From this far away my boobs will look like chicken pox.

November 5

Dear Billy,

This one's true. Not that all the others have been bullshit, but this one's special. Yeah, special.

Spring semester, 1991.

Remember that?

I do. All the time.

My sophomore year marked a noticeable increase in my study time and a noticeable decrease in my drinking-and-debauchery time. As much as my father enjoyed hosting the entire Kappa Delta sorority at his tailgate parties, he hypocritically made it clear that if I didn't sober up and hit the books I'd be home for a semester playing cart jockey in the A&P parking lot. Apparently, there's nothing like a punch-in, punch-out job to teach college pukes the true meaning of life or some such Irish philosophical horseshit.

So I studied.

I continued to party; I hadn't died. Just being around Scoutmaster Kelly meant that one had to be physically and emotionally prepared for a shot of Jägermeister at any time. Rooming with her that year made cleaning up my act all the more challenging, but I managed, and Dad left me alone after I tallied a 3.8 GPA fall semester.

On April 7, 1991, Rutgers hosted Penn State in a fierce varsity baseball rivalry that the rest of the planet had no idea existed. The hype got even more intense when New Jersey's governor, whoever he was, bet Pennsylvania's governor, another memorable fellow, that Rutgers would win or he'd host the last legislative session of the term in a Penn State sweatshirt.

Gripping stuff.

Our honor, nay, the honor of New Jersians everywhere was on the line.

Actually, no one gave a shit, but Scoutmaster Kelly decided to do her part. As a concerned booster of Rutgers athletics, she vowed to attend the game, secure a seat strategically behind first base (not difficult to do, even for the NJ-PA showdown), and flash her tits every time a Penn State infielder made a throw.

Her plan was foolproof. She started with a pitcher of Alabama Slammers. (Many of Scoutmaster Kelly's plans began with something poisonous.) Step two involved getting intoxicated enough to believe that her boobs, when bared in public, might be a distraction to an NCAA Division I athlete. Keep in mind that at the time, Kelly was about a 34B, not nearly the honking D cup her fiancé purchased after she agreed to marry him. *Those* could've changed the weather. But the Rutgers University baseball team wasn't in the market for a rain delay that afternoon, so Scoutmaster Kelly's pert 34Bs did the job just fine.

I went with her.

I didn't drink the Alabama Slammers, well, not many of them anyway.

And I did not bare my titties for any Penn Staters, even though some of those guys probably went on to play pro ball.

Kelly did, the harlot!

After two innings, there'd only been two ground balls to the Penn State infield, and one of those had gone to second base to cut off the lead runner. Rutgers batters had either walked or hit fly balls to the outfield.

I remember it funnier than it was: Kelly, sucking her fingernail, slurred, 'Maybe I need to start flashing the outfielders.'

'Won't work.' I didn't bother looking up from my notebook, a biology lab on woody dicots. 'The outfielders are watching the ball sail over the infield. Your only hope is to get the infielders so riled up they'll overthrow or underthrow or misfire or prematurely . . . whatever.'

'You're right. Damn it.' She considered the centerfielder, a cutie with a scraggle of whiskers and long, lean legs. 'From this far away my boobs will look like chicken pox.'

'Heh. Right. Stick with the infielders,' I said. 'That second baseman looks plenty horny.'

'Bullshit. That's a cup.' She shoved the side of my head playfully. 'You're not even paying attention. Who brings homework to a baseball game on a sunny afternoon?'

Again, I half ignored her. 'Anyone with a C- in biology who needs a B+ in biology; that's who.'

'But you've got bigger tits than I do. You could take care of the shortstop or that little guy way over there.' She pointed across the diamond.

'That's third base.'

The bottom of the third inning brought such a surplus of

ground balls, the teams must have gotten the idea that there was a drunk coed flashing her breasts. Just about every player in the Rutgers lineup gave only a half-assed, wimpy swing at the ball, a bunch of limp-wristed efforts that didn't see one hit leave the infield until the bottom of the fifth. Players from both dugouts watched first base as if the seventh game of the World Series depended on it. In the fourth, the Penn State second baseman actually overthrew first, confirming for Scoutmaster Kelly that her plan for field-wide domination had worked, once anyway.

By the top of the sixth, the assistant AD, a pasty, overweight, twenty-something graduate student with an earpiece and a radio in his belt, arrived inevitably to escort Scoutmaster Kelly and her smallish boobs to the exit. She received a warm ovation from both dugouts and was encouraged never to return to a Rutgers University baseball game. To her credit, she left with dignity, walking out under her own power, a healthy swish to her ass sending every player on the field an affectionate farewell.

I stayed, not because I gave a damn about the baseball game, but because I'd gotten a head of steam going on my biology lab. The sun shone; breeze from the east carried the barest remnants of Jersey shore salt and sea, and I didn't look forward to whatever scheme Kelly might concoct to paralyze the few functioning brain cells left wandering unsupervised inside her head.

That's when Coach Custer put you in right field. Do you remember?

With your hat pulled low and your uniform fresh from the laundry, you jogged past, peeked over. 'Psst! Hey, Red.'

I looked up, found you watching me as if we'd met before but you couldn't recall where.

I smiled, didn't say anything, didn't know if there were rules against chatting with ball players on their way to the outfield. If nothing else, I'm a rule follower.

'Hey, Red.'

I raised both hands in a gesture I hoped said, *What? Aren't you supposed to be playing baseball about now?*

And you unsheathed that deadly, heartbreaking smile, briefly, just for me. You pointed your glove at my notebooks. 'X = 19. Write it down. X = 19.'

Okay, you can kiss me now.

You turned and jogged to the outfield, never heard me call, 'It's biology, doofus.'

A bullpen catcher in shin guards stood by the foul line. The two of you tossed a ball back and forth while the Rutgers pitcher warmed up. I tried focusing on my lab report, but couldn't stop watching as you caught and tossed that ball in such a leisurely, practiced motion. I couldn't help it; I imagined us together, moving in a similar, easy pattern of sway and swish, all afternoon, maybe even in that comfy-looking grass.

I watched you all that inning and the next. No one hit the ball your way, and you didn't get up to bat before the game ended in the top of the seventh. Regardless, it's all etched indelibly in my memory: the way the hegemonic sprawl of perfectly trimmed grass made your red cleats look like holiday decorations. Your smooth athletic movements: readying for each pitch, then relaxing, fussing with a leather tie on your glove, or jogging smoothly toward the foul line when an infielder threw the ball to first base.

Young, clean cut, healthy, powerful, competitive, masculine, animal attraction . . . you were all at once reminiscent of nothing I'd ever known but clearly – slap-me-stupid clearly – what I wanted. Yet I had no idea how to find you, meet you, introduce myself without blowing snot on you or farting indecorously from those sinister eggs they served every morning in the cafeteria.

And then you saved me the trouble.

I know you remember that.

Rutgers won the game on a triple play. You told me later that there was a gazillion-to-one chance of that, but I can't remember the odds, something akin to being struck by lightning while in the jaws of a great white shark.

The Rutgers dugout spilled on to the field; the infielders converged on first base, tackling one another and piling on in that familiar, primitive ritual that says *We won! Now let's jump on one another like primates!*

You ran in from right field, approached the pile of jubilant young men, but before you joined the fracas, you slid a few steps closer to the bleachers, caught my eye – not hard to do at that juncture – and shouted, 'Hey, Red!'

And you tossed me your RU baseball hat. It landed in a wrinkly lump near my feet. I didn't know what to do; I mean there had to have been some university regulation about chucking school property willy-nilly to fans in the bleachers.

But after only a second or two, I grabbed it, felt the coarse cotton and the cool sweat against my fingertips, and stashed it in my backpack.

You were gone, stuck somewhere near the middle of the pile. When you emerged from the melee, you rolled to your feet, jumped lightly on your toes, then looked in my direction. Waving, you cupped your hands near your face and mouthed the words, *Ratskeller later*. It might have been *Anne's here; I hate her*. But that wouldn't have made sense.

My face flushed red to match your sexy uniform pants. I caught your eye, mouthed, *Okay, bye*.

The few fans in the bleachers near me got so involved in the victory celebration, no one noticed as I collected my bags, stuffed my unfinished lab report in my pack, and hustled out – careful to check for that assistant AD. I felt a queasy certainty that he'd seen me steal your hat and figured it was just a matter of a few steps before he'd stop me, demand it imperiously, then lead me away, blushing, to whatever prison cell held Scoutmaster Kelly.

No one caught me.

And I still have the hat.

What great memories,

Jennifer

November 13

Billy –

Richard hit me once. You might be wondering about that, so I'll toss it out there unsolicited. I think he surprised both of us. It didn't hurt much, and before I could react he'd left the room, fled somewhere he wouldn't have to watch me melt down. I want to say that I clobbered him, attacked him with a running chainsaw or a butcher knife. I didn't. Instead, I just stood in my kitchen, watching my watery reflection waver in the smoky glass of the microwave oven. Green numbers, 10:07, shone like a Neon tattoo on my forehead.

I was drunk enough to believe I could see my cheek swell. That should have infuriated me. If I'd been starring in a Hollywood blockbuster rather than a tawdry suburban melodrama, I would either have collapsed in a frothy heap, weeping in jags, or perhaps marched after him, raging.

I did neither, just stood there, wallowed in disbelief for a few minutes, then poured more wine.

A couple of months later, he threw an empty vodka bottle at me. I don't think he meant to hit me; scorn just burst out of him uncontrolled. The bottle – Grey Goose – sailed past my head, cleared the kitchen island and slammed into the sheet rock beneath the window in our sunroom. Before shattering, it left an ugly impression in my wall, similar enough to a vodka bottle that I couldn't pass it off as one of my kids' toys.

My parents came for dinner that Sunday. Mom wasn't in the house five minutes before asking why I'd moved the Claude Cambour painting she loved so much. It worked better above the fireplace than beneath the window.

And did I know that if I wasn't careful the sun spilling into that room every day would cause the paint to fade I might look in to having it treated she knew someone up in Parsippany who treated acrylics maybe he had a website or something where I could learn about the dangers of exposing untreated canvases to sunlight and why did I move it anyway and didn't I think it fit the room better in its old place above the mantel and she worried that the kids might ruin the Cambour if I left it hanging that low and and and . . .

Dad saved me; that's rare. 'Smells good. What's cooking?'

Sometimes he's a genius.

Richard knew Dad'd thrown us a life preserver and poured him a Scotch.

My husband and I have been at one another's throats for over eighteen months now, but he hasn't hit me or thrown anything, not yet. The night before we packed up to move into separate homes, we drank our last bottles of wine together. Sipping politely through an expensive Merlot, we ate pizza with the kids in a domestic display worthy of a Rockwell painting. With the boys in bed, Richard and I glugged less demurely through our final bottle, cheap-o Cabernet Horse Piss someone left after a dinner party. Both empties stood guard on the granite island as we made preparations and tried to avoid insulting or infuriating one another. I'm glad, because on that night I'd have fought back.

Keep well, Billy.

Jennifer

November 25

Hey Billy,

I went to Wegmans the other day, because I hate myself.

Yet, before I get rolling here . . . no, there's no apostrophe in Wegmans (or in Starbucks for that matter). It's not a grammar mistake on my part. It's just a bunch of Wegmans and Starbucks out walking around; I guess. Melville's scratching at the inside of his coffin.

Anyway, I went to Wegmans. I don't hate myself, but these days I struggle to get all aflutter at the grand work of epicurean art that is Wegmans: fresh sushi, wine bar, and pastry chef with his now-you-hear-it-now-you-don't French accent. How that guy manages to keep a job in a neighborhood of anorexic, forty-year-old women remains an unsolved mystery. I mean, how many desserts can be injected to bursting with light-as-air chocolate mousse?

The Wegmans experience used to be a hoot, but after discovering that Richard had spent the past twenty years following his erection around town, I found the store a pinch less invigorating. Sure, it's a cool place, and it's nice to know that I can get imported, whole milk, Camembert or Danish Fontina cheese to go with my freshly drawn coconut milk, but what ruins Wegmans for me is wondering which of the women shopping there, often in absurd, second-skin workout attire, slept with my ex-husband. It's like walking through a 3-D, virtual reality version of a Sluts & Whores wall calendar in an auto parts store:

Turn the corner into the cereal aisle and run into Mrs. July, 2003. Sneak through the bakery to get to the deli and nearly bump carts with Mrs. Autumn, 2008, Miss Barely Legal, 2010, and Mrs. April, 1999.

Fake boobs, expensive mani-pedis, Coach bags, gifted children in soccer uniforms, and authentic, imitation smiles for me, the ex-wife who never knew.

They all call me 'Jenny,' as if the endearment brings us closer together after such a trying time in the foxhole that was my life.

'Hey, Jenny, did you see that deal on free-range shrimp and vegan Chapstick? Do you want me to pass you some?'

'No thank you, Mrs. February, 2005 *and* August, 2006. I'd rather you pass me one or two of those live lobsters so I can liberate them inside your thong.'

Wegmans at 11:30 on a Saturday morning: perfect for a North Korean missile strike:

'Oh, hi Charlotte!' (READ: God, what a tramp in those biker shorts.)

'Heather! You and Paul have to come to brunch next week.' (READ: What is that? A zit? Or a bullet wound?)

Kissy face, pretend hugs, and *KABLAM!* One North Korean dildo for the whole place.

Heh.

I know. I know: I shouldn't get lost in my daydreams.

Anyway, Wegmans. I went last week and ran into Myrna, a good friend who never slept with Richard because, in his assessment, she fell definitively into the not-even-with-a-borrowed-dick category.

I love her.

At Wegmans on a Saturday morning in blue sweatpants, a sweaty, gray T-shirt, grimy sneakers fresh from her flower beds, and an old NY Jets hat, she looked like five miles of lowland bog. Her chubby husband and two bickering kids in tow, they might have been an advertisement for sort-of-happily ever after.

'Jenny!' she hugged me, no air kisses, no embarrassment for the sweat under her arms. 'How're you holding up?' She asked, and she cared, and she listened, and the rest of the place could have spontaneously combusted while she talked with me. She wouldn't have noticed.

And my asshole ex-husband wouldn't have nailed her with a borrowed penis.

With Myrna, the one rare specimen of friend that almost none of us have or appreciate when we do, standing there, I silently promised to be a better person, if for no other reason than to deserve her friendship.

We talked about her kids and my kids and school and math homework and her flowerbeds and her father's rheumatoid arthritis all in the space of about ten minutes. When she finally got round to asking about Richard, I waved her off. 'Fuck him.'

'Ick, no.'

I laughed, needed it.

Myrna's eyes lit with the rising tide of a devilish idea. I knew it before she opened her mouth. 'What?'

'Nothing,' she grinned and somewhere, Richard's penis went limp in his hand. 'Just watch your email later.'

And Myrna was off, pushing her cart in the direction of a gaggle of chatterboxes peeling ears of corn at an impromptu, cardboard display designed to make shoppers feel as though they're making selections at a roadside stand in Iowa. Jesus.

A few hours later, she sent me this. I'll just paste it here so you can read Myrna's original draft. I'm not funny enough to do it justice second hand.

Hey Sweetie,

Kong is napping and the kids are outside. So I thought I'd grab a second and send you a quickie pick-me-up. If it picks you up, terrific. If it doesn't, well, you're hopeless anyway.

When I mentioned Richard this morning, you said, 'fuck him,' which I'm assuming you say anytime anyone brings up his name. What's sad for me is that if you're going to ignore him and avoid discussing him, the brush-off you give ought to be a touch more creative. And let's be honest . . . a touch less offensive. I know you're struggling, but dropping the f-bomb every time someone asks about your marriage will only get you branded as a potty mouth around here.

So while I was thinking about ways for you to paraphrase, 'fuck him,' I thought as well of the many purchases he made (for himself) over the past ten years or so, and figured what a lovely way to communicate what a reprehensible limp noodle he is, but also how selfish, self-important, self-serving, and self- a few other things that aren't coming to mind right now. So Jennifer, my love, the next time anyone (and I do mean doctors-lawyers-Indian-chiefs-your-kids'-principal-your-gynecologist ANYONE) brings up old Lie-and-Screw, I want you to think, 'fuck him,' but share, noisily, one of Auntie Myrna's devious plans for Richard's selfish purchases.

When asked about him, respond with panach . . . panash. (No,

I don't know how to spell it, loser.) Let people know that . . .

1. You plan to donate both of his shiny, imported motorcycles to the first pair of obese, perspiring, Latin American, atheist, illegal-immigrant lesbians you can find. We'll toast their good health as they roar into legally-wedded bliss.

2. His two Porsches . . . similar idea. You find two of those anti-gun, pro-choice, health-care-for-everyone, tree-hugging, Rush-Limbaugh-is-a-fascist lunatics who Tweet inane drivel to Keith Olbermann and Al Sharpton, not any of the intelligent ones trying to change the world for the better, but a couple of the drunk, stupid, unemployed ones who couldn't spell 'Limbaugh' with sidewalk chalk. They drive off to the protest in matching 911s, and we celebrate with wine, chocolate, and Ben & Jerry's Mocha Orgasm Chip.

3. For your house on Wilmette Court and the other on Beechwood Avenue, you can let people know that you're planning to use them as halfway houses for pedophiles and paroled sexual assault convicts. Kiddie porn and hand cream all around! Oops . . . there goes the country club. Some of those golf slacks will be like dick targets. Cigar sales in the pro shop will go way, way down.

4. For all of your diamonds, pearls, and other 'apology' jewelry, that one's easy. You donate it to the Democratic National Committee to help elect brown-skinned activists determined to bring equitable resources to disenfranchised, unemployed, immigrants from sea to polluted sea! (Sorry, I'm getting carried away!)

5. For that 40-foot yacht he brought to seduce unsuspecting Chili's waitresses up and down the Jersey coast, I suggest you let people know that you're planning to sell it to a company that ferries Cuban

refugees (and drug dealers) from Havana to Miami, 24 hours a day, except Easter of course. Because you know how much old Dickie loves our great American melting pot.

6. And finally, truly the best for last, the BMW M-Class Roadster convertible, the very car he bought for himself the same weekend he bought you a Dyson vacuum cleaner, the most powerful vacuum cleaner in the world. What ever should we tell people you plan to do with his BWM M-Class Roadster? Oh, wait! I know . . . you tell them you're planning to put the top down and fill it to the brim with whale sperm. Yes, sweetie, warm, sticky, aromatic, undulating whale sperm. Of course, to pull that off (lol) you're going to have to jerk off a whale, probably a few times. Don't worry. I'll help you.

Anyway, I hope these helped. I've got to run now, but call or text later if you wanna get drunk or hijack a Japanese trawler or something.

Love you!

Myrna.

Oh, PS: If it makes you feel any better, you can let the people at that Monmouth County Animal Adoption Agency know that he gave away the dog you got as a wedding present (Who does that?) because it chewed a corner of the sofa. And then he gave away the dogs you got as puppies, because they jumped up to greet guests . . . and those psychotic PETA crazies will eat his ass on a hoagie roll. No kidding.

Peace.

November 26

Dear Billy,

As direct as I've tried to be in these notes, I realize I'm skirting a couple of issues, because they're embarrassing for me.

On one point of clarification, I figured I'd come clean so you know the depth of the water we're swimming in together.

In a confession written for his therapist, Richard admitted that there were days when he would have sex with me in the morning, have sex with one of his girlfriends during the afternoon, when he was at work, out for a run, biking, going for groceries, whatever, and then come home either for sex with me again, or to masturbate to Internet pornography, sometimes as often as twice a day. He suggested for a while that he was addicted to sex. I call bullshit on that for a number of reasons I'll get to later.

For now, that's enough. I just wanted you to know outright.

Also, just so you know: that was pretty difficult to write.

Keep well,

Jennifer

PS: As far as I can figure, with old calendars and datebooks I've thrown in a cardboard box downstairs, he regularly had sex with a number of women while I was pregnant with each of our boys. In the past few months, now that he and I are willing to shout at one another about anything, I've asked if he ever thought that he might be passing a crippling infection on to me (he did, a few times) or to one of his children in utero.

He wouldn't answer.

December

But what troubled you was Nick's decision to rest in the island of pines with its needle carpet and its splash of diffuse sunlight.

December 1

Hey Billy,

I hope you don't mind that I attached that email from Myrna last week. She always makes me smile; I think it's because she's somehow Teflon coated when it comes to the local Bitch Squad. She does her own thing and doesn't care how it registers on the Richter scale around the community pool. I want to be her.

Actually, I want to be Kate Upton, especially when I'm at the community pool.

Nah. Kidding.

Anyway, I have another bit of old writing I thought I'd send your way, just for another perspective on the tangled web of uncertainty, anxiety, and formative rubber cement that has made me the Upton wannabe I am today. This is a piece of short . . . nonfiction, I guess . . . that I wrote before an especially animated therapy session (with Dr. Lane, you'd love her!) I attended about eighteen months ago. It made for some interesting therapeutic fodder. Rather than re-work the whole thing for your benefit, I'll just paste it in here. You can read this over, and I'll pick up the threads frayed from this bit of history later on.

Oh, but before you start . . . I suppose I should say that this is true. This happened, as well as I can recall it anyway. I don't know if I remember it exactly as it took place, or if my memories have filled in some of the cracks in the pavement with more of that rubber cement. Either way, if you were to put a gun to my head today (that'll make sense shortly), I'd say that this bit is true.

Also, I'm no Emily Dickinson. This reads like whatever they call those articles, *narrative nonfiction*, but if my narration suffers in places, remember: I studied Elementary Education. We don't read Dickinson. Although spending the next ten years of my life locked in my bedroom and wearing my wedding dress doesn't seem like such a neurotic suggestion any more. Maybe Emily knew Richard.

I call this . . .

'Velveeta Processed Cheese'

I don't know what will someday kill me, if I'll go quietly in my sleep or get T-boned by a county garbage truck. I hope it isn't drowning or burning to death or Lou Gehrig's disease (that's a vicious bastard). No thanks.

Around here, if an accident doesn't get you and you don't die from complications due to obesity (it chalks up more pudgy corpses annually than cigarettes and alcohol combined), the Grim Reaper often appears in the guise of a metastasizing invasion of cancerous cells, hell bent to gobble up your liver, lungs, colon, pancreas . . . whatever gets you into the Ziploc baggie.

Again, no thanks.

But I did eat a lot of Velveeta processed cheese.

From 1973 to 1989, I bet I had Velveeta sliced, melted, baked, or casseroled into something at least twice a week. My mother's no slouch in the kitchen. When she wants to, she can hold her own with the slickest of the reality TV chefs eliminating one another over half-baked quail. But with my aunts, uncles, and cousins around, and my brother and me getting involved with sports, music, and friends down the shore, Mom often had to make due with whatever she could cook up quickly and get on the table between softball practices, music lessons, homework tutorials, and Dad coming home hungry.

If you've never cooked with it, there isn't much that melts so agreeably into a mouthful of incipient chemotherapy as a block of Velveeta processed cheese.

One of my mother's staples throughout the 70s and 80s was homemade macaroni and cheese. These days she makes it with sharp Cheddar, smoked Gouda, even Gorgonzola when she's feeling frisky. It's good. I swear my bother can eat his own weight in the stuff, just with a spoon and a six pack of Bud Light.

Back then, however, Mom and Dad didn't have $8.99 to spend on eight ounces of real cheese just to bake it over macaroni. Velveeta came in dense, stackable, foil-wrapped bricks the Mayans could've used to build a temple in the Yucatán. And it was blue-collar, white-trash cheap. No one knew at the time that processed food would kill us or cause us all to balloon into Mama Cass. We just knew it came cheap and it melted smoothly into happiness. The cancer-rotted bodies didn't start piling up until the Reagan administration.

That spring, my brother was away at school. Mom, Dad, and I had the house to ourselves until Gary came home for the summer. (My brother's name isn't really 'Gary,' but Dad's always been a fan of the film version of *For Whom the Bell Tolls*. The name just kind-of stuck when we were kids.)

That house, my parents' old place on the hill above the river, even twenty-five years since I've lived there, so many memories are burned indelibly into my mind. I can even recall the boring bits, the interminable summer days when school had been out for a while, but the clock hadn't quite spun far enough to signify that the time had come to shop for notebooks, pencils, and matching Granimals shirts and skirts: second grade style.

I remember how curious our house felt without Gary around, like a sweater that used to fit. I'd tug at the sleeves of the place, stretch the crew neck, anything to adjust myself in that house, just me and my parents. The walls, floors, windows were all the same, the neat seams in the brickwork my father had done by hand – he used black cement because my mother found it reminiscent of an East Village apartment.

All of it, I knew it: the smells, textures, creaks, and ghostly moans of the doors and floorboards, but it felt oddly off center with just the three of us, as if it had been nudged a bit to one side by a passing earthquake that didn't have the polite decency to shove us back aright once it'd gone up Tamarac Road toward the lake.

Coming out of the bathroom, up the hallway, around the dinner table, in the living room with the blue Berber carpet, some semi-conscious part of me always expected Gary to appear, as if he'd just been in his room reading.

But he didn't show up, and I weathered the awkward silences, the clumsy stops and starts in what had been the steady clockwork of our family routine. Mom and Dad felt it, too, and without my brother around, they adjusted to the unexpected moments of disquiet by sharpening their scrutiny of me.

How many paragraphs did you write?
How many math problems do you have tonight?
Are the odds in the back of the book?

Do you need anything ironed?
How many miles before the car is due for an oil change?
Do you really need to be on the phone for an hour?
Are you really going to wear that to school?
Did you get a C on a history quiz?
Do you think it's because you're on the phone all the time?
Or listening to that nonsense, Purple Rain?
Or skipping class?
Are you skipping class?
Only in my mind, Mom.

And then April 17, 1988.

And macaroni and cheese fresh from the oven, a 375-degree trapdoor to Hell, the house redolent of Velveeta and Parliament cigarette smoke.

Mom cooked. Dad smoked Parliaments and drank Dewar's Scotch and soda over ice, a slam-dunk assurance that any Scotsman worth a damn would have tossed his sorry Irish ass into the North Sea. I did Algebra II homework and listened to Prince's *Purple Rain* on my stereo. I probably had it turned up too loud, irritated him while he poured cheap booze with unsteady fingers. He and Mom discussed my brother, spring break, the leaky upstairs shower, our old dog's veterinary bills, the here and there desultory meanderings of any forty-five-year-old couple who've been together since ninth grade.

My room back then was a sanctuary, a cave I'd escape to whenever he'd get fired up over something unexpected or trivial, usually something he'd forget until the next time he opened his veins and dumped Dewar's into his bloodstream. He rarely came down the hall, though. I think it might have been because my father, for all of his embarrassing affairs, knew comparatively little about women. The thought of entering my room, unannounced, and discovering me in the midst of anything *womanly* would have turned him into a pillar of salt.

He almost never washed clothes, but when he did he wouldn't fold my underwear, wouldn't touch my bras. Rather, he'd leave them in the dryer for me or my mother to discover later on. Dad, like Richard, was never more than ten minutes away from that one drink, the one that would convince him that he was irresistible to nurses or waitresses everywhere. Sadly, also like Richard, Dad often had that drink in a place where lonely nurses and waitresses go to feel love, even ephemeral love that smells of watered down Scotch.

Regardless, I felt safe in my room.

Until that April.

I did math homework and listened to Prince sing about how he would die for me. Periodically, I'd distract myself and watch the gathering darkness beneath the dogwoods outside my window. I've never been creative, have always been awed and mystified at the movies – never cared that this or that actor's wardrobe changed, mid-scene, without warning. I'd forgive them and let myself be carried away for two hours of cathartic escape. But if I did revel in the fantastic notion of breaking free from the working-class chains that I'd drag around forever like Jacob Marley's IHOP waitress, I had those fantasies while tucked away in that room, watching lightning bugs flicker beneath my mother's favorite dogwoods.

Dad came in carrying his drink, interrupted me factoring a quadratic. To this day, I can't factor a quadratic. Without saying anything, he crossed to my turntable (I had *Purple Rain* on LP) and looked down at the spinning record with dull, confused anger. He peeked behind the stereo; I had it propped on a banana yellow milk crate I'd hijacked from my ninth grade history classroom. He might have been looking for the electric cable. I don't know. He hadn't a clue how to turn off the music, so he grabbed the delicate needle arm and yanked it off the record with a visceral screech.

I didn't move, stayed frozen on my bed, determined to weather the storm without provoking him. He wheeled slowly on me, started in with a slur I will hear in nightmares until Satan one day grants my parole.

'You were late last night.'

I didn't answer, didn't look up.

'Yeah. Yeah. I know . . . know what time it was. You were . . . it was 12:20 at least.' He took a half step forward, overcorrected left and braced himself against my closet door. It wasn't much, just a stutter step to the side, but I felt it in my stomach like turbulence: he'd moved between me and the corridor.

I stayed still, argued with myself over whether it'd be wise to make eye contact tonight. Some nights that fostered such a wellspring of pride in him – when I stood my ground – he'd lose track of why he'd gotten angry. But tonight it wouldn't work. Some vestigial, primitive, survival instinct inside my chest told me to stay low and ride this one out.

'Yup. Yup. You did . . . were. And I don't know how many times we have to tell you . . . have . . . how many . . .'

Purple Rain continued spinning on my turntable. He watched it for a second or two, then moved matter-of-factly to the milk crate and kicked the whole works: crate, stereo, Prince, speakers, a cracked plastic toss of wire-strung garbage into the far corner of my room.

I heard Mom coming from the kitchen.

So did he.

The clock wound down; he went sharp and deep in a rare show of efficiency that, had my mother not intervened, most likely would have led to my suicide later that night.

Dad turned awkwardly in his slippers – he'd hurt his foot. 'Whore! Do you not realize . . . understand you're a whore?'

Scotch and soda splashed over his knuckles onto my rug. I watched the drips track lazily toward his wrist, catching my lamplight.

'Letting him touch you like that . . . that's a whore; you cheap . . . and this music, this fucking . . .' He glanced to where the stereo had been, shook his head, too enraged to recall that he'd just corner kicked it like Pele. 'This shit you listen to, fucking shit, fucking him like a goddamned cheap whore . . . you think he really –'

'Gerry, get out here.' Mom stood in my doorway, as angry as I've ever seen her.

As angry as she's ever been.

He ignored her, leaned in to deliver this salvo close up, one he could savor. And God and Christ forgive me, but on his deathbed, I hope my father remembers that he got drunk enough and angry enough one night back in April, 1988 to call me a cunt.

He said it.

The rest of his Scotch slopped over my bedspread. I felt it all night like a puddle of cold piss. His face red, damp with acrid sweat, he said, 'I want you to go out there and call him, call him, have him come get you, because you can't fucking live in my fucking house if you're a whore's cunt!'

If you're a woman reading this little story, take a second – right now – and turn to your boyfriend, husband, father of your children, and make it clear to him that if he ever calls your daughter a cunt, you'll kill him. You don't have to describe it in detail or tell him how you'll manage it. Just tell him: 'Use that word with my daughter, and I'll kill you. God strike me dead a thousand, thousand times if I don't.'

Gloria Steinem and *Ms.* magazine would have me celebrate that word, cunt, because it's spent too many years as a brutal, acrimonious, derogatory term. I, as a woman, should play a role in reviving it as a celebration of my unappreciated sexual and reproductive organs.

Yeah, screw her, too.

Did her drunk, stereo-kicking father ever call her a whore's cunt? Not a *kundi* or a *cunti* or whatever native Indian term means fellowship or some slobbery bullshit? If he did, then he's an asshole too.

Or maybe I'm too hard on Steinem.

I went to see Eve Ensler in *The Vagina Monologues*. I stood up with the rest of the audience and chanted, 'Cunt! Cunt! Cunt!' in that wonderful affirmation of how exhilarating it can feel to shout bad words with well-dressed strangers. We all patted ourselves on the back and said, 'Whew! *That* was invigorating.' But the following weekend at Giants Stadium, I stood, and in my strongest Gloria-Steinem voice, shouted, 'Tony Romo's just a cunt! Cunt! Cunt!'

Security had me in handcuffs in three minutes.

Yeah, that's a lie, but you get the point.

We've got a ways to go before that word is entirely rescued. No one had gone to any lengths to rescue it that spring, when my father used it just after kicking my stereo to pieces.

Mom stepped in, rage and loathing twisting that wonderful woman into something ugly, actually dangerous. She took him by the arm, ordered him, 'Gerry, get out of this room now!'

And he turned on her.

His highball glass dropped to my bedspread; the ice clinked on the warm flannel like shards from a broken window. I still have that glass. I save dimes in it, just dimes, until I collect enough for a bottle of wine, something nice I drink by myself.

You see, he dropped the glass to free his hand.

Mom didn't care.

He swung hard and fast, still dull and sloppy; he didn't seem to make up his mind whether he wanted to punch her or to slap her. At the last instant, he did neither. Instead, he grabbed her, clumsily at first but then tighter, brailling his way around her throat.

I want to remember Mom's eyes bulging or her gasping for breath, but she didn't. Some Mama Bear instinct flooded her bloodstream with enough molten-hot adrenaline to match the cheap, smoky Scotch clouding his. And that fast, clutching one another as they'd never imagined on those naïve nights strolling down Broadway to the river or cruising out 52 to Orange Lake, my parents disappeared from my room.

Still frozen on my bed, I heard them struggle along the hallway, the haunted floorboards groaning beneath them. No one spoke. Dad made a few incoherent, grunting, guttural sounds, the spastic, retarded confusion I'd expect from a lunatic trapped behind those last unintelligible moments that capstone an irrevocable crime of passion.

Something broke.

I heard it snap, audibly crack like Harrison Ford's whip.

I looked for it later, after Mom had gone to bed but couldn't find it. I wish I'd found something broken, cracked, shattered, whatever, didn't like thinking it'd been inside me. But I heard it. And that sound, Indiana Jones whip-assing some NAZI, that crack woke me from my catatonic disbelief. I crossed the hall to my parents' bedroom, only vaguely aware of Dad choking Mom against the neat seams in the brickwork. He'd used black concrete, because it reminded my mother of an East Village apartment.

In 1988, Dad carried a silver Smith & Wesson .357 magnum, a revolver. He left it in his sock drawer, loaded, with the clear understanding that my brother and I were forbidden ever to touch it, never mind remove it, draw it from the soft leather holster, and carry it down the corridor to the living room.

I did.

For an interminable moment, I considered blowing my brains out, just tucking the barrel under my chin and forcing myself to pull the trigger. I'd never have mustered the nerve to put that gaping barrel in my mouth, but beneath my chin . . . that'd show him.

But I didn't, and I didn't because when I turned toward them I caught a momentary glimpse of the kitchen light playing on my mother's white knuckles, gripped tightly on the tanned leathery muscles of his forearm.

Two decades later, I know that was God, whatever He looks like, wherever He is, whatever you think, I don't care. If there's a God, and there'd better be, He let that bit of light catch my mother's knuckles, and I decided to save her.

I half jogged toward them. 'Hey! Hey! HEY!' The gun raised to shoot – no, to *kill* him – I had to scream to get his attention. Yet in the end, it wasn't me running or shouting that did it. Rather, it was my mother's eyes as she saw me coming for him, lunacy, homicide, devastation, utter abject despair in my face. Dad saw her gaze shift, and the few coherent brains cells still firing on all cylinders gave him just enough hesitation to loosen his grip from Mom's throat and turn lethargically around.

Fortunately for him, he didn't yell, didn't even speak. If he'd have said one word to me, I'd have shot him six times in the face, chest, and face again until the gun clicked dryly in my hand.

Mom yelled, but I can't remember what she said. Like the brick wall, the kitchen light, the aromas of Parliament cigarette smoke and macaroni and cheese collapsed into a smeary, uncertain backdrop, like a sloppy acrylic painting. Only Dad stood out in crisp, stark relief, his Monmouth Bluegrass Festival T-shirt as clear as the HD images I get from my Blu-ray player nearly three decades later.

I bit hard on the inside of my cheek; it didn't help to iron the tremor out of my voice. 'Get out. Out now, or I'll kill you. I'll kill you, and if you ever, ever touch her again, I'll kill you, Dad. I swear to God I'll kill you.'

He watched me for a long moment, then sucked at his teeth, shook his head in disappointment, and blew out a long, slow breath that said, *Well, lookee who's Miss Big Britches.*

Again, I almost shot him, killed the werewolf with his own silver bullets. 'Out.'

He collected his wallet, cigarettes, and car keys – to his police cruiser – and left quietly. I suppose he had a .12 gauge in his car he might've used to shoot me, my mother, even himself. He didn't. Instead, he returned three days later, sober, apologetic, and with a $169 Kmart stereo under his arm.

Twenty years later, Richard came home from a three-day bender with a $15,000 diamond ring, a more expensive apology than Dad's $169 stereo, but both washed in on the same bad-smelling tide.

I shouldn't have accepted either. But I accepted both.

Recently, my mother and I discussed what happened that night. I told her how sorry I'd felt for her for so long, and how I'd have given anything – even my own life – to set her free from my father's poison.

She said she was glad I hadn't, that she tried to pry the gun from my fingers but gave up for fear that we'd accidentally shoot one another. She'd followed me dazedly around the house for a half hour until I finally placed the old revolver gently beside the toaster. She'd planned to tackle me from behind if I raised the gun to my own head in the confused stretch of God-awful minutes right after Dad fled.

I don't think he knows that; I'm sure she never told him. Even today, he doesn't realize she's capable of that kind of bravery.

And if there's a silver lining, I never ate another ounce of Velveeta processed cheese. If I smell it, I have to leave the room or risk throwing up.

Oh, *The Vagina Monologues* was excellent. See it if you can.

And that's it, Billy. Granted, there are a few loose ends in there that I'll tie up in later emails to you – assuming, you know, that you're out there somewhere and willing to read anything I send your way. Do I frighten you? I don't mean to. If so, just say the word, and I'll stop writing.

(But I won't want to. Sorry, but I have to tell you the truth; it's a rare commodity around here, and one I need.)

Jennifer

December 10

Dear Billy,

Myrna and I met for coffee today while my older boys were at baseball practice. Homer came along and colored a picture of a reindeer that looked like a collie who had expired from bone cancer just after being run down by a city bus. Yes, my guys play winter ball. Fall ball, spring ball, summer league, winter workouts, we're baseball people.

Anyway, two-hour practices give us an opportunity to catch up, gossip, complain, and ingest felonious amounts of caffeine at felonious prices the dope peddlers at Starbucks slap on every *venti whatever whatever.*

I told her about you.

My hands shook; I had to grip the cup. It was exciting in a hushed-infidelity kind of way.

You know how you have moments that stick with you, unexpected interactions when you can recall every word, every nuance of the day, light through the window, details, the angle of a napkin, the number of sugar packets torn and abandoned beside a spoon still cradling a few drops of tepid coffee?

You know those moments?

I had one of those moments with Myrna this afternoon.

'C'mon, sweetie, you gotta spill it,' she pressed. 'What's going on with you?'

'I've been . . . distracted recently.'

'I can tell. What I wanna know is why.'

I didn't know what to say, Billy. But some part of me wanted her to know about you, so I lied, just a little. 'I've been thinking about re-connecting with an old boyfriend, Billy Klein. He and I dated when I was at Rutgers.'

'I thought you met Dickface at Rutgers.' Her hands working of their own volition peeled the top off her cup, dumped in a third sugar.

'I did,' I said. 'This was before . . . him.'

'It's okay, sweetie, you can call him Dickface. I don't mind.'

I took a quick swallow just to buy time. To me Starbucks too often tastes like burned dirt. 'Billy was a baseball player —'

'Oh I love baseball players, those pants, that sexy squint in the sunshine; yup, they do things for me.' She fanned herself with a paper napkin. 'Might even need a little alone time in the car when we're done.'

'Nice,' I crumpled the napkin. 'Knock it off, will you? There's kids here.'

'Mama's got needs, sweetie,' she laughed. 'And keep in mind, Kong and I've been together since ninth grade. I never had a chance to date any NCAA athletes.' She thought on this for a second, 'not that a battalion of them came calling.'

Behind us, barristas communicated in fluent dope peddler: *grande, no foam, extra hot, half-caf.*

'Anyway . . . Billy and I hit it off right away. We were young and stupid in love and making plans for kids and houses and careers and Labrador retrievers . . . oh God, Myrna, we'd have screwed it up, but at the time, every tiny detail of our life together made sense, as if one of those 1000-piece puzzles had fallen from the sky and magically fitted into place.'

She frowned, nonplussed. 'Damn, you must've been in love, because you're sounding like a dopey Hallmark commercial.'

'No, it wasn't sappy. It was special, right from the start, took me 136 days.'

'Whaddya mean? I don't get it.'

'To know. It took me 136 days to know that I was in love – From April 7 to August 21, 1991 – that he was the one, maybe not the only one, I have to be honest about that. Right? When I met Richard, I got caught up in the excitement surrounding his life and his band. Sure, that was pretty addicting, too. But –'

'But with Billy?'

'He was the guy I should have chosen . . . *chosen* . . . should've begged him to have me and then chained myself to him. It would've been happily ever after, and if not happily ever after, at least a helluva lot more happily some goddamn thing than I am these days.'

'So . . .' She raised an eyebrow.

'Yeah, I buggered it up, the biggest mistake of my life.'

Venti, extra pump, extra foam, java chip, upside down

Myrna reached across the table, took my hand, squeezed hard. 'Call him.'

'No.'

'Why not? It isn't as if you're going to reconcile with Dickface. Or better yet, gimme his number and I'll call him. If he's every bit as sexy as you say –'

'I haven't said.'

'If he's every bit as sexy as I imagine, then maybe he's looking for an experienced woman, albeit a tad toward the Rubens end of the underwear rack at Wal-Mart.'

I scoffed. 'You're not fat.'

'Don't lie, sweetie, it makes your face scrunch up like an old sponge, not pretty.' She fussed with the hot-finger thingie on her cup, 'So?'

'So . . . what?'

'Was he sexy?'

'God yes,' I sighed like Audrey Hepburn. 'Not square-jawed-hero sexy, but 'til-death-do-us-part sexy, better-than-average, and amazing in a few places, you know, a crooked smile here, an endearing dimple there, stuff I could've watched age and change over five or six pretty satisfying decades.'

'Holy shit,' Myrna finished her coffee in a gulp. 'If you don't call him, maybe I will. Old Kong's got his good traits, but he tends to keep them hidden behind that seventy-five pounds of excess blubber he insists on carrying around.'

'Bullshit,' I said. 'Dave's not fat.'

'No lying, sweetie . . . sponge face. Okay? Remember sponge face.'

Grande, Demerol, Percocet, Oxycodone, Xanax, children's aspirin, no foam, decaf

'Anyway, I was in love, and I regret every smoothly varnished mistake I made that year, every last one. I keep them polished and neatly lined up in my memory like porcelain screw ups in a China cabinet, especially these days.'

'Call him.'

'Maybe.'

'You should,' she said. 'C'mon, he's probably married and fat and bald and drooly and unemployed and missing a few prominent teeth. Who knows?'

'Maybe,' I said again, knowing I was full of shit.

Tall, mocha, no whip, ristretto

Again, Myrna squeezed my hand. 'He could be trim, gainfully employed, a great father, and recently divorced from a genuine merciless bitch who tried to ruin his life. A call from you might be exactly what he needs right now.'

And there it was, Billy. Whaddya think? Could I possibly be exactly what you need right now?

Should I call? Let me know. I'm listening.

Jennifer

December 18

Hey Billy,

Tonight I've been thinking about alliteration (my son had some questions on his homework), barrooms (because they're never too far from my mind), and our old friend, Nick Adams. So I decided to have a couple of drinks and scribble a note to you.

My guys are in bed. Richard is . . . I dunno . . . on a date? Who cares? And I'm half a bottle of Merlot into a Tuesday evening – I know; I know: stupid. But I had a couple things I wanted to send your way, and Nick Adams, the wine, and my son's literature homework brought them all back to me in vivid Technicolor.

Do they have Technicolor anymore? I don't think so. That used to be the cool part; remember that? When they'd scroll those blocky, 3-D, *TECHNICOLOR* letters across the screen, you knew you were in for a great show.

Whatever. Sorry. That's the Merlot. I'll muscle through it. Just give me a second here.

Anyway, here's a news flash: Women don't go to bars because we're hoping to find a sweaty, smelly, sloppy, embarrassing, one-night stand with a man we hope will never call us again.

That happens sometimes; Tequila's poison after all.

However, we don't plan on it.

We do – periodically – go to bars hoping to meet someone witty and relatively good looking, who's polite and who truly listens to what we have to say and who looks as if he might even listen to what we have to say *after* we've had sex.

And who doesn't spend all evening talking to our boobs.

But spends some of the evening talking to our boobs.

We go to bars thinking we might meet this fit, polite, funny, friendly, gentleman and that our drinking, fondling, fumbling, and fornicating just might result in a call the next day when we meet, share an embarrassed apology over a nonfat, chai latte and *then* fall madly in love 'til death do us part.

That doesn't happen often.

Nope.

What often happens is that we arrive at the bar hoping for fit, friendly, funny – and if we're lucky – forgiving. But when he's not there (I understand he's been spotted recently in Boston; maybe it was Baltimore) we too often settle for his knuckle-dragging doppelganger: fat, farts, and foul.

I swear to God I'll cut out the silly alliteration. It's just that after homework tonight I figured I'd see if I had any left in me. Pretty cool, huh?

Going to a bar with friends is an act of dishonesty almost every time. Again, many women will say that I've lost my mind or that I've lost touch with the self-actualizing feats my girlfriends and I managed back in our twenties.

I'm trying to be honest.

Women go to bars like we go to Atlantic City casinos. Everyone wants to have a good time for the night, but deep down, bubbling in there with those getting-dressed, pre-game cocktails is the faint hope that the stars will align and we'll go home with the progressive jackpot. Sure, just being there's fun, but we want to win big.

Maybe tonight's the night. Maybe the gods will take pity on me, and I'll meet the man with Sean Connery's accent, Robert Downey, Jr.'s wit, Johnny Depp's looks, and Mel Gibson's ass — minus the lunatic anti-Semitism.

I'll just meander up to the bar, and there he'll be: his shirt tucked in, his nails clean, his belt matching his shoes, and his debilitating neuroses masked either by deft therapy or manageable doses of anti-psychotics.

He'll take one look at me standing alone in a wilderness of cheap, plastic harlots, and we'll wake in each other's arms at sunrise to plan an elaborate, beachside, barefoot wedding — after another half-dozen shuddering, time-bending orgasms, of course.

Yup.

We believe it happens, just like the addict shitheads who believe tonight's the night they'll hit the jackpot at Donald Trump's casino.

I wonder which has the longer odds, actually. I've probably got a better chance of being struck by lightning while in the jaws of a great white shark . . . just like that triple play, Billy.

Think about it: Even if your most loyal, seen-you-at-your-worst girlfriend, playing supportive linebacker on your first night out after the most devastating, soul-crushing breakup of your life will pinkie swear that men are off the menu for the night. It'll be just greasy food and vodka shots until a paramedic is administering chest compressions to both of you.

Well if the *Bull Durham* Kevin Costner, the *Ricochet* Denzel

Washington, the *Oceans 11* George Clooney, or the *Hitch* version of Will Smith shows up looking lonely, even that sworn-to-love-and-protect-you girlfriend . . . bitch . . . will be undone. The next thing you know, it's all hair flips, 'oh my gods!' and forearm touchy.

My least favorite: forearm touchy.

Why do I tell you these things?

Because, sadly, I'm far enough down this path to know the truth. When I was twenty, I didn't appreciate what I had, because I truly believed it would happen again and again. I believed that adorable baseball players would be so smitten by the charming way I wrote my lab reports that they'd be lining up to toss their hats at me – making me feel more special than any barroom drunk ever could, even the semi-evolved Neanderthals who periodically manage an amusing pickup line.

I didn't appreciate you, didn't deserve you.

Even that night in the Ratskeller after the Penn State game, I wore your hat, knew you'd find me, knew we'd hit it off.

We did. On those corner stools, whatever existed between us was organic and powerful enough to shift the tectonic plates – just an inch or two – but far enough that no one in the Keller seemed to notice us. If our friends were there, no one interrupted. No one stumbled over; nothing broke that wonderful, ephemeral plane that closed us off from the rest of the world for a few hours.

Jesus, if we only knew, at twenty, how few of those moments we get, maybe we'd savor them a bit longer and stretch them into the wee hours.

But I was young and dumb and drunk and eventually distracted by alcohol and hormones and the thin, mop-haired, wanna-be rock star who sang in the garage band they'd booked that night in the Keller. Who knew I'd end up dating him after you graduated? Who knew I'd end up married to him for eighteen years?

All I did was look up, just for a second, when I heard him singing some Eddie Vedder tune. You were busy explaining something to my boobs at the time – not that you did too much of that, nope, just enough.

I made eye contact with him, and he winked at me, editing Pearl Jam's lyrics to include the line, 'Nice hat.'

I laughed because I was twenty and I was drunk, and I was over the moon intoxicated with the very idea of you, Billy. With your one lopsided incisor and your receding hairline, you couldn't compete with a rock star who'd change Pearl Jam to hit on me in a crowded bar. Because I was twenty, and all twenty year olds understand that smart, athletic, compassionate, supportive men will line up for them for years. All we have to do is pucker up and feign interest, and it'll be *rainin' men*.

Yeah. Heh. Bullshit.

How many smart, fit, compassionate men have ever lined up for me?

Exactly one.

And I let you get away, because I thought the rock star would bring excitement and romance to my life. I was entitled to excitement and romance, you see.

Bullshit.

I don't know why I couldn't be content just to remain behind that mysterious ephemeral plane that protected us, giving us something special, however temporary. I wanted more.

Now I'd give just about anything to go back to the Ratskeller, April 7, 1991 with you.

Do you think we could recapture what we had in that shadowy corner, in a world lit only by those uncertain candles?

Jesus Christ, but I want another chance.

Why can't we have second chances?

I wasn't selfish; I was dumb. I wasn't entitled; I was naïve and drunk.

Why couldn't some forty-three-year-old woman have shown up in a silver DeLorean, grabbed me by the hair and slapped the stupid right out of me? Why'd I break your hold on me even for a second?

That's rhetorical. I did it, because I always imagined there'd be another square-jawed hero to sweep me off my feet. You didn't have a square jaw, just that one crooked incisor.

If I only knew.

That night, you talked on and on about a Modern American Fiction class you were worried about failing. You'd only enrolled because one of the guys on the team, Pete or Andy, had said it was an easy A. We decided either they'd played you and that the class was genuinely tough, or that you truly were a semi-literate baseball player.

And I a cleat-chasing slut.

We drank Busch Light on tap, donkey piss, while you talked about Ernest Hemingway as if he and Nick Adams might wander into the Ratskeller and order a couple of grappas. You didn't give a shit about the class but were upset that Hemingway's 'Big Two-Hearted

River' had confounded you.

I'd never read it, rather toiled away with the other sophomores in Russian Literature, hadn't met Ernest or Nick yet.

I've read it since that night, though. Thirty-one times. For my two cents it's the only story in that collection, *In Our Time*, worthy of Hemingway's signature.

You did a sweet job describing it for me, as the mop-haired rock and roller lugged amplifiers and set up microphone stands. You'd been confused by Nick's journey out of Seney and into the wilderness.

Seney exists, by the way, up there in Michigan. It's just a one-moped town, but it's there.

We drank and ate handfuls of spicy Chex Mix, probably rife with bacteria, and you described your confusion at why Hemingway would send Nick on the journey, alone, on foot, uphill, with a 'much too heavy' backpack.

The metaphor for life's burdens made sense, even to me who hadn't read the story. But what troubled you was Nick's decision to rest in the island of pines with its needle carpet and its splash of diffuse sunlight. A place where even the sweet-smelling fern had been forbidden to grow, Nick removes his pack, rests on that carpet, and falls asleep with Nature itself keeping watch.

Afterward, Nick reshoulders his pack-cum-metaphor and makes his way to the riverside meadow where he sets up camp.

'I can't figure why he takes that nap,' you said. 'I mean, what's the point?'

I chased another mouthful of Chex Mix with another swig of Busch Light. 'Dunno. Maybe he was tired.'

'Obviously he was tired. He'd just come back from the war. He had post-traumatic stress, a hot day, and a heavy pack. He was freakin' exhausted. But I still don't get it. It's almost like Ernie had two pretty good paragraphs about a guy napping and no place to put them.'

I reached over, put my hand on your forearm, squeezed.

(Forearm touchy. I hate forearm touchy.)

I said, 'Billy, as fascinating as this all sounds, I stopped caring about Dick Adams –'

'Nick.'

'Nick . . . Adams . . . five minutes ago.'

You laughed, toasted me with your pint glass. 'Yeah, well laugh it up, Tolstoy, but I'm gonna flag this exam, because I can't figure out one shell-shocked fisherman's nap.'

We let it drop. I wish we hadn't. The band was about ready to kick start their set, and God knows we had out-of-tune grunge covers to enjoy.

Forty-five minutes later, the mop-haired, amp-lugging rocker sang 'nice hat' to me, and the spell was broken.

What a disappointment.

Do you know how many men have hit on me in a bar by asking my opinion of an inference he's drawn from a Hemingway story?

Yeah, you guessed it again: exactly one.

I have read that story since, and how I'd love to sit with you again . . . not at the Ratskeller, though. There's no amount of amoxicillin that would ever get me back into that dungeon, but someplace else, maybe a nice wine bar, where we'd get a bottle of something relaxing and go line-by-line through it together.

The nap makes sense, too.

Twenty-five years later, we all know that nap.

I bet you know it as well.

Nick, broken and spent and worn to the nub, gets off that train with a sackful of fear, self-loathing, and regret. He's got to walk up that burned hill, alone, lugging that burden, because that's the only way he can earn an admission ticket to that meadow and that river.

And his nap?

Whether it's God or Nature embracing him doesn't matter, because when he wakes he's been granted a moment's grace, a chance for rebirth.

All that's left is to bring order to the chaos at his campsite and then baptize himself in that water.

Holy shit, but wouldn't that be a neat trick? What I wouldn't give to nap like a corpse in a sheltering island of sentry pines, wake reborn, and wash away all my sins and fears in the safe, easy, nonthreatening shallows of a baptismal font. What a useful experience, a hell of a lot more effective than a colon cleanse or an extra couple of Oxycontin to bring sleep down like an anvil on Wile E. Coyote's flattened skull.

The nap's key. It's Nick's bridge from the burned hillsides of his past to the safe, predictable shallows of his present, and the cold, murky depths of the swamp in his future. It's just on the other side of that half-fallen cedar tree, another metaphor worth its weight in Chex Mix.

We spent . . . what . . . sixteen months together?

And I never read that story until I got into Professor Howard's Modernist Fiction class.

Another of my mistakes.

I imagine us discussing it. That's silly; isn't it? But I do. Sometimes we're beside a fire or wading in a shallow stream like Nick Adams. Other times we're at that wine bar. I've never been there, but it's mahogany with heavy-framed mirrors and tasteful linens lit by those same two candles from the Ratskeller.

I still have the hat.

I wear it when we walk and talk or sit and talk, Nick Adams forever young as we get older.

I can't remember if the garage band was any good.

Okay, that's a lie; we both know it. I hope you'll forgive me that one.

From your favorite cleat chaser,

Jennifer

December 26

Dear Billy,

I found a few pennies in my jacket this morning, one brand new and one dating back to 1971, the year I was born.

Just turning it over in my hand, I can't imagine the '71 ever had that enthusiastic, new-penny shine. The edges, letters, and date had been worn to the slats. Abe Lincoln looked like Ralph Fiennes as Lord Voldemort, and the color had faded from cheerful copper to turd brown. I tossed the new penny into my coin jar and taped the '71 to the fridge. Maybe I'll stop by Lowe's later and get some Brasso, shine it up again.

Curse frigging time, huh?

Jennifer

January

I'm the one lunatic who washes her hands every six minutes when two Chinese chicken farmers die out in Wang Fuk Province and Glen Beck promises that we're all going to succumb to avian flu if we don't duct tape our doors and windows shut.

January 2

Hey Billy,

Much about me has changed since the last time we saw one another. Probably most evident, from my perspective, is that damned near everything scares the hell out of me these days.

As a teenager or a college student, I'd try anything. My friends and I surfed on the roof of my mother's station wagon. I rode nearly all the way from Ocean Grove to Sea Girt before a Spring Lake cop yelled at me. Thankfully he'd been on a bike or we all would've cooled off in the lock-up until my father came to get us. That wouldn't have been pretty.

I'd eat anything. Food that would make a Kodiak bear shit his drawers, I'd slather it with mayo, nuke it for ninety seconds, and eat it on crackers. I didn't care.

Amusement park rides. Night SCUBA diving. Skiing back bowls in the dark. Partying on rooftops. Swimming through Hurricane Gloria. Making out with drunk fraternity brothers. Dancing with strangers. Driving home drunk. Drag racing jet skis on a crowded river. Crowd surfing at football games.

You name it, and I'd try it. No matter how reckless, stupid, or dangerous, the more adrenaline charged the better.

When I was seventeen, a couple of friends and I went on a weekend camping pilgrimage to Hope, New Jersey, the one-horse, one-Rolls-Royce town where they filmed the original *Friday the Thirteenth*. We set up camp on a small pond in the wooded hills outside town and spent the weekend skinny dipping, replaying grisly murder scenes from Jason's laundry list of disemboweled teenagers, and basically scaring the shit out of one another.

I loved it. But I wouldn't go back there now for all the money beneath Mrs. Voorhees's blood-stained mattress.

Not a chance.

These days, everything scares me. It's embarrassing how skittish I've become. Something as simple as an unfamiliar shadow on my curtains will keep me up, trembling for hours. I hate loud noises, strong storms, and sinister-looking teenagers in hooded sweatshirts. I can't jog unless I've previewed the route for disagreeable dogs, and I check and double check the electrical outlet before I go mining for a trapped bit of burned toast with a butter knife. I'm nervous around lawyers and rich white men, because I feel like they're stealing my retirement money. I was even scared that Bruce the Shark was going to eat Marlin and Dory.

What the hell happened to me?

I used to leave the toaster plugged in just to see if I could extricate the charred bit of crust without touching the sides, like a real-life game of Operation.

Now I'm a frightened rabbit, hiding in my small, suburban warren with my flanks protected. I hate it when my boys go outside to play. Jesus Christ, they're adolescents; they get injured just standing still. I go to the community pool in case one of them hits his head on the diving board and knocks himself senseless while the lifeguard is chatting up some bikini. I hold my breath when my eldest son cuts the grass, even though I spent nearly three-thousand dollars on a tractor that shuts down every time he so much as shifts his narrow ass on the seat. I'm terrified every Sunday that he's going to end up looking like Oscar Pistorius just getting the lawn mowed.

Microwaves, traffic, hot beverages, lightning, strangers, noisy breezes, snakes . . . good lord, snakes . . . burning candles, Interstate highways, airline travel – bugger all airline travel. I need a double-diphenhydramine-NyQuil-Jack-Daniels-and-Dramamine cocktail just to purchase an airline ticket.

I'm afraid of the ocean, school shooters, drug dealers, low-rent districts, acid rain, large crowds at sporting events or concerts, MS-13 members, and plague bacteria hanging around a public bathroom. I'm the one lunatic who washes her hands every six minutes when two Chinese chicken farmers die out in Wang Fuk Province and Glen Beck promises that we're all going to succumb to avian flu if we don't duct tape our doors and windows shut.

And yes, I'd bet that I have three-quarters of a mile of duct tape in sundry drawers and boxes around my house, just waiting for one-too-many Chinese chicken ranchers to fall over dead. Then it's zip, strip, and stick; my house will be like Travolta's bubble in that old movie.

You see, my imagination is a coke addict with a case of ADHD you could chart from space.

I don't sleep well anymore. That doesn't bother me too much, because adults who sleep well truly aren't paying attention. There's enough nefarious sentiment out there to keep any sane person up all night. But I'm afraid . . . See? Heh . . . that perhaps I take it to extremes.

When I go to my kids' school, I check for defilade and test desks for resilience, literally asking myself what caliber of bullet those bullshit, plastic chairs might be able to deflect. I make the boys show me multiple exits from classrooms, the gym, the cafeteria, just in case their school ends up on CNN.

Who does that?

What kind of message am I sending them? It's nuts and I know it, but keeping my mouth shut isn't an option. I'm their mother.

Last month, I flew to Chicago for a conference, a two-hour flight from Newark. Literally dozens of planes make it safely every day. Yet three days before I left, I sat my two older boys down to review what I wanted them to do in the 'unlikely' event that my plane was the one they'd see cast willy-nilly over some western-Pennsylvania hillside on the evening news. I made them recite contact numbers for my brother, his wife, my mother, and where to find the $276 in cash I'd stashed in the house. They know the various PIN numbers for my credit cards and debit accounts, even the name of the nice receptionist at State Farm who helped me adjust my life insurance policy when Richard moved out.

My middle son started to cry. Why wouldn't he? His mother's a goddamned reject from the Randle Patrick McMurphy Camp for Alcoholics & Sociopaths. I deserve to live in the woods outside Hope, New Jersey, sharpening my machete and wrestling Jason Voorhees for whatever road kill we can scrape up for lunch.

He looked at me – my son, not Jason – and said, 'Mom, why are you going, if you think you're going to crash?' He deplores crying in front of his brother and quickly dried his tears on my sleeve. (I don't mind; I sometimes feel like I've had snot, dried food, spoiled milk, blood, or coagulating spit up on my sleeves since 2000.)

I tried to explain. 'Sweetie, I don't think I'm going to crash. I think I'm going to be fine, but I want you to be ready in case I'm not around . . . you know . . . without warning.' No one said it, but they both read my mind: DO NOT CALL YOUR ASSHOLE FATHER.

Sensing the conversation drifting into the shallows, my eldest son, a trivia genius at thirteen, simply said, 'Mom, you realize that at any given time there are nearly 70,000 people in the air over the United States. More of them die from heart attacks than crashes each year.'

I hugged them both. I do a lot of that, couldn't help it if I wanted to.

My middle son laughed. 'How's your heart, Mom?'

My heart is fine. My heart is full and strong and healthy and ready to beat a noisy symphony until I see my youngest grandchild happily married and living someplace sunny, with leaves that change in October and snow for Christmas. My heart is maybe the only sane, reliable part of me left.

I have to do it. Like the hug thing, I can't help it. It's my job to be scared shitless day after tenuous day. It started when I popped with my first son. Almost six months had passed before I exploded. I stayed skinny. Richard liked that: my belly stayed small; while my boobs got big – new toys for him to toss around while he pretended that we were just a little bit pregnant.

Yeah: stupid Neanderthal.

But yes, it started when I realized, after about six months, that this was the most important thing I'd ever do. I woke one morning, caught sight of my baby bump in the closet mirror and had myself a minor league, junior varsity panic attack. (I've since moved up to varsity; we're coming to that bit shortly.)

I cupped one hand under that immutable, gravity-defying bulge – Richard slept like one of Jason Voorhees's latter-day victims; he never knew – and had myself a momentary break from the confident façade I'd spackled on every day since I pissed on that plastic stick and scored a purple cross.

I'm not ready to be a mother. What'll I do when he gets a fever, breaks a bone, cuts his head open riding his bike, drives his car into a ditch, gets his girlfriend pregnant, smokes pot on my deck, goes bankrupt, gets divorced, has surgery, chemotherapy?

Shit. Holy fustickating shit. Who signs up for this? We could've gone to the movies. Why didn't we just go to the movies? 1999. What was playing? American Beauty. *I hear that was good. But no, I didn't see* American Beauty. *Rather, I stayed home and had unprotected sex, and now . . . well, not right now, but three months from now, it'll start: the most important thing I'll ever do.*

I'm not ready.

So I got scared. But I got over it, three kids over it, if you're keeping a tally.

We've weathered fevers and broken bones and bloody gashes and disappointment and life not turning out the way we had it planned, and we've been fine.

Now though, I'm by myself, and that scares me more than Jason Voorhees ever could. Don't misunderstand, Billy. I'm not scared because I need a man or my kids need a father. Screw that. He slept with nearly thirty women in eighteen years. He couldn't wait to get out of the house each day; his erection could open the front door, unlock his car, and drive down the block. I'm not lonely – well, not unless *you* are; then maybe I can be talked into it – no, I'm frightened because my kids aren't anywhere near done needing me. They're undercooked. I'm probably forty-five years from seeing my grandchildren happily married in someplace sunny.

I can't count on Richard for anything. That's sad. But I can't, so I'm taking it on myself. It's become my only mission in life. Who knew?

I've got to get those boys what they need so that every night at 10:30, I can talk to God and we can agree that all three of them are happy, healthy, and safe. With that done over the next forty-five years, then I can die.

Screw it.

So you see. I can't afford to go down in a plane crash because some drunk mechanic forgot to change the oil in the 737. I can't contract a metastasizing tumor that sidelines me for eighteen months. I can't run away; I can't sustain a serious injury. I can't be abducted by aliens, and I sure as shit can't afford to get distracted by anything as inconsequential as my need for decent orgasms or my untimely death.

Because I am a single mom.

So . . . what am I going to do? As much as it pains me to admit it, I'm going to continue jumping at shadows, continue worrying every time one of them dives to field a ground ball. I'm going to be a slobbering, nervous wreck the first time they take the car for a drive, and I'm going to break their goddamned legs if I ever catch them surfing on the roof of my mini-van as they head from Ocean Grove down to Sea Girt with their friends.

Hey, shut the hell up. You're not the mother; you don't understand. Unabridged, Day-Glo hypocrisy is part of the job. As long as I'm doing this by myself, I'll establish the rules. Thank you very much. Like old Nick Adams, we all have our half-fallen cedar trees separating us from what's safe and what's paralyzing. For a single mother, that tree leans just outside the front door.

In 1982, Aunt Grace took my brother and me to see *Friday the Thirteenth, Part III* in 3-D. We drove up to Rockaway Mall; they had the first, ten-cinema multiplex in central Jersey. Tickets were outrageous at $3.75. Milk Duds and Twizzlers cost $.75, and a medium popcorn, enough for us to share, was $2.25. A $15.00 night at the movies back then would top $70 today, but I'm not nostalgic. 1980s, 3-D graphics couldn't compare with the high-tech, full-body, 3-D, HD experience that runs $14 these days.

Old Jason whipped ass, though. That poor, misunderstood, Hell-spawned boy killed a couple of dozen, half-naked teenagers like a virtuoso. Part III was his first movie in the hockey mask, too, and he didn't disappoint my brother and me. The demon with a cognitive disability (Jason *is* a politically-incorrect, homicidal sociopath) cut, slashed, broke, tore, dismembered, and spear-gunned his way across Camp Crystal Lake, all the while scaring the unbridled shit out of me. I jumped, shrieked, even clutched Aunt Grace in a death grip until the perky, blonde protagonist finally buried that three-quarter-bit axe in Jason's forehead, ending his exsanguinous field day – at least until Part IV, starring Corey Feldman!

What's my point?

I don't have a clue.

Being terrified of a lunatic killer in a hockey mask is supposed to be as bad as things get, but what I didn't realize in 1983 is that I would not understand fear until I had children, and I would not understand terror until I sat up nights wondering if I could raise them on my own.

Jason might be a badass, but what would he do when challenged with a forehead gash that clearly needs stitches, while the baby's sleeping, and the older brother isn't due to come home from baseball practice for another twenty minutes?

Huh?

Right: he'd piss himself.

And what would old Jason do with a screaming baby on a cross country flight or in the fifteen-item line behind some miscreant with twenty-two items because: *those seven soup cans all count as one!*

Actually, come to think of it, that might be the perfect situation in which to have Mr. Voorhees along. He could kill that jackass with a machete, and I could hustle through with my eight items and get the baby in the car for a nap lickety split.

Or . . . heh . . . I could send Jason over to Richard's testosterony new bachelor pad for a visit, just some special time for them together. Then we all could know a little fear, maybe take turns for once.

Oh, and speaking of Oscar Pistorius, did you see that they only gave that douche bag five years for shooting his girlfriend? Five years. Oh well, just another dead girlfriend, I guess. Honestly, I hope someone in there rips his arms off.

Anyway, all this talk of disemboweling teenagers also reminds me that while I was preggo with my first son, back in 2000, my husband considered packing up and getting out. At nearly nine months and ready to burst, I did a lot of crying and self-pitying and self-loathing before begging him to do the right thing and stay with me.

With *us*.

By then, I considered the baby as part of us. I think that Richard, for a while anyway, considered the baby an inconvenient expense.

He'd been making a disgraceful amount of money that year, so I didn't balk when he first told me that he'd have to pay $25,000 to clear a legal issue that had evolved from a clerical error. It hadn't really been his fault, but it had come back to stick on his department anyway. Apparently, some no-good liar had thrown him under the bus for her mistake.

Again, I was comfortably into my third trimester; Richard could have told me he'd decided to run for president of Paraguay and I'd have half believed him because I was only capable of half listening to work-related drama.

Did it seem strange to me that in a multi-billion-dollar corporation, a middle manager would have to spring for $25,000 to keep his department out of legal trouble? It sure smells questionable now. But I was pregnant and sore and bloated and nesting. $25,000 would sting, but it wouldn't ruin us. So I nodded, comforted him (READ: gave him a blow job), and told him to go ahead and write the check. We'd make it up during the next quarter.

You see, Billy . . . he was doing well enough that I thought of the calendar in quarters. Wealthy people do that. I don't anymore. It's better this way.

Years later, Richard weathered a moment of weakness when he decided he actually wanted to be married and to raise children (the children he helped to create, well, the three of them who lived in our house anyway). In a tearful confession he admitted that the $25,000 was payment to keep his inter-office mistress (an executive who'd been skipped over for a promotion) from going to the CEO with news that she and Richard had been involved in a torrid affair for several years, violating about nine zero-tolerance policies in the company handbook. Richard worried, not that he'd raked our marriage over the coals, but that he'd lose his job when whatshername told the brass that he'd lied on travel reports, meeting agendas, presentation schedules, and sales strategies all so that he could justify bringing her along on business trips around the country.

On paper, she'd been listed as administrative support (READ: blow jobs). Truthfully, she never left the hotel room. I'm not convinced she ever brought along clothes; yet she whined like a squeaky motel bed when they passed her over to promote him instead.

Ooops. A woman scorned and all that.

She must have given some full-throttle, exquisite head, because the cost of the raise she didn't receive from the company was $12,500 a year. With promotions not slated to come round again until 2002, old Dickie boy paid her for two years of lost wages, just to keep her mouth shut – when *opening* her mouth was what got the two of them into hot water in the first place.

Cheap jab, I know. But what the hell, I'm jaded.

Anyway, enough fond memories . . . where was I?

Ah yes: nine months preggo.

In 2000, when I was about to swim upriver to spawn, whatshername, Guzzlin' Greta, and Richard decided . . . yup, you guessed it . . . that they were in love, and that if he left me . . . *us* . . . cold, lonely, and carrying sixty pounds of future college tuition bills, that they could make millions, defraud their company of thousands in travel expenses, and live childless as jet-set lovers, recently divorced into second-marriage, do-over happiness. What a lovely idea.

It didn't work.

By 2002, Greta got tired of guzzlin' and wanted more money. Also tired, her husband oiled up his Elmer Fudd .12 gauge and got ready to shoot himself a lecher. That would have been amusing.

Richard lost his job when Greta got passed over for a promotion a second time. She demanded another $25,000; this time Richard turned her down. Greta's husband told the CEO everything, and both of them were sent packing.

Guzzlin' Greta got divorced.

Richard lied to me, told me he was 'downsized.'

And we moved to the suburbs, where he started a new company, went out on his own, made three times as much money, and started boning all the women in our neighborhood, several of them in my bed, in my shower, and on my dining room table.

Lecher, great word.

I suppose it's funny to tell it thirteen years later, but at the time it was equal parts confusion, disappointment and pain. I was about to have our first baby, my husband's son.

It should've meant more to him. Instead he was distracted by the possibility of leaving me for a woman he thought he loved but who extorted money from him just a few weeks later. And despite it all, she still went on gobbling his cock!

(Heh. Um . . . sorry. I'm fired up.)

I dreamed of growing old together, chasing the afternoon sun in an effort to squeeze every possible minute out of each day, just to wake up the next morning and do it again. I planned to buy him ballroom dance lessons for his fiftieth birthday, so we'd be the most graceful, suave couple on the floor when our boys finally got married. Now I'm hoping they elope.

It all made sense; we had the fairytale, and he took a steaming dump on it.

Why?

Because I didn't give head as masterfully as Guzzlin' Greta?

Because he didn't – *doesn't* – love me?

Because a fat, pregnant, homebody wife isn't glamorous? Certainly not as glamorous as a sex-slave co-worker waiting in the hotel suite.

Did he think she just lay there all day, naked and diddling herself while dreaming of him? Did he not realize that she probably went to the gym, wore underpants, took shits in his bathroom, ate tuna sandwiches, watched Oprah, and only squirmed into that uncomfortable Teddy about ten minutes before he got back?

Was she so good that he decided he didn't want his own son?

Or did he just not love me? I know he loves his boys; he seems to.

Just not me. That's fine though. I've got 'No Vacancy' signs hanging from those memories and that scraped up bit of my heart.

Oh, I finally rented *American Beauty* last night. Damn, that was a good film, even better than *Friday the Thirteenth, Part III*.

Jennifer

January 16

Dear Billy,

Do you know what I hope happens in the not-too-distant future? I hope that some rouge member of the CIA or MI-6 or the Boy Scouts of America releases an exposé that describes in detail how all wine comes from exactly the same place: a titanic, Monsanto-owned factory farm somewhere in central Nebraska. We'll all gasp in horror at how there's absolutely no difference between the $800 bottle of *Château Snob & Bitch* from the Loire Valley and the $8.00 bottle of *Dragon Piss Scratch 'n Sniff* from Wal-Mart.

It'll be headline news for weeks. CNN will devote an entire channel to wine snobs' reactions around the globe. And I'll be able to enjoy telling all the snooty bitches in the neighborhood Snooty Bitch Brigade that they can finally stop with all the slurping, gurgling, sniffing, sipping, gargling, and swishing that goes on around here every night between 5:01 and the main course.

Jesus Christ, half of them went to Rutgers while the other half pulled down a 2.00 GPA at Trenton State. None of them jetted in from the *Sorbonne School of Wine Bullshit*. They half pay attention to the sommelier at Wegmans, and they think they can tell the difference between grapes, between years!

Horse poop.

I don't remember what I was doing in 2003 or 2004. I think it had something to do with changing diapers after pumping breast milk in the faculty bathroom before racing to the grocery store, cleaning the house, and begging my useless husband to babysit for an hour while I went jogging to keep my ass from destroying Tokyo. I have no recollection of what that season's grapes tasted like or how much rain fell in the Medoc region, or how that harvest compared with the fabled, wet season of '89.

Shut up already and drink a beer. It goes with everything.

That's all, Billy. It's coming; I'm looking forward to it.

Jennifer

January 24

Hi Billy,

The clock's ticking.

I'm forty three, and I've got to get some of this shit figured out.

Is it possible to live only on the happiness and satisfaction I absorb from my kids? I think so. Millions of women do it. Some of them have to be genuinely happy sucking up the vicarious joy their children bring home each day, riding their ups and downs like a stowaway on a roller coaster.

Find the joy.

That's not a bad motto.

Might even be time for a new tattoo.

It's not too late to start again. Perhaps I won't have to, because I have them.

Find the joy.

Homer and I drove to Newark today; it's on my top-ten list of scary stuff to do with an afternoon. Route 9 and Broad Street were damned near impassable. We are the most densely populated state in the nation after all.

I didn't mind; it was worth it. I found a lovely gentleman, if barrel-chested and a bit hairy, Ira Lefkowitz (I swear to God I'm not making this up) at the jewelry exchange on Clinton Avenue. He picked through the boxes of apology jewelry and gemstones I'd received over the past fifteen years. It took a while, so he sent his nephew down to the corner for coffee. It was good. I had mine with a bit of extra sugar. Why not? This was an adventure.

The coffee tasted like an unexpected day off, a sunny day.

About 3:30, just when I worried I'd have to collect the whole works and hurry home to get the boys from baseball, Ira plucked that creepy eyepiece thing from his face and said, 'Meh . . . it's . . . all together, about . . . twenty eight, perhaps thirty.'

Holy shit!

'I'll give you twenty three . . .' He hesitated, waited for me.

I almost peed. 'Thousand? When?'

Ira laughed, a big, Eastern European wheeze that might have fallen out of a Sholokhov novel. 'Right now, right . . . now.'

I checked my watch, just so he'd think I planned to consider the offer, maybe take my business elsewhere. It didn't do me any good; I'm no actor. 'Done!' I even slapped my palm on the counter, nearly upsetting a precarious display of knock-off Rolexes.

'Done,' Ira echoed, wheeze-laughing again. His suit jacket hung on the back of his desk chair like an exhausted sail. He dug in a pocket for his checkbook.

I could've kissed him, but he was about sixty-eight and smelled faintly of herring and body odor. I decided against it, paid my VISA bill instead.

Find the joy.

Jennifer

February

Thank God for wine. It keeps me from eating myself to death like an Australian dog.

February 9

Hey Billy,

I'm a little drunk tonight.

My sister-in-law made lasagna, the Irishman's downfall. You might think it's Guinness or Smithwick's. Nonsense. The Irishman's downfall is good Italian lasagna with meatballs and thick, pasty Marinara sauce, sloppy with cheese and life-threatening cholesterol.

Why?

Because . . . two reasons, actually . . . because it comes with wine made from grapes that don't grow in Ireland (or New Jersey, come to think on it) and because it tastes better than anything we make in Ireland.

Boiled plants. Yeesh.

Anyway, when it comes to my sister-in-law's lasagna, I'm like one of those Australian shepherds that will eat itself to death. Just fill the trough and I'll host a gluttony clinic.

Thank God for wine. It keeps me from eating myself to death like an Australian dog.

That's a good one; I need to remember that.

Most days when I look in the mirror I'm glad Home Depot doesn't carry over-the-counter flame throwers, because I'd buy one, grill my ex-husband, broil my father, and then turn the flame on myself. I know . . . I know . . . it's difficult to kill oneself with a flame thrower, but what the hell, I'd read the owner's manual. It's got to come with directions. Right?

I love my sister-in-law.

My brother's a genius: he married an Italian girl from Bayonne. She can cook.

I boil plants. My house smells like asparagus piss, not that asparagus does much pissing, but you know what I mean.

What were we talking about?

Wine. Right.

I'm a little drunk tonight, Billy.

And it's not every day that I look in the mirror and hate myself, but most days . . . no, *many* days. *Every* day in 2014, when I looked in the mirror I felt inadequate, old, slow, and ugly. But divorce proceedings have been good for me: stress, cigarettes, caffeine, insomnia, and sheer, unchecked loathing for the man I married have contributed to my diet and helped to melt away sixteen pounds.

I should do a late-night cable infomercial. It'd make millions – The Ex-Husband Diet Plan: Nicotine & caffeine your way to a size 6 or your money back!

Hold on a second; I've gotta get my head on straight.

I'm writing tonight, because I've got a draught of wine courage and I want to clarify a couple of things that I've left out of these scribbles so far.

We can get back to Richard later. I want to talk about my father. By now, you've got to be wondering why I still have anything to do with my father, why I answer the phone, visit him, allow him to see my kids on vacations and weekends, any of it. I suppose there's part of every woman that remembers what it meant to be a little girl, to idolize her father as the first and only man she'd love unconditionally (until her own sons are born).

That's not me.

Well, that's sort of me. Some unincorporated, dry prairie town inside my chest will always love and idolize my father, but I keep the border patrol pretty tightly mobilized around that sucker.

Rather, I stay in touch with my father and forgive my father for two pretty compelling reasons. I often forget them, especially when he's got me angry enough to bite the head off a badger or embarrassed enough to move to the Outback and live among the wallabies.

What's a wallaby?

And where are you, Billy? Albany?

You know what they have in Albany? Neither do I . . . bunch of stuff about the French and Indian War, I suppose. The Hudson's nice, and I think Daniel Day Lewis made a much better Hawkeye than Randolph Scott ever dreamed. Although, Wes Studi stole that movie in my opinion.

And *Ironweed*! I saw *Ironweed* twice. It was awesome; Jack Nicholson and Meryl Streep were amazing.

I could live there, I guess. I've always been partial to the New Jersey coast, but I could learn to love the Hudson and Lake George.

Albany. Okay.

I grabbed some more wine. No idea what this is, *Cuvée du Château Roadkill, mis en bouteille au 7-Eleven*.

But it's wet, and it's purple, and it's here tonight. It'll do.

My parents were married in 1963. By 1966, my grandmother (She drank more than I do) had moved in. Dad was twenty five; Mom was twenty three. Dad worked as a mason during the day and sent applications to police departments all over North Jersey by night. Willing to work hard to prove his GED was a matter of necessity, my father believed that if he could be a cop, he could reclaim some of the self-respect he'd lost the day he finally walked out of high school Geometry and started bagging groceries. Mom believed in him; that was all he needed, just like that goddamned Bon Jovi song again.

When the Asbury Park Police finally bit, the kids – because that's what they were: kids – got a loan, bought a split-level ranch off Route 18, and started going bareback to the pony rides, hoping for a bundle of joy or at least my shithead brother.

Things came together. Life gelled into something special they could hang on to, maybe nurture into fifty years of love, honor and cherish.

But they had my grandmother. At fifty three, unemployed, and living in the room that would one day become my parents' master bedroom, my grandmother drank rye, chain smoked her Chesterfields, and bemoaned her lot in life, louder with each lukewarm blast of woe-is-me. Mom and Dad tried to ignore her, tried to help her find a job, a boyfriend, anything to get her out of bed and into life.

It didn't take.

They spent free weekends making the rounds of local pawn shops, once even going all the way to Clinton Avenue in Newark (where I'd one day hock two bags of apology jewelry from Richard). They went with whatever money they'd managed to save and whatever cushion, however threadbare, remained in their checking account at Freehold National. They carried the few bucks my grandfather (Mom's father) might have slipped her on their last visit to Orange Lake, and they used all of it to buy back my grandmother's wedding rings and family jewelry.

She'd sneak out of the house when Mom went for groceries or to an OB/GYN appointment. They'd had some trouble getting pregnant at first and sat nervously through a clutch of appointments that year.

Once out, my grandmother would hit Delancy's Tobacco Shop on Pond Road, buy a fifth of rye and catch the bus out front of the firehouse. From there, who knows where she'd go? Edison, Elizabeth, Irvington, Jersey City, Dad damned near had to bribe her with booze to find out where she sold the jewels each time.

It was good stuff, nothing you'd find in the imperial *Hofburg*, but decent diamonds, nice settings, two and three thousand dollars in jewels sold for thirty-five-dollars-worth of Chesterfields and whiskey.

Mom and Dad hung in there until my brother was born in '69. Grandma had gotten worse and often stayed sequestered in her room for days at a time. At twenty eight, Dad had his hands full. He'd been with Asbury Park PD for two years, made $12,000 a year, and worked nights on Memorial Drive and Springwood Avenue before rioters burned it to the ground in July, 1970.

My Aunt Grace lived with them. Ten years younger than Dad, she was getting ready to graduate high school and wanted to attend the beauty academy over in Belmar. She had a good after-school job at a local ice cream parlor and already showed signs of the same hard-nosed work ethic that kept my parents on their feet for the past fifty years. If nothing else, Billy, they earned every dollar they ever had.

Beauty school costs money. Kids cost money. Vacations and penicillin and slat-sided, Country Squire station wagons cost money, more money than they brought home each week and certainly too much to be shelling out hundreds to rebuy my grandmother's wedding rings on Sundays.

My Aunt Molly – we'll get to her shortly – was twenty three and lived in California. Dad had two sisters; Aunt Grace was too young to escape.

Aunt Molly was, too, but no one knew that yet.

By mid-autumn, Mom was pregnant with me. Aunt Grace had enrolled full time in the Monmouth County Beauty Academy. Dad was in year three with the Asbury Park PD, and my grandmother stayed in bed all afternoon and evening. Generally drunk by the time Dad got home from work, she'd shout for him, berate and insult him, blame him for not sending Aunt Grace to a proper college, and accuse him of leaving her alone, lost and lonely all day. My parents' room, the bed where I'd sometimes crawl in with them as a toddler, smelled of ashtrays, stale farts, and the withering disease of hopelessness.

Dad did his best to make her comfortable. He brought her dinner on a tray and yes, even freshened her glass from time to time if only to shut her up

He never drank rye.

Forty-five years later, and he's drunk, sipped, swilled, gargled, or gulped just about every spirit known to the western world, but he's never drunk rye, not an ounce.

Dad would have given anything to mend the broken place my grandfather left when he chased some young hottie down to Florida. But there was nothing he could do for her. My grandmother's heart had been broken. Rather than fight it, she let it debilitate her, embraced the reality that she'd never been good enough.

Grandchildren couldn't heal her.

My father's love, money, and attention couldn't heal her.

Only booze and Virginia cigarettes soothed her, eased her pain and carried her off to sleep like the fond mother in that Longfellow poem.

She'd sleep, but only after she raged at Dad night after night. Her flesh yellowing to jaundiced leather, her liver spots alarming maps of discolored constellations in the lamp light, she barked at him through cracked lips and disintegrating teeth.

Good Christ, what a nightmare for my father. Sixteen years younger than I am now and saddled with all that – on his embarrassing GED and his Asbury Park salary. How he must have hoped for a future with my mother, my brother and me – even with Aunt Grace and Aunt Molly. But like a paroled convict he was shackled to a past he couldn't erase.

Escape wasn't an option, not with a baby and another on the way, and not with his own mother committing excruciatingly-slow suicide in the bedroom he'd planned to share with my mother 'til death did them part.

So he wished it.

And it happened.

Dad's a Christian, not always a good one, but a steady one, a lifer. He's not a Christian because he believes the doctrine or enjoys the smoke-and-mirror rituals. Nope. Dad's a Christian because on the few occasions in his life that he's spoken out loud to God, God has listened and responded.

I know, Billy. I can hear you all the way down here: 'That's bullshit, a coincidence at best.'

Nope again. This is true.

In the autumn of '70, my dad came home from a rough stretch in the city. Asbury Park's black population had risen up together that summer, and throughout the year there were skirmishes, small battles following the war when folks west of the tracks fought to show the traditional, white establishment on the boardwalk that the city could no longer be split by Memorial Drive. The West Side wouldn't be ignored by whites who had hired them to clean hotel rooms and collect garbage for a hundred years.

As a cop, Dad fought to put down the civil unrest. Whether he agreed with it or not, that was the job, and he did it with a three-foot, ash billy club and a leather-braided, lead-tipped sap. What today would be condemned as a human rights violation was essential equipment back then.

We don't need to go too deeply into it, but I remember him describing West Side rioters breaking panes of glass that they'd throw, horizontally, at the police line like razor-edged Frisbees.

Anyway, my father came home after a nasty day of trying to keep peace in Asbury Park. My brother had a fever, just a tooth breaking through, but he howled and screeched until the children's aspirin got a toehold. My Aunt Grace had brought home a boyfriend – he'd later become my Uncle Mike, but no one knew that at the time. Mom, pregnant and exhausted, made dinner, even put out the nice plates and clean glassware. Until she finally chucked them all in 1982, many of our everyday glasses had spent their formative years as Flintstones grape jelly jars at the A&P.

Dad saw the nice plates, the good glasses, the new boyfriend, and realized he'd have to wear a few hats.

Father: He picked up my brother, held him close, tried to comfort him through the fever.

Husband: He saw that mom had the table set and dinner cooking. He didn't help her but did offer up a brief kiss and a pat on the swelling tummy for me.

Brother: Aunt Grace wanted to make an impression on the new boyfriend. She idolized Dad, looked up to him as the father she never knew, and hoped he'd go easy on this new boyfriend. Dad took one look at my Uncle Mike's callused hands, figured him for a worker, and offered him some iced tea. Aunt Grace was happy.

And Son: Before Dad had a chance to change out of his uniform, he excused himself, turned on Channel 9 news out of New York, and told Aunt Grace to help my mother while the new boyfriend watched TV. When no one was looking, he fetched a fresh bottle of rye from the cabinet and sneaked it down the hall to my grandmother's room.

By dessert, my mother, my aunt, and my father had been humiliated. Between my brother's wailing, my aunt's clumsy efforts to impress my future Uncle Mike, and my grandmother's abuse, Dad had poured a second, then a third, and finally a fourth Dewar's and soda.

When Uncle Mike finally left, thanking my mother and scoring points with my slowly collapsing father, mom cried. Aunt Grace cried. My brother finally fell asleep. And my father turned down the interminable corridor from the kitchen to the bedroom where my grandmother's background music still rang in echoes of abuse she'd slung at him for four years.

He didn't love me . . . and you don't love me!

He'd had enough.

He'd drunk his share of bravery, but not a cell in his body wanted to walk that hallway ever again the victim of my grandmother's incoherent raving. He didn't hate her; he understood. He loved her, but Dad couldn't live with it anymore.

You don't . . .

Disgusted and hating his own father for leaving her alone, he wished it. My sleeping brother rested in the crook of his arm, and the man who would one day call me a whore's cunt took a few steps down the hall, enough to ensure some privacy. Then he turned his eyes to Heaven and said, 'God, please, just take her. Take her tonight.'

On the television, Lawrence Welk's orchestra tooted and bopped through their *Good Night; Sleep Tight* closing credits. Bobby and Sissy danced, she in a fuchsia ball gown, he in a baby blue tuxedo.

Two hours later, my grandmother was dead.

It's true, Billy.

Sealing his future, Dad had cracked open that bottle of Dewar's. A young cop in a difficult situation, in a violent city, with a promising life ahead, he'd poured just enough to muster the courage to pray for his own mother's death, an unthinkable and ironic end to her already heartbreaking story.

And it worked.

I don't know what else to say except that it haunted him for most of his adult life, still does – I suppose – when he lets himself remember.

My mother told me that story when I was in ninth grade. I don't know why except that maybe I'd been a bit judgmental about Dad's drinking one weekend, and she wanted me to know. I even remember how she started off: 'Jenny, everyone's behavior makes sense when you have enough information. You don't have to forgive him, but you have to understand.'

Since then, I've understood and too often forgiven my father's behavior, because I can't imagine the ration of guilt that comes for a half-educated, Catholic boy who prays for his mother's death, then sees it happen two hours later. (Not to mention that I've got my own sprawling collection of dumbass decisions. If you've been following along at home, my friend, letting you go is near the top of that list!)

Anyway, agree with me or not, I don't care. What's the ebb and flow of a lifetime when scribbled in a few pages of shitfaced email?

Besides, there's more: another reason. This one's worse.

In vino bullshit!

Jennifer

PS: Just because I can't go to bed on such a downer tonight, did you know that Randolph Scott lived with Cary Grant in a torrid bromance? I suppose I shouldn't be surprised; they were both snazzy dressers. Imagine if word had leaked about Cary Grant. Geologists could have charted breaking hearts on the Richter Scale at Cal-Tech!

February 20

Hey again Billy,

I bought a house by myself this past fall. Ever done that? It's a novel and unsettling feeling knowing that so much about our survival hinges on me.

So I bought a tool kit at Lowe's.

It's banana yellow. Groovy!

And a drill. Drills are sold separately from tool kits. Who knew? The drill's yellow, too. I love them both.

My house is a small, split-level cottage on about two acres of middle-of-nowhere New Jersey farmland. It's the biggest yard I ever imagined owning. My sons played baseball there every day, right up until freezing temperatures drove them inside for the winter. It's the smartest purchase I've made since old Dickie boy moved out. It's got a whitewashed, corral-style fence and a wonderful screen door on a rusty spring that slams like a judge's gavel, letting me know when someone's coming or going. Behind my yard, the landscape rises in a gentle wrinkle, leading to a neighboring farm. By late October, the fields behind our baseball diamond were rife with brilliant, yellow-and-green soybeans, thigh deep as far as I could see. When the morning light hits them, I feel like I'm supposed to feel in church and want to have the entire congregation over for donuts and coffee so they can await sunrise and watch God leave for work.

I bought the house in September and was overwhelmed shortly afterward by the sheer number of cracked, broken, dismantled, disfigured and rattly, noisy moving parts that needed fixing. We've already established that I've got three-quarters of a mile of duct tape. But soon after moving in, I discovered that the T-shirt lies: Duct tape can't fix everything. Now and then you've got to have tools.

I do, banana yellow ones. You'd love them.

What I didn't notice, because I was busily trying my hand at simple, in-home repairs, was that outside my two acres of lawn continued to grow. As an intervention strategy, I waited for goats to arrive and start eating. They didn't.

Or cows. Nope.

Eventually, I went back to Lowe's, this time for a $2600 tractor with a lawnmower attachment vicious enough to mow Iowa without coming up for air. My tractor's green and yellow; they didn't have camouflage. The Lowe's guys delivered it. A nice kid with KENNY stitched above the pocket of his shirt asked if I wanted him to put it in my shed. Rather than embarrass myself by making my ignorance a matter of public knowledge, I said simply, 'No, I've got it.'

Kenny unsheathed the cutest *bullshit, lady* smile, then glanced at my lawn. The grass wasn't quite knee high, but most ankles would disappear two steps in. 'You sure?'

I took the manual and keys, signed his manifest. 'Yup, no problem.'

Kenny piled back into the Lowe's truck and drove off, while I questioned whether my determination to fend for myself was the wisest course of action with two acres of fourteen-inch grass and a $2600 tractor in my driveway like a beached whale.

I needed two days to read the manual, 136 pages that might have been written by a room full of learning disabled chimpanzees. By page 112, I figured I could get gas and oil into the thing, start it, raise and lower the mower blades, and all of it without losing any fingers or toes. I read the last 24 pages anyway, just to be thorough, even though most of that bit was about the sundry things I might do to invalidate my warranty.

As an aside, one of the clear warranty no-nos included running over foreign objects with the mower. Heh. I hadn't mowed a half acre before mutilating four baseballs, popping a tennis ball, beheading a G.I. Joe (he lost an arm in the procedure, too) and sending a rock into the side of my house like a Tomahawk missile.

I had to cut the grass twice, because it had grown so tall. When I finished that first afternoon, I seriously considered selling the tractor and maybe picking up a goat or two. The lawn couldn't look any worse, and maybe the goats would do a better job ironing the place to a uniform height.

At forty-three years old, I'd never cut grass. That realization didn't occur to me until after I'd gingerly pulled the tractor into the shed. (When it came time to mow again, I had to use REVERSE, another comedy show for my neighbors' viewing pleasure.)

To celebrate, I took the boys for ice cream. Afterward, on the white board in my kitchen, I used a dry erase marker to write, *I CAN:*

Beneath it, in green, I wrote: *CUT LAWN.*

Standing alone in my new kitchen, with my boys in their beds, and my dog in the yard, I had myself a quick, but therapeutic and soul-affirming cry. A good one. I didn't try to stop, just let it run its foamy course through my body, and when I bent to wipe tears off my linoleum floor, I thought, 'Hmm . . . next up, tile.'

In the months since the boys and I left Richard's 5,400-square-foot McMansion and moved into our 1,850-square-foot ranch, I've tackled dozens of home improvement and repair projects on my own.

A few of my favorites were:

1. I hung a light fixture in my dining room. This was my first varsity level Mama Fix (my sons' way of making fun of my projects). The light wasn't my first foray into electricity, but it was my most technically-demanding dismount to date. I shut down power to the entire house for three hours to do it, made the kids and the dog play outside with instructions to call 911 if they heard a thunderclap or saw a flash of lightning through the windows.

2. I fixed a leaky toilet. Not a big deal, but I mention it here, because most of the women I've known in adulthood have no idea that sticky ring of space-age polymer exists. That stuff could hold NASCAR engines together. I also mention the toilet, because that was the project when I finally learned that all of my home improvement endeavors require at least two trips to Lowe's. If I can buy two of something cheap – like space-age sticky toilet ring donuts – and save a trip back there with Homer in his car seat and the dog in the back, it's worth it. Buy two; it saves time.

3. I drilled a hole in the floor to run TV cable and stereo wire downstairs. Again, not a big deal, but it's scary deciding to do it. I spent twenty minutes finding the spot to drill, then ten minutes sitting there with the drill in my hand, drumming up the courage to press START. Holes are permanent; the old toothpaste trick doesn't work when you're the owner.

4. I took apart my kitchen sink to retrieve my engagement ring. If it had been my wedding band, I might've just turned on the water and washed it down the River Jordan. But it was my engagement ring, my sentimental connection to the night Richard proposed, on his knees, hope and love in his eyes as he

slipped that ring on my finger. Heh, nope. I need the diamonds to buy back-to-school clothes next summer. Oh, and dismantling the sink wasn't too challenging, but holy shit what a Stephen King nightmare of greasy, aromatic, putrefied, organic disgustingness accumulates down there. Jesus Christ, some of that stuff had hair growing out of it. Thankfully, diamonds rinse off.

5. I put up my own Christmas tree, watered and decorated it, and it stayed up, without collapsing or bursting into flames, until the boys went back to school in January. I mention this because like cutting my own grass, I'd never put up my own Christmas tree before. (The mini holiday shrub on my desk at Rutgers doesn't count.) I don't own a good saw, not yet. So I borrowed one from my neighbor to cut about an inch off the trunk before putting the tree in the stand. I kept all ten fingers, and while the tree leaned a little to the left – not unlike a drunk Bill Clinton – no one complained.

I watch a lot of HGTV, and at some point in every episode, I find myself saying, 'Hell, I could do that. I just need . . .' What gets filled into that blank generally determines how quickly and loudly my two older boys will shout, 'No way, Mom!' and slap me back to reality.
    But if I just had a mitre saw! Or my own lathe!

I hope you're well, Billy. And remember: if you can't fix it with Duct tape, hit it with a sledge hammer and start over.

Jennifer

Oh, and postscript . . . One of my favorite things about having my own – albeit used, slightly dented, and wrinkly – house is that I no longer have to sneak time to email you. I haven't mentioned that yet, hadn't planned to, but those last few months, while The Deadbeat Homewrecker and I lived under the same roof, I had to email you in secret (early mornings, late nights, when he was out). He's such a controlling asswipe that he'd often find an excuse to look over my shoulder while I was on the computer, snooping to be sure I didn't have a boyfriend. If he knew I'd been writing to you, he'd have been irretrievably pissed, even though his penis has stickers on it from exotic locations it's visited, like an old steamer trunk. And no, I don't believe that I was being unfaithful to him when I emailed you.

That would have been fine with me, though, I'd have been up for a little infidelity.

February 27

Dear Billy –

I dropped the boys off at Richard's new place today. It's an attached townhome in a chi-chi neighborhood near the beach called *Belle Terre*. I didn't go in, didn't have any breath mints to erase the vomit flavor from the back of my throat. So I dumped the guys off at the porch and backed out of the driveway.

Richard peeked out the door, invited me in. He wanted to gloat; I could smell it on him from across his manicured evergreen shrubs. I lied, claimed I was late for a chemotherapy appointment and had to run.

May God strike me dead if I ever step foot in that place.

You know what pisses me off about it? His new house has a tidy, antiseptic, clean-fingernails feel to it, as if people can be rich enough just to forget all their mistakes and start over with a shiny new whateveritis. I know it's true; we all do. It's why we hover over the television or the Internet when a rich, white guy is held accountable for his sins. It's not news, but it feeds a persistent hunger in our culture: to see the untouchables take a punch from time to time.

I remember that heartbreaking chapter from *Gatsby*, when Tom and Daisy plot together in their kitchen, just drinking beer and eating chicken. They're planning to buy their way out of trouble. I've always hated them for that, Daisy especially. She's got a chance at love, and she buggers it raw, because she's addicted to Tom's money. Jesus, what an asshole.

I'll take my baseball yard and my rusty screen door any day.

Sorry, it's not doing you any good to hear me complain tonight. I'll sign off.

Jennifer

Hold on, just one last thing: *Belle Terre?* I'm no linguist, but that means 'beautiful earth' in French. Right? Do you believe that people in Paris are lining up to live in a neighborhood called *Beautiful Earth?* Of course not.

I can hear the Parisians now, 'Ah, belle terre . . . zat meanz lovely ground, non? What a strange name for zee home place.'

Beautiful Earth. Pretty Dirt. That's even better: *Pretty Dirt*. Very French.

March

And another memory rose from the swamp water to punch me in the guts.

March 5

Hey Billy,

Today, my sons took two boxes of Mike & Ike candies, spread them over aluminum foil, and melted them in the oven. They wanted to stir them into a rainbow soup of Mike & Ikeness and create a giant candy they could impale on a stick, allow to cool, and become the envy of every kid in the neighborhood.

  Groovy idea. Poor execution.

  When the oven didn't work quickly enough, they dumped the softening candies into one of my ceramic salad bowls and nuked the whole works in the microwave for five minutes.

  What emerged, at nearly 400 degrees, could have doubled as a rainbow-colored, Mike & Ike cannonball, if they'd have been able to get the concoction out of the bowl. Sadly, it'd been permanently fused to the ceramic.

  Time to give up?

  Don't be silly.

  The boys decided that since unspeakably hot temperatures had attached the candies to the bowl, freezing everything ought to make it easier to set their new Frisbee free.

  That didn't work either, so they gave up, filled the bowl with water, and left it for me in the sink while they played downstairs with the dog.

  For a few minutes, I tried to clean the remnants out of my salad bowl, then gave up and eighty-sixed the whole works.

  I guess those *Baby Mozart* DVDs aren't worth a damn.

Living the dream!

Jennifer

PS: Did I mention that I adore my little house? I do. It belongs in the Hundred Acre Wood with an overweight bear and a neurotic pig in a pink sweater.

March 12

Dear Billy,

This one's sad, but you need to know.

I like staying in hotels: the impermanence of living out of a nylon suitcase, using miniature soaps and shampoos, packing the right number of shirts, socks, pairs of pants. I've always enjoyed the feeling of being displaced without threat, an adventurer who drinks from safe, cellophane-wrapped glasses.

There are few things in western culture that say, 'I'm only here temporarily, just moving from Point A to Point B in my life' as effortlessly as the cellophane-wrapped drinking glass, the mini fridge, or the travel-sized deodorant.

One of my earliest memories is of a hotel room. I know it was a hotel room, but I can't recall where. It must have been either a Route 9 flophouse across from Newark Airport or a cockroach ranch adjacent to LaGuardia, out in Queens. I stayed there with my mother, my brother, Gary, and my Aunt Grace the night before we met my father on an inbound red-eye from California.

My friends will sometimes sit around and discuss our earliest recollections of school, church, the beach, our childhood friends, whatever. Some claim that these memories are good or bad, happy or disheartening.

I don't get it.

My earliest recollections are fringed in dark browns or black and tinted the sepia color of the daguerreotype photos we used to see at wild west shows. They are jerky, insubstantial, stop-action movies, often only a few seconds in duration, and frequently forgettable. Unless I run headlong into a throwback aroma, a trigger texture, or a friend who encourages me to think back four decades, I don't spend much time rooting around in the swampy mud of my childhood. My memories generally politely agree to remain buried.

Except this one.

In the early '70s, as far back as I can cast this net, jet airplanes took off after burning an enormous amount of fuel. I read somewhere that it takes 40,000 pounds of jet fuel to get a 747 through a ten-hour flight and that a large plane can burn over 6,000 pounds just getting into the sky. Today, jets use a similar amount but modern fuel burns so much cleaner, departing jets don't leave the same twin trails of ugly, ash-colored pollution that they did in the '60s and '70s.

That's the memory.

I'm standing in an airport. It's either Newark or LaGuardia, because I can see the uniform gray of boring skyscrapers in the murky distance. Either way, it's a city airport in 1974. Planes depart and land, and I watch them with my brother, our hands and faces pressed against a pane of concourse glass large enough to act as a front window for Rhode Island.

I remember the departing planes best: that passionate roar as they raced down the runway, the clone contrails of dark smoke they left behind, looking as if they were already ablaze and about to come crashing down in a collapse worthy of the *Book of Revelation*.

We'd stayed overnight in a hotel. The desk stationery had a colorful logo in the corner; my brother's milk left perfect circles of condensation across the page my Aunt Grace had set out for us to use as a placemat. Mom bought us each a bottle of milk and a cake donut from a vendor in the lobby. Gary's left crumbs on the piece of writing paper that spilled on to the wooden desk surface when Aunt Grace cleaned up.

It's my earliest memory: a hotel room, colorful desk stationery, milk and donuts, departing jets, filthy exhaust, and my father arriving home from California.

Six or seven years later, Gary and I came home from school to watch old reruns on WWOR, Channel 9, out of Manhattan. After-school programming included *Woody Woodpecker* cartoons (he died the death of a thousand, politically-correct lashes), *Gilligan's Island*, *The Brady Bunch*, and *The Partridge Family*. M*A*S*H played at 7:00, after dinner.

One afternoon, an episode of *Gilligan's Island* came on – the one where a gargantuan spider terrorizes the castaways until Gilligan's tiny carrier pigeon faces it in battle and frightens it away. As ever, the denouement offered the Professor a chance to explain what had happened and how they wouldn't be rescued after all. He suggested that in this case spiders are afraid of birds no matter the size difference. I always thought it was bullshit, because that spider looked like a hairy, spindly-legged Volkswagen and could have eaten that pigeon and his entire extended family and still needed a snack before lunch.

Anyway, when Gary saw the bit where the bird attacks the spider, he said, 'Hey, this is the one we saw that time . . . you know . . . on those *Lost in Space* TVs at the airport that day with Aunt Grace.'

And another memory rose from the swamp water to punch me in the guts.

Another ten minute slice of that morning returned in an out-of-focus recollection of those coin-operated televisions. My brother was right: the contraption that attached the TVs to the molded-plastic chairs, their conical skulls, the curved plastic arms all in a line looked like something Will Robinson would have watched in his cabin on *Lost in Space*.

For twenty-five cents you could get local TV for thirty minutes on a private screen. Either Dad's plane had been late or Mom had gotten us up early, because she rooted around in her cavernous pocketbook - Mom never called them purses; rich women carried purses – mined up a few quarters, and sent knucklehead and me to watch TV with Aunt Grace while she watched the arrivals board for news of Dad's (and Aunt Molly's) flight.

We watched *Gilligan's Island*, Gary yelping for another quarter every time the screen flickered then faded out. The spider episode was a barn burner. That thing had emerged from the jungle and might have killed every one of the castaways (starting with Mrs. Howell, if you ask me. That woman was a pain in the ass).

When Gilligan's pigeon attacked, I screeched, dove into Aunt Grace's arms, and hid my face until Dad arrived, picked me up, and took us all home in Mom's Country Squire station wagon.

I don't remember my Aunt Molly, can't remember her coffin, am not certain Gary and I ever saw it or if it just went from the plane to a hearse, and then to the funeral parlor or the cemetery. When I close my eyes today, I can see the baby blue of a Pan Am logo, a fire engine red *TWA* scripted on a fuselage, even the brilliant maple leaf of the Air Canada planes, but I can't remember Aunt Molly, alive or dead. I want to say her coffin was white, but that's a guess, just my brain filling in details it picked up in movies or books in the forty years since.

I don't know.

I do know, however, that my father blamed himself for her death. He blamed himself at that airport in 1974, and he blames himself now.

It's Reason Number Two why I (too often) forgive him for his self-destructive behaviors, his affairs, his drinking, his inability to communicate, and his mistreatment of Mom, Gary, and me.

Dad believes that if he'd been a better brother in the years after his mother died that his sister, my Aunt Molly, would still be alive today. And in typical, tragic Dad fashion, he's probably correct.

All of that is true, even the gargantuan spider that crawled from Gilligan's jungle like a bad dream. I'll admit that spider didn't make sense as a metaphor for some of this silliness until I started writing to you, Billy. But it happened.

The rest of this is my imagination filling in half the gaps, only half, because I never met Aunt Molly, not that I can recall, anyway. So I don't remember her voice well enough to insert it into this interaction with Dad. Regardless, I imagine that half of their last phone conversation together went something like this:

Aunt Molly: *Polite conversation.*

Dad: Yup, fine. Thanks. Fine.

Aunt Molly: *Polite conversation.*

Dad: Doing good. Both good. Gary's reading his books, and Jenny's figurin' some of her letters, mostly using that animal book you sent her; it's got most of them in there. Dunno what she'll do when we try'n show her that letters apply to other things as well.

Doesn't ask how she is. Doesn't ask why she called.

Aunt Molly: *More polite chit chat.*

Dad: It's fine. I'll have ten years pretty soon, might make sergeant then. Seven in now. Gotta good raise at five. Not like the lieutenant, but we're doin' okay.

Aunt Molly: *Pause.*

Dad: Moll?

Aunt Molly: *Backs off, asks about Aunt Grace.*

Dad: She's good. Gotta nice ring from Michael. She takes it off at work, sets it in a little ceramic dish Maggie got her at the flea market a coupla weeks back. I worry she's gonna forget it an some asshole's gonna steal it, but so far she's kept track of it.

Aunt Molly: *Asks about Grace's wedding.*

Dad: Dunno yet. March sometime.

Aunt Molly: *Pauses again.*

Dad: *Waits.*

Aunt Molly: *Asks.*

Dad: Now . . . you know, Moll. I've got Maggie, the kids, your sister, the wedding. I've got all that and–

Aunt Molly: *Suggests.*

Dad: Nope. Nope. Now . . . you know, Maggie and I can't . . . we can't have you bringing that, all that . . . into . . .

He finds a wellspring of courage. He'll regret the next fifteen seconds for the rest of his life.

. . . into our house. We can't have it.

Aunt Molly: *Waits.*

Dad: *Continues* . . . We're doin; our best here, keepin' afloat; you know. And I'm a police officer, Moll. I can't . . .

He trails off . . .

Aunt Molly: *Asks.*

Dad: No. Sorry. I'm sorry.

Aunt Molly: *Pleads. Suggests. Pleads again.*

Dad: What is it? What're you on?

Aunt Molly: *Evades the question. Calms. Asks again.*

Dad: What is it? Just pot? Or pills?

He doesn't ask about booze. Booze doesn't factor into this equation.

Aunt Molly: *Answers truthfully. Cries.*

Dad: *Steels himself* . . . No.

This moment's a flat, black eternity between them.

No, Moll. I'm sorry. But that shit's poison, and your sister's still a kid, and Gary and Jenny're here all day with Maggie. We can't have it . . . won't have it. They're just babies, and I'm doin' my best.

Aunt Molly: *Cries.*

Dad: *His mind racing* . . . I'll send you the insurance information. I can add you to our policy; it's just a few bucks a month. I made a Xerox in the office last week. You get to a doctor, get in to see someone. Get yourself cleaned up. Then we'll talk. Gracie's wedding's in March. You gotta be here for that anyways.

Aunt Molly: *Cries. Pleads.*

Dad: *Doesn't want to be angry* . . . Where you living? What's this phone number? Where can I send that insurance stuff? C'mon, Moll, you gotta understand my side of this.

Aunt Molly: *Hangs up.*

Three days later, Dad sat at Nagle's Café in Ocean Grove. The lieutenant had a policy against taking Asbury Park cruisers south of Wesley Lake, but the coffee at Nagle's whipped anything Asbury's lunch counters had to offer. He kept his handheld radio close, just in case, and knew he could be on Kingsley in twenty seconds or less.

Dad just drank coffee, $ .35 a cup, never ordered food. There wasn't enough money to go out to lunch. He had two peanut butter and jelly sandwiches on Sunbeam bread in a brown paper bag in his car out on Ocean Avenue. He could've brought the sandwiches in and eaten them at the Formica counter with his $ .35 coffee, but he left them for later. Too proud to have even the pimply-faced high school kid working the grill see him packing lunch, he ate in his car rather than pony up $1.99 for a tuna sandwich.

The kids at Nagle's made some hellaciously good tuna sandwiches, though.

His radio burped. 'AP 429.'

'Shit.' He keyed the handheld. '429.'

'429, you've got a telephone call you need to take.'

What the hell?

The dispatcher had gone nuts. Cops on duty didn't take phone calls.

He clicked the channel open. 'Can you take a message?'

A pause. 'AP 429. What's the nearest number? The watch sergeant will call.'

Shit.

Dad asked the kid working the grill for the number on the counter phone, passed it on to the dispatcher. Less than a minute passed before the telephone rang. Pimples, gripping his spatula, nodded toward it. Dad gestured to his coffee cup, then slid down two stools to take the call. 'Cooper.'

'Cooper? It's Laboda.'

'What's up, Sarge?' The first tendrils of unease uncoiled in his guts. 'My wife call?'

'No, no, nothing from her. Maggie's fine. Fine, I'm sure.'

Shit. What's this?

'What's up, Sarge?' He repeated, uncertain what else to ask.

'Listen, Cooper,' Sergeant Laboda said, 'I need you to come in.'

'Sarge?'

'Just come in.'

'How 'bout it, Sarge? Don't hang me out like this. Huh?'

Laboda sighed. The unease in Dad's stomach tautened. He watched Pimples freshen his coffee, watched the creamy fluid darken to the color of shit. No way he'd drink it now.

'Sarge?'

'I got a call from a lieutenant with the Santa Monica PD, out in California . . .'

No. Not today. Not now.

'Yeah? She dead?' He managed. 'OD?'

'Yeah. Sorry.'

'Suicide? Or . . .' He didn't know how to ask. Dad and his co-workers lived with similar incidents every day. But none of them knew what to say when lightning struck close to home. For cops, embarrassment warred with pride and a sense of privacy until any useful communication had been whittled down to one- and two-word phrases.

'Listen, Cooper. They don't know. But you gotta get out there. You know?'

'Yeah,' Dad ran his finger back and forth across a crack in the Formica counter top.

'Your parents –'

'No. But thanks, Sarge. I'll be right there.'

My Aunt Molly had been twenty-three years old, twenty years younger than I am now. My father doesn't discuss it these days, but photos around his house, even instamatic shots in picture books that have grown mildewed and stuck together, even there, it's not a difficult inference to draw. He blames himself, and maybe he's right. Perhaps she would have lived if he'd played his hand differently. That's not my judgment to make; yet forgiving his bad behavior – granted, too often – is my choice.

How forty years of forgiving him have left tire tracks up and down my heart and how those skid marks played a role in my marrying, suspecting, and forgiving old Dickie boy (again and again) for his transgressions is another matter – albeit one inexorably linked to my father. Unraveling those intestinal coils is why I write to you. Let's get back to it; whaddya say?

Are you still with me?

Jennifer

March 22

Billy –

Drunk tonight. Sorry.

You in Albany? I want to go running there, maybe next summer. It's my favorite way to see a new city, running. I started running after my second baby. Love it. Try to get out a few times a week. I think a run through Albany would be nice.

      Wanna come?

      You used to run for baseball. Do you still?

      Maybe we can run together.

Nite,

Jennifer

Just reread this. I like that one sentence up there: 'I started running after my second baby.' That's a good one. Where was he running? I wonder if I caught him.

Gotta get off the Cabernet. But it's yummy.

Okay, bye.

April

I don't hold him accountable for me being a single mom, and he doesn't feed his dirty underwear to the dog.

April 1

Hey Billy,

In 2010, Richard and I bought a beach house in Avalon. We could have found something closer, a cottage on Long Beach Island or an attached townhome in Manasquan or Sea Girt. But central Jersey beaches get overrun during the summer months. Tourists swarm like fleas on a dog. While they're mostly harmless, just local families who've had a week down the shore since the Second World War, we decided to head farther south. We hoped to find a place in a quiet neighborhood on a quiet beach – as quiet as the Jersey shore gets in July, anyway. Richard looked in Stone Harbor, even as far down as Cape May, but eventually took me to see a homey cottage a block off the sand in Avalon.

Avalon, New Jersey is all about families. It's a family town with a family-themed marketing strategy: an alcohol and tobacco-free beach, a kid-friendly boardwalk, and only one bar, a tiki-style place on the pier beside the Avalon Hotel, with its whitewashed shutters and Mansard roof.

Growing up in New Jersey – and any true Jersey native will agree with me – one develops the innate ability to differentiate between a breeze and a sea breeze. The skill gets into our bloodstream like the ability to calculate a common denominator or to ride a bike with no hands. I don't doubt that were I to be arrested (let's say for killing my ex-husband with a Samurai sword) and imprisoned in central Kansas in a windowless room for thirty years, the day a sympathetic, probably-divorced guard finally allowed me outside, I would, in ten seconds, be able to discern between any old breeze and a genuine sea breeze.

As an added bonus, an energetic onshore breeze, redolent with sticky, salty, organic decay and sand and pizza and Coppertone suntan lotion, yeah *that* breeze gets me horny, not just okay-let's-do-it horny, but rather don't-make-any-plans-because-we're-going-exploring horny. *That* kind of horny.

By 2010, Richard and I had navigated a bumpy path through some challenging marital trials. So I felt confident that buying a place in such a Pollyanna town was a clear step toward responsible adult behavior for both of us . . . well, for Richard, anyway.

I was hopeful. I felt good about being married, hadn't felt that for a few years, and believed that perhaps another baby (a baby girl) would give us just the clarity of purpose we needed to weather the next twenty years, see the kids off to college, and then find a comfortable spot to get old and die.

A beach cottage in Avalon, New Jersey, the perfect place to conceive an infant baby girl who would win my husband's heart more thoroughly than I or any secretary, flight attendant, co-worker, or IHOP waitress ever could.

Then he'd stay home.

Then he'd be good.

Even Richard couldn't ignore a baby girl calling him 'Daddy.'

And I'd have a daughter.

I prayed for it: nights, mornings, even driving my van around town on errands, I'd ask God, out loud, to send me a daughter, because I thought that a little girl and a beach house might save me.

Yeah, I'll be working through this shipment of glassy-smooth guilt with my therapist until Homer's graduated from college.

By now you've got to be fairly sick of my inane rhetorical questions. But how could I have been so deluded?

My boys are happy, healthy, energetic, intelligent, beautiful young men. I couldn't be more blessed with a star in the East and a camel out behind my manger. Yet I found time every day to pray for a daughter. With a daughter I'd never be lonely. I'd never lack for companionship, never have to worry that I'd have someone who'd go shoe shopping with me or who'd tell me honestly that my ass had gotten too big for this or that pair of slacks.

I'd have someone who thought of me like I think of my mother. Not that I've ever asked my mother, but I know that's got to be proof of divine intervention. Having a daughter love you has got to be the closest thing we get to being singled out by God. It's just for a second, but it scars your heart as deep as a branding iron. God opens the heavens, slaps you hard across the face, and says, 'Ready or not, here she comes: the wellspring of all your worry, love, fear, anxiety, and contentment. Brace yourself for a lifetime of unconditional love . . . and suffering; let's not forget suffering.'

With sons it's different. Granted, it's still pretty special, but with boys, I'll get to protect them until they decide to protect me. That relationship will shift based on our age and stage. But with a daughter, there'd be threads we'd weave through our lives together that would stay in place forever, evidence of our connection that no one could ever pluck apart.

Certainly no man.

Needless to say, God heard me, decided to teach me a valuable lesson in greed, avarice, or whatever He calls it, and He sent me a boy.

Homer Watson Teasdale, super evil genius, friend to all dogs, and archenemy of fragile porcelain heirlooms everywhere.

And I'm an asshole.

So is Richard, but we knew that.

I had no business praying for a girl. The implication that makes about my boys embarrasses me today, especially now that they've been my rock through this separation and divorce. Like I said, they're happy, healthy, and beautiful. I've not had to suffer the stomach-clenching ambiguity of knowing one of my babies had scored high on the amniotic fluid assessment for Down syndrome, fragile x, autism, Tay-Sachs, muscular dystrophy, even ADD. Although we have our share of hyperactivity, particularly when the Red Sox play the Yankees.

My boys do well in school. They ride their bikes with their friends, play guitar, read the occasional book (if there's a cool monster or an amusing reference to farts), and trade in baseball knowledge and trivia like brokers on the Commodities Exchange. My highest highs have been with my boys, and I know now that they're all I've got, at least for the time being. Not to mention, they're already better people than I've ever been, and if you think I'm just being sappy here, you either don't have kids or you can go screw yourself.

There; that's better.

Anyway, I prayed for a daughter. I shouldn't have been allowed to. Some faction of Judeo-Christian-Islamic scholars should get together to draft then circulate an altogether new Tri-Partisan Policy that says, 'no more praying for selfish bullshit. No praying for lottery numbers or great boobs, good seats to the Super Bowl or short lines at Six Flags.' We can pray for health, happiness, and safety. Everything else we've got to figure out on our own. Call me an agnostic, but I'm betting God doesn't give a damn if Duke beats North Carolina or if Bono tosses a guitar pick at me because I got seats right up front.

Homer Watson Teasdale.

He's three; I'm forty three, and we're figuring some things out together. For example, I don't make unreasonable demands that he rescue me from my self-inflicted depression and disappointment, and he won't poop on the living room floor, or the kitchen floor, or the patio behind the BBQ grill.

It's all negotiations with your third child. I read that somewhere.

I don't hold him accountable for me being a single mom, and he doesn't feed his dirty underwear to the dog.

Easy peasy.

I remember the night he was conceived.

Richard and I had sneaked away for the weekend. We shacked up at our beach house with a few bottles of wine, some nice bread from the Italian bakery, and a couple of lobsters we bought on the lazy drive down through Long Beach Island.

I lit candles, while Richard opened the windows and deck doors, inviting the sea breeze in to charge me up and confirm for him that he was getting laid later. Conditions were favorable; we had a green board. We were go for launch. I'd lost a few pounds that summer, and Richard rewarded us both with a shiny, new set of 34-Ds. Granted, I carried them around, but he helped whenever he got even remotely horny, which was most evenings and three or four afternoons a week.

I'd trimmed the hedges in the Promised Land, worn some slutty undies, and basically went topless five minutes after getting the groceries put away and clean towels in the master bathroom. We skipped dinner to hump like teenagers. The lobsters both died in the cooler sometime during the night, poor buggers. But neither of us cared. Neither of us was hungry at all. Richard was in his element: screwing for God and country. And I was deliciously out of my element: mothering and domesticking and wondering where my wandering husband might be. I knew exactly where he was, because I had the bald head of his chubby penis in my hand, in my mouth, and in my neatly-trimmed twat for most of the night.

In case you weren't aware, most wives and mothers can pull off *slutty whore* pretty admirably when we put our minds to it. We're often too busy with the mothering and domesticking, and many husbands — check that, *my* husband — didn't give me a reason to want to.

Also, as an aside: I think it's probably for the best that men don't have a clitoris. It's far too powerful a force. Most women know enough to keep the damned thing holstered under normal circumstances, only taking it out when the time's right to let go with a 'yippeekiyaay motherfucker!' or two, or if we're fortunate and truly relaxed, even three. But then it's back in its cave, safely tucked away so our IQ points can climb back into triple digits.

If men had a clitoris, holy crap. Wars would be fought. Laws passed. Taxes levied. Supreme Court justices bribed. Planet Earth would come to a gear-squealing halt. Crops would rot in fields. Grave-silent factories would gather dust. Golf courses would grow thick with weeds into dangerous, suburban jungles, and world markets would collapse, because half the population, 3.5 billion men, would be home touching themselves during every commercial break on ESPN.

Richard doesn't have a clitoris, but he knows where to find one . . . *them* I should say. Yes: *them*. He doesn't have an enormous, gratifying horse penis, and he can't stay hard for four hours like those suicidal old farts who overdose on Viagra. No, Richard quite simply paid attention during Anatomy & Physiology class one sleepy autumn day in tenth grade when his teacher covered the male and female reproductive organs.

I'm sure he caught on to God's unfair discrepancy before any of his classmates. He might even have raised his hand, asked, 'um . . . Mr. Johnson . . . um, why would women have that . . . you know . . . when all it's used for is feeling . . . um . . . well, good? I mean, why don't men get one?'

His teacher, a man with a penis, would have responded with something appropriately antiseptic. 'Well, Richard, it's very simple. By having the clitoris near the upper edge of the vagina, women experience greater pleasure during intercourse, thereby securing their willingness to participate in the act with predictable frequency – around their monthly ovulation cycle, of course – and thus ensuring the procreation of the species.'

Heh. Nope.

I like imagining a girl in that class, a junior or a senior who'd failed and needed the re-take for graduation. A sloppy, parking lot whore in a black bra and a white tank-top, she turned her Gothy make up to old Dickie boy and mouthed the words, 'I'll show you.'

And it began: Richard's career as a human clitoral compass.

That breezy night in our beach house, it was my clitoris that took center stage. Richard couldn't wait to oblige: I was his wife, but I'd shown up with new boobs. I might as well have been a stranger, which excited him and invited even more up-close and personal attention from the Clit Fairy.

Everyone had a wonderful time, and by morning he'd forgotten that a weekend with me meant a weekend away from one of his local trollops. That Saturday, I woke, naked, on my couch and took a minute just to revel in the fact that I'd had a round of pretty gratifying sex. Then I sat up and realized without any doubt that I was pregnant.

Now I know that even the Michael Phelps of human sperm can't swim that far that fast, but I also know my body – all the creaks, groans, echoes, and radar pings – and I determined (after a lightning-fast tally on my fingertips) that the time had been right.

A little girl.

The possibility rose in my mind like a fogbank over a beach town, clouding all logic or reason. I couldn't see clearly, didn't hear Richard turn on the shower down the hall, didn't smell coffee brewing in my kitchen. Confusion and strangely-cool ambiguity swallowed me up.

I was pregnant, or could be.

Just to put the stem on the apple, I wore a bikini bottom all day, well part of the day, and nothing else. Every time Richard got even the teensiest bit horny, which he does with staggering, *Deutsche Bundesbahn* regularity, I let him have me: on the couch, on the floor, in the shower, even once on the deck. Why not? He'd paid over six-thousand dollars for my tits. What the hell, he might as well enjoy them. My clitoris spent the weekend calling all the shots. Its IQ reached three standard deviations above the mean; while my brain's ability to complete even the most mundane tasks, buttering bread or folding socks, seeped slowly beneath the fogbank.

Finally, we quit.

He went out to the tiki bar for a beer and a smoke, and I took a shower and went to bed with my legs propped up on three pillows. I'd spent the day getting filled with baby-daughter sperm; there was no way even one of those tiny Xs was going to fall out.

Exhausted but happy, I dozed, then fell asleep, believing that a daughter would do the trick. The beach house and the sea breeze had worked wonders. A baby girl would wrap everything up with a tidy pink bow. Finally, after fourteen years, we'd turned that godforsaken corner. We'd be okay.

Less than six hours later, I discovered how wrong I'd been.

This happened, no bullshit.

She called herself Arella. I don't know if that really was her name, but she spoke little English and got by using German and Hebrew with her boyfriend, husband, manager, whoever he was – a portly, overdressed German named Karl.

Karl spoke enough English to decide that my husband was just about the most engaging fellow he'd met in months. What Karl and Arella were doing at a neighborhood tiki bar in a place like Avalon escapes me, but to hear Karl describe it in broken sentences, they were on their way to Manhattan for a photo shoot with some modeling agency. They'd been in DC visiting the monuments and decided to take the scenic route up the coast before driving into New York and international modeling fame.

For Arella anyway.

Karl couldn't have modeled shoelaces. He must have been wealthy, well endowed, or exceedingly powerful in the modeling, fashion, or filmmaking industries. Otherwise, I was at a loss for why Arella would be traveling with him.

Power, money, influence, or penis length had something to do with this odd couple. I didn't bother staying up late enough to find out.

Richard did.

We didn't discuss it on Sunday, though. We didn't discuss anything on Sunday.

Arella – I don't know if she had a last name – remains the most exotically beautiful woman I've ever seen. Tall and athletic, she exuded youth, vigor, and feminine sexuality, much more powerfully than the starving, emaciated, stick figures in the *Victoria's Secret* catalogue. Arella might have been a basketball player, a volleyball player, even a tough Israeli soldier out for the night in a cocktail dress. With lean, gorgeous muscles and exquisite thighs, hips, and tits, she wore Mediterranean olive skin like the promise of a mind-numbing, ten-minute orgasm crammed into about thirty seconds of once-in-a-lifetime physical pleasure.

They claimed she was on her way to fame as a supermodel. That might have been true, but I've not heard of her since. The one-name thing was a good start, I guess. Arella had drunk enough appletinis, however, that for the night her rise to supermodel stardom would be derailed by the need to vomit in the street. I bet she looked great doing it, though.

Karl wanted to hump her like a rutting Bichon Frisé. Richard might not have survived the night without humping her.

Even I wanted to hump her – well, not hump her so much as savor her, but you know what I mean, Billy - after speaking awkwardly with her for less-than five minutes. And I was pretty seriously pissed off at my shithead husband at the time. I'd gone to bed excited and feeling connected with him (having mistaken sex for love . . . again), overjoyed at the possibility of being pregnant, and hopeful that I might get a little girl. I woke up six hours later, 4:00 am, to find him drunk and hosting strangers in our living room, where we'd made love multiple times the previous evening.

Dumbass dropped a glass. I woke, pulled on a robe and joined them, worried that they might be drug dealers, killers, felons on a tri-state crime spree. I wasn't thinking *sex*; I was thinking *home invasion* or *Truman Capote*.

Arella closed quickly on me, embraced me, murmured some Israeli greeting. She smelled of cigarettes, vodka, and lilacs. She hugged me hard, with unapologetic, full-frontal commitment: breast on breast, belly on belly, *mons pubis* on *mons pubis* (I had to look that one up). She pressed hard enough that I got the message like a static charge from my carpet: Arella wanted sex, but she didn't want Richard *or* Karl. Sure, a mini, pre-dawn orgy would be fine with her, but she'd had enough appletini poison to give in to a different appetite altogether.

On any other night I might have gone for it. Why not? Arella was drop-dead gorgeous, compellingly, memorably gorgeous. But that night I'd been transfixed by the possibility of having a baby and saving my marriage and maybe even discovering that Richard still loved me, all of me, not just my new boobs or my engorged clitoris.

So I kept it polite, at first, tried the c'mon-hey-nah-not-tonight strategy that I'd used for years to get my father out of the Scotch bottle and into bed. I wanted Richard to myself, even drunk as he was. Whatever. He'd had a few too many, I hoped, in celebration of his personal decision to stay married or his hours-long contemplation of his favorite baby names for little girls

Karl and Arella needed to go. All would be forgiven if they'd just finish their drinks and get out of my house.

They didn't. Karl draped his Abercrombie & Fitch blazer over the back of my sofa, placed his glass on my coffee table, splashed booze across Hugh Jackman's face, ruining my weekend copy of *People*.

Arella flopped into our lounge chair. Her silk chemise shifted charitably; she looked good enough to eat. I considered it; I'm not lying to you, Billy. Just watching her pout and drop into that chair, if I'd have tried it, I'd have looked like a giant squid with one boob peeking out of my top and too much pasty thigh exposed awkwardly.

Arella sat like the love child of Gene Kelly and Gabrielle Reese.

I tried again, politely, 'It's pretty late, you know. And I'm sure you two have important things to get ready if you're heading up to the city tomorrow. So I'll just say good night. Richard can show you out when you finish your drinks.' Polite, but done.

I didn't want to go back to bed angry. I knew I'd not get to sleep, not with strangers in my house, but I wasn't irretrievable, not yet, just a bit overwhelmed with their last-call-nightcap party at my house while I slept.

The hug and the dress and the *mons pubis* bit threw me off as well. I admit it.

So I shot Richard a look that said, *it's okay; just get rid of them and I'll take you to breakfast later.*

He didn't get it.

Instead, he handed me a cosmo, cupped my ass with one hand, and slurred, 'I'll give you $3,000 to fuck her, right here, while me and Karl watch.'

He might as well have punched me in the stomach. I focused on the drink in my hand, the fun, fruity color, the delicate stem on the glass. I bent slowly to place it beside Karl's, careful not to spill any on Hugh. It took a few seconds for me to trust my voice; I tried the Dad strategy again. 'C'mon, Richard . . . I'm not . . . no, not tonight.'

He draped an arm across my shoulders, breathed muggy, Marlboro Light and nacho cheese into my face only inches away. 'C'mon, baby. You can do this. $3,000 cash tomorrow. No, Monday. Bank's not open tomorrow.'

'No.'

Karl said something to Arella in German. She turned brown eyes, lovely eyes, to my Frumpy Alice bathrobe, assessing me through the flannel. Her eyebrows rose, almost imperceptibly; her eyes widened, *Yes?*

'Three grand,' Richard broke whatever spell Arella might have woven with another blast from his cigarette-and-Dorito-flavored breath. 'You guys get naked, maybe some nice kissing, a little gropety-grope, and we'll all see what happens. C'mon, baby. Whaddya say?'

'Out.' I shrugged free from Richard's arm. 'Both of you, get out of my house. Right now.'

'Hold on. Hold on,' Richard started.

'You, too,' I cut him off. 'I don't care, but they've got to go. Immediately.'

'But, sweetie, I invited –'

'Out!' I turned, tried to retreat.

Arella caught my eye, said something intended for me. I was too angry to know if it was German or Hebrew.

Karl apologized noisily in broken shards of nervous English that wedged between Richard and me, enough to release me. I escaped to my room, closed the door but didn't slam it. I couldn't have a bilingual woman, taller than me, prettier than me, in better shape than me, and better with nominative and objective case pronouns than *I* . . . see me slam the door. I'm not a door slammer. Take that, Boobs One Name.

Richard left with them.

He showed up around 10:30 Sunday morning, still drunk, disheveled, and carrying a half-dozen bagels and two *venti* mochas from Starbucks. I'd already packed, cleaned the house in a blizzard of Clorox wipes and disparaging comments. I'd been disillusioned by the same disappointing conclusion again and again; now I just wanted to get home to my boys.

We never talked about it, went a couple of weeks without talking at all. I figure he and Karl took turns with Arella until the three of them passed out in their hotel room. I should've checked his phone. A man like Richard would never let a woman like that, a legitimate, big-game trophy, get away without photographic evidence. He'd want one with his dick in her mouth and one full-length shot, Michelangelo's masterpiece photo for nostalgia.

That began the end for us. Pregnant, disgusted with myself, and as alone on planet Earth as I'd ever been, I felt my options dwindle. We sold the house in Avalon. Richard told the agent it was for economic reasons, but we both knew better. I'd never go back there, didn't even want that furniture. We sold it fully furnished.

I'm not sure if an ocean breeze still does the trick. Since then I've only been to the beach on Mom duty with a diaper bag full of toys, towels, and SPF 50.

As for Homer Watson Teasdale, daredevil, interpretive dancer, and Cheerios dumpster . . . he and I are fine. He landed on my life like a frigging depth charge, but since I was in dire need of a little demolition, I decided not to mind so much. Most days, he's just so goddamned thrilled to be here, I forget that I ever wanted anything but him. A few times I've wondered if there'd ever be anything cathartic (for either of us) in a frank discussion of where my life had been when I decided to have unprotected sex with Richard one last time.

Probably not.

I'd been in the toilet, had believed a baby girl would save me, and maybe she would have. Or maybe I'd have screwed her up so thoroughly, she'd have been the only Kindergartner in I-hate-my-mother Goth makeup, snake tattoos, and pierced eyebrows that look like a fly fisherman's hat band.

Homer is the exact, diametric opposite of what I thought I wanted from life. God pissed me off when he sent me a boy. Hadn't He been listening? I distinctly said, 'Girl. Vagina. Field Hockey. Prom Dress. Kappa Delta Sorority.'

Nope. He'd been right again.

Getting what I wanted would have left me (and my daughter) on a dirt path to surefire misery. When Homer emerged, looking like a lizard with a tiny penis, I had no choice but to take another road.

Thank God.

And that's where we are. But don't worry, there's much more where that came from.

Keep well,

Jennifer

April 17

Dear Billy —

I read over that last email and decided to send a quick follow up. Some mornings as the sun rises over the baseball field we've mown into the yard, God tries to convince me that I've bought another beach house.

I didn't realize it when I chose this place; the soybeans looked like a rolling expanse of green, knee-high shrubs. By late October, they matured, changed colors, and those back fields shone yellow-green in the sunrise like slow ocean rollers at dawn.

When the wind shifts and blows in from the northeast, I can get a taste of salty air in my face and the occasional confused seagull out slumming. It's not bad.

The boys swing hard, trying to clear the fence. They like watching their homerun shots splash down in that sea of sunlit gold and green. I like it, too. They'll crack a deep drive over the corral fence that lands like a falling star. Every few days I organize a search party, but we don't find too many baseballs out there.

Who cares? Wal-Mart's got racks of them for $2 a-piece. It's worth it for me to see the guys hit one into the soybeans here at my beach house.

I'll spring for the two dollars.

See you,

Jennifer

PS: Well, shit. Just once I'd like to write to you and be able to omit a detail, not lie as much as leave something unsaid. But I can't.

Reading my last email, I reflected (polite verb) on Richard's propensity to go in without a shower cap, if you get my meaning. Anyway, I'm fairly confident that my boys might have at least one half brother and perhaps a half sister they don't know about. There, I said it, and I feel better. I'm sorry, but I'm not quite ready to plow that ground just yet. So all you get today is my suspicion/confidence that it's true.

April 26

Dear Billy,

I'm writing from a hotel in Boston tonight, couldn't wait until I got home.

I brought the boys up here for a weekend of Red Sox games. They're rabid, manic, sociopathic fans who watch, read about, research, and discuss the Red Sox incessantly. I don't mind and figure I'll one day convince them to read Toni Morrison or Ernest Hemingway by mentioning that the Sox play important roles in both *Sula* and *The Sun Also Rises*. What the hell, I'm not above deception if it gets them hooked on good writing.

Anyway, at Fenway Park tonight, we sneaked down to the rail beside the first base dugout. The game had ended a couple of minutes earlier, and the crowd filed out around us. They'd played the Blue Jays, pounded them 12 – 4. So a mostly-sedate group of fans wandered out without much ado: they'd known the Sox had it in the bag for two hours. That helped us. Security guards near first base watched the crowd with detached interest, almost bored. The one closest to us might have been asleep on his feet, if his eyes didn't periodically shift from ass to ass as drunk women made their way up the worn concrete steps.

My middle son, who already wants a Red Sox tattoo, asked, 'Mom, do you think I can jump over and steal a handful of dirt? I'll be really fast.'

'No, Buddy, we'll get arrested.' I tried to sound convincing, but didn't believe our ass-watching guard would move from his spot if Al-Qaeda operatives stormed the locker room.

My son surprised me. 'Will they keep us together?'

'Whaddya mean?'

'If they arrest us, can we stay together?'

'Yes, Buddy, I'm sure they'd keep us together.'

'Okay then.' And he took off, down the aisle, over the rail, on his knees, and back in less time than it took me to call after him. Spider-Man couldn't have maneuvered it more fluidly.

'Hey!' Ass-Watcher yelled, turned toward us. 'Hey, kid!' But that's all he had. He didn't come after us, just shook his head disapprovingly at me, then returned to his vigil.

'Look!' As wildly enthusiastic as I'd ever seen him, my son had two handfuls of reddish, sandy-clay mixture that he quickly dumped into an errant beer cup his brother found beneath a nearby seat. 'Mom! I did it!'

I hustled them up the aisle, wanted out of there before the local storm troopers arrived to take me into custody. 'Nice work!'

'Can we put it on the mantel?'

'We can put it in our cereal, if you want,' I said. 'Let's just get out of here before we're slapped with a criminal trespass citation.'

'Okay, Mom.' They followed me out, planning what style vase they'd purchase to commemorate the moment. And we escaped like career criminals from a Chicago speakeasy. It's the most fun I've had in years. I can't wait for tomorrow's game.

I brought them up here, because Richard's been spending money on them like cash itself was invented six months ago. I can't keep up and have to budget and deny myself all sorts of wants and needs. Otherwise I'd not be able to corral enough money to compete.

Actually, I'm not kidding anyone. I can't compete. Richard made over $260k last year. I made exactly $0. Once the judge signs our paperwork and I'm free from him forever, I'll be entitled to twenty-eight percent of his salary, or $72,800. It's not bad, but he still wins in the let's-see-who-can-buy-their-affection-faster competition.

So I'm not playing. I refuse to play.

Okay, bullshit. I'm playing a little bit this weekend, showing the boys that they can enjoy life with their mother, even if I can't buy them a new space shuttle every other weekend.

Insufficient Funds. Ever get that when they run your debit card? Yeah, I hate that.

I suppose that's what I enjoyed most about tonight. The best part of the evening didn't cost us anything. It was our time together, committing a criminal trespass in the sandy clay of Fenway's foul territory. There's no amount of money I could throw at them that could replicate their joy at making it out of that stadium with two handfuls of dirt.

That's the joy I've got to be able to show them. Screw the space shuttles.

Maybe tomorrow, we'll try for a handful of grass!

Find the joy. It's going to be my new tattoo. I've mentioned that; I know. I've just got to muster the courage and the money. I'll send a photo when it's done.

Go Red Sox!

Jennifer

May

Are you joking? If Jesus can't help me keep my panties hiked all the way up, no one can.

May 8

Hi Billy,

There was a time, about three years ago, when Richard tried to convince me, his therapist, and himself that he is a sex addict.

     I'll wait while you laugh.

     Or do you believe in that nonsense?

     Sex addict. Heh.

     And I thought about writing a letter to you and attempting to describe my embarrassment, outrage, and eventual laughter at his unbridled, unfettered, unmitigated, and un . . . some other stuff . . . selfishness. Instead, I surfed the Internet from cover to cover, reading the research and investigating the veracity of the claim, 'I am a sex addict.'

     Holy crap. You wouldn't believe the gold-plated bullshit floating around in cyberspace (most of it written by men, excusing their behavior) on the issue of sex addiction. I read confessions, angry outbursts, blog posts, Facebook comments, indictments, divorce arguments from both sides in public records, and even a Dr. Phil transcript that I couldn't get through, because every time I think of him commenting on sex, I imagine him flopping around like a beached tuna in the shallow end of some king-size bed.

     Anyway, my favorite was a blog post/raging rant that I enjoyed so much I decided to copy and paste it in here for your entertainment. Whoever this guy is (I'm betting it's a woman in disguise), he/she has no shortage of frustration with selfish sex addicts or Christian groups' claims to have a therapeutic answer to every ailment known to modern medicine. It's the old duct-tape-fixes-everything adage applied to Bible thumpers and those they hope to heal.

     I love it. And yes, I think that makes me a bad person, but I don't care.

     He/she sounds like me when I've had a few drinks and get myself riled up. I think that's why I had such a good time reading this and hope that I can get every spoiled asshole on Earth to read it, too. Anyway, here it is (oh, it's Rated R; brace yourself):

My Loyal Readers,

Recently, I found an article about a rich, gated-community pussy who didn't have the stones to admit that he'd been boning half the women in his wife's mahjong crew as well as her faux-Gucci-bag-party friends. He'd been tallying co-ed naked time with the Tuesday afternoon white-wine-and-Lunesta girls and had nailed a few of the hired cleaning ladies – just for a taste of foreign cuisine.

Brace yourselves, friends, we're going where no man has gone before, like in Star Trek, but with condoms.

This Rogue Penis is white. He's a golfer with a boat, a pair of jet skis, and a beach house in the Outer Banks of North Carolina. He's got honking big-assed televisions all over his house and a car with a price tag higher than most bachelor's degrees.

Perhaps you've met him, slept with him, Rogue White Penis like the shark from Jaws. Where's Robert Shaw and Roy Scheider? We need a few of those barrels and maybe that spear gun.

What's infuriating about this particular species of shithead is that when confronted by his wife, instead of saying, "Yes, dear, I've been humping my way through the neighborhood, often with your close friends," Rogue Penis joined the ranks of Post-Millennial Absurdists who suggest that they are addicted to sex, just not the kind of sex one has with a spouse.

Now loyal readers, I don't know what team of crack psychologists determined that being addicted to sex – but not to sex with one's regular partner – was a bona fide disabling condition, like blindness or Multiple Sclerosis. But one or more of them must have been shaft deep in all manner of nubile hoo-ha from around the research campus, because psychologists, unlike professional basketball players, aren't renowned for their ability to attract underwear models. Getting a bit every now and then (in a polite missionary position) is probably a refreshing break from all those null hypotheses. Psychologists aren't giving Matthew McConaughey a run for his money with the Los Angeles Laker Girls.

But these days, when pharmaceutical companies pay millions of dollars on incoherent marketing campaigns for drugs to treat invisible ailments, sex addiction has become the irresistible flavor of the month.

Find someone living below the poverty line who screws half the women on his street, and you know what you've found? An adulterer piece of shit who can't get through the day without unzipping his fly. Move that same sorry slob to the suburbs and prop him up in a big house with a convertible in the driveway, and what is he? A sex addict.

Critics will say, "So what? Sex addiction is just another in a laundry list of bullshit excuses to purchase medical happiness over the counter. We're perfectly content to spend tens of thousands of dollars so our therapists can afford the monthly dues at the country club. Where's the harm in crazy people paying their own money to treat imagined illnesses, particularly if they're willing to write the check for the pretend drugs or the pointless group-therapy discussions?"

Slathering oneself with authentic-imitation pity, particularly previously-purchased pity is fun. Hell, it's the American way. Tom Joad would have done it too, if he could have found ten cents for a decent bowl of soup. It's difficult to sustain an erection when you're starving.

My problem with Rogue Penis and his sex addiction isn't that I take a judgmental position on people nailing each other. Shit no! I'm all for people getting as much ass as they can fit in a suitcase with a plunger. Rather, my problem with sex addiction is that people out boning used to own the decision, if not proudly. Many of our own parents back in the 70s and 80s, got drunk in a local bar and nailed a skank or two, just for the calisthenics. You know what they did when they got caught? Well, that's another story; many of them behaved pretty badly. But I'm betting that none of them ever put on their best victimized-by-my-culture countenance and said, "Sweetheart, I'm tragically addicted to sex, but sadly not sex with you."

Today, these palseated nose pickers actually continue catting around the neighborhood *after* they've been caught, because sex addiction is a disabling condition, and they just can't help it.

Yeah. Right. Like I can't help queuing up the chicken-fried steak as opposed to the side salad. If you're going to jerk me off, at least put a little panache into it.

What can we do to help these people overcome the irrepressible need for a blow job from a different woman every day? What can we do to help them curb their desire for fleeting, meaningless physical engagements with clients or neighbors? And what can we do to stop them from looking in the mirror and seeing a victim?

I've been researching this, and it's almost unspeakably ridiculous . . . almost.

Evangelical Christians.

I'm not joking. Because in this country,

when I think *sex addiction treatment*, I
immediately think evangelical Christians.

Salt, pepper. Eggs, bacon. Starsky,
Hutch. Packers, Vikings. Sex addiction,
evangelical Christians.

It's almost perfect: I'm rich and willing
to pay whatever's necessary to feel better
about myself. Enter the church, an
organization willing, as ever, to take my
money and lie to me.

God bless America.

No, really . . . God bless America. We've
paid. We want it done.

Anyway, back to Rogue Penis (aka: rich,
golfer, sex addict, dickhead who fell in love
in 1988 and regrets it now, twenty-five years
and twenty-five pounds of softened midsection
later). In the article, the *victim* (no shit,
the author called him a *victim*) had plans to
spend a month in rehab, but not rehab for the
usual suspects: coke, smack, Oxycontin, weed,
booze, or Percocet. None of those made the
list.

Sex rehab. Sexual addiction
rehabilitation over thirty days at a facility
in Arizona, hosted by evangelical Christians.

I'll pause here while you look around for
a good place to vomit.

Sex addiction treatment for men and women
at a private (wicked expensive) facility in
Arizona, without spouses, for thirty days.

Loyal readers, here's where I have a
question: If Rogue Penis creates opportunities
to sneak out of the house for a handful of
fake suburban boobie, won't he find a
convenient laundry list of available options
when he checks into a rehab facility filled to
bursting with women who *claim to be
motherfucking sex addicts*? That's like sending

those pudgy lardasses from *The Biggest Loser* down to McDonald's to pick up a healthy salad and a low-fat yogurt parfait.

Oh sure, no problem. I don't want a Big Mac. No thank you. I never developed a taste for the Big Mac.

Good lord, what have we come to? James Madison, Thomas Jefferson, George Mason, Benjamin Franklin . . . any of them would take a flame thrower to the lot of us, and be justified doing it!

Look around, loyal readers. We live in a culture that encourages people to make excuses for inexcusable behaviors. They're chasing tail around the neighborhood, strange tail; so they don't have to invent any meaningful chit-chat, wetting the wick, nibbling the titties, and humping to happiness. Rather than summon the fortitude to say, "Yeah, honey, I screwed your golf partner," they cry and wonder if they're addicted to sex.

You know what I'm addicted to? Beer and donuts. Wanna know why? Because they taste great – like magical, frigging, Harry-Potter-enchanted-them-super-dooper GREAT. I'm not making excuses. Do I wish I wasn't addicted to beer and donuts? No. I love them both. The hell with it. I've got to die of something.

Anyway, when sex addicts decide to "fix" themselves . . . Why they want to do that, I don't understand. They're getting laid, after all . . . but when sex addicts decide to do something about it, where do they go?

Arizona. Into the waiting embrace of the evangelical Christians. A salt-of-the-earth organization known for their level-headed approach to myriad social issues.

Screw the Jews, Muslims, Hindus, and anyone who hasn't accepted the Caucasian,

English-speaking Jesus as their Lord and
Savior! Now, turn Bill O'Reilly back on.

I want to go. Don't you?

I mean; I'm not jonesing for thirty days
sequestered with a dorm full of crazies,
talking out loud to Jesus about the fact that
they've been struggling to keep their pants
on. That's just silly. If you're going to talk
out loud to Jesus, how about asking for
health, peace, happiness, social and cultural
stability, a cure for hunger, deadly ailments
or diseases?

Nah. Are you joking? If Jesus can't help
me keep my panties hiked all the way up, no
one can.

Actually, that's a pretty good point.

But I want to go anyway. Imagine the non-
stop boning going on in a place like that.

When I think about it – the addicts and
the Christians, not the actual sex – I get so
embarrassed about who we've become that I
honestly feel a little disappointed Mikhail
Gorbachev didn't say, "Intercourse the
infidels!" and nuke us to dust in the Kansas
wind.

Not Yeltsin, that drunken gunslinger.
Gorbachev.

If it had to be someone, I wish it had
been Gorbachev. He could have gone to a
private screening of *Rambo: First Blood, Part*
2 with the Politburo, got himself into a
pretty good froth, and just pushed the big red
button. Why not? With that map of Vietnam
tattooed on his forehead, he was ready to
rumble.

Did six-hundred-thousand Americans die in
the Civil War so we could send sex addicts off
to Arizona for treatment from evangelical
Christians? If so, I think a whole rack of

those soldiers would want their money back.

Healing, loyal readers. That's what they call it: Christian healing. Because when I think: *how can we help someone overcome the selfish need to indulge at the Poon Palace while the wife and kids are at Grandma's*, I think: *of course, the teachings of Christ, our Savior*. Because no one quite had a handle on self-medicating, self-centered, childish, bullshit behavior like . . . oh, wait . . . that's pedophile priests looking to avoid prison, not Jesus. He can't stand those dopey bastards either.

Do you know a sex addict, loyal readers? Perhaps you know Rogue Penis himself. If so, slap him hard (you suburban pussies) and give him a look of genuine, indignant disappointment. Or better yet, buy the self-indulgent prick a case of beer and drop him at Dunkin' Donuts. Maybe the jackass will explode.

May 9

Dear Billy,

Okay. Forgive me. I know it was awful, but I couldn't help it.

I want to meet the writer (woman; I know it was a woman) who came up with that. I mean, she must have just snorted an entire suitcase full of fat-free cocaine and gone to work at that keyboard.

Sorry. I admit: it was a bit heavy handed. But she's my kind of girl!

I'll tone it down for a while. I promise.

Jennifer

PS: Poon Palace? Tell me you didn't love that line!

May 26

Hey Big Guy,

Heh, sorry. I blame the cosmopolitan martinis. They're malicious poison.

Do you drink? I hope so. You used to, but not so much, not so much as I do now, anyway. Shit, no one drinks as much as I do now. Actually, that's an exaggeration. I don't drink too much. I just make the mistake of sitting down at this computer when I've gone a gallon or two beyond my limit.

I need some kind of software on this thing that keeps me from writing email, logging on to Facebook, or Twitter, any of it, unless I'm sober enough to calculate a nasty, big-boned equation. The two-by-three-way analysis of covariance, that'd do the job. Or maybe the area beneath the curve, from calculus; remember calculus? Neither do I. But that one was a bitch: $f(x) - g(x)$ and all divided by the derivative of some shit I didn't know in 1991, never mind today after a jolly visit from the Ghost of Cosmopolitans Past.

I read a story about Winston Churchill once. A famous drinker – champagne, I think – he asked one of his attendants, bodyguards, secretaries, somebody how many boxcars they could fill with the empty champagne bottles in his wake.

The attendant answered something to the effect of, 'not even one, sir.'

Cool. I like that story.

Don't worry. I don't drink that much, but when I do, I tend to go off the high dive. I enjoy the high dive; it gives me a chance to take in the view.

After the boys went to bed tonight, I even wrote a little song to commemorate all those years of play-pretend-happy. If I knew how to play the guitar or something, I'd sing it for you. You remember my singing? Be glad I don't have your cell number, or you'd be in for an unpleasant and frightening serenade tonight, Big Boy.

I think of it as a country-hip-hop-Barry-Manilow-operatic aria with a side of bacon. Here it is:

You bought a ring, a perky little diamond, when we were twenty three.

We rented *Barefoot in the Park* and talked of possibilities.
But lately those dreams have checked themselves in for some out-patient surgery.
Anything to laser, scalpel, scope, or chainsaw what was *we* into *you* and *me*.

Now I don't want to set things right, or make up over a beer.
Just get your flabby ass up from my chair, and drag it out of here.
I'm saying it wasn't worth it.
Boy, you know it's true.
How in the name of Jesus Christ did I frigging fall in love with you?

Though the last twenty years have seen us through three healthy pregnancies,
They've also seen us weather the storm of thirty grim adulteries!
That's three children and a bouquet of stretch marks to remind me for the rest of my life
That twenty years are the price I paid to play your trophy wife.

And I don't want to work things out, or hear your silly lies and cheer.
Just get your perky ass out of my chair, and light the goddamned thing on fire; I don't give a shit!
(That line doesn't quite work. I'll edit it tomorrow.)
I'm saying it wasn't worth it.
Dick, you know it's true.
How in the name of all that's holy did I agree to marry you?

There's more, but that's all I have drafted tonight. Maybe I'll sing it at open-mic night at the café over behind Wegmans. After all the insipid poetry the Bitch Squad reads every other Friday, my song might be just the dose of inappropriate revelry this town needs.
    Oh, and nothing rhymes with 'cocksucker.' Ever notice that? Well, 'long-distance trucker' works, but how do you fit that into a poem about love?

To the point. Finally.
    You're probably wondering how I've written you the equivalent of hundreds of pages in the past year and never mentioned my sons' names – except for Homer. Everyone knows Homer.
    Have you wondered that?

166

I haven't been lying to you, Billy, so I feel a little embarrassed that I've been dodging that bit of truth since I started scribbling these notes. My eldest son is named for my husband, Richard Daniel Teasdale, and my middle son is named for my father, Gerald Cooper Teasdale.

My friend Myrna asked whether I'll change the boys' last names to Cooper. I changed mine a few weeks back, just after the ink dried on the divorce agreement.

I can't, because Gerry's name would be Gerald Cooper Cooper. That'd be great if he had plans to star in a Dr. Seuss poem, but for anything else, he'd sound like a hiccup.

So they're Teasdales, like their father.

And I'm sorry I kept that from you. It's just humiliating for me that I would spend a hundred pages bitching about my father and my ex-husband after naming my children . . . you know what I mean.

Although I suppose if I had things figured just right, I wouldn't be here, tipsy, and writing to you in my PJs with a disconcerting stretch of empty acreage on the other side of this bed.

But enough for tonight, or I'll get myself into trouble.

Love,

Jenny

May 27

Hey Billy,

I'm sorry.

Danny, my eldest, (we call him Danny, thank God) wanted to watch some old videos last night, home movie stuff. I got swallowed by an unanticipated sneaky wave of sadness. It crept up from beneath my sofa as I watched Richard and me in our first house, bringing Danny home from the hospital, playing in the yard, the works. I'm sure you understand.

Anyway, I had a few drinks, one for each pang of loneliness, depression, anger, whatever emotion took its turn (after waiting politely in line) slapping me hard across the face.

And I wrote to you, called you 'Big Guy.' Sorry.

And I sent a copy of my poetry, such as it is.

And I referred to myself as 'Jenny.' I hate that name; I'm not a 'Jenny.'

And I wrote 'love.' Jesus.

I'm glad you know my sons' names, though.

Let's start again. And I promise I'll think about cutting back on the alcohol, especially before I write to you.

Jennifer

June

You can get the fashion designer out of the Kmart panties, but you can't get the Kmart panties out of the fashion designer!

June 2

Hello William,

Do you know what I thought about this morning?

I'm waiting for you to answer. You're not going to, because in here you're actually a second-person apostrophe. The reason I know that is because I paid attention in English classes that you ditched to drink beer and carouse with your friends at the Ratskeller. As much as it might pain me to remind you, if you'd gone to class more consistently, my friend, you'd know about second-person apostrophes as well.

Not that anyone anywhere gives a shit.

Well, maybe that Lynne Truss woman over in England. She does.

But that's not what I thought about this morning.

Rather, I thought about Day 137. Do you remember Day 137? I bet you do.

August 22, 1991. You helped me move into my room: Monmouth Hall #317. I can't remember where Scoutmaster Kelly was that morning, probably off leading Cuba to democracy or pouring pitchers of kamikazes down her throat.

Anyway, I recall it vividly, even if you don't.

I had two boxes of books, two suitcases of underwear, socks, belts, and bathing suits, and about three hundred articles of loose clothing, jackets, and shoes tossed capriciously into the back seat of my Honda.

Remember that Honda? The Green Goblin's Dildo? I loved that car, although it rattled like a malfunctioning sex toy.

We carried the boxes up to my room; I left the driver's side door of the Dildo open, thinking we'd be right down for the rest of the stuff. We weren't.

You pressed against the wall outside the women's restroom. I sidled past, mining in my shorts for the key. I'd worn your red RU baseball hat; I used to wear it all the time. And you watched me go by, just a couple of steps.

That's what got us, those two or three steps.

I gnawed on my bottom lip, cursed at my stupid box full of

books, and finally managed to get the key into the lock and the door open.

You didn't come into the room right away, Billy. I crossed to the empty desk – the Scoutmaster had summarily dumped all of her belongings onto one of the beds, claiming that bed, desk, and armoire like a laundry room Neil Armstrong. She'd not done much else to unpack but had hung a U2 poster on the wall. To this day I swear Scoutmaster Kelly can't get fully aroused without Bono peering down at her.

I dropped the box onto my desk, turned, and found you there, a little sweaty, a little flushed, but still hefting my collection of modernist fiction.

'I love you,' you said.

I didn't answer, not right away.

So you said it again. 'Coop, I'm in love with you . . . all over the place.'

I'd known you for 136 days, Billy Klein, and your timing couldn't have been more perfect: not too early, too eager, too horny, and not too late, too slow to commit, too uncertain. Nope. Perfect.

Day 137.

Forty-five minutes later, I begrudgingly let you pull your shorts on. Shirtless and sweaty, you took two wobbly steps and collapsed onto the loose pile of Scoutmaster clothing. You exhaled with a sound I want to hear in the thirty seconds before I pass away, and I couldn't help myself, couldn't have held back with a gun to my head. 'I'm in love with you too, Billy. It's hard for me to believe there was ever a time when I wasn't.'

And the wheels came off the wagon.

Instead of rolling languidly onto your side to watch me dress, to remind me how much you loved me, or to ask me to marry you, to bear your children, or to open a joint checking account at Chemical Bank, you sat bolt upright, as if jolted with a cattle prod. I'd been wrangling myself awkwardly into a bra, and your sudden look of terror had me thinking I'd developed some unsightly skin disease.

Hey, screwing on those old plastic mattresses, anything is possible.

'What?' I said, panic daring me to move. 'What's the matter?'

You stole a pink T-shirt from Kelly's flotsam, pulled it over your head – it fit like a coat of sexy paint – and took off barefoot through the corridor.

'What?' I shouted, casting about on the floor for my shorts but only coming up with your baseball hat. 'What's the matter?'

'Your car!'

We found it. Remember? The Scoutmaster and her *boyfriend du jour* had come looking for us. When they discovered the Green Goblin's Dildo, double parked with the door open and the keys inside, they decided to have some fun with me. Kelly moved it twelve miles across New Brunswick to a seedy parking lot in the kind of strip mall that gives central Jersey its reputation as a place where civil zoning officials go to get paid off by mafia bag men.

I couldn't have cared less. Although, cab fare to the triple-X porn shop where they left it on Route 18 was almost twenty-five dollars. The Scoutmaster never covered that for me, the bitch.

Day 137. I'd go back tomorrow if I could.

What the hell, tonight.

I would bring sheets this time, though. Those dormitory mattresses were like petri dishes.

A long time ago in a galaxy far, far away . . . wasn't it?

Keep well, Billy,

Jennifer

Oh, and I don't know if you were keeping score that day, but I pulled the trigger three times in forty-five minutes, not a Guinness record, but worth the price of admission. You only managed one, but from my vantage point it looked like a good one.

Let me know if I owe you those other two. It's been a while, but I could probably be convinced to square up our accounts.

June 12

Hey Billy,

I'm a sucker for a happy ending. I am. It's embarrassing, because I haven't had many. But any given Friday night when my boys suggest we hit the movies, I'm invariably up for a romantic comedy, even at $65 a crack for all of us to go.

I should mention that when Danny and Gerry convince me to take them to the movies, we almost never see a romantic comedy, or worse, a love story. Nope. When I pony up $65 for popcorn, Whoppers, Swedish fish, and movie tickets, it's usually to see an aging Bruce Willis shoot three dozen people without his shirt coming untucked.

And don't get me started on Sylvester Stallone. My middle son, Gerry, loves him, saw the first two *Rocky* films and decided that Stallone was an American icon worthy of Brando, Pacino, or De Niro – lasagna eaters, all of them. Gerry can't get enough curled-lip, sweaty-browed, Human-Growth-Hormone-injected Italienglish drawl.

I can, however.

I put a stop to Stallone movies last year with *The Expendables VIII* or whatever it was. Jesus, the guy looks like an Army Surplus duffel bag, one of the mildewed, canvas models. Jack LaLanne and Arnold Schwarzenegger had a love child they abandoned on Passyunk in South Philly. Rather than leave well enough alone, Talia Shire and Burgess Meredith raised the boy, convinced him that life as a disco bouncer required too much Algebra, and helped him sound out the really hard words in that first *Rocky* screenplay.

As for Bruce Willis, he's all right, still attractive in a pasty-Michael-Jordan kind of way. I can shell out $65 to see him blow stuff up. But I prefer romantic comedies.

Particularly since my divorce.

Heh.

Growing up – and by 'growing up' I mean the time between my first menstrual period, when I got emotional, and my recent divorce, when I got emotional – I've seen hundreds of cookie-cutter love story and romantic comedy films. Because I'm a sucker for a happy ending.

Unlike the rest of the theater, I honestly believed Richard Gere would sweep into that God-awful whatever-it-was factory and carry

Debra Winger away. I did, because college educated, Naval officers in their dress whites often stop by grungy, $5.00-an-hour factory floors to find a fiancé.

And Debra Winger . . . what woman didn't want to be her? My mother's in her seventies, and she still gets herself all akimbo just thinking about the possibility that Richard Gere might wrestle into that uniform one more time and carry her away.

Since my divorce, though, I've begun to see some of those films from a different perspective. For example, when Richard Gere strutted through blue collar Puget Sound to rescue Debra Winger from a mundane life in her mother's footsteps, do you think he mentioned that she would spend the better part of the next twenty years in Norfolk, Pensacola, or every Navy wife's favorite: sunny Cyprus, where trips to the grocery store are a gamble, but the flak jackets come in an assortment of fetching spring colors?

Nah. Richard just waltzed in there, looking like a twenty-five-year career in San Diego, with drinks on the veranda at the Del Coronado, and weekends sailing to Catalina Island with their 2.5 above-average children.

I bought all of it, drank the Kool-Aid every time Hollywood served it up in a convenient 32-ounce cup. You get the extra 8 ounces for a measly fifty cents!

Stupid.

Anyway, since my divorce, I've watched a few of my favorites again – some of them a couple of times – and have compiled for you a brief list I'm calling **The Single Woman's Guide to Hollywood Romance**.

An Officer and a Gentleman didn't make the list, but I mention it here as an example of how my perspective on happy endings has changed since my attorney called to tell me that I was single again *and* that I owed her $17,329.

In no particular order . . .

1. *Meet Joe Black*

Stunning, emaciated, overworked, billionaire scion, Claire Forlani finally, against pointlessly-challenging odds, finds true love for the first time (because gorgeous, educated, wealthy women can never get dates). Sadly, her true love is Death enjoying a weekend off. In the end, though, only the fat, old man dies, because Brad Pitt is just too cute to kill, even after being struck by several cars.

SWGHR Bullshit Rating: Utter Nonsense.

2. *Something to Talk About*

Kentucky Horse & Hound heiress, Julia Roberts, catches husband, Dennis Quaid, catting about with others from the local Millionaires' Equestrian Club. So she poisons him in a clearly felonious act of attempted murder. But since rich girls don't go to jail, she attends her sister's wedding, enjoys one breathtaking dance with Quaid, realizes just what a catch he truly is, and agrees to forgive and forget. Afterward, she lives happily ever after with the man she tried to murder, and who might still be involved with any number of women from adjacent plantations.

SWGHR Bullshit Rating: The poison bit was clever.

3. *Sleepless in Seattle*

Widower, insomniac, Tom Hanks's meddling son communicates with desperate lonely-heart, Meg Ryan, who dumps the perfectly-marryable Bill Pullman (didn't she see *While You Were Sleeping?*) to rush to the top of the Empire State Building in a clear rip-off of an already saccharine-sweet Cary Grant film. Once there, she finally meets Hanks, who's just given a stern reprimand to his eight-year-old son for . . . get this . . . flying alone across the country and taking a taxi from LaGuardia Airport to Midtown Manhattan without Dad's permission! Yet when Meg shows up, Hanks (and the audience) forgets what a shitty father he was to have an eight year old pull a stunt like that, and falls in love with her almost immediately. This is tough news for Ryan, though, because social services case workers and the New York City Police show up ten minutes later to drag Hanks off to jail and his son to a foster placement in Seattle.

SWGHR Bullshit Rating: He's eight for Christ's sake. Focus!

4. *Pretty Woman*

Billionaire, Richard Gere can't operate a manual transmission, so he pays $20 to a six-foot streetwalking Julia Roberts to drive his Lotus Esprit to Beverly Hills, where there's an apparent shortage of eligible, disease-free, educated, horny women. He falls madly in love with the witty and compelling Roberts (out of character for his jaw-clenching, monotone, even-keeled worldview) without ever asking if she's even the tiniest bit HIV positive.

SWGHR Bullshit Rating: We didn't even believe this one when Disney did it in crayon. And Gere is already married to Debra Winger. They live in double-wide base housing down in Pensacola.

5. *Sweet Home Alabama*

Perky, adorable, fashion designer, Reese Witherspoon, is engaged to marry square-jawed, gazillionaire and NYC mayor's son, Dr. McDreamy. But first she's got to get a divorce from her sloppy, banjo-pickin', BBQ-stained husband, Josh Lucas, who just happens to be the only brooding, Byronic artist and would-be underwear model on the bayou. Will she choose Dr. McDreamy and his mind-blowing *Tiffany & Co.* crackerjack box? Or malaria and crawdad omelets?

SWGHR Bullshit Rating: You can get the fashion designer out of the Kmart panties, but you can't get the Kmart panties out of the fashion designer!

6. *Titanic*

This one will confound me until I find a way to let it go. A honking, big-assed boat (and metaphor for Man's overconfidence & perhaps a penis-length thing) sinks in freezing cold water. A handful of rich people allow over fifteen hundred poor people to drown in bitter agony, and James Cameron still wants us to give a shit about Jack and Rose. Is he joking? Arnold should have terminated him when he had the chance.

SWGHR Bullshit Rating: Sell the necklace; move someplace warm.

7. *13 Going on 30*

Teenage outcast, Jennifer Garner, breathes the magic fairy dust her chubby, awkward neighbor has apparently used in constructing an absurdly-elaborate-but-equally-unappreciated doll house. The dust fires Garner seventeen years into the future where she ends up trapped in her own, sexy, thirty-year-old body. When she discovers that she's grown into a selfish bitch, she turns to now-adorable Mark Ruffalo, the dollhouse architect, who honorably refuses to dump his fiancé, even though Garner promises that she's not selfish anymore – just before asking him to leave his fiancé at the altar! In the end, she pouts so convincingly that she's dragged back in time and given a second chance.

SWGHR Bullshit Rating: I'm waiting for that to happen to me.

8. *Hitch*

I have a problem with films set in New York City, especially films featuring a gossip columnist, a date doctor, and the *Mall Cop* guy. I'm as happy as the next person to suspend reality at the movies. Like half the planet, I cheered for Frodo as he deciphered incoherent messages, dodged those evil, black-cloaked things, and sneaked into that mountain cave just to get his finger bitten off by the lizard guy. I was all in, edge of my seat. But movies about people dating in New York City shouldn't require that level of suspended reality. *Hitch* does. What real estate agent works with these people? Will Smith has an 1800 square-foot apartment on his salary as a date doctor? Okay, fine. Let's say he makes enough every month to cover the rent. How is it possible that he's draped in $3000-worth of designer clothing in every other scene? Does he have a trust fund? Are his stocks paying off? Is he carrying $50k in credit card debt? Maybe his father is Wilt Chamberlin. I don't know. But I've been visiting Manhattan since I was old enough to walk. I have dozens of friends with apartments in the city, and even with lucrative corporate jobs, they live in phone booth closets where they have to fold up the bed and the ironing board just to make a piece of toast.

SWGHR Bullshit Rating: Eva Mendes was nuts to play hard-to-get with Will Smith. Where's her head? Oh, and Frodo should have known that lizard guy would be there. He wasn't thinking straight either.

9. *Fools Rush In*

Matthew Perry gets drunk with Salma Hayek. They have sex; she gets pregnant, and they marry in a civil ceremony without telling her abundantly Catholic parents or inviting her abundantly Catholic family.

Up to that point, I followed the story all right. Amusing, ironic, silly, and Chandler from *Friends* was convincing as the bumbling American who buggers things up. Where the story lost me was that after Salma told her parents the truth, Chandler was allowed to live. He'd deflowered a virgin (so they believed anyway), dishonored her family, disrespected her father, and essentially gave the finger to God, the Catholic church, and the core values, traditions, and beliefs of the Mexican people. But they didn't kidnap him or dismember him with a chainsaw. Instead, they shouted and stamped their feet in irritation like white people from Connecticut. If I had pulled a Salma Hayek with the varsity quarterback, my father would have learned how to build a tactical nuclear device, and detonated it in my new husband's underwear.

SWGHR Bullshit Rating: Love doesn't conquer all, amigos!

10. *Jerry McGuire*

Basket case, disenfranchised, disillusioned sports agent, Tom Cruise implodes when, at thirty five, he realizes that his life has been one long wade through shallow, stagnant water. Renée Zellweger, single mother at twenty six, finds Cruise's breakdown so irresistible she quits her job, joins him in a doomed business venture, marries him, and gets wildly fortunate when Cuba Gooding, Jr.'s football (and acting) talent saves them both, proving that complete boobs can make millions without much effort.

SWGHR Bullshit Rating: Am I crazy, or did Tom and Cuba have the more convincing relationship? Oh, and that deaf woman in the elevator didn't sign, 'You complete me.' She signed, 'I want fish tacos.' I swear to God.

11. *Dirty Dancing*

Jennifer Grey can't dance. Patrick Swayze can. Jennifer is a bit of an ugly duckling. Patrick is built like Hera's wet dream with wash-and-wear hair. They connect against the backdrop of the Catskill Mountains, and after much teeth-gnashing, a botched abortion, and some slow-motion sex, Jennifer Grey still can't dance. In a risky but bold career move, Swayze sings, *She's Like the Wind*. It used to give me goose pimples. Now it just frightens my dog.

SWGHR Bullshit Rating: You're humming it right now; aren't you? God, you're predictable. All right . . . everyone together! Don't hold back!

12. *Ghost*

Thank God for Whoopi Goldberg, or that would've been two hours of Swayze and Demi pouting introspectively. I can't believe I saw it seven times. Oh, wait: the pornographic ceramics class! Good storytelling, but it only got me a D+ on my clay salad bowl at Monmouth County Community College. You can't believe how surprised my instructor was, nearly gave him a heart attack!
SWGHR Bullshit Rating: Would you stop singing already?

13. *The American President*

This one was unbridled silliness from the start, because if a trim, widowed Michael Douglas truly had been elected president of the United States, the entire federal system would come to a tooth-rattling halt. The sheer press of eligible women lined up along Pennsylvania Avenue would shut down everything north of the National Mall from the Potomac to Union Station. They'd be coming in by bus from Ottawa. The FBI would have to check IDs like a taxpayer-funded bartender.
SWGHR Bullshit Rating: 'Pick me, Mr. President! Pick me!'

14. *Message in a Bottle*

Kevin Costner misses his dead wife. She drowned near their home, so rather than move to the prairie, he tosses love letters to her that wash up on the beach where Robin Wright Penn happens to be jogging. Penn, a journalist, confuses Costner's letters with a legitimate news story and commits several weeks to hunting down details of one lonely guy living ten feet from where his wife offed herself. Apparently, Penn's editors don't realize that there's genuine news happening on Earth either, because they continue to pay her despite the fact that she begins sleeping with the subject of her investigative research. (Don't worry; lots of credible journalists do that. And no one cares, because they both look fabulous naked.) Regardless, it's Nicholas Sparks:

Everyone dies tragically, even the dog, the milkman, three strangers biking by, and the teenage kid scooping ice cream down at the Tastee Freeze. I can't believe Cool Hand Luke agreed to appear in this bowl of warm whipped cream. He must've needed to make a payment on his boat.
SWGHR Bullshit Rating: Come to think of it, those Stallone movies are looking pretty good about now.

15. *The Notebook*

No, really . . . let's run over Nicholas Sparks with a snowplow. He's diabolical! Women of the world, unite with me on this! There's got to be a cure for these movies.
SWGHR Bullshit Rating: All right, damn it. When's the next one coming out?

See? It's all a matter of perspective, Billy. And these days, my perspective's pretty much buggered.

Jennifer

June 17

Dear Billy,

I don't have much for you today except a quick afterthought, an enlightening moment I had last night while watching *Footloose* with my sons.

I won't torture you with my post-divorce interpretation of Kevin Bacon's lascivious hips. Rather I was thinking that this refreshingly-new lens I've been using to re-watch romantic comedies also provides me an unexpectedly humorous perspective on old music. Last night's culprit: 'Total Eclipse of the Heart' by Bonnie Tyler.

God, I loved that song. I'd sing along in the shower, in the car, even in the grocery store a decade later when some virgin loser recorded a Muzak version to hum in the cereal aisle. I owned the LP, the cassette, the CD, and have – I confess – watched the original music video on YouTube a couple of hundred times.

Who didn't want to be Bonnie Tyler? It was 1983, and she was living in that powder keg and sparking or sparkling or whatever the hell she was doing. We didn't sing it; we bellowed it. How often do we get to use the verb 'bellow' and have it fit perfectly? Almost never. That song gave every teenage girl an opportunity to bellow.

I played it for my sons last night. Between them, they couldn't agree whether Bonnie Tyler had smoked too many cigarettes or if she really needed to use the toilet. Indignant at first, I played the song again and realized that they were right. She sounds like she went into the studio while battling both lung cancer and constipation. How did I not hear that thirty years ago? Did anyone?

I'm off to dig up that old Rick Springfield album!

Jennifer

June 29

Hey Billy,

I used to be what most people would call wealthy, if not downright
rich. My husband made a one-percenter's salary, plus commissions,
plus whatever bonuses the executive staff decided to dole out,
especially around the holidays.

Today, I'm poor.

Richard still does well; he's just determined not to share as
much of the spoils with me. That's fine. I don't mind . . . much. If you
recall, I grew up comparatively poor, lower middle class anyway, and
I'm good at it. I'm more comfortable living paycheck to paycheck than
I ever was having tens of thousands of dollars lying around.

Is that odd? It feels odd now that I think on it. I'm not being a
martyr; having money was great. It's just that realizing I'm no longer
able to afford anything is strangely comforting. Predictability breeds a
sense of security; I suppose.

Regardless, I'm not writing to you today to gloat over how
much money I no longer have. My last email, the one about films I've
re-interpreted now that I'm divorced, inspired me to think of eight or
nine additional movies I should've added to the list.

Don't worry; I'm not going to do that to you. But I am going to
bend your ear a bit about movies for poor people, a discovery I only
recently made about myself and my mother.

When I was a kid in the '70s, Mom used to iron our clothes on
Sunday mornings. It was her TV time, just about the only time all week
that she had control over what channel we watched. She ironed
everything while standing in our living room with either a black-and-
white creature feature, an old western with Gary Cooper or John
Wayne, or one of the laundry list of cookie-cutter *Tarzan* films. *Tarzan*
movies ran through late morning. NFL football games were broadcast
Sunday afternoons, and *The Wonderful World of Disney* came on after
dinner. Gary and I liked to watch Giants games which came on at 1:00.
If they played on the west coast, the game didn't start until 4:00, which
presented a problem for us, because every time Mom turned on a hand
mixer or used a blender in the kitchen, our television picture got fuzzy.
So for twelve years, Mom did all her ironing before 1:00 in the
afternoon and all her mixing and blending during commercials.

I swear to you I'm not making this up.

Mom and Dad rarely took clothes to a dry cleaner. Sweaters, delicates, and winter coats were either hand washed and line dried, or they went to the cleaner once a year, generally in late April before Mom stacked them in the closets for another summer. Everything else went into the washing machine, the dryer, and then across that ironing board.

She didn't mind; it was her TV time, and no one messed with the show until she announced that the ironing was done and it was time for her to get busy cleaning the house or preparing dinner. Then Gary and I would dive for the TV, each of us getting a mild shock every time we touched it. We'd thunk through the other three channels in hopes of finding anything more compelling than a mostly naked man and his pet monkey.

My mother ironed every week. She had dozens and dozens of clothes pressed and hanging all over the living room until our house looked like one of those moveable racks at the dry cleaner. Just about the time that Johnny Weissmuller and Cheetah were defeating whatever band of European evildoers threatened the jungle, Mom would finish the last of her ironing, summon everyone to the room, and assign stacks of laundry to get put away. I placed my stuff in drawers and hung dresses, blouses and pants in my closet. Doofus Gary simply stacked his entire pile of clean laundry on top of his dresser where it stayed until he wore something and dropped it on the floor, signifying to Mom that it was dirty again. My sons use this exact strategy today.

When I graduated high school and went to college, I lost track of those memories: black-and-white images of my mother ironing with *Tarzan* on the television. Her work represented a massive charitable undertaking, something no one else who lived in our house would have considered, never mind attempted even once. Yet it didn't impress me enough as a kid that I remembered it until I started ironing our clothes this year.

I do it on Sundays, just like she used to. Although, I reserve a week night as well, just to catch up. I think it's because kids today seem to have more wardrobe changes than we did back in the '70s.

Like my mother, I watch movies on TV, not DVDs, DVR recordings, or streaming films. Rather, I turn on the television, flip through the channels, and find something I can watch while I iron everything I've hauled home from the Laundromat. Who would've thought I'd end up here, wrapped in a plush, comforting memory of my mother as she completed a thankless task week after week? Not me. From the day I left for college, I never ironed a stitch of clothing. Richard and I sent everything to the dry cleaner, even Gap shirts and cotton pants that could've just as easily been washed at home. It never crossed our minds that we were spoiled brats.

My favorite ironing-board movie? *The Outlaw Josey Wales*, the 1976 western starring Clint Eastwood. It's a knuckle dragger of a film. Clint's facial expression never changes, and his voice doesn't move from the same three-note range he perfected in the Sergio Leone trilogy, but I love it anyway. First off, it's nearly three hours long, which gives me plenty of time to iron shirts, khakis, whatever. Second, it's young Eastwood in a bristly beard and a cowboy hat. And third, it's exciting as all get out. He kills over two hundred guys, and never once does he fall off his horse, lose his hat, or inadvertently swallow his tobacco juice. He only runs out of ammo in the very last scene, after firing his pistols 9,473 times. For his heroics he's rewarded with Sondra Locke, the only blonde, skinny, waif of a white girl for a thousand miles in any direction. They've got about four awkward lines of dialogue between them throughout the movie, and it's clear by the closing credits that if Clint survives and marries Little Miss Muffett, he'll get more scintillating conversation out of his horse.

Awesome.

I used to make fun of my mother for her Sunday-ironing love affair with Johnny Weissmuller. I mean the guy was a great swimmer, but he looked ridiculous in that Tarzan getup with that smelly chimp hanging all over him.

I half dread and half hope for the Sunday afternoon when Mom will stop over and catch me ironing Danny and Gerry's T-shirts while Clint Eastwood negotiates a peace treaty with Ten Bears, the guy who played Chief Bromden in *One Flew Over the Cuckoo's Nest*, not a good ironing movie if you ask me.

I hope she laughs at me. She'll probably want to take over my iron, and change the channel.

I know I haven't mentioned her much this year. But she's been a superhero all my life and most of her own, certainly since she married Dad. As much as she wanted me to go to school, find a career I loved, and make it further up life's ladder than she ever did, I've got to admit: I'm sometimes overwhelmed that she and I have Sunday ironing in common. Yeah, it's a stupid thing to cry over, but I like knowing she's inside me, still pushing and kneading, albeit silently and behind the scenes. I'm abundantly aware that I've got plenty of Dad's genes. I see them staring back at me every time I catch a glimpse of myself in the mirror behind the bar down the street. Yet I'm comforted knowing I've got Mom's ironing DNA. It was one of my life's more powerful realizations; there was no fanfare, no shouting, no drunk driving citation, none of Dad's pomp and circumstance, just a stack of shirts, a clutch of hangers, and Clint Eastwood.

Ya gotta get plum, mad-dog mean, William Klein, if ya wanna get the ironin' done by noon hour.

Jennifer

July

I don't know what it is about poorly-educated, white-trash shitheads who believe that everything about their lives will be all hospital corners if only they can get to Florida.

July 7 - 8

Hey Billy,

Speaking of my ironing . . . I'm writing this morning from the
Laundromat in Freehold. I haven't quite saved enough for a washer
and dryer yet. We sold the old clunkers with the house; that was dumb.
I should've known that I'd only be caught up with my laundry until
Homer ate an Oreo, which happened about thirty-eight seconds after I
signed the agreement to include all of our appliances in the sales
contract. Oops. I bought a dishwasher right away. I figured that if it
came down to me washing dishes every day or washing clothes at the
Laundromat twice a week, I'd prefer sitting here with the winos, the
poor housewives, and the college kids.

I know myself well enough that if I'd bought a washer and
dryer and promised to do the dishes by hand, I'd have Mount Pork &
Bean in my sink and three hundred dirty paper plates drawing a
battalion of flies to my recycle bin every Monday.

A dishwasher was the clear choice.

With that said, the Laundromat's pretty nasty. I haven't visited
one since my junior year in college and forgot how disagreeable these
places can be. I think someone slept on this table last night, because
there's a half loaf of Italian bread in a plastic baggie that looks to have
been used as a pillow. Beside it is a long contrail of snot or drool – I
don't want to get close enough to figure it out. Either way, it has the
consistency of that stuff Victor Frankenstein used to preserve body
parts and appears to have been excreted by whoever slept on the bread.

Hopefully, he isn't coming back for a nap, because I'm typing
this about eight inches from where he marked his territory.

Homer's watching Fox News on the cruddy TV in the corner. I
pray he doesn't develop a liking for Sean Hannity's suits.

Anyway, since I have a couple of hours (and $14.00 in
quarters!) I figured I'd write with another example of why I've turned
out this way, why I'm here – on a Thursday morning – in a
Laundromat in Freehold, New Jersey, and why I'm so determined to
make sense out of my relationships with my father and my ex-husband.

I don't know if we'll ever meet again, Billy. But if we do, I want
to have all of this nonsense behind me. I'm determined to feel healthy
again. I can't goddamn remember when I last felt healthy, but I know
I'll recall the sensation when it happens. Feeling like damaged goods is

a definite step up from feeling like a trophy wife which was a clear promotion from feeling like I could never please my father. However, at forty four (I had a birthday recently!) and starting over – Jesus, let's not mention that again, or I might decide to take a nap here in the Wash & Go – I've got no one to turn to but myself, and myself has decided that all of this has to get burned to ashes, bagged up, and buried in the yard.

I don't know who I'll be when I see you again – *if* I see you again, sorry – but it isn't going to be the me I am today with my laptop perched just down the block from a six-inch trailer of snot and my three year old watching Sean Hannity stare at Ann Coulter's boobs. (They're nuclear reactors, like in *Terminator*. Hannity clearly wants his own pair.)

Anyway, among the things I love are two items that might seem disconnected for everyone else on Earth, but which remain irrevocably attached to one another in my mind. They are the New York Giants football team and Johannes Brahms' *Symphony Number 4 in E-Minor*.

Don't worry; I'll tell you why. I've got ninety minutes before the underwear'll be clean and nothing good's on TV. Homer's got Sean Hannity and a Ziploc baggie full of Oreos, guaranteeing that I'll be back here before Sunday.

On December 19, 1981, the New York Giants hosted NFC East rivals, the Dallas Cowboys in a barn burner that ended in overtime on a thirty-five-yard field goal from Giants' kicker, Joe Danelo. Anyone who decided that football is America's favorite metaphor for bloodthirsty, warlike conflict must have been in East Rutherford, New Jersey that afternoon, because the only thing that kept those two teams from killing one another was a lack of medieval weaponry, a shortage of cocaine, or some combination of the two.

I love the NY Giants. I have since I was old enough to understand how football works. Lawrence Taylor, for all his faults (drugs, women, a volatile temper, he might even have shot a man in Texas just to watch him die; I dunno) was a god around our house. Phil Simms, Dave Meggett, Carl Banks, Rob Carpenter, Harry Carson, Michael Strahan, Justin Tuck, the list goes on for me. My son, Danny, until he was six, actually believed that our National Anthem ended with the words *o'er the land of the free and the home of Eli Manning*.

Nope, not kidding. He still sings it that way just for grins.

On December 19, 1981, Brad Van Pelt emerged as the Giants' hero. The all-pro linebacker had Danny White's number, and intercepted the Cowboys three times, saving the game for New York.

I was there. Dad took me with him.

We had season tickets for years – until the Giants finally won a Super Bowl in 1987 and the price went up. In 1979, seats were available for just about anyone willing to drive up the Turnpike. By 1981, LT's coke habit turned him into a homicidal lunatic every Sunday, and fans across the region tuned in to watch our brutal defense. That group of marrow suckers represented the skeleton of the team that eventually won it all after the '86 season.

Sadly, this story isn't so much about the Giants-Cowboys game as it is about what happened afterward. Believe me, I'd much rather write about football.

Dad had two tickets. Normally, he took me or Gary with him. Mom never went; she disliked tailgate parties, tailgate partiers, cold weather, the Turnpike, you name it. Four or five other officers from the Asbury Park PD had seats as well. They'd bought them as a package deal, which enabled Dad to get his seats at an affordable rate for a few seasons. With a half-dozen cops attending games together, the pre-game party raged for hours, swallowing up four parking spaces in the stadium lot, a bag of charcoal, ten pounds of ice, five pounds of grilled farm animals, a carton of cigarettes, a quarter keg of beer . . . oh, and a couple of Cokes for Gary or me, whoever went that weekend.

A Cowboys game was a big deal. I don't know how I drew that straw, unless maybe Gary went to see the Redskins and had to give up the Dallas ticket to me.

We arrived in the main lot by 9:30 for a 1:00 game. Dad and his friends set up their tailgate apparatus: tables, awnings, hibachi grills, a kegerator, lawn chairs, a stereo system, and a massive banner strung between several cars that read NY GIANTS FOOTBALL in garish, patriotic letters two feet high.

I admit; I loved going with him. Once we got into the car (his police car . . . yeah, we'll get to that shortly) and put a few miles of Route 9 between ourselves and my mother's disapproving glare, I allowed Dad's enthusiasm for partying and my enthusiasm for football to rile me up. Like everyone else, I bundled into a parka, wore heavy wool socks, ate too much beef, and drank my Cokes in a foam beer cozie like a die-hard fan.

Dad and his friends were shitfaced by 11:30. They had to be: none of them earned enough as Asbury cops to buy beer during the game. Sure, they might queue up one or two, but at $4.50 a pop inside the stadium and $ .75 in the parking lot, that choice was easy: either get drunk early and stay inside for the entire game, a must for the Cowboys, 49ers or Redskins, or drink a bit, see the first half, and wander outside for beers during halftime. This was more appropriate for Cardinals, Saints, or Patriots games. (The Patriots sucked back then. Drew Bledsoe was in grade school; Tom Brady hadn't started Kindergarten yet! Steve Grogan still has nightmares about blood-red drool dripping from Lawrence Taylor's chin strap.)

Thanks to Brad Van Pelt's interceptions and LT's brutality, the game made it to overtime, and Joe Danelo, a shitty kicker on any other Sunday, drained the thirty-five yarder for the victory.

The New York metro region went ape shit. Dad hefted me up, kissed me on the cheek, and raised me above his shoulders, so I could watch the players celebrate, dog piling on Danelo until he disappeared from view. Fans lingered in the stadium and around the parking lot for a few hours. The Asbury PD tailgate still had some hot coals in the grill and plenty of ice in the coolers. Another round and another round and another round got poured; while another cow gave its life for the victory celebration. I didn't have any Cokes left, but I ate another cheeseburger and another hot dog, the reason I turned down the salad later . . . you'll understand shortly.

Dad reveled in the day, the game, the time with his friends and me. None of the other officers brought their kids, certainly not their ten-year-old daughters. Dad always did. Either Gary or I was with him, too often learning about his habits and appetites, more than we should have known at that age, but a price both of us were willing to pay to spend time on one of his adventures.

And December 19, 1981, like van Pelt's three interceptions, ended up an unexpected and memorable adventure.

I knew we were in trouble when we finally packed up and started down the Turnpike. Giants Stadium is off Exit 16W – yeah, I know: cheap NJ joke, but I couldn't help myself. By the time we reached exit 15, Dad and his friends were rolling south at nearly 120 miles per hour. Two of the other guys finally dropped out of the race. They drove in one of the cop's pickup trucks; it just didn't have the wherewithal to maintain that speed for long. The other cars, Dad's unmarked cruiser and another officer's personal car, a Buick or something nondescript, ran side by side down the Jersey Turnpike as fast as they could go.

No one wore seatbelts.

Dad drove one handed, while holding a beer with the other. Some friend, I don't remember who, sat beside him with a cold six pack between his feet. He periodically passed one over to Dad.

They tossed empties into the back seat beside me.

At first, I found the race exciting. I'd been in his car on hundreds of occasions and knew that he drove too fast. All cops did. But I'd never gone quite this fast with him quite this drunk.

Then, in what might have killed us, another of Dad's shitfaced, shithead friends – some cop I don't remember – rolled down the window in the Buick and shot at us with his service revolver.

I know it didn't hit Dad's car. I checked the following week when he finally came home.

It might have killed someone in the northbound lanes, though. I don't remember hearing or seeing a crash in the other direction, but we were going so fast, and I was (now) so frigging terrified, that a *Lufthansa* jet could've landed in the northbound lanes and I wouldn't have noticed.

Dad yelled, stepped on the brakes, just for a second, then sped up again, changing lanes to pull in behind the Buick. He swore like a drunk hip-hop artist and revved the police cruiser until I thought he would simply slam into the back of the other car and send us all ass over tea kettle onto the runway at Newark Airport.

The Buick shifted right, a mistake on their part. I remember watching the driver-side window, waiting for it to roll down, so they could shoot at us again.

Thankfully, it never did.

Instead, Dad's doofus friend rolled his window down. A smelly amalgam of frigid winter air, diesel exhaust, and North Jersey pollution rushed into the car at 120 mph. I ducked behind the seat, had no idea what might happen next, but the list of possibilities sucked.

I didn't beg Dad to slow down. I don't know why. Actually, I might know why: I wanted him to take me along on his escapades. Even at ten years old, I understood that it wasn't normal for a father to disappear for three or four days at a time, to return home from work at 8:00 am the morning after he left, or to miss school conferences, musical performances, or church events because he was 'at work,' my mother's way of paraphrasing the word 'missing.'

I liked being with him, loved him. I still love him, even though I don't go on any merry chases with him anymore. (Actually, these days he drives like any seventy-three year old: slow, cautious, and with an unkind word for any young person doing anything even remotely dangerous. How quickly he forgot that he *invented* dumb and dangerous on the roads.)

Anyway, as I ducked behind his seat, holding my breath, Dad's companion drew his own service gun and fired twice at the retreating Buick. He scored at least one hit, in the trunk, just above the right taillight. When we parked outside the Blue Caboose later, I saw the neat bullet hole, its abrasion of scraped paint clear evidence that it had come from behind and off to the left. Similar to the shot fired at us, I don't have any idea what happened to the second round. It also might have killed someone headed north toward the airport.

Thirty minutes later, we made it to Asbury Park and the Blue Caboose, a railroad-themed bar on Kingsley Avenue, near the old Baronet Theater. The football game had ended in overtime, about 4:30 pm. We spent another two hours in the parking lot as Dad and his friends tried to finish their quarter barrel, then drove for an hour down the Turnpike to the Parkway and out Route 33 to Asbury Park. When we sat down at the bar and Dad ordered his first beer, it was 7:40 pm. I'd left home with him at 8:15 that morning. Eleven hours later, we still hadn't called my mother.

She knew where we were, though.

Laundry's done. I'll finish this later, after I get Homer to bed.

Okay, Billy . . . back to it. This one's a marathon. Sorry. I didn't realize I'd go on quite this long, but as I've said before, we're in it now, and as long as you're willing to read, I'm willing to scribble.

My mother always knew when Dad had a girlfriend. I guess it wasn't difficult to deduce; for thirty years my father either had a girlfriend or was on the prowl for a new one.

Richard frequently sneaked girlfriends past me – literally dozens of times, now that I do the math – because I wanted to believe that we were happy, living our idyllic life with our two boys, our boat, our beach house, our matching Trek mountain bikes, and our neatly-tended, suburban flower beds. When Richard told me that he and some woman were, 'just talking,' I believed him because I wanted to believe him. Mom didn't buy that bill of goods from Dad, not once. When he was out drinking, he was out chasing women. What's sad is that for years she wanted him to give up the girlfriends but didn't mind if he blew the foam off a few beers with his friends from the station. By the time I was in high school, those tables had turned. She just wanted him sober. My mother had given up on the women; it was the booze she figured would get Dad dismissed from the police force, keep him miserable for the rest of his life, or kill him outright.

Today, I'm not sure who had it worse: Mom, who knew Dad was humping every warm-blooded slut from Hoboken to Seaside Heights, or me, who thought my husband was faithful and never quite realized the depth and breadth of his infidelity . . . until the confession. We're almost up to that bit, too. Just hang in there.

Anyway, one of Dad's warm-blooded sluts hailed from Tom's River, down the Parkway a good thirty miles from Asbury Park. What she was doing driving all the way up there just to drink until her panties fell off never made sense to me, until I woke up in my mid-forties living alone for the first time in my life.

Her name was Regina DeMario. In 1981, she was probably thirty-two or thirty-three years old, married but not happily, halfway raising a couple of Catholic school kids, and scraping by on her daily dose of blackberry brandy, abject depression, cheap pot, and dreams of escaping to Florida with my father. Her list of if-onlys must have been inspired. I imagine they ran something like this:

--*If only my husband would pay attention to me, listen to me, touch me softly, even once a week.*

--*If only someone would love me. I'd prefer it to be my husband, but at this juncture I'd take just about any gainfully-employed, disease-free, fun-loving man with an active heartbeat.*

--*If only my kids would pick up after themselves, maybe clean a cereal bowl or wash a towel every once in a while.*

--*If only I could move from this town, maybe try someplace where I don't see everyone I knew in high school every day of my life.*

--*If only I'd gone to college, even Ocean County Community College.*

--*If only I had a better job, something challenging where I had to think creatively now and then.*

--*If only Harrison Ford would swing by on that bullwhip and carry me out of here. I'd show him a few things about bullwhips!*

(Okay, I stretched that last one a little.)

--*If only I could hook that Asbury Park cop, I could live on the beach, have some self-respect, enjoy life, rediscover good sex, even find a job with a*

window that opens or a view of the boardwalk.
--If only I could hook that Asbury Park cop, we could get a little place
down in Florida, not much, just a cottage for romantic vacations, just the
two of us. My mother would watch the kids. She'd understand.

As an aside, I don't know what it is about poorly-educated, white-trash shitheads (like Regina) who believe that everything about their lives will be all hospital corners if only they can get to Florida. What's Florida got that's so special? St. Louis encephalitis? Tourists? Old people? A mouse the size of a Chrysler? I don't understand. Regardless, Regina didn't wish for millions of dollars, a seat on the stock exchange, or a mansion on a hill. She didn't hope to marry a vascular surgeon or an escape to a billionaire's ranch outside Plano, Texas. Rather, she knew herself well enough – even that's poignant in a stomach-turning way – to understand that those dreams were outside the regulation field of play for her. She didn't waste time pursuing fairy tales. But driving up to Asbury Park every Friday and Saturday night, and even a few weekday afternoons, to catch my father made abundant sense to Regina DeMario.

Sadly, it makes sense to me now, too.

As a cop with a steady job, a comparatively flat stomach, and a good attitude about booze, travel, and fun, my father was a catch for someone with Regina's resume. Driving drunk down the Parkway three times a week was an easy tab to pay for a holster sniffer of her caliber.

God-awful; I know . . . couldn't help it.

She dressed to accentuate her three marketable features: her hair, Italian black, Prell-silky and long; her boobs, full from going a touch heavy-handed into the cannoli plate or the meatballs; and her legs, healthy, shapely, and destined to look like hanging pig corpses before her fiftieth birthday, but for now, encased in Sheer Energy Leggs, they dangled off that bar stool like uprights in an overtime field goal.

Dad, the moron, thought he was in love again. As a ten-year-old kid and only knowing Regina for an hour, I could already tell that my father was in trouble. It took me a while to get over the shock of seeing them together, of realizing that he'd brought me to meet his girlfriend (there was an earlier instance I'll get to later), and understanding that his friends, fellow cops, guys my mother gladly fed pot roast on Sunday afternoons were in on it. Everyone knew but me. And before the end of the night, when Mom picked me up, I understood that this time Dad was a goner. He was in love, enough to insist that this woman meet his daughter. Regina's kids weren't there, thank Christ, or I would have had to 'play' with them, making nice while our parents sneaked out back to go down on one another.

Regina didn't love him; she might've thought she did. Rather, she loved the *idea* of my father, the promise he represented for her life. Dad ate it up, reveled in it like a grass-rolling mutt. They kissed; they fondled one another. She made him a salad in the kitchen behind the bar. Dad devoured it as if it had come from the sous-chef at the Four Seasons, when all it contained were a few bits of iceberg lettuce, chopped tomato, sliced cucumbers, and a handful of Velveeta cheese chunks.

I hate that stuff. But you knew that already.

I didn't eat any. Dad slathered it with blue cheese dressing, tried to share it with me. I told him I was full from the second and third helpings of grilled farm animal I'd eaten in the parking lot. What I should have said was that I would rather have died from starvation while crossing the Rocky Mountains on all fours than ever eat anything Regina DeMario chopped as his pretend wife in their pretend kitchen at the Blue Caboose.

I want to say I handled this all well, but I didn't. Meeting Regina kicked off what were the worst three days of my short life.

Oh, and if you're wondering why the management of the Blue Caboose allowed an insufferable badge bunny like Regina access to their kitchen, it's because Dad and his friends were Asbury Park cops. Bartenders, bouncers, bar owners, even waitresses love it when their bar becomes a 'cop bar.'

Police officers, as I'm sure you've read, heard, seen on television, the Internet, or the movies, make for some of the planet's worst barflies. (Teachers and nurses do, too, but teachers and nurses don't carry handcuffs, guns, tasers, and pepper spray. There's nothing like five or six cops at the bar to mitigate drug traffic, gang activity, or drunk and disorderly behavior.)

And what's the cost? Not much. Every third or fourth draft beer is free. Hell, it might even be a write off.

Dad never carried much money. He and Mom didn't have much. He did, however, carry blank checks. Back then, people still wrote checks. He told Mom that he needed them for emergencies. Obviously, in that cavern he called a brain, drinking for three days without coming up for air periodically constituted an emergency.

My mother took me aside the following summer to show me a series of checks that had arrived as part of the previous month's statement. Dad had been on a three-day bender in some bar – not the Blue Caboose; he never went back there after breaking up with Regina. Anyway, over the course of three days at another cop bar, somewhere in Belmar, Dad had written three checks for twenty dollars each. Draft beers (for cops) were eighty cents for ten ounces. My father would write a twenty-dollar check. I know that doesn't sound like much, Billy, but do the math. At eighty cents for every ten ounces, Dad could buy twenty-five beers on one twenty-dollar check. And with every third beer on the house, that's thirty-three, ten-ounce drafts for a grand total of three-hundred-thirty ounces, or two-and-a-half gallons of beer for twenty bucks.

Not bad.

Over a weekend's debauch, Dad would write three checks and be able to drink seven-and-a-half gallons of beer.

Nope, not kidding.

Mom showed me the checks, because she wanted me to see what alcohol did to Dad. I guess she never knew that I'd been with him in the car, at 120 mph, with colleagues firing live ammunition outside Newark Airport. Rather my mother pointed out the change in Dad's handwriting over three days of Old Testament hedonism. It was true: Dad's meticulous, blocky, 1950s-grammar-school penmanship did get progressively more seasick with each check, amusing my mom. I didn't have the heart to tell her about the car chase.

What kept him alive? I have no idea.

He drove shitfaced all the time. He'd leave the bars at closing time, sometimes walking down the boardwalk, sleeping in the sand, or passing out at a girlfriend's apartment. But most often, he'd pile into his police car, drive to the station to sleep, or race down the Parkway or the Turnpike, chasing whatever inebriate woman had promised him a blow job and a plate of fried eggs, if he could just get to her house in one piece.

I hated everything about Regina DeMario, her boobs, legs, hair, even her salad. I hated the way she cuddled up with him right there in front of everyone, as if they'd been married two weeks earlier and she'd met him in the driveway after a hard day's work. I hated my father for bringing me with him, hated his friends for allowing him to make such a fool of himself and my mother, and hated the Blue Caboose, their inane railroad theme, the absurd mounted deer above the bar, and the blocks of Velveeta stacked in their refrigerator, just waiting to give some unsuspecting salad-eater a tumor the size of a tennis ball.

I didn't yet know how to be angry at Dad; that I learned later in life. He'd been my hero, my protector, the man I would love unconditionally for the rest of my life. Yet I'd never experienced hatred, pure, unfiltered, high-test abhorrence quite as fluidly as I did that Sunday night, December 19, 1981 after enthusiasm for a Joe Danelo field goal parted Regina DeMario's thighs in an Asbury Park police cruiser behind a dumpy neighborhood bar in a shitty town, on a dangerous street, beside a dying boardwalk and an empty beach in a post-industrial back water where none of this mattered in the grand scheme of things – except to me and my mother.

(See? I still get so pissed off, I start sounding like bad Raymond Chandler. Sorry.)

Mom showed up at 9:45, took me home.

Shell shocked, I sat in the back of her old Caprice. We didn't speak; Mom was too angry and embarrassed. She'd stood there, silently, until one of his dumbass friends noticed her and elbowed my father hard in the ribs. He had one hand around Regina's waist and one up the side of her skirt, admiring the faux-silk texture of her Sheer Energy Leggs pantyhose.

Dad turned, irritated. 'Hey, dafuk?'

'Coop!' someone warned, a brusque whisper.

Realization and disappointment hit him from two sides, mute stupefaction making him look like a slasher victim in a B movie. Finally, his shoulders slumped and he turned to where I sat, two stools down, his half-finished salad like a plate of cold vomit. 'Go ahead,' he whispered, 'grab your coat.'

In the parking lot, he and Mom fought. It was a good one, but nothing that merits mentioning here. Mom wanted him gone. He hurled insults at her until he ran out of nasty shit to say and had to recycle some of his previously-used material.

I held my ears, but not at first. I waited a few minutes, heard enough to know that they were done, then held my ears.

I didn't cry, though.

On the way home, two pieces of odd evidence confirmed for me how furious my mother was. First, she drove out Cookman, across Memorial Drive and through the ruins along Springwood Avenue, a part of the city they never rebuilt after the riots. It's still pretty dangerous to drive around there today, and was on a Sunday night in 1981. She must have been damned near blind with anger, because I'd never known her to drive that way, not since Dad came home so bloody and torn back in 1970.

More convincing, however, was the radio station she had on in the car. Normally, a Frank Sinatra, Bobby Darin junkie, Mom must have decided to rescue me, probably angry with herself for waiting all day to do it, and just cranked on whatever station had been punched in. She often listened to the weather on AM stations out of Manhattan – these days, she watches the Weather Channel as if it's got the same plot structure as *The Godfather* movies. That late on a Sunday night, whatever AM station had dealt in news and weather all week would have switched over to high-art music, chamber orchestra and symphony stuff for city snobs to relax before another week of exploiting the Third World for billions, or whatever city snobs do all day.

It's when I first heard Brahms' *Symphony Number 4 in E-Minor*. I'm not sure my mother heard a note; she just drove, both hands on the wheel, an advertisement for 10-and-2 safety. I can't remember which orchestra played or who conducted them, but the opening movement must have just started, because we were able to hear the entire piece before arriving back at the house, a good forty minutes from the Circuit in Asbury Park.

That piece of music saved me. Looking back on it, the feeling I had is more difficult to explain. I'll never do it justice in an email at 11:15 pm, but it was as if someone, somewhere wanted me to know that there were beautiful things, things bigger and more important than me out there in the world, and that I didn't have to be a ten-year-old prisoner in the back seat of my mother's '77 Chevrolet. Johannes Brahms composed that work outside Vienna in 1885, and I knew from the moment when the Whoeveritwas Orchestra slam dunked those final chords that he had written it for people like me: lost and frightened souls needing a lifeline.

Everyone needs a lifeline from time to time, Billy, even superheroes like us. I find it sort of disheartening that a ten-year-old girl would need a lifeline to heave herself out of the hole her own father had mined into her heart – and if that's a mixed metaphor, keep in mind that it's late, and I've already folded laundry beside a runner of wino snot. So I ought to get a free pass on a few split infinitives and whatever.

Dad's selfishness, alcoholism, adultery, all of it hit me hard. I stayed in bed for two days, unable to move, as I poured again and again over everything I had said and done, combing through all of my comments, decisions, and behaviors as if I might find the one thing I could have done differently that would have kept them together, that would have kept him away from Regina, or that would have seen us leave the game, get an ice cream, and drive home in time for a second dessert with Gary and Mom.

When I didn't find anything at first, I tried again and again and again.

Mom let me stay home from school that Monday. It was close enough to winter break that I only missed a couple of boring worksheets, a film strip on the history of Christmas trees, and a holiday party with red and green cupcakes.

Dad called Monday afternoon. Finally sober enough to realize what an irretrievable screw up he'd been, he asked to come home.

Mom, in a rare show of anger and frustration, decided not to forgive him. At thirty-seven years old, she'd taken one too many hits. Thirty-something years later, I wish she had stood her ground that week. But you already know she caved. I suppose moving back to Newburgh with her tail between her legs was more than my mother was willing to pay that time around. What strange things motivate us; my mother decided to tough it out with Dad rather than go home and look like a failure in front of her sister.

That afternoon, though, she stood up to him, threw him out, refused to let him come home or to forgive him.

I've never asked, but I bet that shocked the hangover right out of his system. I bet he left tracks in his tighty-whities when Mom finally told him to hit the road. God, I wish I could remember the conversation. I heard it from my room – well, one side of it – but can't remember how she put it. Mom doesn't swear, so any interpretation I'd offer here would be exaggerated too much for posterity. Regardless, it must have been a shocker for dear old Dad, because the last thing he ever expected to hear – hell, it might have been the only time in his life he heard her say it – was my mother telling him to pack up and bugger off.

How much happier would she have been in Newburgh, raising Gary and me with her sister and our cousins? I can't begin to speculate. But she's tough; she'd have found happiness there. I know it.

My parents arranged for Aunt Grace to stay with Gary and me, and for Dad to come pick up his things on Tuesday after school. Mom would be out of the house, but she understood that Dad wanted to see us. So she agreed to have us wait at the house while he collected enough clothes to live on his own for a while or to shack up with Regina in some beachside motel room. Mom knew Dad would eventually realize that Regina looked quite a bit different sober, with sunlight on her body, than she did in the fantastical hazy shadows of the Blue Caboose. Dad and Regina would only be able to stand a few days of one another's sober company before the sheer, wearisome, mundanity of their personalities made whatever No-Tell Motel room shrink smaller and smaller. I think I mentioned before, you can pretty easily get the girl out of the cheap Kmart panties, but you can't . . . well, you know.

Damn, I wish I'd known then what I know now. It might even have been amusing.

But I was ten, an innocent kid, and the whole works nearly ruined me. Actually, no kidding, I can still feel the dying embers of that weekend today, keeping some thimble-full of hatred at a low boil. I don't suppose it's good for me, but then again, I don't give a shit. Whatever keeps me warm on those chilly December nights when the Giants are on.

Dad, because he's an immutable putz, showed up early. Mom was still in the house, which made her attempt to escape even more embarrassing: he physically forced her to stay in the driveway. She didn't come inside with him and eventually got away, but not before Aunt Grace (and a handful of neighbors) watched the fireworks of my parents *discussing* terms of Dad's departure.

Yup, you guessed it: Four days later, he was home for Christmas. Aunt Grace and Uncle Mike were there, and everyone acted as if nothing had happened, even though it had happened dozens of times before and would happen scores of times in the decades to come.

Gary and I opened presents, felt – didn't feign – genuine enthusiasm for home and hearth and family and Christmas, and dreaded going back to school the following week as if winter break had come and gone with the same seamless ebb and flow of food, presents, snow, and Jimmy Stewart movies we'd expect from any other year. Dad does Christmas well, did it well in 1981, and by New Year's Eve, Mom had forgiven him again.

I don't know when he broke it off, but I'd bet it wasn't that week. Nope, I'm sure Dad told my mother he had plans to dump Regina, but he most likely kept it up, called her from the station, even trysted in their No-Tell Motel until he got bored of the same vacuous expression after the same sloppy sex on the same musty sheets.

After all, there were many other fish in that sea. And life's too short for tiresome afternoon humping. And some other platitudes . . . whatever. You can fill in the blank.

The good news is that I still love the Giants and haven't missed more than a half-dozen games in over thirty years. Also I bet I own ten different recordings of Brahms' *Fourth*. My favorite has got to be Herbert von Karajan conducting the Berlin Philharmonic, but there are a few others that run a close race for second place. I listen to that symphony most often when I'm out jogging. At about forty minutes, it's perfect for a quick five-mile run, or a four-miler if I'm feeling fat. I often wonder if I'd have discovered the Brahms symphonies if Mom had switched off the radio that night. Probably not. Johannes Brahms doesn't get a lot of air time in our neighborhood. Sure, he was popular with music and orchestra geeks at Rutgers, but even at work, amongst teachers, I don't run into too many fans who stop by my classroom in the afternoons to watch YouTube performances on my Smart Board.

Find the joy; I guess.

Oh, and what's amusing about Regina DeMario that I found frightening and exotic back in 1981 but which is simply trailer-trash awful today, particularly given that she's about sixty-five and working at a 7-Eleven on Route 22 outside Plainfield, is that Dad was transfixed by the small rose tattoo on Regina's left tit. He couldn't take his eyes off it, and she struck me (even as a kid) as a woman who chose outfits around her boobs.

Greeting cards they aint, Billy.

Anyway, in the years since then I learned that the rose on her breast is called a Rose of Jericho. Ever heard of one? They're designed to look like a rose, but their innermost folds are actually the labia of a moist and worked-up vagina. They're popular with tattoo enthusiasts around the world today, but in 1981 a Rose of Jericho would have pegged Regina as a woman who periodically went head first into home plate, if you get my meaning.

There's no chance my father knew that. If he had, he never would have slept with her. Lesbians, in his mind, represent the perfectly irresponsible waste of two otherwise-bangable women. Who would want that?

Heh. Diabolical.

All right, William, it's now after midnight, and I'm just getting to the point of all this rot. Shall we press on? Or should I toss it all and get to the punch line tomorrow?

That's one of the frustrating things about writing emails, essentially writing in second person, is that no one answers my questions. Bugger. It'll be my choice then.

Let's keep going. Anger and frustration with Richard have kept me up for twenty years. One more night isn't going to kill me.

I promise I'll keep this bit brief.

In case you missed it, a common denominator in my father's breakneck, crash-and-burn path through life has been his desire – no: *need*; that's better: *need* – to come home to Gary, my mom and me. He can't make it on his own. His love for us and his guilt at his mother and sister's deaths are the fundamental truths that keep his compass pointed north. It's why we forgive him, and it's what keeps him coming home decade after decade. He knows my mother will love and forgive him forever. Call her a madwoman, or call her the toughest soul the Universe has yet to spawn, it doesn't matter. She's chosen her path through life, and it runs over and through and around my father, come Hell, high water, broken plates, wrecked cars, and holster-sniffing whores from Tom's River.

I don't understand her, have never been her, and can't live my life as she's decided to live hers.

Which brings us to Richard, the shadowy, mirror image of my father, save for one critical difference: Dickie never wanted to come home. Time after bloody time, he believed he would be better off without me, without the boys. Some variable eludes life's equation for him. I still don't believe he knows what it is. But he's determined to crash face-first through every opportunity for happiness that life presents him, because he can never quite get the color right, can't get the exact shine on the wife, the house, the car, the bank account, the kids' report cards . . . none of it gleams with just the right luminance he feels he's entitled to, just because he's walking around with an erection in his pants and a five-digit balance in his checking account.

I hate to admit it, but I hope he dies some day never having found it. That's a terrible thing to wish, but right now my divorce is fresh enough and I'm angry enough that I hope it happens. Because he's never going to find the Utopia he believes every time he watches a Brad Pitt movie or a Kate Upton photo shoot on YouTube. He thinks that shit's real. God help him.

Actually, no. God can roast him. I don't care.

Eleven years ago, Richard and I were thirty three. We had moved out of our hip little townhouse in Bayonne to the first of our absurd McMansions in Manalapan. I found a teaching job in a local school, and Richard joined Manhattan commuters on the train, the bus, even the ferry from Perth Amboy. With two little boys and an eighty-pound Labrador retriever, we needed more room. The suburbs felt like the right place, even though we both knew we'd miss the easy accessibility of the city and the nightlife in Hoboken.

Having gone from 1,800 square feet in Bayonne to 3,800 square feet in Monmouth County, we filled the place with Eddie Bauer, L. L. Bean, cool antiques, fun, quirky art, and a 1912 Duncan Phyfe dining set – all mahogany – that I stripped, sanded, stained, and refinished myself while the boys napped in the afternoons. Word got out around the neighborhood that Richard and I had moved in. We were young, attractive, comparatively wealthy, and drunk from Thursday to Sunday.

The party began. Our basement bar became the hot nucleus of an organic disaster that has since seen seven marriages in ruins, dozens of STDs treated with handfuls of amoxicillin, and even one depression-fueled suicide attempt that led to a seventy-two-hour Hold and Treat at a Long Branch psych hospital.

Lovely.

As ever, I know what you're thinking: How much of what I'm imparting here could have been avoided if I'd been a couple of nautical miles closer to sober?

Probably quite a bit of it.

But I wasn't sober; we've already established that.

Onward.

The first friend I made in the new neighborhood was Margaret, a chemist working on a grant from a pharmaceutical corporation to develop an affordable anti-depressant for marketing to economically-disadvantaged areas of the world. Apparently, being poor and living in squalor leads to sadness. Margaret's company wanted to capitalize on whatever kopeks these miserable bastards had left in their pockets. I guess when alcohol and locally-grown cocaine aren't enough to lift you out of the doldrums, a fat, American-based dope company will be there to separate you from your last pennies.

I liked Margaret a lot. Smart, funny, and a bit homely, she never slept with Richard. He doesn't like them ugly or smart. Smart women frighten him. He's uncertain what we might say if we have a creative or an independent thought. Being a geek and a touch socially awkward, Margaret latched on to me, the party girl and weekend hostess. We hung around together, drank too much wine in the evenings, and had one another for support when the weekend's festivities got out of hand. I can't remember how many nights I'd catch her eye across the bar, just to share a conspiratorial glance when one of the neighborhood regulars danced on my coffee table, peeled off a shirt, showed off a t-back thong, barfed in my flower bed, or grabbed the wrong ass, the wrong boob, even the wrong penis bulge. She'd sit at the end of the bar while I washed glasses, and together we'd bear witness to the dancing, the groping, the furtive kisses, and the fondling that started up about 2:00 am and generally petered out by 3:30 or so.

No one got hurt, at first. And by brunch the following morning, we'd mopped up the vomit, emptied the dishwasher, hauled out the trash, and forgiven one another. Truth be told, we were young; we had too much money and no mentors or role models to guide us. As long as we laughed about it over bagels and coffee after church, everyone would start making plans for next week's debauch. Chicken or BBQ? Vodka or bourbon? Should we hire an exotic dancer? Maybe a guy-girl stripper team?

It had to end. Not one of us had any idea how it would end, but par for the course of my life, that chapter unraveled from an unexpected thread: Margaret.

Early one morning, perhaps 2:30 am, Margaret's husband, Charlie, was dancing with another of my friends, Debbie. If you recall, she was the one who finally blew up her own marriage on the deck of Richard's 40-foot Chaparral in Barnegat Bay. I suppose I should have seen it coming; she was all over Charlie, who, married to Margaret, hadn't had his hands on a body that lithe since the senior prom. They were both shitfaced – we all were – but that night Debbie's husband, Mike, cracked.

It might have been the Wild Turkey he'd been mainlining for five hours. It's been known to cause fights from time to time. Perhaps he'd gotten wind of Debbie's afternoon adventures along our street; they were the stuff of legend back then. Hell, she might already have been with Richard for a quickie blow job behind the kids' playset out back. He's certainly near the top of my list of possibles when I recall Debbie's Orgasm Scavenger Hunts.

Regardless, Mike had fifty pounds on Charlie, and decked him handily, a one-punch knockout that sent him sprawling across my Eddie Bauer sofa and into one of Richard's stereo speakers.

Some of us laughed; some screeched. Debbie started scratching and slapping at Mike so viciously that once the smoke had cleared on the incident, she had to take him home to patch up his face. He appeared at church the following morning with two butterfly bandages on his cheek, looking much worse than Charlie, who just had the souvenir black eye.

Yet by halftime of the Giants – Packers game that afternoon, Richard had grilled three pounds of burgers and brats. Charlie and Mike had shared several pitchers from the keg in the basement, and the thirty-something crew from Beechwood Avenue laughed together and swept another embarrassing incident beneath the neighborhood carpet.

Margaret had been horrified. She staggered from her perch at my bar, half helped, half dragged Charlie home, and then spent five hours shouting at him while he half dozed and half applied ice to his face in their living room recliner. I don't believe she'd been angry that Charlie and Debbie groped a bit on the dance floor. That sort of nonsense was expected, accepted. No flag on the play.

Rather, what pissed Margaret off was that Charlie had behaved badly in front of Katherine, Margaret's young and impressionable sister who'd been visiting from Georgia for the week. A nineteen-year-old college kid, Katherine had seen her share of parties, but she hadn't seen her elder sister sit, shitfaced, at the bar while her brother-in-law danced with the neighborhood slut, copped a feel, and got his face punched for his troubles.

Katherine hadn't seen that.

And she didn't see it that morning in my basement either.

Again, you've probably guessed why. Young Katherine wasn't in my basement at 2:30 that morning when her shitfaced sister, embarrassed, dragged her semi-conscious brother-in-law home from the party, bruised and bleeding from one nostril. Nope. Katherine hadn't seen any of it, because she'd been upstairs, in my guest bedroom, with Richard's face planted firmly between her barely-legal thighs.

Bear in mind, Billy: she was nineteen, a college kid.

Richard also missed the impromptu fight in our basement, because he was helping Katherine get off, and even worse, securing an invitation to visit her residence hall at Georgia Tech later that semester. Getting her to bark like a dog in my guest bedroom was just the beginning of his barely-legal adventure. By Wednesday of that week, my husband had convinced his supervisor that he needed three days in Atlanta to secure a new client for the company.

What a virtuoso liar! Can you believe that?

And the goddamned executive staff approved the trip!

Richard didn't have a client lead in Atlanta any more than he had a client lead in Shanghai. Yet off he went, as cocksure as a human being can get, to spend three days boning and sucking in a college residence hall, surrounded by coeds – all of whom probably loved him, because he supplied the entire floor with beer, wine, pizza, Chinese food, pot, pills, dildo batteries, you name it, all weekend.

Actually, I'm making that last bit up, because I still can't get over it. While Richard did hang around the residence hall, partying with Katherine and her friends, he wasn't allowed to sleep there. Apparently, the Head Residents at Georgia Tech draw the line at thirty-three-year-old married men sleeping over.

Instead Katherine stayed in his Peachtree Street hotel room, on the company expense account.

Who does that? Who hits on his friend's barely-legal sister, sodomizes her while his other friends beat the shit out of one another in his basement, and then arranges a fraudulent business trip to spend several days screwing her *after* buying booze and dope for her entire dormitory? How does one grow balls that enormous? Okay, I get it: she's hot. She's young. She's horny, and she's willing. You go down on her in the guest bedroom while you're both shitfaced, and she barks endearingly like a Bichon Frisé before jerking you off all over her perky little tits. I get it. Drunk and stupid can explain a majority of the world's collective sins.

But to sober up, shower, shave, and commute to work just to lie to your boss that you need thousands of dollars for business travel to Atlanta to get laid?

That's a varsity-level shithead right there.

And what's worse – we're not quite to ground zero of this debacle, but it's coming up quickly now – what's worse is that on the flight home from Georgia and the drive down from Newark Airport, Richard planned, actually scripted, how he was going to tell me and his two toddler sons, that he had decided to leave us, our home, and our life together to move to Atlanta and live with Katherine, the nineteen-year-old college student he had fallen in love with over a bottle of Absolute in our guest bedroom.

Nope, not kidding. I wish I was.

And Katherine, the mind-bogglingly-stupid kid who believed him, confessed all of it to her sister, my friend Margaret, who showed up with a bottle of Bordeaux and a half-pound Hershey bar that we shared while she gingerly passed on the details of their dough-headed conspiracy.

Richard, like my father, gets caught up in the moment. He drinks; he revels in his friends; he allows his enthusiasm for the celebration to get the better of him, and he willingly casts good judgment out with the empty whiskey bottles. Where my father's different is that when the sun comes up and sobriety pries its immutable way back inside that hollow cave he calls a head, Dad regrets his transgressions, because he fundamentally hates the idea of hurting his family and friends. That hasn't kept him from doing it over and over again for the past fifty years. Alcoholism has infected him to his bone marrow; at this juncture there are no other paths. I'm not making excuses for Dad. He has left more broken bodies in his wake than Richard can count. But my father regrets every screw up. (How self-loathing hasn't killed him is a frigging mystery that only comes into focus by about 4:58 pm every afternoon. Thankfully, it's washed out to sea again by 5:05.)

In subtly different light, Richard doesn't regret his cataclysmic boneheadedness. He's proud of it. He sees Katherine's invitation to fly to Atlanta for a blow job as a conquest, an achievement he might immortalize on a plaque and hang in his office beside the framed certificate he received for coaching the 7-U kids for the Monmouth County Youth Soccer Association.

Dad's an addict and a shithead.

Richard's something worse.

On dozens of occasions, my husband has stared into my face, implored me to forgive him, begged me for another chance – because twenty-seven chances just aren't enough – and told me how he would love me and our children forever.

And I believed him, because when he said it, he believed it.

Even though it wasn't true, not a word.

Discussing any of this with him is diving into the deep end of human neurosis. Head first, ready or not, over my head without a lifejacket or a mixed metaphor to get me out of there.

I don't know what kept Richard from leaving me and the boys when he returned from three days with Katherine at Georgia Tech. I used to comfort myself by thinking it was because he realized that he truly loved us and wanted to be a husband and a father. But I don't believe that anymore. Now, eleven years down this muddy path, it's evident that Richard's decision to abandon his Atlanta plan came in a moment of complex confusion that hit him in the chest when he drove into our driveway, maybe when he saw whatever toys Danny and Gerry had left in the front yard. He pulled in, took a look around, and said, 'Oh yeah, I'm married with two kids. All of this is mine.'

If hindsight can be trusted, I bet he sat for a few minutes and stared, slack-jawed, at the house, the lights in the kids' rooms, the neatly-mowed grass, the sidewalk chalk left in broken bits on the macadam and said, 'Holy shit, I have to do this . . . *have* to do this. This is what I'm supposed to be doing.'

And he got out of the car, put Katherine entirely out of his mind – even though five minutes earlier he'd believed that he was in love with her – and braced himself for another week of domesticity, until the beer flowed and the BBQ crackled Friday night.

Because Fridays meant another adventure.

And another and another and another.

And here we are, Billy, lost and alone and craving Herbert von Karajan's rendition of Brahms' *Fourth Symphony* to lead me through the darkness one more time.

It's 3:27 am. I've been writing to you all day.

You don't write back. I can't blame you, though. I must sound like a frigging basket case.

Sound . . . I *am* a basket case, whatever that means.

I hope this explains . . . well, what . . . me? Part of me? An important part of me . . . to you.

I'm off now for a quick visit with Herr Brahms and then to bed.

Jennifer

PS: Sorry. As if I haven't gone on long enough . . . my father came out of this one smelling sweeter than I'd intended when I got started yesterday morning at the Laundromat with the bread pillow and the snot runner. Sure, I told you the Blue Caboose story to get to the barely-legal story, but it wasn't my goal to have Dad look anything at all like a hero once we'd wrapped up. So I've got one point to add before signing off. You see, December 19, 1981 was not the first time my father introduced me to one of his girlfriends.

In late 1979 – I can't remember the exact day – Dad brought me along on a weekend trip to Newburgh, ostensibly to pick up a truckload of planks from a high school friend who'd opened a lumber yard in their old neighborhood. My father did a number of renovations to my parents' house; he's pretty handy with a trowel and a hammer.

Anyway, we spent that weekend in a cabin in the Catskills, somewhere near the resort where Jennifer Grey still can't dance.

Claire Somethingorother joined us. I don't remember much about her, except that Dad and she played the same silly game of pretend-married that he played with Regina DeMario two years later at the Blue Caboose in Asbury Park.

What stands out in my memory from that weekend was sleeping in a bunk bed. I'd never done that before. Dad let me have the top bunk, while he and Claire Somethingorother shared the bottom.

On our way home, Dad bought me McDonald's, a big deal for us, and made me promise not to tell anything about Claire's visit to my mother. I agreed because I was eight and afraid that if I blew the secret Dad would never take me with him again.

That was dumb, but what would you expect from a third grader?

Mom needed about fourteen seconds to infer that something was wrong. Naturally, she opened with the same Call to Worship that's served her well for over seven decades: 'Do you need to use the bathroom, Jenny?'

Heh, Jesus.

Later, after Dad had gone to bed, she took less than five minutes to get to the bottom of our whirlwind run up the Thruway.

I'll remember it until they burn and bury my bones.

Mom, trying not to sound upset: 'Tell me, Jenny, was she wearing underwear?'

Me, fearing Dad, but unable to lie to my mother: 'She was, Mom. I saw them, just on the side, by her . . .'

'Hip?'

'Yeah, hip. I saw them there in the morning, while they were sleeping.' On the small, black and white television behind her, President Carter promised to see American hostages safely home from Iran. It would be another fourteen months before they were released.

At eight years old, I'd slept in my first bunk bed. I've managed to avoid them ever since. I just can't do it, not unlike Velveeta processed cheese.

And we're done for the night, Billy.

Jennifer

July 21

Hi Billy,

Sorry. This one's blurry . . . don't know why, just too many years, too many miles.

As much as I bitch, you'd think I was always the one on the receiving end of my father's misadventures. That's not true.

My brother took his share of hits, too.

I wish I'd known it thirty-five years ago, wish we'd both been better at reaching out for one another rather than retreating into whatever Fortress of Solitude we'd constructed around ourselves. We might've helped one another through it, made it easier on both of us. You know?

Late one night, maybe '78 or '79, I woke to my parents shouting in the kitchen. They did that often enough; it wasn't a big deal, certainly nothing worth immortalizing here. I rolled over, tried to get back to sleep. And I must've been fading, because I can't remember how their conversation ended, who won, who gave up, whatever.

Vaguely, I recall hearing my mother say calmly, 'You know you're killing your son.'

It wasn't a question.

I've searched the dusty shelf where I keep all my treacherous memories, trying to recall how Dad responded, but I can't find it up there.

The next day, I wasn't any kinder to my brother. I should've been. One of these days, when Gary and I finally get to sit Shiva for some of those low times, I hope I'll have the courage to tell him how sorry I am that we didn't find one another much earlier.

Jennifer

July 23

Hello Billy,

In December, 1981 my mother was still in her thirties, a touchdown younger than I am now.

With two kids at home and Dad either working or waist deep in cheap Scotch and harlots, I cannot fathom what kept her on her feet.

Imagine it: You're almost forty years old. You have a punch-in, punch-out clerical gig to make ends meet, two young kids at home, and a husband whose job it is to go to work, earn a salary, keep his pants zipped all day, and remain in the shallow end of the bourbon bottle.

Easy. Right?

Nope.

What crosses your mind the first time you realize that you're too far along to turn back? You're too confused to turn left or right (if you'll allow me to bend that metaphor, just a pinch) and you've got to stay the course or blow up your own life just to get out from under the layers of musty, damp, mildewed flotsam that have accumulated since the evening you said "I do" a decade and a half earlier.

I wish . . . how I *wish* I had asked Mom that very question thirty years ago. Jesus, Billy, I'd have been so much better equipped to deal with Richard and all of his selfish insecurities, his addictions, his parade of brainless lonely women.

But I never did.

Not until a few months ago, and by then it was too late.

Mom was young in 1981; I was just a kid. And I suppose if I ever rub a Cabernet bottle just right and a genie pops out hawking wishes, that's what I'll ask for: I'll go back to Christmas break, 1981, so I can stand in my mother's kitchen that holiday season, learn to cook, and talk with her about motherhood, wifehood, fortyhood, and living one blood-spattered day at a time.

I've rubbed a lot of Cabernet bottles in the past twenty-five years and have never found a genie, but I did drum up the courage to ask Mom about it one afternoon this spring.

Her response surprised me.

She'd come over to spend the day with Homer. Danny and Gerry were off somewhere; I can't remember. In a rare show of humanity, Homer decided to take a nap. Mom and I were left standing in my kitchen, drinking tea and making plans for dinner. (When Dad's around, Mom can't go far without arranging their next meal. I tease them about it now, but check with me in thirty years and maybe I'll be living plate to plate as well. I do love to eat, Billy.)

With an hour to kill, I decided finally to clean out my lazy Susan cupboard. Homer had gotten inspired shortly after we moved in and dumped about two cups of almond-vanilla cooking oil all over the plastic racks in there. Rather than empty it and clean the whole works, I periodically removed a spice I needed, wiped off the bottom of the jar, scrubbed the place where it had been, and then replaced it. At that rate, I would have spotless lazy Susan racks in thirty-seven years.

Oh, and just in case you're like the host of middle-aged men around here and have no clue what a lazy Susan cupboard is, go to your kitchen; that spinny, round thing in the corner cabinet, where you and your wife –

Do you have a wife, Billy? I have to admit; I kind of hope you do. Otherwise, I've been wrong about you for a long time. But then again, maybe she's an insufferable bitch and needs replacing.

– keeps all of her spices, jugs of olive oil, extra sugar and flour, baking soda, garlic powder, cooking essentials . . . that's your lazy Susan.

It's probably cleaner than mine.

Anyway, my strategy failed, because while I cleaned beneath each spice as needed, I overlooked the fact that garlic, sugar, flour, oregano, basil, the draft horses of the American kitchen often spill a bit when commuting to work beside the stove. So shortly after Homer's cooking oil incident, the semi-circular racks were also caked with slimy bits of oregano, gritty smelly garlic powder, granules of hardening brown sugar, and colorful flecks of crushed red pepper.

It was a mess; I didn't want to clean it.

Mom did.

What would have taken me eighteen months, she wrapped up in fifteen minutes. She just did it. Armed only with a container of Clorox wipes, a plastic trash bag, and a roll of paper towels, she emptied every canister of spice, every oil-soaked bag of flour, sugar, and cylinder of salt, and every decorative, cork-stoppered bottle of goofball cooking oil that I'd won at some Mothers' Mafia wine-and-utensils party in the old neighborhood.

Now over seventy, my mother crouched – it's easier than kneeling, I guess. Her lower back and knees creaked with the effort, but she never complained. And while I stood by, drinking tea and spectating, she wiped everything off, tossed the bits that needed tossing, cleaned the plastic racks, and had everything returned, closed tightly, with labels out.

'There,' she said, 'your Italian stuff is on this side, top shelf. The Cajun spices and gumbo fixings are down here. Your grilling spices and seasonings are next to the silly oils, and your flour and sugar, vanilla, cinnamon, and other baking stuff is all against the right side of this upper rack.'

'You didn't have to do that, Mom,' I said.

'What? It's fine. I came to play with my grandson. He's sleeping. I can be useful.'

'It's been a mess for months.'

'Meh,' she shrugged. 'Now it's clean.'

'Thanks.'

She wiped her hands on a crumpled paper towel, dropped it toward the trash bag. It missed and lay like a stained memory on the tiles. 'I figure, if you were still living with Richard, you'd've cleaned it that very day, right when Homer spilled it.'

I didn't answer, just nodded.

'So there's no harm done in leaving it for a while. You know?' She glanced left and right through my kitchen. 'Around here, who cares if you gotta little olive oil spilled in the cabinet?'

'Nobody.'

'Right,' she smiled. 'And that's good.'

'You think? Really?'

'Are you happy?'

'Jesus, Ma.'

'Happier?'

'Yeah,' I said, 'happier, definitely happier.'

'Then, it's good. And who gives a damn if Homer spills?'

'Am I wrong?' I didn't want her to answer; I knew – thought I knew – what she'd say.

'Are you happier?'

'Yeah.'

'Are your boys okay? Healthy? Safe?'

'Yeah.'

'You feeding them, sending them to school, making them read books?'

'Of course,' I let myself be led. Mom amused me when she played psychologist. For a woman who claimed to watch the Weather

Channel all day, she'd clearly been sneaking some quality time with Dr. Phil.

'Then you're not wrong.'

'But you'd never have abandoned Daddy.' As soon as the words left my mouth I longed to reach out with both hands, grab them or slap them to the tile with that crumply bit of oily napkin. What the hell good was it to bring up thirty-year-old pain now?

She surprised me. 'I thought about leaving him, even planned it, a few times . . . few . . . a hundred times, but I didn't.'

Still irritated with myself for asking, I kept quiet, let her decide to say more or change the subject.

She went on. 'He couldn't have made it without me.'

'What? Mom, he's not your . . . responsibility.'

'Sure he is,' she wagged a finger. 'It's what your generation doesn't understand and why you find fault with ours. You don't think that your spouse is your responsibility, that your marriage is your job, full-time, for the rest of your life, but as a girl – yes, *girl* – growing up in the 1940s, that's all I knew. My husband would be my responsibility. My marriage, too. Leaving him would say more about me than it did about him.'

'But Mom,' I tried a different tack. 'He took advantage of you, lied, drank himself stupid three times a week, had girlfriends, ignored you, your goals for yourself, your family –'

'No he didn't,' she cut me off. 'I wanted children. I got them, and you and your brother with your educations and your travel, your families and your outlook on life . . . the whole world . . . we never imagined the whole world back then. The world was five blocks long and three blocks wide. New York City was an adventure, once or twice a year, and that was it. You and Gary have been so many places, seen and learned so many things, experienced so much, and you're teaching your own kids, my grandkids, ten thousand things I was never able to teach you.'

'You taught us plenty,' I said.

'I got what I wanted.'

'But Ma –'

She interrupted again, uncommon for her, but she was clearly fired up. 'And so did your father. We got what we wanted, what we started out to do together a hundred years ago.'

'For better or for worse?'

'Used to mean something.'

'Bullshit.'

'What was I gonna do? Leave him and become a corporate lawyer? A surgeon? I graduated high school with a diploma in clerical studies. I wasn't going to college. My parents knew it before the end of my ninth grade year. I was getting married, having children, and maybe, *maybe* getting a job as a secretary.'

'It was wrong. They were wrong,' I said, sounding young and corny.

'It was 1958,' she frowned. 'You can't look back and call it wrong. If you were there with us, you'd have done the same things, honey.'

'But all those weekends, the parties, the weddings and vacations, didn't you ever get . . . exhausted?'

She laughed.

Getting my mother to laugh out loud, Billy, is a big deal. Perhaps she's seventy years old and philosophical now with a healthy perspective on the past six decades. But she wasn't always able to find the joy or the humor in life. Life took a stick to her early and often. Standing in my kitchen with my semi-circular, lazy Susan racks wiped clean and smelling of bleach, we both knew it.

'What's funny?' I asked.

She took a stabilizing breath, pressed a palm flat against her breastbone, an old lady gesture, but a good one. 'Exhausted? Did I ever get exhausted? Oh, Jenny, I've been exhausted, emotionally, physically, in so many ways, since the mid-1960s. I'll have to be dead for fifteen years before I feel entirely rested.'

'But –'

'But nothing. That's fine with me. I'll have an eternity to rest. Being tired now is par for the course.'

Again, I couldn't think of what to say. I wanted her to admit that she'd been wrong. But why? Did I want it for her? Or did I want it for me? Because I hadn't been able to make my marriage work, and here she was, seventy years old and looking down the barrel of old age with a smart, tidy, healthy perspective on a half million miles of dirt road that would've killed any average woman, certainly the selfish princesses who used to live next door to me and Richard.

She rescued me. 'You're living your life. I lived mine. If you're happy, then I'm happy. I'm at the other end of the road, honey. The view is different looking back.'

'But then I should –'

'No, you shouldn't.' The woman who'd not stood up to my father a dozen times in her life had interrupted me six times in five minutes. 'The view is different looking back, but you gotta get there first. There's no cheating. You gotta put in the miles. It's the miles that make the difference.'

My *papier mâché* convictions unraveled. 'Mom, I want to hear you say I'm doing the right thing. I mean, what if I've got this all wrong, and I should tough it out like you did.'

She didn't take my hands, didn't hug me, didn't create some Hallmark moment for us to cherish like coffee drinkers in a Maxwell House commercial. Nope, instead my mother crouched down again, started collecting up her soiled Clorox wipes, crumpled paper towels and throw-away plastic canisters of oregano and garlic salt. 'I said that if you'd grown up in the 40s, with me and Daddy, you'd have been like us. But you didn't, honey. And if I'd have grown up in the 1980s, like you did, I'd have been more like you, and maybe . . . things would have been different for me, too.' She bagged the trash, tied it neatly, and pressed it into my garbage can. 'Who knows what might have been different for me?'

And there it was, Billy. In one breath, my mother confessed her regrets, confirmed her integrity and her victories, and – sadly, holy shit, goddamned sadly – dreamed of being me, of breaking free, and finding out what the future might hold for those of us who dive (or stumble awkwardly) into the deep end of the pool.

She sipped her tea. 'But I got what I wanted, honey. Don't forget that.'

'I won't, Ma.' Done arguing, I decided to think on it a while before I told her again that she'd been wrong.

'Comparing your life to mine isn't fair to either of us. We're apples and oranges or whatever, but I got everything I wanted. And so did Daddy.'

Before I could beg her to clarify that revelation, Homer padded into the kitchen, his Cookie Monster underpants sagging from his non-existent ass. 'Nana?'

Mom beamed. 'Yes, Mister Monster Man?'

'Nana, can we make a cake?'

'A cake?' He might have asked her to sack Troy, single handedly, armed only with an array of filthy insults. 'Of course we can make a cake. I am an expert cake maker.'

'Can we make a police car cake?'

'No problem.'

'With a light that lights up? A red one?'

'Do you have a red light?'

'In the flashlight, in my room.'

'Then, yes, we can make a police car cake, with a red light that flashes.'

'Can it be a big cake?' He gestured with his arms as if to demonstrate that anything smaller than a Volkswagen would be inadequate.

'Bigger than you,' she said.

'C'mon, Nana,' he took her hand and led her from the kitchen.

What comforted me, Billy, wasn't that my mother confirmed I'd been right or wrong to leave Richard. Rather, what made me feel better was her apparent belief that the view backwards over the decades is pretty good. I sincerely hope that wasn't bullshit, because from where I'm standing, the view pretty much stinks. What do you think? Was she straight with me? Telling me what to expect for better or worse over the horizon? Or was she protecting me? Sheltering me again from the bruises and busted bones of life?

I wanted to ask her, but she was busy baking a cake the size of a four year old.

I'm going to bed confused on this one, pretty sure she spun me around that lazy Susan one time too many. I wonder if I'll do that to my boys one day, spin the scraped up memories and details just so until they all line up, clean, with their labels neatly pointed outward.

Keep well, Billy,

Jennifer

August

But Farrah would have rolled over and wept if she'd have come home from the grocery store to find Lee Majors passed out on the couch while their two-year-old son ran naked in the back yard, chasing the dog with a handful of poop.

August 1

Dear Billy,

Working without a net these past couple of years, I've learned a number of things about myself, too many to list in one email, but if you've been following along at home, you'll pick up most of them in these letters. A few of the more important lessons I can cram into one note.

I realize that there are a few survival skills that I've mastered pretty well. Among the most important are:
--Delay gratification and
--Tolerate ambiguity.

Similarly, I've learned that there are a few survival skills that I haven't mastered worth a nickel-plated turd. Among those are:
--Tap sources of support or resistance and
--Forgive myself for being human.

Growing up, I was never very good at delaying gratification or tolerating ambiguity. I used to wish that I could pick up my life and shake it like a wrapped holiday present, just to figure out what might be hidden inside. I didn't do well setting long-term goals or waiting around for rewards or positive outcomes. I needed a metaphysical pat on the head most days to keep me energized for another week, another year pushing the rock up the hill. I never went more than about fifteen or sixteen weeks working at anything. In that much time, I might play on a sports team with the goal of winning a playoff game, or I might study a textbook and a series of lecture notes in hopes of acing a final exam.

Sixteen weeks. That's about right.

These days, I've changed. I'm not sure when it happened. It wasn't as if God flipped a switch and I could tolerate ambiguity. Rather it happened over time, without me realizing, until one morning I woke and made plans to save money for ten months so I could take the boys to Boston and Fenway Park the following spring.

I'd never been a saver, a planner, a wait-arounder, if that's a word. (If it isn't, it should be.) Yet there I was, tossing handfuls of coins into a glass jar on my mantelpiece, planning for a vacation I wouldn't take for ten months.

People who can delay gratification well, I believe, actually end up happier, assuming things work out as they had planned. I'm not sure about you, but I'm staggered at how often things don't work out the way I envisioned them, almost never. So I've been slow to embrace this newfound super power.

What finally did it for me was that glass jar full of coins. (It's a big one, at least a gallon. Pickles, I think.) My rules are simple: I pay cash as often as possible, so I don't get into hot water with the VISA Corporation, who clearly don't care that I'm divorced. And I never use exact change. If I buy a cup of coffee that rings up at $2.05, I pay with three dollars and dump the $ .95 in my jar. Also important is the understanding that no one can remove coins once they're in the jar. That's sometimes difficult, because there are mornings when the boys need lunch money, or weekends when I have to dig up $14.00 in quarters for the Laundromat. We've actually left the house twenty minutes early on school days, just so we can get to the ATM, withdraw $20.00, find a place to break it, and give everyone lunch money, rather than steal a few dollars from the jar.

And slowly, wonderfully slowly, (if you don't mind me wallowing in a couple more unnecessary adverbs), the jar fills up.

It's exciting, much better than driving through the bank ATM and withdrawing cash.

Delay gratification and tolerate ambiguity. I think they must be resiliency skills most people never consider until life clobbers them, and they have to regroup, refocus, and re-whatever else just in the interests of getting through the day without stabbing innocent bystanders.

You know what else is interesting about it? After delaying my need for quickie gratification for ten months, things that would have bothered me earlier in life *didn't* bother me this time around. For example, when the boys and I got to Boston, I was pulling into a parking space just a couple of blocks from Fenway Park. God smiled down at me and said, 'Heck, look what a nice thing you're doing with your kids today . . . have a great space.'

I had to wait two seconds for some old woman walking an equally ancient dog to cross in front of us, and in that stretch of time, the Universe said, 'Oh, no you won't, either.' And a fat guy with a fat wife and a fat son in a fat Toyota Camry pulled into the space God Himself had reserved for the kids and me.

Three years ago, I'd have drawn my flame thrower and roasted the entire chubby clan.

But this time I didn't. I just shook it off, drove around the block again, and found a space in another lot.

Holy crap.

You'd think that ten months of saving coins to take my kids to Boston would have caused me to rage at any inconvenience along the way. I'd indignantly shout back at the Universe, 'Dammit, I've been stockpiling nickels for almost a year to get here. That was my parking space!'

But I didn't. Surprisingly, the need to delay gratification helped me see the chubby clan in their chubby Toyota as a minor obstacle rather than a rage-inducing carload of jackasses who need to be murdered in a sociopathic killing spree, which is how I would have seen them before my divorce.

Who would've thought that having my life blown up would teach me so much? I want to go on a lecture circuit just to tell the world about it: *You think you're healthy with your running and your P-90X and your yoga? Nonsense. What you need is a handy-dandy lesson in Tolerating Ambiguity & Delaying Gratification, and all for the low, low price of $69.99.*

What the hell, maybe they'd pay.

With that said, what I don't do well is tap sources of support, and I don't forgive myself for being human. Mistakes I overlook in others, simple things, daily buffos, I couldn't care less. My boys break glasses, track mud on the carpets, crash their bikes, or spill blue Gatorade on their white shirts, and I don't care. I forgive them. I forgive all kinds of people for all sorts of transgressions. But I almost never forgive myself.

And I don't let others help me.

I have no idea why.

Actually, that's a lie. I know exactly why, and I'm betting you can guess the reason as well.

My friend, Myrna. Remember her? She's the one who's going to help me masturbate a whale so we can fill Richard's BMW Roadster with cetacean sperm. I mean, *that's* a good friend.

But I won't let her help me, not as much as she'd like, anyway.

Myrna's honest and good hearted. She's got a healthy sense of herself, despite the local Bitch Squad, and she's raising her kids to be credible *before* they're pretty or popular. I love that. Myrna emails a couple of times a week; she stops by with donuts or coffee or Ben

& Jerry's Chocolate Opium Lifesaving Heavenly Miraculous Fudge Chunk ice cream. We grab two spoons and throw the top in the bin with the promise of eating until it's gone or until we're both knocked insensible by a diabetic coma.

Yet I don't tell her the truth all the time, and I won't let her lend me money or babysit Homer when I need a couple hours of quiet. I don't let her do stupid, easy things that I'd do for anyone who needed help: cut the lawn, gas up the car, grab some groceries, or let the dog out on weekends, when such simple gestures would make my life easier.

Why can't I let Myrna (and a few others) help me punch some of the unutterably tiresome tickets I have to punch day after day?

I'll tell you.

It's because I'm shithouse at tapping sources of support, and I'm even worse at forgiving myself for being human.

And why?

You guessed it again: my asshole ex-husband and my doofus father.

Do all roads lead to them? Am I truly going to live the next fifty years of my life discovering that every nuance of my personality has somehow been trodden on by those two Clydesdales?

For now, yes, I think so.

But maybe not forever.

When I was a kid, I tried to do things perfectly, because I thought it would keep my father home and sober, where I needed him. Tens of millions of kids have experienced these exact feelings growing up with alcoholic parents. Some of us learn to lie, cheat, and manipulate like intergalactic champions – they're survival skills as well. While others, like me, believe the great lie: that I can work hard enough, long enough, and perfectly enough at school, sports, or helping around the house that my drunk parent will see the error of his or her ways and decide that being home with me is more appetizing than getting hammered in a bar with the likes of Regina DeMario.

Bullshit.

But kids around the world believe it; we always have. It's nothing new, and in this regard there is nothing special about me.

The tragedy occurs fifteen years later when kids like me become type-A, lunatic, overachiever adults, and marry egomaniacal douche bags like Richard Brad Pitt Teasdale. What do we get when we combine my deep-seated need to please with his equally-deep-seated need to experience pleasure and gratification every day? We get nearly twenty years of dysfunction, resentment and a BMW M-Class Roadster full of whale ejaculate.

Heh. There you have it. I'm a forty-four-year-old woman who's finally figured out how to follow life's compass from my dad's tire tracks to my husband's car wreck. I'm not sure yet if my newfound superpowers – delaying gratification and tolerating ambiguity – will eventually save me from this Poe novella. But with every handful of nickels and dimes I toss into that pickle jar, I'm betting on it.

And around we go again,

Jennifer

August 15

Dear Billy,

Yeah, I know: I said I had super powers, that I can tolerate ambiguity and delay gratification and find joy and decipher incoherent plots of *Mission Impossible* movies. But sometimes I'm full of baloney.

Despite all my boasting and all my carrying on to you about how strong I am, I still want to shoot him. I just want to drive over there and shoot him in the neat tile foyer of his ridiculous *Belle Terre* bachelor pad.

That'd work.

Or maybe I can beat him to death with that Mike & Ike cannonball the boys made in the microwave a couple of months ago. That'd work, too.

I'll call you from prison and let you know how my rehabilitation is coming along.

'Pretty Dirt.' Jesus wept.

Jennifer

August 20

Hello Billy,

Don't worry. I'm feeling better. I didn't shoot anyone, not even Richard. Heh.

I'm writing today, because I have coveted information that inquiring minds across the world would like to possess.

I know what Victoria's secret is.

Yup.

Victoria, whoever the hell she is, Teutonic, goose-stepping torture queen of lingerie designers, has two secrets she keeps from the world. One of them she keeps well, one not so well.

The secret most of the planet has already inferred is that Victoria doesn't own any pants.

I know; right? Not much of a secret.

But Victoria's Secret Number Two is a doozy. You see, Victoria endorses the cocaine-and-water diet or the less-popular but abundantly-effective, crystal-methamphetamine-and-water diet for all of her front-line employees, namely, the Silicone Seven. You know them better as the boob-and-bone models pouting at the camera, abject starvation tugging their airbrushed faces into grimaces that approximate faux sexual arousal. In the meantime, women of every shape, size, color, demeanor, and age are out there actually getting laid in their Jockey underwear.

Go figure.

Who hires these flavor straws?

And who decided that the Silicone Seven should be the benchmark against which the rest of us are measured? That's absurd. It's akin to comparing all men to LeBron James or young Sean Connery.

Unfair. Unreasonable. Stupid.

When I was a kid, healthy, appropriate role models for girls were scarce– they still called us *girls* back then; we didn't become *young women* until the Clinton administration. Sure *Charlie's Angels* looked cool chasing bad guys and toting guns, but not one of those angels ever got married, delivered a baby, tried to finish her Master's degree, or rushed home to clean the house after picking the kids up from basketball and before taking the dog to the vet.

Farrah Fawcett. She was the angel against which all other angels charted their progress up the Angelometer. But Farrah would have rolled over and wept if she'd have come home from the grocery store to find Lee Majors passed out on the couch while their two-year-old son (READ: Homer) ran naked in the back yard, chasing the dog with a handful of poop (Canine? Human? No one knows.) Farrah might have broken Lee's six-million-dollar legs if she'd have made breakfast, done the laundry, vacuumed the dog hair, got the kids on the bus, and dressed for work, only to pick up his sweaty running clothes from the bathroom floor and his wet towel from the bed.

Life's easy when all you have to do is exercise, keep your skin clear, exercise some more, nap, do your hair and makeup, then spackle on flirtatious undies for a photo shoot. The Silicone Seven don't need much energy to half dress and then flop on the divan. A cocaine-water-rockstar diet is appropriate for them.

The rest of us (READ: the Human Race) have bodies that need to convert food to glycogen, life-giving carbohydrate molecules that kick start our mitochondria, so we have enough energy to heft the vacuum cleaner up and down the stairs, get the kids fed and through their homework, and still have enough wherewithal for sex with the dumbass husband who left the sweaty shorts on the bathroom floor for the fourth time this week.

Glycogen. Sugar. We can't live without it. Well, we can, if we don't have to worry about pulling up our pants. The Silicone Seven require almost none. The rest of us have got to gobble down a peanut-butter-and-jelly sandwich and a bean burrito from time to time.

As an aside, remember that your body doesn't care where that sugar comes from. Beer, pizza crust, beer, donuts, Ben & Jerry's Chocolate Banshee Wail, and beer are all effective sources of fuel for your mitochondria.

Victoria's super secret diet will leave you prostrate on your Eddie Bauer sofa, in your undies, with your mouth hanging open. If you happen to have expended the sum total of your snort-n-go energy getting your hair just right, before collapsing from exhaustion and starvation, you'll look fabulous when the coroner shows up to snap your picture for next month's underwear spread.

Anyway, role models. We didn't have many. *Charlie's Angels* were tough and pretty, but they didn't have real lives, and they worked for men. Even Bosley, a dork, outranked them in Charlie's hierarchy.

Three's Company. I liked it. Two young, professional women, living with a guy they weren't attracted to sexually. It's a great premise. What bothered me about it was that the blonde had to be a knucklehead, while the brunette was smart but nearly devoid of sex appeal. Why couldn't Janet have been smart *and* sexy? Why did Chrissy have to be a dipshit? Did they both have flaws because America wasn't ready for John Ritter to share an apartment with hot, smart women without wanting to get laid all the time? Or did American audiences, including women, need the girls to fit existing stereotypes, again, so we could explain away the fact that they weren't humping in a three-way every afternoon?

Cagney and Lacey came along in the 80s. Those two were about as close as we got to women who resembled professionals trying to juggle all the balls today. Tough, gun-toting detectives, ready to fight, swear, and spill coffee in the car without giving a shit, both women had families, husbands, houses they had to clean, and kids they picked up after soccer practice. They were closer to the real deal: glycogen-burning creatures who don't own Eddie Bauer sofas, never mind get all dolled up just to lounge around in their underpants looking sexually unsatisfied.

The problem I had with *Cagney and Lacey* was that they tried too hard to be like men. I remember watching that show and wondering how female detectives might truly act, and if they'd be fundamentally different from Colombo, Crockett and Tubbs, or Barnaby Jones. Might women actually be better at solving crimes and capturing felons if they behaved like women rather than mimicking the men they'd seen in the same roles?

Meh. Then I switched the channel. Honestly, I was too young to care, especially if *The Love Boat* came on, and I could watch dim-witted women give in to shirtless, hairy men for an hour.

Princess Leia? Yeah, she was a badass with her laser gun and her sexual manipulation of Indiana Solo. I liked her. As a princess, she was set to inherit a leadership position (until her planet got blown to dust by her own father, a sociopath with troublesome power and control issues). Leia knew what she wanted from life, and she didn't struggle to tell men the truth about what she thought, what she needed, and how things were going to be once she took over the galaxy.

Then she let George Lucas put her in that goddamned bikini thing, and the wheels came off the wagon. For thirty-five years that's the only way she's been remembered. It's sad. Carrie Fisher used to get hammered, I guess, after her relationships and her career took a header into the concrete. I sometimes wonder if her career fell apart because she wouldn't take traditional sex-symbol film roles. Maybe things came unraveled because there were no good roles for her, so she started getting shitfaced all the time. Or perhaps she was just typecast and no one wanted to hire her, because the entire planet remembered her choking Jabba the Hutt to death in that wrought-iron bra.

I like thinking that Carrie got ostracized in Hollywood because she wouldn't drink the bullshit Kool-Aid and refused to take roles where she had to play an airhead, a sex symbol, or a reward for a man doing something heroic. I mean, how many women can Sylvester Stallone have? The guy can't conjugate verbs without a cheat sheet.

In sports, women had to sift through male-biased media coverage for good role models. Sure, Billie Jean King gave birth to Chris Evret and Martina Navratilova, but unless they were playing in the last round of a major tournament, Evret and Navratilova didn't get nearly enough air time to make an impression on girls my age. Television networks didn't give a shit about women's tennis, because American sports enthusiasts (READ: men) didn't give a shit about women's tennis. Instead, we got figure skating, with its over-the-top femininity, bad music, goofy uniforms, and pretend gymnastics. The flips and spins were impressive, but the arm waving and the lip pouting and the tiny skirts made figure skating just another circus sideshow.

Until Mary Lou Retten and a handful of Eastern European and Soviet simians came along, female athletes had Dorothy Hammill, Tai Babilonia, and a smattering of blonde tennis stars. Gabrielle Reese, Deena Kastor, and the Williams sisters were still little kids. A few years later, we had Nancy Kerrigan, yawn, and even she only merited real network coverage *after* she'd been beaten with a stick.

I suppose I've got to admit that Joan Benoit made a lasting impression on many of us. An elite athlete and grade-A badass, she whooped the rest of the world in the women's marathon at the '84 Olympics. But that was it. Afterward, she faded into the hazy gray of women's running, at the time a warm bowl of *who really cares.* Joan needed a better agent. Who gave a damn that Patrick Ewing and Michael Jordan won gold medals in Los Angeles and ended up on a cereal box? Together, they couldn't have run a mile in Joan Benoit's sneakers. She was amazing, but we didn't hear nearly enough from her.

That Michael Jordan character went on to great things, though.

Didn't he? Imagine if he'd moved to Nowhere, Maine to raise a family, and Joan Benoit had become the undisputed champion of sports, media, Bugs Bunny movies, and Hanes underwear.

The worst of the female role models we had as kids was Lynda Carter as *Wonder Woman*. I'm sure there are plenty of people who'd disagree with me, plenty of women who couldn't stand Edith Bunker, Ginger & Mary Ann, Julie the Cruise Director, or the barnyard full of Bond girls Roger Moore talked out of their undies. Carol Brady was an airhead, 'Oh, Mike, what are we going to do about Marsha? I know she's *my* daughter, but I'll defer to you, because you're an architect with a den, a housekeeper, and a station wagon.' What blue collar kid could look up to Marge Roukema, Millicent Fenwick, Geraldine Ferraro, or Bella Abzug when she had *Dallas*, *Knot's Landing*, and Madonna videos on television every night?

Yet Wonder Woman sent the most powerful negative message.

Created by a white, male psychologist in the 1940s, the absurd, bee-sting version of the comic book superhero probably shouldn't have merited a television show. Powerful, independent, credible-*before*-sexy women around the world should have come together to say, 'Hell, no. We won't have it. It's base objectification of an impossible version of our bodies, and we've seen where that nonsense gets us. Morgan Fairchild is a Fem-Bot for pity's sake!'

Yeah, right.

When Lynda Carter came along with those boobs, that ass, and that waist, men across America swallowed their gum. Her waist was a class-A felony in twelve states. It was nearly non-existent. You could take a Geometry test, cook a pot roast, and conduct an orchestra around that waist. How she did it, without glycogen, remains one of the twentieth century's unsolved mysteries. And Carter donned that ridiculous costume twenty-five years before the advent of the crystal-methamphetamine-and-water diet so popular among the toothless members of the Victoria's Secret stable of scrawny bitches.

Everyone wanted to be Wonder Woman. Who wouldn't? Her lasso made men tell her the truth. Let's write *that* again, because that subtle factoid merits another go-around: her magic lariat made men tell her the truth. She had an invisible plane and a secret island full of misfit Amazonian she-babes at home, all of whom sat around doing nothing, because Earth would have ground to a pointless halt if they'd have shown up together. Men everywhere would have been struck dumb and stared, open-mouthed and drooling, and women would have fallen collectively silent, each of them making plans to kill the wonder tribe off before they could procreate and establish an entire province of six-foot, high-breasted, Lynda-Carterian wonder chicks.

I remember . . . and I swear I'm not making this up . . . buying Jordache jeans I had to pee, lie down, and exhale vigorously just to zip up. I'd wear them with a cheap, gold-snake latch belt, pencil thin and fabulous. I'd crank that belt as tight as a hoop on a barrel slat and march around the middle school, pretending to be Lynda Carter, with my perfect ass, my emaciated waist, and my golden lariat to make men tell me the truth. It's not surprising that I struggled in pre-Algebra. I couldn't clear a fraction from a two-step equation until I got to tenth grade and discovered baggie jeans. What the hell, there was no blood getting to my brain. Once blood got pumped to my legs, it stayed there; nothing got north to my torso, past that belt. No way.

It's a wonder my feet didn't explode.

Looking back now, I realize that women like Toni Morrison, Gloria Steinem, Joyce Carol Oates, even Oprah Winfrey did a lot of work to inspire women my age to stretch ourselves beyond the silly stereotypes and narrow expectations nurtured by our parents and so many of the celebrities, athletes, and musicians on television or FM radio. Because I grew up in a lower middle class neighborhood with dads who worked and moms who raised kids, often while holding down a job, I had less exposure to Millicent Fenwick and more exposure to Michelle Pfeiffer. I'm not sure why, just the tidal flow of media noise through our town. We'd see a hundred breathless-blonde-waif movies before we'd ever read a Toni Morrison novel. *The Color Purple* wasn't Morrison, but it landed on my life like a hand grenade. I scoured local libraries for a copy, finally stealing one from my sixth grade teacher, a genius (we'll get to her shortly), and reading it on the bus to and from school.

I can't say whether the female leaders of the '70s and '80s intended for me to inherit a world in which I was expected to be a college-educated mother, professional, wife, and comic book superhero. I can't imagine Gloria Steinem ever wrote a speech hoping that I'd one day have to starve myself after running five miles, cleaning my house, driving my kids around, and hauling a laptop everywhere so I can get work done. She'd be embarrassed if she knew I felt pressure to do it all so I'll have a tidy McMansion, above-average kids, a fulfilling career, a narrow waist, clear skin, great hair, enviable boobs, a tight ass, and a high rating on the Neighborhood Bitch Squad's compliance-o-meter. Oh yeah, and an employed, upwardly-mobile, compassionate husband with a flat stomach, decent hair, limitless love for our children, and a genuine desire for me before all other women, Kate Upton included.

Who decided this was a good idea?

And who decided that it's *our lives* that have to come apart when our husbands flush their end of the bargain down the toilet with the used condoms?

I mentioned once already that I had to turn down a great teaching job this year, because Richard refused to share the costs of child care with me. How can he get away with that? They're his kids. I should drive to his house at 6:30 every morning and drop them on the front stoop.

(No, I'd never do that.)

I could ring the doorbell, and say, 'Good morning, Dickface. Your kids are here. If you want them to have child care, give me a call, and maybe I'll agree to split the costs with you.'

Why is it my job to find child care, pay for child care, and have to ask him to help me pay the bill, thereby giving him a gift-wrapped opportunity to say any of the following:

Nah, you wanted custody. You figure it out.
I told you that you couldn't make it on your own.
Oh, now you need me?
What have you been buying?
Where'd you learn to budget?

They are his kids. He was there when we made them; I remember those negotiations vividly. Why do I have to be the one who quits her job, chases the boys around six days a week, gives up my career, my dreams, my hobbies for Christ's sake?

I'm not complaining. Okay, I'm complaining. But I don't want to complain. I genuinely want someone to answer my question:

Why are women expected to be Wonder Woman, when men can gain seventy-five pounds of chub, ignore domestic responsibilities, and still covet every nineteen-year-old woman who walks by?

Something's rotten. It's been rotten for generations; I get that. But it shouldn't be rotten today, still. And what's worse is that it didn't *feel* rotten when we were married and pretending to be happy with our house, our jobs, our kids, and our Labrador retrievers. We participated in the Really Big Lie, hiding the fact that when we got divorced, at forty three, he'd be able to escape with ten percent of the responsibilities, while I got saddled with ninety.

I can read your mind: 'It's your own fault, Jennifer. You should've worked harder in the divorce agreement.'

Bullshit.

The values, traditions, myths, value-driven behaviors, and core beliefs of everyone in this lying-to-ourselves culture dictates that I be the one to give in, to abandon my plans, to back into a corner with my victimized haunches protected. Richard gets a new house, new car, new gym membership, and new girlfriend, all for the low price of one-check-a-week, planet Earth's only penalty for asshole husbands who chased their erections into divorce court. Our culture expects my house to be the one with diapers piled in the nursery, while Richard has a wine rack, a porn channel and a cleaning woman.

I didn't commit adultery. I didn't bang members of our wedding party two days before the ceremony. I didn't pay thousands of dollars to keep a lover quiet and save my career. I didn't solicit male *and* female partners on Craig's List.

Yet I get shafted, because our culture expects my soul to be comforted in motherhood.

It is.

But fuck you anyway.

(Sorry, not you, Billy, everyone else. You know what I mean.)

I've been whining about role models for women, but I'm wrong. I've got to look deeper. Our role models didn't do it all; none of them did. Even Lynda Carter as Wonder Woman fell short when it came to cleaning her house, satisfying her husband, and avoiding Wendy's cheeseburgers as she hustled her kids to afternoon activities. Yet I – and tens of millions of mothers out there – try to do it all.

We must be sick; something's wrong with women today.

We hold one another accountable on every point in the tally:

When a working mother at an evening little league game shows up in a suit with a baggie from McDonald's, do we think, 'Wow, she must have come right from the office'?

Nope.

Instead, we think, 'That shit's going right to her ass. I hope she knows that. If I ate a Big Mac, I'd have to run from here to Manitoba. What's she thinking? And thank God my ass is smaller than hers.'

When a working mother has guests over, and her house is a bit messy, do we think, 'I'm not surprised. When does she ever have time to clean up'?

Nope.

Instead, we think, 'Look at this place. It's a disgrace. She can't get her kids under control. Their shit's everywhere, and does she not understand that animals shed every day? And thank God my house is cleaner than this dump.'

Don't shake your head at me, William Klein. You know this is true.

When a working mother shows up at a neighborhood cocktail party in an old dress that doesn't quite fit as well as it used to, do we think, 'Hi, Working Mother. It's great to see you. Thanks for coming'?

Nope.

Because there's something wrong with us. Because we've embraced The Really Big Lie that makes it okay for my husband to continue catting around our neighborhood while I raise his sons. Because we don't truly care if someone else's life implodes as long as everyone in our own house continues moving roughly west together.

What do we think? We think: 'Jesus, who dressed her?'

And as a bonus kick in the metaphysical balls, we add, 'And thank God I don't look like that.'

Finally, when a working mother's kids get into trouble at school or fail a class or struggle to understand Algebra, do we think, 'Well, it's got to be hard for her. She's got so many balls in the air. I hope things work out for the best'?

Nope.

This time we blame the teacher first, because teachers are easy targets. Then we think, 'I'm not surprised, really. Those kids have been trouble since INSERT EX-HUSBAND'S NAME left with that woman from his office. It's no wonder the kids are turning into criminals. Oh well, less competition for colleges when applications go out.'

And we invariably add, 'Thank God my kids aren't messed up like that.'

Wonder Woman didn't do it all, because she couldn't have been Wonder Woman with a college degree, a husband, three kids, a dog, a house, and a career as a super hero. Not a chance. Wonder Woman was a candy ass. If she had any courage, she'd have married Superman, pumped out a few wonder kids, and tried keeping the Fortress of Solitude picked up while Superman was out fighting crime and helping Catwoman out of that leotard in the parking lot behind the Justice League of America.

That would have been a comic book worth buying for our daughters.

All right. I'm going running before Danny and Gerry get home from school. I push Homer in the stroller and dream of the food I won't be converting to glycogen later, since I want to fit into my old jeans before winter. The *Victoria's Secret* catalogue arrived this afternoon, so I'm inspired to run a bit harder. I imagine myself chasing the Silicone Seven off a bridge.

Jennifer

PS: Okay, that wasn't funny. The guy who founded Victoria's Secret actually jumped off the Golden Gate Bridge when he was just a year or two older than I am. But it's okay to write disparaging stuff about the flavor straws. They don't read; burns too much glycogen.
Credible before sexy!

August 25

Hi Billy,

When I last wrote to you, I mentioned Alice Walker's book, *The Color Purple*.

Don't worry. I'm not going to drag you through my thoughts on what you'd clearly consider a chick book. Rather, thinking about *The Color Purple* takes me back to middle school, feeling lost and disconnected, and finding a ray of inspiration and hope in an unlikely place: school.

My sixth grade teacher, Joan, is a genius in the classroom. She's been working with adolescents for thirty-five years, has been awarded Milken Educator honors, and has won recognition from parent groups and teacher organizations. Yet I've never known her to rest on her accomplishments. In a career where more and more parents, legislators, corporate executives, and college professors blame teachers for the vast, yawning plain of half-literate dough heads graduating from high school, Joan has stayed the rigorous course, held students accountable, and found joy in her work year after year.

Find the joy. There's that phrase again.

I once went to see Bruce Springsteen and the E-Street Band at Giants Stadium. Being from Freehold, going to Springsteen shows is a rite of passage. He's not a musician in Monmouth County, New Jersey; he's an oracle, a prophet. Near the end of the three-hour epic, Bruce, sweaty, manic, exhausted, introduced members of the band one by one. As always, he saved saxophonist, Clarence Clemons for last. After riling the crowd into a hedonistic froth, he shouted, 'You wanna be like him, but you just can't!'

That's Joan.

I wish I could go onstage at Giants Stadium with 70,000 lunatic, screaming, passionate middle school teachers and introduce Joan that same way: 'You wanna be like her, but you just can't!'

Joan saved me in sixth grade. It wasn't a big deal; she saved dozens of us from ourselves, from our community's low expectations, from adolescence. Saving twelve-year-old girls was a daily occurrence in her life. She didn't have to work too hard at it either. Joan kept me after class one afternoon, handed me a copy of *The Color Purple*, and said, 'Don't let this place determine who you have to be, or what you have to become. It's a big world out there. Try the deep end before you acquiesce to Freehold, New Jersey.'

Acquiesce, unorthodox vocabulary for sixth graders from our town. I ran down to the library to look it up.

I didn't understand Joan's challenge at first, but I read *The Color Purple* anyway, falling head-over-handlebars into the Deep South and the lives of Celie and Nettie, sisters who had it much worse than I did.

Then I read it again, and three or four more times in the past thirty years.

Saved by Joan. Easy peasy.

I remember one class period late that year. She'd been disappointed by a writing assignment we handed in, half done and sloppy. Clearly irritated, she looked around the classroom, asked, 'Are you proud of your work?'

No one answered; it was middle school. We didn't have a clue what it meant to be proud of our work.

She shook her head, then charged us. 'Look at the person next to you, your friends. Will that person be your friend in ten years? Twenty? Will you surround yourself with people who have a meaningful influence on your life? Or will you settle for half done, half effort, just good enough?'

I had no idea what she meant, but didn't say anything. Joan was pissed off and disappointed; saying the wrong thing could land me in traction.

She went on, 'Think about it. What use is a friend, a wife, a husband – not family; you can't pick your family – but the people you'll *choose* to spend time with? Why spend your life surrounded by people who do things halfway, with half effort, half accountability? Who wants to be around people like that?'

Embarrassed now, many of us looked down at our shoes. You remember that, Billy? When you looked at your shoes the teacher couldn't see you.

Joan knew she had us, the ones she wanted, anyway. She passed back our crappy papers, adding, 'Start now becoming the person you want to be. Start the way you want to end up.'

My face reddened. She was talking to me; I could feel it in my bone marrow.

She dropped my lamely scribbled paper on my desk, said, 'Who will you choose to be part of your lives? People who bring positive attitudes? Huh? Who's it going to be?'

Joan stood beside me as she asked this question. I didn't look up, couldn't do it. I'd be too embarrassed if my girlfriends heard me. But I wanted to look at her and say, 'Yes, I'd pick you.'

But I didn't. Because I was twelve, and I was lost, and I didn't get it until years later, after I'd spent a couple of painful months face planted in Rock Bottom, New Jersey.

Three decades down the road, Joan stepped up to save me again. When word of my divorce got round the county, thanks to Facebook, Twitter, and the Bitch Squad's Thursday Afternoon Drinking Club, I heard from her. Joan and I had kept in touch periodically, not as often as I would have liked, but enough that she felt comfortable sending me a note when she heard that my life had come apart. She hadn't changed, but my understanding of her as a woman, a teacher, and a leader had evolved until I finally understood who she was and what influence she'd always worked to have in her students' lives.

She was the role model I never realized I had. All my silly prattling about Wonder Woman and Farrah Fawcett and the Silicone Seven, a role model I'd never known lived three miles down the road.

Joan writes letters, on paper. It's a quaint, old fashioned practice, and she knows it. When she finally, grudgingly embraced social media, a few of us who'd known her laughed about it over drinks one Sunday afternoon. What made it amusing was that we all knew Joan would never use Facebook for anything more serious than a quick hello, a funny vacation photo, or a description of her tomato plants' catastrophic failure again this season. Serious correspondence was done on paper, nice paper.

She wrote me a letter that I'll keep forever. I might even make arrangements to be buried with it in my pocket. I never knew that she'd lived through her own difficult times. That's funny; isn't it? When we're kids, we think that our teachers sleep, eat, and live in the school. They don't have families; they don't go to the grocery store or buy tickets to Yankees games. When we run into them at the movies or at a community event, how many of us stop, stare, and wonder, 'What's she doing here? She's supposed to be at school.'

As a forty year old, I knew that Joan had a life outside of the Monmouth County Public Schools, but I would never have imagined that such a powerful, bright, independent woman would have been run down by life's locomotive, even a few times.

She wrote of her own visits to Rock Bottom, New Jersey, but clarified that those lowest-of-the-low periods were invariably the genesis of the next good thing.

I'll let her tell you:

'. . . There are worse things in life than being alone. One of them is living with the wrong person . . . The tough work that lay ahead was on myself. And that was nothing to laugh about. I had to ask myself some hard questions: why had I remained in a relationship where I questioned my love for this person? (Questioning love is, by default, knowing it's <u>not</u> love.) Why had I stayed with someone who caused me pain with his drinking, broken promises and slick words? Most importantly, why hadn't I heeded that inner voice that had told me from the first date that this was not the sort of man I respected?

All these questions snarled with feelings of anger, hurt and knowledge of being duped and betrayed. One thing I had going for me was that I knew the score and could move ahead. I was free and out from under the weight of a bad relationship.

This time I listened well to my inner voice and made conscious choices following that turning-point weekend . . . The greatest gift I gave myself was that of linking up with a counselor. I didn't want to pour these troubles out to my family: they would worry even more about me. My friends had their own problems. Paying a neutral counselor to listen to my thoughts brought healing itself; the insights and advice he gave me were treasures.

I prayed, I wrote, I thought and I healed. Spirituality and belief in my talents and abilities grew, and so did my literal and figurative strength. Within less than half a year I was reborn: like the legendary phoenix, I had risen from a baseline of life stronger, more self-confident than I'd ever been. I liked who I was, and I was prepared to spend the rest of my life alone rather than compromise happiness and this sense of well-being by spending it in an unhappy relationship.

Best of all, I was totally comfortable in that knowledge. I'd learned with certainty that one doesn't have to be part of a couple to be a whole person or to lead a rich and fulfilling life.

Out of that bizarre weekend came a badly-needed rebuilding of self (and the miraculous love of my life . . . but that's another story). Sometimes pain gives us an opportunity to grow. Sometimes it leads to knowledge that we'd never have found otherwise, and that knowledge transforms our lives. Pain is not something we seek or look forward to, but when it's imposed on us, we have choices how we handle it . . .

Every choice I made, every moment lived – good, bad, or something in between – brought me to right here and right now. I can visit the past in my memory, but to relive and change any part of it would make the 'now' very different.'

When I married Richard, I believed in our vows.

(No laughing!)

I'd chosen him: the one person who was supposed to bring Joan's meaningful, positive influence to my life for the rest of my life. It didn't happen, and I've spent the better part of the past two years feeling angry at him and sorry for myself.

So I went to see Joan. She's in her sixties now (she'd kill me if I told you exactly how far into her sixties) but she's still among the best mentors I've ever known. She's been down this road herself. That makes her wisdom and advice more credible for me.

And she doesn't take any bullshit from life. I love that about her.

I'm inspired. I've got to get myself together. Being angry with Richard won't kill me, but feeling sorry for myself has got to end.

I'll keep at it, maybe read *The Color Purple* again this weekend. Celie and Nettie were strong women, worthy of Joan's recommendation thirty years ago. I hope I'll emerge from this as resilient as they were, as strong as Joan – that's an empowering goal. And I know I sound hokey today. Sorry about that. I'll get back to my normal scathing indictment of all things suburban next time.

My sixth-grade teacher and Clarence Clemons . . . who'd have thought?

Jennifer

September

When I run, I don't perspire or glow or any of that happy horseshit women are supposed to imply politely over lemonade after tennis. Nope. I sweat like an obese Bavarian trombone player.

September 9

Hey Billy,

The other night I enjoyed a few minutes of 'alone time' after the boys went to bed and I finally convinced Homer to stay in his room.

I'd finished just one glass of wine, but it was enough to stoke the fires, and I settled onto my stomach with my mother's little helper and my favorite HD, Blu-ray, full-color fantasy playing in my mind. You know the one, where Bradley Cooper in a torn T-shirt and stubbly whiskers settles down for a nap between my thighs. *Shazam!*

I was nearly to the top of the cliff and ready to throw myself off – hopefully two or three times – when I opened my eyes briefly and found Homer standing less than a foot away. In just a pajama shirt, he watched me with detached curiosity, looking as though he might dial up the nice lady at 911. He held a half-empty water bottle he'd found in the fridge and a half-soiled Pull-Up, redolent of pee.

I screeched. And yes, that's the only verb that works in that sentence; I tried others.

Startled, Homer jumped backwards, looked as if he might cry, then started laughing. Why not? His mother had gone from soft moaning to deer-in-the-headlights surprise to shrieking, electrocuted baboon in the space of four seconds.

Using my knee for leverage, I found the OFF switch on the Hogwarts Wand of Contentment, pushed it deep beneath the covers, and said, 'Hey Buddy, what's the matter? You okay?'

'I was thirsty,' he said, considered the Pull-Up, still held aloft, and added, 'I did a poop.'

Switching on the bedside lamp, I gave the Pull-Up a closer investigation. 'Where is it?'

'In my room.'

'Oh, good.' I searched with my toes, hoping to discover my wadded-up underwear. No luck.

'Mommy?'

What the hell. Homer didn't care, so I tossed back the covers and followed him down the hall to his room. 'Did you poop in the bed, Buddy?' I whispered, didn't want Gerry or Danny to wake up and find their brother and their mother streaking through the corridor.

Playing along, he whispered, too, in barely audible conspiratorial tones that made me want to buy him a puppy. 'No,

Mommy. It falled out when I took off . . . took down my pants. It falled on the floor, Mommy.' He led me into his room, reached on tiptoe to turn on his Lightning McQueen lamp. 'There it is.' He gestured to a turd that lay off center on the Buzz Lightyear area rug, obstructing Buzz's view through his space helmet. 'Sorry, Mommy.'

I snagged a wipe and a fresh Pull-Up from the bag beside his bed. We chatted quietly while I cleaned him up. 'You tired, Buddy?'

'Can we watch *Cars 2*?'

'It's 11:15 at night, time for sleeping.'

'I want goldfish.'

'Bed.'

'Okay,' he knew better than to argue, and climbed beneath the mess of covers.

I used the nasty diaper to scoop up the turd, flushed it down the hallway toilet, and washed my hands. I'd forgotten that I wasn't wearing any pants and began to giggle at the absurdity of my life here on Earth. Homer had fallen asleep by the time I peeked in on him. Already engaged in one of his epic blanket battles, he'd wrapped one leg as tightly as a burrito and let one leg jut crazily off the bed.

'Good night, Buddy,' I whispered.

Back in my room, I took a few minutes to try and recapture Bradley Cooper, but he'd left the comfortable space between my thighs, probably had a date with some Hollywood starlet. Maybe he'd return the next day. A girl can hope after all.

Instead of mining for my magic wand, I pulled my undies back on and spent the next several minutes imagining Bradley, pantsless and creeping through his Beverly Hills mansion to pick a turd off Buzz Lightyear's face mask. The giggles got me again, and I had to spend the next half hour reading nineteenth-century Russian literature – one of the epics, with all the freezing and the starving – to get to sleep.

As much as I bitch, Billy, I wouldn't trade places with anyone . . . well, except Bradley Cooper's girlfriend, but just for a weekend, maybe a long weekend.

Jennifer

September 12

Hi Billy,

I reread my last note and figured you're probably wondering if I was kidding, or if I actually do have a mother's little helper holstered in my bedside table.

I do.

I bought it at a sex shop in Manhattan one afternoon on a whim. The first time I used it, you'd have thought I'd discovered the mind-expanding power of crystal meth. I got myself off – memorably, catatonically, boisterously – about eight times that first hour and seriously considered never leaving my bedroom again.

These days, I break it out when I need a quick, brain-melting explosion of liberty and justice for all, which isn't too often. And I deliberately don't use it when I'm depressed or battling my weekly brigade of bone-deep regrets. If pulling that trigger becomes the only way to face my regrets, I'll have to rewrite my monthly budget to include $600 for double-A batteries.

But that's not why I'm writing today.

Have you ever been in a sex shop? I hadn't been until I bought my first and only vibrator. And my decision to pop in for the Hogwarts Wand of Contentment didn't have roots in a lifelong addiction to porn; porn is Richard's bailiwick. Rather, I stopped in, because I'd never visited a place like that before, and I was separated and alone, and who gives a shit; right?

Holy crap.

It was amazing. I'd never imagined how many different ways there are to get off. Granted, I was married to Johnny Wad for eighteen years, so I'd been well schooled in a couple of dozen. But a lower East Side sex shop is a sociologist's dream: anal plugs of ascending diameters, like training wheels, rotating, spurting, vibrating, even pre-heatable and electrified dildos, blow up dolls, and portable vaginas and stiff penises from multiple ethnicities. This place was a Sherwin Williams of creative plastic, silicone, leather, and latex.

And the magazines? You name it; they've got it. If you get off watching men in raincoats skydive into swimming pools filled with obese German hausfraus named Greta, they've got every edition archived, some back as far as the Eisenhower administration. At first I was embarrassed and sneaked behind a rack of magazines so no one would see me. But then I decided that I didn't care and began exploring like Indiana Jones in a South American temple.

The Hogwarts Wand of Contentment cost me twelve dollars, making it one of the best deals I've made in thirty years of shopping. Yet the model I really wanted was forty-eight bucks, too much at the time, but thinking back on it now, I wish I'd picked it up. Shaped like a slightly-flattened egg, it fit comfortably in my palm, a readily-hidden handful of smooth plastic, nearly seamless, like a milk-white scoop of Italian marble. I wondered why it was so much more expensive than the buzz-buddy version in my bag. Then I turned it on.

The Holy Egg of Avalon revved slowly like a motorcycle engine in low gear. It started gently, slow, and quiet, then sped up, vibrating more powerfully over about fifteen seconds, until it downshifted again to a gentle massage. And so on and so on and so on.

Standing there in my first Manhattan sex shop, I held this magical device and thought, 'I want this permanently affixed to my underwear, all day, every day, certainly while I'm driving, folding laundry, washing dishes, or pushing a vacuum.'

I didn't buy it. I should have. I enjoy the Hogwarts Wand of Contentment, but the Holy Egg of Avalon could have provided me with hours of transcendental, transformative enjoyment, loosing my soul to float lightly above central New Jersey like a fluffy, happy cumulus cloud out for an explore.

And you see why I can't have one. I'd be reduced to idiotic similes inside a week.

And it was forty-eight dollars. I didn't have forty-eight dollars. Shit.

In case you're looking askance at your computer and wondering if I'm a pervert, keep in mind that if men could get off using vibrators, they'd be everywhere. Horny men would line up outside the Volvo dealership every September, pushing and shoving to be first to glimpse whatever in-dash innovation had rolled off the assembly line in Stockholm. Male-vibration devices would be traded openly on the Commodities Exchange. Dentists' offices would have advertisements for them hanging on the ceiling, so you'd never have to go more than a few minutes without being publicly bombarded with vibrator images or marketing strategies, even while having a root canal.

So no making fun of me because I've got a mother's little helper and a dirty little secret. They're only secret because so many middle-aged women can't get off with their husbands in the room, and we live in a culture where men's orgasms are the only ones that count.

Keep well, and good vibrations to you, Billy!

Jennifer

Oh yeah, and . . . did you ever notice how many affluent, suburban and snooty rich women are willing to accompany their husbands to the Sharper Image store or to peruse their *Sharper Image* catalogue every couple of months? Yessir, the next time that magazine arrives at your house, just flip through and count the number of polished handheld instruments they sell that vibrate vigorously. Back massager; right, it's a back massager. The executives over at Sharper Image live or die thanks to polite, upper-middle-class women who have chronic back pain.

September 13

My dearest William,

Yes, okay, dammit . . . I had a drink with Myrna, just one.
A double cosmo. It might've been a triple. I dunno.
But they're yummy, and good for you, just bursting with real cosmo flavor and fortified with eight essential vitamins and minerals.
I know; I know.
After my last two letters, you might think that I've exhausted the topic of feminine sexuality and satisfaction. I certainly thought I had, but then Myrna mixed me a mind eraser, and I realized that I could go on for some time about inequities in that lopsided department.
I'm feeling pretty good about myself tonight, so I surfed around a few poetry web sites I found last month just for fun. I've never been much for poetry, but as an education major who took a stack of lit classes, I had to wade through my share of musty turds from dead white men. I have a few favorites I read from time to time, just for dramatic philosophical renewal.
I really enjoy some of the new poetry that's coming out of the spoken word genre, and there's lots of good slam stuff around these days, particularly among young people.
(Anything to feel young, Billy. You know?)
Tonight, I came across this one – heh, that'll be a good pun in a few minutes – on a slam site, and since I'd finished Myrna's Cosmopolitan Death Potion, I'm gonna share it with you.
As a disclaimer . . . if this poem doesn't align with your philosophy on the issue of feminine sexual gratification, that's fine. I'm still hoping we bump into one another in the cereal aisle some day soon.
However . . . if this poem happens to capture your philosophy on ringing the old bell, well then, William, I'm gonna be needing to run out and buy myself some cereal right away.
(Heh, okay, sorry. It's the cosmo talking.)
Here it is. Enjoy.

The Cosmic O.
Michael Adams

Orgasm,
A Greek word meaning male or female sexual climax.
But not hers.
Hers make an impression, the cosmic O.

It's an odd word, though,
One whose morphology yields clarity, unabridged commitment.

Let's explore.

Or – an alternative, an option, a different path:
Or – we could invade Western Europe, lay waste to vast tracts of
French countryside,
Or – we could build a ritzy China shop on the San Adreas fault, ride
rhythmic shock waves to financial ruin,
Or – we could balance atop miles of freshly-cut timber lumberjacking
along the Columbia River,
Or – we could blow up the Hindenburg.
There was no electrical spark or atmospheric friction.
Rather,
Some animated woman failed to keep her seat back in the fully
upright and locked position.
One gesture of innocent, demure self-help and *Eureka!*
Lakehurst, New Jersey was in flames.

Gas – whether you prefer *flammable* or *inflammable*, it couldn't
matter less.
That stuff explodes with tooth-rattling enthusiasm.
Gas – thrown on a campfire,
Gas – on a bonfire, riling fifty thousand supplicants into religious
fervor,
Gas –refineries throughout the mid-west, blasting into such profound
brilliance that a cosmonaut orbiting twenty miles up peers out his
porthole and proclaims,
'What the Christ was that? I must meet one of these American
women!'

Perhaps it's not Gas, however.
Perhaps all the fuss is about
A Gasp.

As in:

Gasp – for breath after swimming the English Channel in record-shattering time,

Gasp – for soul-cleansing hope,

Gasp – for love mingled in a salad bowl with ardent passion – dull, thudding, burgeoning, unchecked,

Gasp – for all-over-body-twitch-sweat-moan-grasp-yank-tug-squeeze-bite-grip-never-let-go-not-ever lust,

Gasp – for the peace she's gotta feel in your presence, the love she's gotta reserve, deep down, just for you, the faith she's gotta have that you're hers alone, the trust and understanding she's gotta hold if she's gonna let you bear witness to that thrashing, contorting, primitive, pernicious, perfect end,

Gasp – driving home from work, 4:00 on a Wednesday and knowing it'll happen before dinner,

Help her, trust her, love her, tell her, let her go;

Get outta the way, boy.

You'll wreck the whole works if you can't turn from the mirror.

Gasp – at your good fortune;

You may never be so lucky again.

Once you've been there, you can never go back,

No return.

It's Hamlet's undiscovered country.

He wasn't considering suicide;

He'd just helped Ophelia dig deep and conjure herself a bone shaker.

What dreams may come, young Prince?

Good ones.

Then there's M.

Mmm – Delicious sound,

Soft consonance and transitive verbs in a marriage of feminine ecstasy,

Mmm – Onomatopoeia at its doughy, pliable finest.

Mmm – the hickory smoked flavor of anticipation, the Book of Revelation, the sacred spot deep within her chest, swollen places touched with gossamer sweetness, the transcendent magic when all her tumblers fall together, animal hunger and that sharp-across-the-tongue tangy knowledge that you're the one.

Inscribe her face in the dream you would dream for ever,

Then tell her you did.
It'll help as she squeezes quarts of delicious blood out of that
precious, holy stone.
Mmm – feminine ecstasy,
The cosmic O.,
More than any Greek morphologist could ever corral into one word.

Yeah, okay, so it's not Wislawa Szymborska, but *Shazam!* If only all
men could be Michael Adams, whoever he is.

     Oh bugger, you don't think he's really a woman; do you?

Damn.

Jennifer

September 26

Hi Billy,

Myrna and I ran the New York City Marathon together last year. It was one of those bucket-list items that doubled as a healthy dose of therapeutic self-abuse.

I felt pretty good for the first eighteen or nineteen miles. By Mile 20, I realized I'd made a mistake, and by Mile 22, I was talking out loud to God, albeit incoherently because I'd stuffed both of my cheeks full with Gummi bears I begged from a kid somewhere around Fifth Avenue and 98th Street.

Thankfully, I wasn't the only one.

Marathon runners are among the planet's most diabolical self-loathers. I think I've already written to you about Joan Benoit, one of my childhood heroes. At the '84 Olympics, she'd run a full lap of the LA Coliseum, Mile 26, before the second place runner, Grete Waitz (who'd never lost a marathon she finished) even entered the arena. *That's* an ass kicking. I admire Benoit and Lornah Kiplagat and Deena Kastor and any of the amazing women runners I've followed. Granted, few of the best have children and even fewer hold down day jobs, but nevertheless, the strength and single-minded determination they embody, the uncompromising nature of their commitment are inspirational for any athlete, not just women runners.

Sadly, I'm not a marathoner. There is a distinct and painful difference between a marathon runner and a fourth-grade teacher who's run a marathon. I used to wear a yellow LIVESTRONG wrist band; Myrna wore pink, some breast cancer deal from the Susan G. Komen Foundation. I tossed mine after Lance Armstrong's embarrassing confession to Oprah. It's in a drawer, stapled to my marathon bib. Myrna wears her pink version every day.

What I enjoyed most about the marathon was the training. Granted the two million spectators and fans were motivating, but training taught me more about myself than anything else I've done in my life (apart from motherhood, which kicks the shit out of me with staggering regularity).

Even the beginner's training regimen requires over four hundred miles in the sixteen weeks prior to race day. For Myrna and me, that translated into Tuesday, Wednesday, and Thursday runs of five or six miles, Saturday runs of at least thirteen and up to twenty-two miles, and Sunday runs of three or four miles, just to blow out any lingering lactic acid and residual agony. To mix things up, we also ran hill repeats on alternate Wednesdays, dashing like half-naked Marines up a quarter-mile hill near my house. Our first night running hills, we guiltily believed we were giving ourselves a break from a scheduled six miler. Five hill sprints later, my heart rate reached 180 bpm, and I threw up leftover Chinese food on some woman's lawn.

Hill repeats. You don't see many people (outside football practice) running them. It stands to reason: you don't see many people snorting Cayenne pepper either. Sometimes the Universe makes sense.

While I didn't finish anywhere near the front of the pack – at 4:56:38, I came in around eighteen-thousandth place – I considered the experience, the sixteen-week training schedule, the 4:30 am runs, the treadmill workouts while Homer napped, the babysitters I paid just so I could suffer for three hours, and the actual race, with my boys cheering me on, my dad drunk with seventy thousand Italians on Fourth Avenue in Brooklyn, my finisher's medal, and my post-race photo with Myrna, the two of us sharing a Mylar blanket outside the Dakota on 72nd Street . . . all of it was a brightly-wrapped victory for me as I dragged my life out of the mud with both hands (and two reasonably-toned legs).

Thinking back now, it isn't the finish line or the two million spectators or those awful miles through the Bronx that stand out for me. Rather, I remember unimportant formative bits along the way. For example, I'd drive around on Friday nights, leaving two Hershey's *Nuggets* every three miles beside the road and a small Gatorade every seven. Myrna and I both can make one chocolate *Nugget* last three miles. However, we have a different approach to the challenge. For me, I nibble about one-third of a *Nugget* at the beginning of each mile. This convinces me that I've got enough sugar in my system to jog another mile to another nibble. After each bite, I wrap the rest of the candy in the gold foil and tuck it inside my jog bra. (Yes, gross; I know. But you can't imagine what reprehensible things you're capable of doing when you've reached Mile 9 or so of a twenty-two-mile training run. By Mile 18 or 19, you could easily agree to murder a close relative. Eating chocolate dipped in boob sweat is nothing.)

My nibble strategy has one drawback: for some reason, I have to muscle through the awfulness of every third mile, knowing that I don't have any chocolate left. I'm not sure why this is, but I invariably feel better once I've reached Mile 4, 7, 10, etc. to fetch my next *Nugget*.

Myrna, on the other hand, stuffs the entire *Nugget* into her cheek, like a makeshift wad of chewing tobacco. Over the next three miles, she slowly sucks on the chocolate, keeping the flow of sugar into her bloodstream steady. About two-and-a-half miles later she gives in to temptation, chomps and swallows what little remains, and then curses for a quarter mile that she should've stuck it out a few minutes longer and that she'll never make it to the next cheekful.

Strange, I know, and it's just a little thing, a thimbleful of memories I wouldn't have if I hadn't agreed to run that silly race. A year later, I remember each of our *Nugget* runs fondly; I'm glad to have suffered over hundreds of miles with Myrna. We were two, over-forty women testing our limits and doing okay.

Although I'll grant that there were dozens of times when I wanted to collapse on the side of the road and beg God to ferry me across the River Jordan.

I miss those times, too.

There are embarrassing, painful, and less-motivating aspects of training for a marathon that I don't recall quite as fondly as I recall nibbling on nuggets of milk chocolate.

For example, I discovered that I'm deft at the right-handed snot rocket. Particularly important on cold mornings, blowing snot out my right nostril, without a tissue or handkerchief, rarely presented a problem. I could fire a shot glass full of watery boogers across the sidewalk and into the grass without much effort. The left-handed snot rocket, however, frequently aborted its trajectory shortly after launch and splashed across the back side of my left shoulder.

Who cares; right? I'm running. What difference does it make if I have three ounces of coagulating mucus on my sweatshirt like a phlegmy turd from a sick seagull?

Well, it mattered when I ran to Starbucks for a coffee, or when I ran by the boys' school to check in with a teacher or to surprise Danny and Gerry for lunch in the cafeteria. Some Starbucks barista or office secretary would gesture in polite sign language, *Um . . . Ms. Teasdale, you've got boogers or seagull shit on your arm. You might want to wipe that off before one of the sixth graders uploads a photo to Instagram.*

Also embarrassing was when Danny would do the laundry. Gerry hasn't yet embraced the notion that clothes don't wash themselves. But Danny will periodically clean a load or two of whatever castoffs have made the floor of his bedroom impassable (except to Sherpas or oxen). Oh yeah, after almost a year in my new house, I finally bought a washer and dryer . . . no more trips to the Laundromat; no more Italian bread pillows; no more homeless drunk's snot rockets. But don't get the wrong idea. Danny doesn't voluntarily come into my room to collect my laundry. Rather, I shout directives at him when I hear water running into the washing machine, and he begrudgingly adds my stuff to the load.

Have you ever run twenty miles without stopping? Ever done it in the summer? Yeah, me too. And without all the sordid details, running clothes (including underwear) get funky. That about captures it: *funky*. *Crusty* is excessive, but not by much. When I run, I don't perspire or glow or any of that happy horseshit women are supposed to imply politely over lemonade after tennis. Nope. I sweat like an obese Bavarian trombone player. I sweat and my underwear gets nasty and my socks smell like a North Jersey mafia hit. I often have dried snot on the left shoulder of my shirts and dried chocolate in the hollow cups of my sports bra.

While on long runs, I have peed in bushes and fields, fallen in mud, thrown up and splattered my shoes. I've sweat until I appeared to have been dunked in the Homely Pond, and wiped up all sorts of human excretions with my shirttail. My laundry is disgusting, and my son lets me (and his friends) know it when he's forced to reach into my laundry basket and pluck out the worst of the offenders.

Tough. I birthed him, fed him, protected him, taught him to read, ride a bike, shoot a basketball, and ask a girl on a date. I'll one day teach him to parallel park a car, factor a quadratic, negotiate a deal on a house, read a Dickinson poem, roast a Thanksgiving turkey, and tie a bow tie for his wedding.

He can handle an encounter or two with my foul underpants.

Regardless, the Hershey's *Nuggets* are better memories than the snot rockets, the bloody toes, the vomit, or the grimy unders.

Myrna swears we'll never run another marathon, but she's tough, and I'm tougher than I ever imagined. Between us we'll come up with $3.99 for a bag of chocolates.

Keep well, Billy.

Jennifer

PS: I hate adding these post scripts. They're always so goddamned depressing. This one's no different. Sorry. As much as I loved the New York Marathon and training with Myrna, I got into running because Richard couldn't help but make comments about how slowly I lost weight after Gerry was born.

See? Older women shouldn't get pregnant.
Damn, girl, you lost it in three months last time.
Who's doing the eating around here? You or the baby?
You planning to wear those rolls into the grave some day?
I thought breast feeding was supposed to burn fat.
Lovely, isn't he?

Anyway, I started running, because I got sick of him editorializing to me and his friends (and his frigging girlfriends; I know it) about the length of my stretch marks. I sincerely, sincerely hope that he marries some young hottie who gets pregnant and tubby. That way, he can be in his late forties, have a newborn child and *another* portly wife.

What the hell, if she gets into jogging just to please him, maybe she can join Myrna and me on our next *Nugget* run.

September 30

Hey Billy,

Portland, St. Augustine, London, Denver, Quebec City, Washington, DC, San Francisco, Key West, Madison, Boston, Cincinnati, Manhattan, Chicago, Atlanta, and San Diego. Those are a few of the cities I've explored on foot. I mentioned it to you before: running is my favorite way to see a new place the first time. When I can manage it, I like to arrive in the evening, so I don't take in too much from the airport shuttle. That way I can wake at dawn and lace up my Asics for a couple hours of exploration. Pick a town and I'll meet you there for a few miles.
    For you, Billy, even if I have to crawl.

Jennifer

And small places: Helen, Georgia; St. Albans, Vermont; Boothbay Harbor, Maine; Roanoke, Virginia; and Leadville, Colorado (but I was sucking serious wind up there).

How about Paris? Or Cairo? I dream about running there. Or Albany; I'm good with Albany, too.

Inbox

william.klein@twkfj.org

October

Dear Mr. Klein,

October 2

Dear Mr. Klein,

I apologize for contacting you out of the blue and on your company email. However, I have information of a personal nature to share and ask that you indulge me for a few lines. I'm not selling anything or soliciting your support for any political or humanitarian causes. This is a difficult and awkward message for me to send, because it might well cost me a relationship that means a great deal to me. I've spent the past year supporting a good friend through a trying divorce and think that you might be interested in what she's been through.

My name is Myrna Caroline. I'm from Manalapan, New Jersey, and I'm close friends with Jennifer Teasdale. You'd remember her as Jennifer Cooper from Rutgers University, class of 1993.

She remembers you.

If you recall her senior year, you had moved to Chicago to work, and she started dating Richard Teasdale. They were married in 1996. Afterward, Jennifer lost track of you; although she mentioned you (fondly) in passing a number of times since I met her in 2006.

She and Richard recently divorced, after several years of bitter acrimony. As part of the healing process, Jennifer has been writing to you and sending the letters to an inbox somewhere in Gmail cyberspace. No one read them until last week when she finally invited me to log in and scroll through the hundreds of pages she's drafted to you since she realized her marriage was hopeless.

She'd kill me if she knew I'd contacted you, and you might think I'm a horrible person for even suggesting that you log in and read my best friend's most personal and private thoughts. I can't believe I'm suggesting it. (My hands are shaking as I type this.)

But I think you should read them anyway. According to Jennifer, the two of you missed a chance at happiness twenty years ago. I'd hate to know that it happened to her twice. Naturally, everyone's different after twenty years, so perhaps nothing will come of this. Perhaps you'll delete this message and forget all about me. Perhaps you'll read what Jennifer's written and decide that your life is moving along just fine without her. That's okay, too. I'm hoping you'll read over her letters (they're to you after all) and decide to reach out to her, make contact again.

If things work out, wonderful. If not, that's fine. I just can't sit on my hands any longer. I love her too much for that. So . . . I'm passing you the ball, Mr. Klein, and either way, I promise I won't contact you again.

To read her letters, log in to Gmail under this account: **letterstobillyk@gmail.com**. The password is: August181992. She doesn't have a Facebook account. She deleted it a few years ago, but if you're on Facebook and decide to 'friend' me, there are a few photos on my page of the two of us slogging through the New York Marathon last year. I'm sure you'll recognize her.

I wish you all the best and appreciate you considering my suggestion.

Myrna Caroline

Inbox

letterstobillyk@gmail.com

October 17

Dear Billy,

Writing to you the other night about my marathon experience, I got a little nostalgic and flipped through some old photos of Myrna and me after the race. I found my ING NYC Marathon bib and my finisher's medal in the drawer with my yellow LIVESTRONG wrist band, and I got to thinking about Lance and his conversation with Oprah.

Did you watch that? I think half the planet did.

What an insufferable egomaniac.

It's too bad Oprah didn't invite a Justice Department attorney to swear him in before the cameras rolled. A few years in federal prison, that'd show the cocky bastard he isn't all that Heaven-sent. Although federal lockup isn't the one where thugs stab you or giant men gang rape you in the shower. Those are state prisons. Too bad. Lance could use a good rogering, teach him to be nicer to people.

What bothered me about Lance's confession isn't that he finally admitted to doping. Much of the cycling world already believed that. Rather, I was irritated by the cocksure, smug responses he gave, as if he wasn't on television with his life in ruins.

Bill Clinton did the same thing when he got caught lying about blow jobs. Monica Lewinsky had serviced him in her role as a White House intern, a skill I'm sure she listed near the top of her resume. Bill lied about it, got caught red-penised, then told the truth.

But Bill, like Lance, did it with that same I'm-a-big-deal-so-you-can-screw-off look on his face.

I've said before that I'm content to think of culture as the values, traditions, myths, beliefs, and value-driven behaviors established by any group of people, anywhere, and any time. It helps me understand why people behave as they do, even when they look like lunatics to anyone observing from outside their value system. I'm no historian, but National Socialism made sense to many Germans, because Hitler spoke to the values, traditions, beliefs, and myths the majority held close. They bought Fascism, because he wrapped it so neatly in *Hakenkreuz* paper (they don't sell that shit at Hallmark). And for years, it didn't much matter that he was a sociopath who only needed a hockey mask and a machete to complete his ensemble. People behave according to what they value. Germans in the 1930s did as well.

To anyone peeking in the windows, they must have looked like a corral full of nutters. To them, however, on-time trains, imprisoned Jews and low unemployment made sense.

If that's the case, how then does our culture (again and again) forgive douche bags like Bill Clinton, Lance Armstrong, and Richard Teasdale? What do we value about confident, white men that makes it okay for them to lie, cheat, deceive, and screw at will? They get caught; they apologize, and we forgive them. What the hell is that about? How often do you read the cover of *People* or *US Weekly* and see some doofus who's spent eighteen months stoned, has divorced, slept around, been arrested, made disparaging comments about minority groups, maybe even punched a cop? They wile thirty days puking in some rehab center, shave, put on a clean suit, shrug, and say, 'Gosh folks, I'm sorry.'

And we forgive them.

How stupid is that?

I wanted Oprah to waggle a richly-bejeweled finger in Lance's face (not really; it's just fun to write the word 'bejeweled') and say, 'You are an egomaniacal turdface, and I'm pleased to remind you that your life is over. Go live in squalor somewhere with the other manipulating liars, senators, and Mel Gibson fans.'

She didn't say that.

In 2006, Richard and I went to marriage counseling, largely because Richard wouldn't admit that our domestic problems stemmed from his propensity to insert his penis into any warm, damp orifice he could find. What we needed was for him to spend several years in serious analysis and therapy. What we got was couples' counseling, which will probably cease to exist once Viagra is available at 7-Eleven. The couples' therapist kept asking about sexual attraction, sustained erections, libido, and conjugal time in the sack. I tried explaining that Richard's ability to sustain an erection wasn't the problem. Rather the problem was that Richard too often sustained erections in the parking lot behind the Chili's on Route 9. We had all the erections we could handle; Richard could have decorated our Christmas tree with the erections he'd passed out to those less fortunate.

You get the idea.

Anyway, in a rare display of genuine concern for our marriage, my former husband surprised Dr. Lane, our therapist (and me) with a written confession of his *sexual transgressions*. That's what I used to call them, back when I had a marriage worth saving. Nowadays I refer to

Richard's adulterous wanderings as his *Dick Olympics*. He medaled in six events.

I don't know when he finished his notes, but they read as if they were scribbled in a mad, 3:00-am dash through a decade and a half of bone-deep regrets. He must have sneaked out of bed, crept to his office, and wrote on a legal pad to avoid waking me with the clickety clack of his keyboard.

I didn't get to read them at the time; Richard gave the pages to Dr. Lane during a one-on-one session while I waited in the lobby. Later, she suggested to me that she had a better sense about the root cause of our difficulties – sure, *root* cause – but she never let me read those notes and never guided us through the carnage left by Richard's erections.

A few years later, counseling had failed several times, and my husband was back in the saddle with another crop of willing victims: divorcees, discontent housewives, and half-literate waitresses he met in the city.

Anyway, after a nasty fight late one Friday – we were both drunk, so I'll take partial credit – Richard rose early to go running. Terrified of gaining a pound or two, he needed to blow out the hangover, burn off the calories, and get away from me.

Stupid with dehydration and my skull cracking to spill vodka-flavored brains on my carpet, I crawled into the bathroom to pee, glad Dickie would be gone for an hour. I needed to get my shit together and didn't have the strength to handle it with him hovering around.

And there they were. I have no idea why. On the floor beside his vanity, Richard had left his leather messenger bag. (I bought it for him on a weekend trip to Boston when we were dating. The tanned cowhide had aged well, more gracefully than Richard, me, or our dysfunctional union.) The pages hung limply, half in and half out of the leather pocket, as if he'd fetched them after our fight, perhaps poured over them, digging for something he could use against me.

I don't know why, never asked him.

Regardless, I copied the pages, returned them to the messenger bag, and spent the weekend pretending I'd not found anything. I used the desktop copier in Richard's office. My fingers shook from adrenaline, depression, self-loathing, and alcoholism . . . almost too violently for me to press COPY or feed the pages into the machine. I couldn't read them until later; I'd have barfed and wept all over his desk if I'd seen even half a paragraph during that anxious dash down the hall.

With the copies tucked beneath my mattress, I returned shithead's confession to his bag. My knees tried to buckle. I leaned close to the mirror, stared myself down. Waited. I had to slow my heart, or he'd know right away that I'd been snooping.

It worked. I didn't manage to read Richard's confession through until Monday. But I've read it hundreds of times since. It's gotten easier. My lawyer's flipped through a copy as well.

Years later, what's amusing and sad is that Richard wrote those pages during a time when he'd decided to make an honest effort to reconcile with me and save us from a lifetime of regret and animosity. He offered them to our therapist as evidence that he understood how unforgivably he'd treated me, the boys, our family, and the promises we'd made during our engagement. Those pages are the one piece of evidence I have that he wanted to try, and yet they are the main piece of evidence I used to discredit him in our divorce proceedings.

Yup: amusing and sad.

He never saw it coming, never knew I had them.

Billy, I've been writing to you for over a year now, and I've tried not to hold anything back. I want to type Richard's confession, word-for-word, for you to read, but I can't do it, not yet anyway. First, I've got to give you a thumbnail synopsis in my own voice. I have to. I'm not sure why, except that there's something about you reading his words that makes me feel as though I might lose . . . shit, what? . . . some imagined status I might possess in your memory.

Yeah, I suppose that's it.

I can't let you read his confession without first giving you a ballpark description of what it contains. Call it a weakness of mine. I swear to God that I'll trust you with my heart if I ever have a chance to give you my heart, but for now, typing this email, I can't have you bypass me and hear directly from him. It's just vanity. I need to control – or at least try to control – your response to my ex-husband saying that I wasn't good enough for him. I'll fumble around, paraphrasing what I've read hundreds of times, because I don't want you to think that I was a bad wife or a boring sex partner. That's the conclusion I draw when I read his confession. I don't come away feeling confused or sorry for him or concerned that there's something deeply and irretrievably wrong with Richard. I should; that much I know. Rather, I come away feeling as though I didn't give him what he needed. And I don't want you to think of me as a woman who can't bring her A-game when it counts. How odd that I haven't seen you since April, 1993, and yet I worry that you're going to believe him instead of me.

Sorry. I can't help it. Just please don't think less of me.

Christ, I'm a basket case. It makes me wonder if all jilted women are this insecure. They might be, men too for all I know.

The good news is that I'll try to keep the synopsis amusing. If I can get you laughing for a page or so, maybe you'll breeze through Richard's notes without a wrinkle. (That's my plan, in case you haven't inferred it on your own.)

Shit. Now I'm calling you stupid.

I'll shut up and get to it.

You're probably wondering, 'Why is she so nervous now? She's been honest about everything so far.'

That's true. However, up to this point, you've only heard from me, never from Richard. I've not allowed you even a glimpse at his side of things. Tonight is a test of my resilience. If I've told you the truth and I believe I can trust you, I ought to be able to hand over Richard's confession and not worry that you'll sympathize with him or pity him or attempt to discern a valid reason why he went off in search of other women so frequently.

And I trust you. And I trust that I've been honest. So here we go . . .

I met Richard the semester after you graduated. We saw one another often, because his band played the Ratskeller almost every weekend, and I hung around the bar with Scoutmaster Kelly and the rest of the KD house. He and I started dating in October, and I was a fully-fledged groupie by Thanksgiving break. I'm convinced now that he targeted me, but I also know that I let it happen. I let you go and flushed *us* down the toilet for a good time, a few drinks, and a chance to date a rock star.

Jesus, if only I had a time machine, I'd swoop in there and beat the shit out of myself. But we've been over that already.

You were in Chicago working and studying, and I respected your request . . . promise. Remember that? It was about the dumbest thing we ever decided to do, but it's decades of massive floods beneath our bridge, and there's no sense crying over spilled blood.

(It was my fault though, Billy. I wish I knew how to whisper in an email. I'd whisper that here.)

I have to begin all the way back at Rutgers, because Richard started sleeping around before he and I graduated. He slept with several of my KD sisters, including my own roommate one weekend when I visited my brother in Philadelphia. I never knew they'd spent that weekend in bed, so I invited her to be a bridesmaid when Richard and I got married, and they nailed one another again on the morning of the ceremony.

We were all down the shore in a rental place, barbecuing, drinking, and behaving like fools. Richard showed up late that Thursday night. I had no idea he was around (I'd been pouring lemon drops down my throat all afternoon with Scoutmaster Kelly and a couple of bridesmaids and was pleasantly incoherent.) He got a room down the beach from our hotel, partied with his groomsmen, and then hooked up with Beth for a hump down memory lane.

My roommate, KD sister, and bridesmaid, Beth Parsons . . . she's married today with three kids. I have no idea if she's still involved with Richard. Probably not. The last I saw her, she'd picked up a pair of baby-making saddle bags. Richard doesn't go to bed with chubby women. Yet I'd bet she's still carrying that torch, the dumbass.

The years Richard and I lived outside Bayonne, he had sex with two co-workers, a nurse from the Jersey Shore Medical Center in Neptune, and a waitress from a restaurant on the Asbury Park boardwalk. He started making some decent money, so we moved to a nice neighborhood, closer to the city. With a golf course, an exercise facility, miles of bike paths, and a community pool, we figured it was a place where our kids could grow up with decent friends and good opportunities.

That was a mistake. In the gated community, old Dickie was like a porn star in a country full of frustrated women. At thirty, he discovered two species of equally beddable hausfraus: the forty-year-old lonely hearts, and the recently-married-now-bored-twenty-seven-year-old party girls. He thought he'd died and gone to Heaven.

The list of women in McMansion Number 1 would be a record setter, if we hadn't moved into McMansion Numbers 2 and 3, where he endeavored to establish a personal best again and again. A short list of highlights includes:

--Pharmaceutical sales rep, MILF, 33.
--Divorced, housewife, PTA President, 41. (We made *Toy Story* cupcakes for bake sales together.)

--Pretend journalist, freelance lay, 29. (Horrid dresser, cute car.)
--Barely-legal sister of my good friend, 19. (I mentioned her before.)
--Barely-legal dormitory mates of barely-legal sister. (No idea how many he managed that weekend.)
--Little league coach's wife, MILF, 38. (When the coach is away . . .)
--Organist from our church, 52 (Sexy for her age.)
--Debbie, my friend the boating enthusiast, MILF, 32. (Remember her? From the $150,000 yacht?)
--Guzzlin' Greta, the MILF co-worker, 38. (At $25,000, that's some expensive tail.)
--Lisa, another friend of mine, tax attorney, MILF, 37. (She moved in the week I was on vacation.)
--A bookstore clerk from Barnes & Noble in Freehold, 22 or 23. (He's not a reader; must've been the coffee.)
--Debbie again, another vacation-week sleepover.
--The wine clerk from Wegmans, 40. (Anti-MILF, but she knows wine.)
--Assorted other women, totaling twenty nine between 1993 and 2013. (Twenty nine that he's willing to admit, anyway.)
--And at least one *curious, athletic hetero or bi* gentleman he met on Craig's List before the 2010 Belmar Five Miler.

Yeah, a guy. I damned near peed my pants when I read that one. Apparently, Richard decided to experiment with more than one of the appetites that plagued him in the wee hours. And what's amazingly coincidental about this particular tryst is that my brother found the listing.

I swear to God this is true.

Gary runs, not like Richard or me, but he gets off the couch every now and then for a 10k or a neighborhood fun run, Turkey Trot, whatever. In 2010, Richard and I had plans to run the Belmar Five Miler, a great race, because it starts at the beach, is pancake flat throughout, and ends at a beer truck beside the boardwalk. Naturally, my brother didn't register in advance, so he got on Craig's List three days prior to the race to search for an unwanted bib.

I can't recall exactly how it was worded, but Gary sat in my kitchen, surfing Craig's List, when he announced, 'Hey, listen to this:

Curious, athletic, hetero male seeks curious, athletic, hetero or bi male for post-race oral. Belmar 5 Miler. Holy shit!'

Apparently, Gary had never visited Craig's List before.

He showed us the listing. 'I can get laid on this thing?'

His wife, Maria, slapped the back of his head, and we all laughed at the absurdity of hooking up with a sweaty jogger for a sweaty blow job after a five-mile run in July.

The bacteria would be colossal, disagreeable enough to lay waste to Rome.

Laughing at my brother, I never thought to look over at Richard, couldn't picture him swallowing a penis, particularly an unknown penis that had just run five miles. I didn't look at him that morning but enjoy imagining him choking on his coffee when Gary read the posting. He never admitted to placing a personal ad for a tryst with a curious, athletic friend. (You'll understand when you read his confession.) We haven't spoken a civil word to one another in the months since he discovered that I photocopied his pages. So I guess I'll never know, but it is entertaining for me to imagine the two of them sneaking behind a convenient hedge or to a secluded parking space. What the hell, Richard nailed every third woman he ever met. Why not enjoy a blow job from a fellow runner?

There you have it, Billy. From a nineteen-year-old college kid to a fifty-two-year-old church organist, Richard wrestled ravenous demons, and fed them women, cars, boats, elaborate vacations, and opulent houses. None of it satisfied him. No amount of money, no corner lot, no shiny BMW Roadster was enough to quiet whatever needs burned in his belly.

We had children and it didn't matter. Not even they were enough to coax him off the ledge. How could I compete? What chance did I stand as a woman, a wife, a friend, a partner, anything?

Please keep that in mind as you read these next few pages.

Here they are, with nothing held back.

April 8, 2006

Dear Dr. Lane,

I have never written this kind of letter before. I've not ever been this honest about anything, and I don't know how to begin. I've read books and seen movies about people who make these kinds of confessions, and they always start by admitting there's a problem. So I'll go with that. I have a problem.

I am a Christian, a father, a husband, a son, a brother, a businessman, an athlete, and a sex addict. I'm keeping that list short, because I want to stick to the things about me that I believe I can never turn off. That's the list. I am many other things, but I can only think of these few that I will always be. That scares me. I don't want to be a sex addict. Yet I feel as though I don't have any choice in the matter, and I believe it is ruining my life and my family. I have prayed about this daily since I felt my marriage was in trouble. I admit I never asked God to help me with my sex addiction prior to that. However, I want to save my marriage. I want my wife and sons to forgive me one day, and I want to be free from this need to covet other women.

Actually, that's not quite correct. I have to be honest. I covet, in some way, almost all women. I even covet you, Dr. Lane. I can't help it.

I can't remember when it started, and I will get to my childhood urges, but I feel like I should try and explain what I mean by covet. I long to touch women, to undress them, to feel their bodies as I work myself to a climax. I don't covet knowing them. I don't want to learn their names, their life stories, or their dreams for careers, families, or apartments in the city. I covet their physical being, their shape, and their touch . . . almost to the point of being distracted while I drive or as I push my shopping cart around the grocery store on weekends. They don't have to be perfectly shaped. I admit that I do covet shapely women more frequently. Those who are thin, with narrow hips, slightly wider thighs, and full breasts are women who have the deepest impact on me. If they are working mothers who have stayed in shape into their thirties, I covet them most. I think it's because I know how much they have to sacrifice to look that good, and part of me believes they are keeping trim for men like me, men who stay in shape and who desire (even need) to touch them. I believe all heterosexual women want to be touched by powerful, fit, confident men. Mothers, especially, who still give off that vibe after having kids, those are the ones I can't clear out of my mind.

Yet I covet almost all women I see. Dirty, overly heavy, women who don't care about their appearance, those are about the only women I don't long to touch in some way. What's strange is that I don't respect them either. I don't hire them to work for me. I don't listen to what they have to say, and I tend to dismiss them entirely, as if they don't exist. I can't remember the last time I had a conversation with an overweight woman or a woman who didn't seem to care about her appearance. It's not that I hate them or dislike them. It's more that they don't exist. I'll say again that I know this is wrong. I know all of this is sick. It's why I'm writing this testament for you and why I'm committed to our therapy together.

I covet teenage girls and college co-eds. I spend hours each day on web sites devoted to the debasement of high school and college girls. Men (sometimes boys) get women drunk or drugged and encourage them into bestial sexual situations. The girls in the photos and videos appear to be enjoying it. I enjoy it, even though I'm fully aware that some of them are only teenagers, and that most of them probably regret their decision when the sun comes up. I know this is wrong. My own sons will be teens one day soon. Yet I frequently find myself staring at teenagers, not twelve or thirteen year olds (I'm not a pedophile), but at girls who know what they're doing. There are sixteen and seventeen year olds who dress provocatively and who (obvious to me) have sex with their boyfriends. They dress the part. They walk and carry themselves in a particular way, and I find that I have to force myself to take my eyes off them, not their childish faces, because they still look like kids. Rather their bodies take control of me, the rounded, softening parts, the space beneath their growing breasts or the high swell of their buttocks, not yet ruined by motherhood, age, or gravity.

I know that I must sound like a monster, but I'm just telling you the truth. I have a problem, and I need help, and to be perfectly honest with you . . . I don't think that I am all that different from many men, certainly not the men I know. Friends of ours go to football and basketball games at the local high schools. They say they're going to watch neighborhood kids compete, but that's not true. They watch the cheerleaders. And I think the cheerleaders know it. Cheerleading uniforms have grown more and more provocative in the years since I went to high school. Volleyball shorts are pornographic. High school girls wear pants so tight that little is left to the imagination. If girls had dressed this way when I went to high school, I'd have ended up arrested. (That's not really an exaggeration.) Even today, with equality in every aspect of our lives, sex is selling better than ever. Everyone knows it. Teenage girls know it. I'm just the one willing to write it down and confess to it. I wonder if you work with other men like me, maybe dozens of us. That wouldn't surprise me.

I couldn't begin to guess how many orgasms I've had. It's at least 15,000. That's about two each day since my thirteenth birthday. There are days when I've had four or five and days when I've only had one. I can't remember the last time I went twenty-four hours without having at least one orgasm. It might have been 2003, when I had a nasty flu for a couple of days. But even then, I think I managed.

I learned to masturbate when I was about eight years old. Nothing much spurted out, but it felt almost the same as it does today. I didn't have a hard childhood. We weren't poor. My parents weren't abusive or drunk or out sleeping with lots of partners. I grew up in a nice neighborhood outside Philadelphia. I went to good schools, had nice friends, and played sports year round. For the past several years I have been asking God to help me zero in on the reason I retreated so often to my room to masturbate, even as a little kid, but I can't remember why, except that it felt good. It was just a little reward I gave myself for finishing my homework, cleaning my room, or helping my mother do the dishes. Self stimulation became as much a part of my daily routine as brushing my teeth or playing basketball with my friends. By the time I hit puberty, I was hooked. I did it most often in the shower, especially when I first started ejaculating, because I was never quite sure how much would come out. I had fears that I'd get started and not be able to stop, or that my mother would come in and find me there, spurting into a puddle on my bed.

My father never had girlie magazines, and Mom threw out most clothing catalogues the day they arrived in the mail. Strangely, the *J. C. Penny* catalogue was the best. I salvaged a few from the trash can before Dad took the garbage out and kept a stash of them in my bedroom. I figured if Mom found them, she wouldn't think twice. The women's underwear advertisements were located near the middle of the magazine, just a few pages of thin, pretty women in bras and panties. It was nothing compared with the material I've watched on my computer in the past several years. Yet at the time, I was in Heaven. I was fourteen when I discovered hand cream. I'd not had sex with a girl yet. So I didn't know that warm cream could approximate the feel of a vagina. Instead, I tried the cream one day when I'd nearly rubbed my penis raw. I needed to have an orgasm, but the pain was pretty bad. So I sneaked into my parents' bathroom and shot a few pumps of Lubriderm into my palm.

It was amazing. I'm embarrassed to write it. I feel as though my life is a car wreck. My wife is about to leave me. My business is threatened. I often can't stand the sight of myself in the mirror. Yet I know that sometime between now and tomorrow morning when I leave for work, I will either sneak out of our house to meet a woman, or I'll masturbate to porn images on my phone . . . with a fistful of that same Lubriderm lotion I stole from my mother's bathroom twenty years ago.

Middle school is when I learned that there is a difference (for me) between being in love with a girl and simply enjoying an orgasm every day.

I know this sounds strange, but I need you to understand. I had, and still have, perfectly "normal" feelings of love, sexual attraction, and human desire for women. I love my wife and will for the rest of my life. That's different from needing to feel sexual pleasure every day, as often as possible sometimes. In seventh grade I fell in love for the first time. Her name isn't important, but she felt the same for me, and what we had was innocent and fun and exhilarating. We bought each other little presents for Christmas and birthdays. We went to the movies with friends, but sat beside one another, held hands, and sneaked kisses in the back of her mother's van on the way home. I used to write her long love letters that I'd sneak inside her locker, her textbooks, or her backpack, just silly kid stuff. Yet when I got home from the movies or the roller rink, I'd jerk off two or three times to images of twenty-five-year-old models in the *J. C. Penny* catalogue.

My girlfriend's face, small breasts, child's ass, or skinny legs never entered my imagination as I stimulated myself. It was as though she existed as a real person, a person I loved rather than an object to stimulate me to a climax. There was a distinct and clear difference between the two. She was a girl I loved and wanted to be with, because we held hands, sneaked kisses, and felt overwhelming desire for one another. But we never acted on it. The women in the magazines, the bra and panty ads, were the tools I used to satisfy my need for that mind-numbing sensation. Those two things were separate. They're still separate for me today. It is the hardest thing for me to explain to my wife. It's as if she can't hear the words when I try to help her understand. I love her. I'll love her forever. But I can't stop the wanting, the coveting, the needing that plagues me every day.

In high school, I still loved XXXXXX. But by November of my freshman year, I'd discovered curious, willing, even aggressive girls who wanted to know more about their bodies and mine.

That's where it started. I'd given my whole heart to XXXXXX. (What's funny is that part of me still loves her, too.) She was in possession of my soul, but for me, there's distinct separation between my soul and my penis. It had become an instrument for feeling good, and I had relations (blow jobs, cunnilingus, hand jobs, mutual masturbation, anal and vaginal sex) with every willing teenage girl I could find in high school . . . and even more in college. College was easier, much easier. Too often in high school, I'd give some girl her first real orgasm, and she'd believe she was in love with me. When word got out that I might have had sex with someone else, she'd be hurt, upset, even violent (a couple of times). I'm not proud of the lives I ruined in high school, but I am hopeful that they've all gone on to happy marriages, in good relationships with kind-hearted guys. I doubt that's happened, because I doubt the existence of many kind-hearted guys, but I hope for them all regardless.

College. If I could have grown old and died at Rutgers University, I would have. By Thanksgiving break of my freshman year, XXXXXX broke up with me. She'd gotten tired of hearing rumors that I was involved with other women. So she dumped me about ten minutes after I arrived home for break. I was upset. I loved her. But I didn't let it stop me from hooking up with another of my high school girlfriends after dinner Thanksgiving night.

Dr. Lane, I wish that none of this was true. Reading it over now, I don't know how this can help you help me get my mind right. I sound like a madman. I'm not a madman. I'm a good Christian guy. I pray every day and go to church every Sunday. I'm good to my children. I work fifty hours a week, sometimes more, to provide for my family, and I think I'm a good son to my parents and a good neighbor to the people who live on our block.

But I've had sex with three different women from our block. Why is that? How is it possible that I can make love with my wife in the morning, and by noon I'm finding an excuse to leave the house so I can have sex with a neighbor's bored wife. Then, when I get home, if I finish up files on my computer or send emails to co-workers about investment research or closing numbers, I end up watching Internet porn and masturbating into a hand towel beneath my desk. There are weeks when this happens three times. My wife asks if I had unprotected sex with other women when she was pregnant. Yes. She asks if I came home and had sex with her afterward. Yes. She asks if I understand that I could have passed on a crippling infection to our unborn children. Yes. But she never asks if I think I can help myself. No. No. No. Sure, I can go a few weeks, even a couple of months from time to time, but like any addict, I'm back on my drug of choice (women) just a few weeks later.

In college, I continued my pattern of questionable behavior. It was easy. Unlike high school, where girls wanted to believe they loved me before they'd agree to sex, college women were experimental, curious, willing, and often drunk or stoned enough not to care. All the questions I dreamed about asking women in high school, I could ask college women. Many of them appreciated my honesty, the forthright manner in which I'd ask permission. I admit, I'd ease my path a bit with a few beers, some pot, or a couple of vodkas, but in the end, I learned to get my own engine revving with a risky game of dangerous foreplay. Sometimes it failed, and whatever woman I'd chosen for the night/weekend would storm away, offended. But often, more often than not, the half-drunk, fully-honest policy worked like a charm. I'll list a few of my college requests here, so you can understand how deep this goes. They're not pickup lines. Rather, they're foreplay:

-Can I see what kind of panties you wear with that dress?
-Your bra is visible through that blouse, will you show it to me?
-Your workout clothes fit like a second skin, can I run my hands over them?
-Can I feel that small hollow between your breasts?
-Do you trim your pubic hair? Can I see it?
-Do you shave your pubic hair? Can I help?
-Can I explore that narrow overhang beneath your ass cheeks?
-How large do your nipples get when they're soft?
-How small do your nipples get when they're hard?
-Can I trace that wonderful, smooth, curving highway from your armpit down to your hips?

-Your T-shirt doesn't quite reach your jeans. Can I touch that ribbon of tan skin peeking out?

You get the idea, I'm sure. My hedonistic behavior in college led to nearly two decades of cheating on my wife. Every free night I had, every time my wife went away, even for a few hours, I'd either dial up Internet porn or I'd masturbate to whatever porn channel she allowed on our monthly cable bill. When she got tired of me having orgasms without her, she canceled it. I still watched it, though, the fluttery, wavering images of people having sex. Even Comcast's scrambling software couldn't keep me from catching a glimpse of a vagina, a bare breast, or an erect penis behind the hazy jumble. The easiest outlet for me to find a regular fix, however, was other women. (I'll try to make a comprehensive list for you at the end of these notes.) Our neighborhood and similar neighborhoods around central New Jersey are filled with discontent, frustrated housewives and working mothers who just want to feel (for a few minutes each week) like they felt when they were nineteen and full of sexual energy and enthusiasm for life.

I help them, and they help me. I don't like talking to them. I don't like thinking that I've cheated on my wife so many times, because in my opinion most of my encounters with other women aren't affairs. I don't make love with other women. I don't kiss them. I don't hold their hands and promise them a lifetime together as soul mates. I have intercourse with their bodies. I stimulate their clitorises until they orgasm, and then they suck my penis until I orgasm. It isn't cheating. My mind gives me permission to consider these transgressions filling an addictive urge. I hate myself afterwards. I used to blame alcohol. I'd get drunk. I'd get women drunk, and we'd have sex in my car, on the community golf course, or in the grass behind my house. I'd do it anywhere. Anywhere that a drunk might go for a drink, I'd go for a blow job. It sounds like lunacy, but it makes sense. The first few times I cheated on my wife she wasn't even my wife yet. We were engaged to be married, but I was still involved with one of her good friends, a bridesmaid, actually. When I went to see Beth in the days before I got married, I didn't think I could get an erection. I believed I had beaten it. I was getting married, and married men have got to struggle to sustain an erection with another woman. What married man doesn't hear and see his wife in his mind while he's helping some stranger out of her panties? I knew Beth wanted a last romp with me, and I knew she'd been drinking with Jennifer at the bachelorette party. The test for me was to determine if the promise of my wedding vows would cure me, and I'd stand in that hotel room with a flaccid penis and a clear conscience.

I was disappointed when it didn't happen. I took the elevator up to my room. I'd called Beth, told her where I'd be, and asked the desk clerk to leave her a key. When I arrived, Beth was already naked, lying on my bed, and watching television while she drank directly from a bottle of white wine. I had an erection in less than ten seconds. So I blamed the booze. I'd not be able to get hard if I was sober. Things would be okay. There was no way I'd be able to sustain an erection, sober, with a woman other than my wife.

Two days later, I met Beth in her motel room, about twenty minutes before she drove to my in-laws' house to help Jennifer get her hair and makeup ready for the ceremony. It was 8:30 in the morning. I was sober, even a little hung over, and I managed an erection without a second thought. It wasn't the alcohol. I drink because it gives me a convenient excuse for my transgressions. I also drink because it's easier to be charming and seductive with women when they've had alcohol. It softens up their resolve. Many women are unwilling to consider adultery when they're sober, because they think it says something awful about themselves. They don't really care if they screw up their husband's life. Most of them already fear or believe that their husbands have slept around. It isn't the vow to the husband that keeps them from having sex with me; it's their self-respect. I use alcohol or pot to help them relax, just enough. Dr. Lane, you'd be staggered to know how many women only need a slight nudge in the right direction. I'm no Don Juan. I stay in shape. I take care to look presentable. I have a good job and a nice house, and I truly listen when I'm talking with a woman. I listen, and I respond to what she says, and I get her a few drinks, and I allow her to meet my needs while I meet hers. Often she doesn't admit she has those needs until she's loosened up with a couple glasses of wine.

Am I a monster? I don't think so. I'm an addict who's figured out how to get the drug I need. I love my wife. But that's separate from my orgasms. Working round the clock to set an international record, my wife would never be able to give me as many orgasms as I've given myself, or as many as I've taken . . . taken . . . from willing high school, college, newly-married, divorced, or middle-aged women. I'm a drunk in search of my next drink or a junkie in search of my next fix. I'm a sex addict, and I hope you can help me. I don't want to be the victim of this curse any longer. I need to find a way to break free.

Dr. Lane, I apologize that I've gone on for so long, but I need to make you a list. You'll probably find it redundant, given all I've confessed in these pages, but I want to feel as though I've not held anything back. You can't help me unless you have all of my cards on the table. Therefore, in as close to chronological order as I can remember . . .

* * * *

Me again. Sorry to interrupt, but the next bit was just him typing out a humiliating list of names. You've heard about many of them from me, so there's no need to re-plow all that ground here. I do want you to read his big wrap up, after the list, when he comes full circle and decides that he's the victim. As you read it, imagine me running him over with the Partridge Family bus. I'll be back shortly with your color commentary.

* * * *

And that's all of them, as honest as I can be, even about Mark. I only saw him that once. We emailed for a while, but then he

283

dropped off the face of the earth. His wife probably grew suspicious about why he'd been in such close contact with an investment banker who didn't handle any of their accounts.

I don't know what to do next. I will continue to come to therapy and continue to be truthful with you as we work to help me find a way through this. I know friends who have managed to quit smoking or alcohol, after having been victimized by their addictions for decades.

* * * *

Sorry again! But good Lord, now he's a victim! Don't mind me; I'm just gagging.

* * * *

They ask God to help them, and they tackle the problem one day at a time. I used to laugh at the stickers they'd put on the backs of their cars, as if it was important for anyone sitting in traffic to know that the driver in front of them was battling drug or alcohol addiction. Now I'm sorry I laughed. I get it. Everything good about me has been taken over and sacrificed for a few minutes of pleasure each day. I'm a mess. I'm losing this battle, and I need your help.

Yours sincerely,

Richard Allen Teasdale

* * * *

Cue the orchestra. Cue Tyrone Power who gently takes Vivien Leigh into his arms as the sun sets over the Pacific, and the friendly natives of Guadalcanal join hands to sing *Innsbruck Ich muss dich lassen*, and . . . pass me a barf bag. I'm gonna hurl!
    I don't know about you, but reading Richard's tidy manifesto reminds me of a few lines I found on a blog site a couple of months

back. I sent it to you; remember? One of my favorite quotes is this one:

```
Find someone living below the poverty
line who screws half the women on his
street, and you know what you've found?
An adulterer piece of shit who can't get
through the day without unzipping his
fly. Move that same sorry slob to the
suburbs and prop him up in a big house
with a convertible in the driveway, and
what is he? A sex addict.
```

I don't know what it is about affluent people to make us think we can excuse every bad behavior, blaming someone or something rather than standing up and taking responsibility for ourselves.

Addicted to booze? My mother didn't love me.

Addicted to Percocet? My life is too stressful.

Addicted to cocaine? I can't keep up with the demands at work.

Addicted to overeating? My parents got divorced when I was a kid.

Addicted to sex? My mother bought Lubriderm lotion, just left that shit out on the counter with the *J. C. Penny* catalogue. Anyone could have gotten hooked. Life was tough in our white-bread neighborhood.

Bullshit. Bullshit. Bullshit. Bullshit.

(Sometimes, it's cathartic for me to type that word.)

Anyway, I used to cry when I read his confession. They were full-body crying jags that left me exhausted. Not anymore. These days I just get disgusted with him, with myself, with the idea that I lost so much time trapped in such an impossible situation. And I know I wasn't in a Turkish prison, and I wasn't being persecuted by NAZIs or tortured by Soviet interrogators. I get it. My blip on the radar screen is comparatively small, but it's still my blip, goddamn it. It's the only blip I've got, and now it's forty-four years old with a kid named Homer who drops snotty tissues into the fish tank.

I apologize that this email has gone well beyond the legal limit in all but six states. I'll sign off soon, but indulge me for just a few more lines as I type out a couple of important codas that need to get written. As I mentioned earlier, I don't believe that you're going to ignore everything I've written in the past year and feel pity for my jackass ex-husband. I'll just sleep better tonight if I mention a handful of omissions he made in his confession.

He said he'd participate in therapy and work with Dr. Lane to get through his addiction. Nope. He went to about three more sessions. When he realized that Lane had no sexual chemistry with him at all and that he'd have to share some of these revelations with his wife, he quit.

He said he never talked with his girlfriends and that he believes these trysts aren't cheating, because 'My mind gives me permission to consider these transgressions filling an addictive urge.' Nope. Just prior to entering couples' therapy in 2006, I printed twenty-two pages of illicit messages from his email archives, all of them sexual, intimate, personal conversations with women he'd been nailing for years. They talked plenty. They talked and cared for one another and (sometimes) even fell in love before they (sometimes) passed STDs around like canapés at a cocktail party.

Yeah, I had my share of amoxicillin, too.

And finally, Beth Parsons, my former roommate and Kappa Delta sister . . . the whore. I introduced her to her husband, Dave. She was all weepy fall semester, senior year, that she just couldn't summon the courage to speak with Dave Parsons, Greek god of fraternity row. Yawn. So I approached him one afternoon at a kegger outside the Deke house. They'd set up a beach volleyball court, trucked sand in and had a tournament. Beth and I played for the KD team. Well, I played. Beth just jumped around and tried to keep her bikini top on. I'm the one who finally approached his Holiness. I'm the one who arranged for them to hook up while I played wingman and fended off hoards of horny frat brothers. Not once did I get a 'thank you' from Little Miss Bang Your Fiancé.

What Beth doesn't know is that during senior week, when graduates have the run of the campus for three, blurry, puke-stained days, I came home one afternoon to find Dave Parsons and Scoutmaster Kelly riding one another like cowboys in a Larry McMurtry novel. Kelly even wore a straw hat and a pair of leather boots. Nothing else. At the time I was horrified. The Scoutmaster made me promise never to tell Beth, and I never did. Poor Beth would have been scandalized.

Dave's a lawyer now, out in the Lehigh Valley somewhere, and about as boring as a handful of overcooked rice.

I should send him a copy of Richard's confession, just to stir things up.

Good night, Billy.

Jennifer

October 19

Dear Billy,

Just another thought on Richard's confession. Then I swear I'll let it go. That's high on my list these days: letting things go.

One night back in 1996, we'd been married less than a year. Richard went out drinking with some friends after a Jets game. It was Sunday night, so I stayed home to get my papers graded and lessons planned for Monday morning. I'd been in bed for a few hours when he finally crawled in.

He must have struck out with whatever woman he'd tried to seduce, because he half entered, half fell into our bedroom drunk, stupid, and horny. He smelled of cigar smoke, bourbon, and fresh vomit. I turned him down and suggested he take a shower before passing out or throwing up in bed.

Richard didn't want to hear that. According to him, he was horny and needed sex.

I reiterated that I wasn't about to have sex with him, as horrible as he smelled. I wasn't angry that he'd partied. What the hell, he was hammered, but he'd had fun with friends at a football game. He'd feel awful for work the next day, but I'd forgive him. I sneaked to the living room to sleep on the sofa, but he grabbed me, roughly, surprisingly so, and yanked me into the bedroom, a first for us. Richard had never manhandled me, hit me, or shoved me around. I flashed back to high school and Dad choking Mom as they careened down the hallway. Without thinking, I moved around the bed, kept an open pathway to the apartment door in case I had to run.

He threatened me in a milky slur, then distracted himself trying to get out of his pants. While he fumbled with the belt and zipper, I called 911. I didn't want him arrested, but I also didn't want to get raped in my own apartment by the one man who's supposed to understand when I say 'no.'

By the time the police arrived, he'd tried again to get me out of my clothes, so they charged him with attempted rape and attempted kidnapping. Apparently in New Jersey, if you forcefully carry a person somewhere against his or her will, it's kidnapping, a felony.

Yikes!

They handcuffed him, dragged him down the stairs, and shoved him into the back of the police cruiser while our neighbors watched, giggling to themselves. I nearly died from embarrassment that I'd had my own husband PCed, but I slept through the night with no fear of sexual assault. I'd never thought to tally that as a good thing, but married life has taught me a whole laundry list of unexpected lessons.

The following day, I convinced the assistant district attorney to drop the charges. It cost me a few hours of personal leave and a humiliating meeting with my principal at work. When they finally released him at about 11:30 that morning, he looked like an animated corpse and smelled just a tad worse.

He apologized, showered, and promised never to do it again.

I believed him, made us both lunch, then slept with him.

I should have seen much of this coming.

Jennifer

And no, I never had anyone ask me, drunk or sober, if he could help me trim my pubic hair. Jesus Christ, I pity any and all of the women who ever fell for his bullshit.

And we're done. See you.

October 27

Dear Billy,

Okay, I lied. I do have one last comment on old Dickie boy's confession and *then* we're done. I promise.

People (and by 'people' I mean Myrna and Gary, the only two bold enough to ask me outright) have asked if I miss sex.

Um . . . duh.

I spent twenty years with Johnny Wad. I've had more sex than a crack-smoking, teenage nymphomaniac. Of course I miss sex, just not sex with Richard.

Wait for it . . .

And there it is, Billy. If I miss sex, but I don't miss sex with my ex-husband, then I can only miss sex with a few other people:

1. **Myself.** Nope, I still have that. Thank Christ. Without it, I'd have already greased sixty-two Wegmans customers with an Uzi.
2. **The Varsity Quarterback.** Nope, too much river mud in my butt crack, sort of takes the polish off the experience.
3. **A Couple of Not-So-Memorable Guys During Sophomore Year.** Um . . . yeah; they weren't memorable. I think one of them, Eddie Something, might have been a poetry major.
4. **You.** Yeah, okay. Who knew how resilient fond memories can be?

Strange old world, isn't it?

Jennifer

October 30

William –

Got laid last night.

That quickie email I sent you the other day is what convinced me.

Yup. I got myself good and slutted up – Halloween party; I went as a middle-aged, very redheaded Rita Hayworth – got drunk on godforsaken white wine (no joke, Billy, I'm pretty sure that God Himself forsook this stuff), found a nice boy of about twenty-eight years old, convinced him I was thirty one, took him home, had my merry way with him, READ: 7 minutes of fumbling, 63 seconds of awkward intercourse, 4 seconds of spastic, palsied jerking, and two hours of nap time before I woke him up, and poured him into his car with one of Richard's favorite travel mugs full of black coffee.

I hope he's not dead in a ditch somewhere, now that I think on it. He seemed like a nice boy.

Why? You ask. Why did I do it? Why did I go out specifically to have meaningless, base, improper, and culturally-unacceptable sex with a younger man dressed as Bruce Willis from *Die Hard?*

I'll tell you.

Because Bruce Willis is hot.

Nope, kidding.

Because I can.

And because Richard's done it 163,000 times.

And because it's perfectly acceptable for men to go off whoring when they're lonely, depressed, drunk, horny, or irritated that the Eagles lost to the Cowboys.

But women? Nope. We're never supposed to be horny, never supposed to go off in search of cheap, meaningless human contact, never allowed to enter a bar and shout, 'Who's the lucky sumbitch gettin' some of this tonight?'

Okay, I didn't do that. But I did get laid, and I don't regret it.

All right . . . you got me . . . I do regret one thing; we'll get to that shortly.

Slut, whore, cheap, loose, easy, party girl, tramp, they're just a handful of the derogatory terms our society finds appropriate for women who go to bars, get drunk, and have sex with strangers.

You know what we call men who do that same thing?

Yeah: stud, hero, badass, gigolo, manly, buck, sex addict, Richard Teasdale.

I have to be a harlot; while he gets to be a stud? I don't think so. I spent the past twenty years promising my body, my soul, my love – bone deep, unreserved, full throttle love – my passion, my family, my hopes, my faith, my desire, and my future, my God-whoring future to a man who couldn't wait to get to a bar, get drunk, and "bone a skank" (to quote a phrase from my favorite blog post of all time).

And now where am I? I'm middle aged, lonely, horny, and ready – no, not ready, *needing*, yeah, needing – to get my *self*, my body, my body with all its mileage, back into the game. Why can't I be coveted? Why can't I be sexy? Why can't I get drunk and objectify twenty-eight-year-old men?

Because I'm a mother?

Bullshit.

Because if I do, my friends and neighbors will call me a slut?

Well, you know what I wanna be for Halloween, William Klein? I wanna be a slut.

But not here in Freehold. Maybe up there in Albany.

Because truth be told – and I do tell you the truth, Billy – my only regret last night . . . yeah, you guessed it.

Please, please tell me you think of me every now and then. Please. Because I'm thinking about you.

And no, I don't plan on hitting the bars again any time soon. It was nice to know I've still got it in me, but those 63 seconds weren't worth the $42 I spent on God-awful wine.

We'll do it better, though. Won't we? I think so.

Jennifer

November

There are enzymes that help to convert alcohol into fatty acids. These then cling to my ass, hips, and thighs, because God hates me.

November 3

Hello Billy,

I have some news for you today. I quit drinking.

I didn't quit today; that news would travel about as well as the *Hindenburg*. I quit twenty-nine days ago (well, except for that one slip off the wagon at Halloween, when I had some pretty disappointing sex with a kid who looked like Bruce Willis).

I read somewhere – okay, *People* magazine – that addicts have to go twenty-eight days before they can truly suggest that they've got a handle on their illness. I don't know what makes four weeks the magic number. Perhaps a month off the juice gives anyone's metabolism time enough to say, 'Holy shit, this feels better. Maybe I should keep it up.'

I want to say it's been easy. It hasn't. I've quit before and failed dozens of times. Yet I never thought of it as failing. I simply figured I'd gone back to drinking, on a few occasions triumphantly. I'd never gone two weeks before, never mind twenty-nine days . . . one full day into Week #5. Maybe that's the secret: our bodies need to feel like we've got a month in the books. Month #1 leads to Month#2 and so on until we die, sober and fit and looking fabulous (except for the dead bit, naturally).

A few things helped me get this far, and since I'm writing to you, I won't sugar coat any of them.

Number 1: You. If I ever see you again, I'm determined to be sober. I've more than hinted at my willingness to come find you. If I ever work up the courage to drive to Albany and knock on your door, I'll need all my IQ points intact to make an indelible impression that convinces you how wrong you were to leave me in New Brunswick that summer. Showing up hammered and drooling feels like it'd be a mistake. Right?

Number 2: Drinking from a wine glass between 5:00 and 7:00 pm. I haven't a clue why this works, but every time I get a craving, I pour some fruit juice or flavored water into a crystal wine glass, and I sip as if it's just arrived from the Loire Valley. Does it bother me that I'm deliberately lying to myself or trying to fool my brain into believing I'm sipping wine? Not at all. I've been lying to myself for over three decades; at least this time it might lead to something useful.

Number 3: Lots of different sugars. This took some legitimate research on my part, and I was interested to discover that my body isn't addicted to feeling drunk. (That's good news; otherwise, just shoot me.) Rather, my body is addicted to the process of converting alcohol into fatty acids, and then – because I often starve myself when I drink – into glycogen to fuel my cells. I joked with you about this in an email a few weeks back, when I talked about drinking beer and wine to train for the New York Marathon. Who knew how right I'd been? The cravings I feel at 9:15 in the morning aren't cravings to get drunk or to feel drunk or to vomit into the snapdragons. Instead, cravings are my body's way of saying, 'Good morning, we're awake now and ready to convert more of those alcohol molecules into fat so you can stay alive, dumbass. How about a Bloody Mary?'

To fool my body at a molecular level, more difficult to do, I've started mixing up the sugars I ingest, diversifying my diet in an effort to retrain my cells to behave themselves. Some days it's fruit and sugar-free fruit juice. Other days it's dairy, plenty of lactose, and yummy cheese. And sometimes I mainline sucrose, just for the abrupt metabolic shift, and eat handfuls of M&Ms, Gummi bears, and Skittles. My sons enjoy those days particularly. With a bowl of ice cream at night, I can combine lactose and sucrose, and ensure that if I do succeed in beating alcohol, I'll be a dyed-in-the-wool junk food addict and type-II diabetes victim.

You see, there are enzymes that help to convert alcohol into fatty acids. These then cling to my ass, hips, and thighs, because God hates me. However, they don't cling long, because I often refuse to eat when I'm drinking heavily, so my body engages in a diabolical process called Gluconeogenesis, a fancy way of saying, 'survive without carbs.' By mixing up the sugars in my diet, I keep my cells working on all different kinds of carbohydrates while I slowly, slowly, slowly clear those alcohol-processing enzymes from my bloodstream.

Think of it like this: The amount of enzyme the average non-drinker needs to convert an occasional alcohol molecule into fat is, let's say, one shot glass full. The amount of enzyme currently flooding my system like an Old Testament disaster is, let's say, one football stadium full. Unless I keep my cells on a strict glycolysis regimen, my body will crave alcohol molecules just to give those chemicals something to do.

As long as those nice people in Scandinavia keep storing alcohol molecules in convenient, easy-access vodka bottles, I'll most likely struggle to walk past a liquor store without pressing my face to the glass like a kid outside the Wonka factory.

As an aside, did you know that IHOP customers pour over 2.5 million gallons of syrup each year? I can lay claim to nearly a gallon myself in the past four weeks. Mama's gotta have her sugar.

Number 4: Being busy during cocktail hour. This one's easy. As a single mom, I'm never at a loss for stuff to get done. Shifting errands, workouts, reading time with Homer, *anything* to the hours between 4:00 and 7:00, I can fool myself into adopting a manic desire to finish unfinished tasks rather than a manic need for alcohol in my bloodstream. The boys groaned at this for a few days, because we don't eat dinner now until nearly 7:30, but all the Skittles, Gummi bears, and pancake syrup helps to quiet them down.

Mother of the Year, that's me!

Number 5: Use my own obsessive nature against me. This one's self-destructive but effective. For every day that I manage to go without a drink, I put a red X in our family calendar. The boys and I do it right before going to bed, and it's quickly become an important shared ritual. After a week, my obsessive need for tidy, orderly task completion took over, and I actually craved a neat row of red Xs more than I craved a glass of wine.

How goddamned crazy is that?

I know my sons will come to me at 9:00 every night, looking for confirmation that I've earned another red X. I don't want to let them down, so I fight off the need for booze, go running, or stuff a handful of syrup-covered M&Ms into my mouth. Now that I've nearly filled the calendar with red Xs, I don't know that I'll ever drink again. Missing a day, failing to earn my X would mean leaving a space blank in the calendar. That'd be inexcusable among my sons and upsetting enough for me that I'd have to get back into therapy, just to deal with my tidy-X compulsion!

Don't worry; if you ever see me again, I promise not to be insane.

I admit that I am just a bit anxious about what I'll do when we turn the page to a blank month in the calendar. Without any red Xs on the page, I wonder if it'll be more difficult to avoid drinking and how many Xs I'll have to accumulate in a new month before my compulsive neurosis takes over again. I'll let you know.

And finally, Number 6: My father. I bet you hadn't expected him to show up again, particularly in a letter about tallying four weeks of good behavior.

Yup, Dad. He's been great. I'm staggered. He calls or texts a couple of times each week just to encourage me. He came over one morning when I was two or three days into this adventure and took all my booze, every drop, in a cardboard box. He loaded it into the bed of his truck, handed me a box of Dunkin' Donuts and made me promise to call him before buying a drink, accepting a drink, or beating a bottle of Mad Dog 20/20 out of a homeless person. I laughed; he didn't. Instead, he stood there, waiting for me to promise.

I haven't called him yet. He checks in frequently enough that I don't have time to get a craving, to accept a drink from a friend, or to go slumming for chemically-aged wine. I've only seen him four times since I started, and each time he's either handed me a bag of candy, a half gallon of ice cream, or a dozen donuts. The man knows his sugars; I've got to give him that. Last week, I jokingly asked if he had any cigarettes. He said, 'No, but I'll get you a pack if you think it'll help. You won't get hooked on the nails after just one pack. Although, they might make you sick.'

He's rooting for me, and I love him for it. The man I swore I'd one day run over with a bulldozer wakes up every day wondering how he can be a better support system for a daughter who's decided to sober up. Not bad. And while neither of us has mentioned it, we both know that I haven't been to his house for dinner in the past twenty-nine days. Dad can't get from 4:00 pm to 8:00 pm without drinking. He lost that battle years ago. We both know that I'm not yet ready to stand around while he drinks a half bottle of red wine by himself. My liver would bust out and splash on the floor. So I've stayed away, and he's not mentioned it. That's been good for both of us; he feels as though he's helping (he is), and I feel sober (I am).

When I do see him, it's generally pretty early in the morning. Like any seventy-three year old, he's awake by 5:00 am. The boys and I get moving by 7:00 most days, giving Dad two hours to get to the store, the Dunkin' Donuts, or the coffee shop to pick up whatever polysaccharide he's decided will help my body outdistance its morning craving.

He's a bit heavy handed on the donuts. I prefer the pumpkin-spice lattes, but I'm not complaining.

Also, Dad doesn't call in the evenings. For years he'd get a little drunk, then sit at the kitchen table with the phone and whatever bottle he'd opened while helping Mom get dinner ready. He'd make drunk phone calls to my brother, me, his old friends, whomever, as he finished the bottle and grew ever less coherent. He's not called once after 4:00 pm, not since the evening I told him I was going to quit and he showed up to collect all my bottles. Some of those evening phone calls can be trying. He gets himself pretty loose, decides on the evening's topic – anything from Middle Eastern politics to the Lehman Brother's crash to Aunt Grace's tendency to serve ham rather than turkey for Thanksgiving – and he holds forth for anyone who'll listen. I listen. My brother listens, so he calls and stammers and repeats himself in an embarrassing display of what six decades of alcohol can do. I don't know what shoulder angel has been shouting in his ear that it's a mistake to dial my number during happy hour, but he's been listening. Once I get a handle on my cravings – which still amount to every cell in my body screaming in unison, 'Give us wine!' – I'll start calling him. He'll appreciate that.

The past four weeks have applied a much-needed salve to my relationship with my father. I wouldn't have believed it could happen, and while we're not chummy and hanging out together on weekends, I do believe he's determined for me to avoid a couple of his more crippling lifelong mistakes.

What's also interesting as I look back on the past four weeks (and ahead to the next four) is my dire need for effective interventions that do not involve drinking. I've been shocked at the number of times in the past twenty years that I've avoided stressful, painful, or embarrassing situations simply by reaching for a wine bottle. Until last week, I'd never admitted how deftly alcohol became my go-to strategy to deal with life's challenges. Other than running and writing to you, Billy, I've not had a coping strategy other than drinking since I graduated from high school in 1989.

Stressful day at work? Oh, look there's wine.

Richard misbehaving? Hey, who needs a vodka tonic?

My father driving my mother crazy? No worries, there's tequila.

Imminent nuclear attack coming to North Jersey? Tap that keg, and grab your SPF 8,000!

People magazine failed to mention that particular tidbit. Sure, my body might be addicted to the process of converting alcohol into fatty acids. Groovy. But my softening brain is addicted to reaching for that bottle every time I experience discomfort, pain, or stress.

That's alcoholism.

It's a big rock up a steep hill, but I'm pushing.

I'll buy you an iced tea when I finally see you. (I like them best with crushed Oreos and maple syrup.)

See you at the juice bar,

Jennifer

November 28

Hey,

I hate not drinking. My body's in full retreat. I had to pull over today just to barf on the side of Route 9 in Freehold. (Remember those enzymes I mentioned? Yeah, they're not quite flushed out yet.) Only about 800 cars went by while I dry heaved into the bushes. Probably sixty percent of them knew me, knew I'd been screwed by my douche bag ex-husband, knew I'd been coping for the past two decades with booze.

Shit. Shit. Bugger. Shit.

I hate these regrets. With no wine, they're bigger, brighter, more vocal, better dressed, nicely appointed, well educated, shiny, fuck, shit, fuck, shit.

I hate regrets. Regretting takes so much out of me, and all day I've got Homer, Danny, and Gerry needing me to keep my act together.

I'm not going to make it.

Come save me. Come save me; I'm damaged goods. I'm in my forties. Jesus, that's a long time, a long list of regrets, Billy.

Ugh. Some days are harder than others. I can't do too much more of this. I'm taking down the mirrors in my house; they make it worse.

Jennifer

December

I have no idea if pregnant gorillas get furious. I imagine they must.

December 11

Dear Billy,

Not drinking for the past nine weeks has brought some much-needed clarity to a few areas of my life that had been alarmingly out of focus.

I'm thankful for that.

Also, I've softened a bit on my father. When I'm not scratching at my palms, drinking tomato juice from a wine glass, or gobbling Swedish fish, I've been able to reflect soberly enough to understand Dad better. Sure, I've always known that his upbringing and his background essentially doomed him to alcoholism and nicotine addiction as early as the mid-1950s. Yet it wasn't until I tried quitting that I understood how challenging it must have been for him, how often he had probably tried to beat his habits, and how disheartening it would have been for him to fail again and again. He didn't have an alcoholic father to inspire him to quit. Amusingly, I do. And one of these days I'll let him know what an odd and unexpected role his demons played in my getting at least this far.

I'm not suggesting that I've got my Booze Beast whipped. Shit, no. While my cravings have eased off in the past week, they've certainly not vanished, just throttled back. The wrong comment from Richard, a bout of self-loathing, a difficult night with my boys, and I could be right back in that wine bottle, swimming for Calais.

About six months back, when Richard and I considered 'pistols at dawn' a reasonable clause in our divorce agreement, I needed help. If you read over some of the emails I sent, you'll not have to look far to find bitterness, anger, frustration: my most appealing traits. We'd gone to all points of the compass trying to reach an amicable settlement agreement. Filing 'irreconcilable differences' with a signed agreement would save us each $25,000 in attorney's fees. It made sense. We needed a divorce; we *didn't* need another indigestible helping of pointless debt.

I drafted a plan he hated. He drafted a plan I hated. We forced ourselves to sit together (in a public place) to draft an agreement we both liked – at first – but then hated the next morning. I edited it. He edited it. We drove over the same dead cats, flattening them *ad nauseum* until we agreed that we disagreed, then agreed to hire lawyers.

By that time, *amicable* had disappeared from our lexicon, must've been erased during one of those furious 4:00 am editing sessions.

My lawyer, a coked-up grizzly bear with clear anger management needs, advised me never to speak with Richard again, to communicate through her only, and to go for the kill.

I considered this for about an hour, beat my compassionate nature senseless with the help of an Alabama Slammer, then called her back to say, 'Okay, kill him.'

Through the phone I could hear her sucking marrow from puppy bones. 'I'll redraft the agreement and give him a week to sign it. If he doesn't we'll file and go to court.'

'Irreconcilable differences?'

'Hell no,' CHOMP, SUCK, SPLASH (another baby Labradoodle in the stew pot). 'We're filing abandonment and adultery. I wanna add that buggery reference as well. That'll shut him up.'

Oh, shit.

You remember that confession I let you read? Yeah well, I let my lawyer read it, too.

We knew I was going to win.

But I feared that Richard would read the court papers, realize I'd photocopied his confession, and show up at my house with a gun or a howitzer. I had no idea what to do. He didn't have a long and storied history of getting drunk and beating me up. However, he did have a track record for losing his temper and lashing out. The night he threw the vodka bottle at me, I'd argued with him about whether or not to hold Danny back from Kindergarten for a year. We'd navigated ten thousand similar conversations about similar topics throughout our marriage, just day-in, day-out stuff that husbands and wives have to sort through on the road to side-by-side cemetery plots. Why Richard decided to bean me with an empty Grey Goose bottle wasn't because he truly cared whether Danny spent another year at home. It was because he was drunk, and he knew I was right. My ex-husband has never been able to stomach the notion that I've outwitted him. I rarely tried to make him feel stupid; I simply argued my side of whatever topic we discussed. When he realized he'd been wrong, Richard lashed out. Most often he used insults: typical asshole guy stuff. But periodically he'd take a swing at me, throw a bottle, break a glass, smash a vase: spoiled brat stuff.

When he received court papers listing every girlfriend, every tryst, every last scrap and sentence of his confession, he'd know immediately that he'd lost to me. That's what would drive him to homicidal rage. (I use the phrase lightly, but that frames it well: *homicidal rage*.) He'd drink a bottle of bourbon, load his gun (a Glock 9 mm my father helped him buy at a gun show out in Warren County), and he'd drive over here, shoot me and then shoot himself. Our boys would watch the whole grisly scene unfold.

I prayed he wouldn't shoot them, didn't honestly believe he would, but prayed regardless.

I joke about it now, mention it in passing, shrug, shake my head, pass it off, whatever. But that night I kept the boys in the house, pulled the shades, turned off lamps and unnecessary lights, and hunkered down in my bedroom with my sons huddled around me.

Then I thought of my father; any port in a storm, right?

I called him, and he arrived fifteen minutes later. He wore an Asbury Park PD flak vest and carried the same silver revolver I'd used to frighten him out of the house the night he called me a whore's cunt and nearly choked my mother to death. (I sent you that bedtime story a few months back. I call it 'Velveeta Processed Cheese.')

The boys thought Grandpa looked ridiculous. He smiled and told them he was thinking about coming out of retirement and wanted to know if they liked his old outfit.

When we got them to bed, Dad and I tiptoed to the kitchen.

'You think that's necessary?' I asked.

He fussed in the cabinets, looking for coffee. I didn't help; it gave him an opportunity to say what he needed to say without looking at me. I grinned while I watched him, tallying yet another gene he and I shared: Be busy during serious conversations.

I asked, 'You want me to make you some?'

'Nah, I got it.' He spooned enough grounds into the filter to fill a fifty-five-gallon drum. It'd be strong enough to kill cancer in an elephant. 'Where's the pot?'

I found it in the dishwasher. 'Dad, I don't really think that –'

'Never mind,' he cut me off. 'It's not worth taking the chance. Just when you think it can't happen to you. You know?'

'Yeah.'

'Anyway,' he turned his back to me, poured water slowly into my coffeemaker. 'Anyway, it's my job to protect you, honey. There's no . . . I dunno . . . nothing at all, you know, that can keep me from that.' He slid the pot into place, pressed BREW. 'You'll understand one day.'

'I understand, Dad.'

He changed the subject. 'You can go to bed, honey. I'll wait on the porch.'

'Dad –'

'Don't worry. I'm not gonna shoot him –'

'Yes, you are.'

'Hmm . . . yeah, okay. Maybe I'll shoot him.' He rooted around inside the fridge. 'You got any of that Irish creamer stuff?'

'Ah . . . no, just the Hazelnut.'

'Damn,' he found it, shook it, looked it over distrustfully. 'All right.'

'Dad?'

'I'll be on the porch. I brought a book.' My kitchen ballooned slowly with the aroma of strong coffee.

I shook my head in amusement. The folks over at Maxwell House wouldn't be broadcasting this commercial. I said, 'Thanks, Dad. You need anything?'

'Irish creamer. I'll get you some tomorrow.'

'Really?'

'Nothing. I'm fine.'

'He won't show up.'

'I hope he does.'

'You'll go to prison,' I warned.

'Nah,' he poured coffee into a Rutgers University travel mug, topped it with about three ounces of hazelnut creamer. 'I'll just scare him.'

'He knows you aren't here all the time.'

'Exactly,' he sipped. 'God, that's shit.'

'Whaddya mean? Exactly?'

'I'm not always here,' he started for the front door. 'Who knows when maybe I'll be at his house? Or behind his house? Or in his garage? In his closet? I'm retired. I've got lots of bullets and lots of time.'

'Good night, Dad,' I hugged him, careful not to spill his motor oil.

'Good night, honey.' And the man I'd blamed for my neuroses, my alcoholism, my perfectionist's urge to please, my tendency to place others' needs before my own, and my derisive outlook on marriage stood an all-night vigil on my front porch, waiting for my drunk, estranged husband to show up for a gunfight.

I lay awake for an hour or so, worrying, then slept soundly.

At 7:30 the following morning, I found my father and Homer eating coffee cake and drinking milk on my front porch. Dad looked worn to the nub, but he propped Homer up on his knee and read him 'The 500 Hats of Bartholomew Cubbins.' Bright, exhilarating relief walloped me, and I braced myself against the door jamb to keep from falling into the hedges.

I made breakfast; it was the least I could do. Homer fed pancakes to the dog and asked for a hat that would change shape and color every time he pulled it off his head.

Dad spent the next two nights on my porch until I finally heard from my lawyer that Richard had signed the papers. We popped open a bottle of champagne to celebrate. The boys chased the cork like a fly ball into the back yard.

I opened another bottle when a friend texted that Richard had flown to San Diego to celebrate his divorce in warm weather. The Universe had been flashing TILT, but I could feel it righting itself, and strangely, I was pleased to have Dad around. Mom stopped by in the evenings, helped me make dinner and get the kids to bed, but she didn't sleep over. My father did.

That last night, I watched shadows morph across the ceiling in my bedroom as I tried to recall exactly what he'd said. It's curious what sticks to my Teflon-coated brain, but I think I retrieved this one whole, without any dings: *Anyway, it's my job to protect you, honey. There's no . . . I dunno . . . nothing at all, you know, that can keep me from that. You'll understand one day.*

I like that bit. It's another memory for my bottom drawer. Remember the bottom drawer, Billy? You been paying attention?

By the weekend, I'd been the recipient of enough incendiary texts from Richard that I felt safe. If he was angry enough to call me an 'obese bitch' in twenty-seven drunken texts from the veranda of the Del Coronado, he probably wasn't angry enough to drive over here and shoot me. I tallied that as a good thing and encouraged my father to go home and sleep in his own bed. He'd earned a couple of nights' vacation.

He hung around for a pizza and a bit of goofing off with the boys. My mother showed up later with ice cream, and they watched a movie with Homer while I ironed shirts in a watery reproduction of a forty-year-old memory. Later, when they left, I hugged Dad and thanked him again. I wanted badly to take him by the shoulders and say, 'Your mother's been dead for forty-four years, and Aunt Molly's been gone over forty. It's about time you forgave yourself and moved on. You and Mom have a bunch of good years left. Why not enjoy them?'

But I didn't. Perfectly planned and delivered lines like that only exist in the movies. Out here on planet Earth they're among my best laid plans, which often spoil before the expiration date. So Mom piled him into the truck, and they drove off. Dad carried his APPD duffel bag. I figured that's where he had the silver revolver stashed, that .357 werewolf killer that had never killed a werewolf.

I finished the last of whatever bottle of wine we'd opened and stole another slice of pizza. The boys slept; the dog wandered off somewhere, and in the quiet moment God allowed me to enjoy before kicking me back onto the field of play, I let fear battle with anticipation for possession of my soul. I figured one of them would win, but it wouldn't be soon. What the hell, I had time. And my life back.

Dad called when they got home. I knew he would. I didn't talk with him for long; I'd been touched by his protective Papa Bear compulsion, but like anything, he didn't know when to crank the volume down a notch. Before hanging up, I missed another chance to tell him how I felt. I opened my mouth to deliver my perfectly-planned line, and nothing useful emerged. What if I encouraged him to forgive himself and he couldn't do it? No sense in making things worse, right?

I know: I'm such a pussy.

As much as I wish he could learn to forgive himself for bonehead moves he made four decades ago, that line's a lot easier to type than to execute. How often do you manage to forgive yourself for being human, Billy? If you're like me, it isn't too often. Some of us get to pay a long, hard mortgage for mistakes we made in our youth.

(But you could help me overcome one of them. Whaddya say?)

Anyway, I failed to reach out to Dad, but I don't mind much. I keep telling myself that he could read my thoughts. He knows what I hope for him, even though he gets me pregnant-gorilla furious several times a month.

And I was divorced. Nothing to it really.

Okay, that's a lie. It sucked snot off a grasshopper's ass.

These days, I'm happy to report that anticipation has a solid lead over fear. Although fear's a tough competitor and, like a drunk Cossack, might never give in. Oh, and I have no idea if pregnant gorillas get furious. I imagine they must.

Soberly (heh),

Jennifer

January

'Good morning, Grandpa,' he grinned like the pathological, career criminal he is, and asked, 'What the hell are you doing?'

January 3

Hey,

Yeah, shit: I fell off the goddamned wagon again. Just for the night, and I climbed back on, but I'm pretty frigging disappointed with myself.

Do you remember being a kid and having your mother serve you food with the burned side down? Did she ever do that? My mom did from time to time, not because she was malicious, just because it was all we had. We could never afford to throw food away, no matter how scorched. Anyway, remember that disappointment, the first time you realized your mother would resort to sleight of hand to get you to eat a blackened grilled cheese sandwich? That's how irritated I am with myself.

And I've got 43 metaphors for falling off the wagon. I might scribble them all out in a boring slam poem about drunk, middle-aged losers. But not today.

Today, I'll leave you with that highball full of disappointment: burned-side-down disappointment.

That's me today. Don't worry, though; I'm back on the wagon. And hopeful.

I'll be a confident jackass again tomorrow or Monday. I promise.

Jennifer

PS: It was wine, by the way. I took the boys out for pizza, and the aroma got to me. Strange how powerful those sensory memories can be. I had Diet Coke at the restaurant and knew before we got home that I was a goner. I should've called my father but didn't have the strength to listen as he slurred me through a craving. (Okay, that wasn't fair; he's been pretty great so far.) So I put the guys to bed and poured a glass – a big glass – from a nice bottle I'd been saving for Danny's college graduation. Stupid.

I dropped the rest off at Myrna's this morning, did it on purpose for the cathartic walk of shame up her driveway. She frowned appropriately. Duly chided, I slinked away. I'm sure she'll finish it off later, maybe even toast my sobriety.

January 11

Dear Billy,

The delicate soap bubble protecting my father and me the week of my divorce popped a few days later.

I told you it would.

He called that Wednesday evening, drinking, drooling, slurring, and voting Democrat. Okay, I'm kidding; my father's never been *that* drunk. To him, a planet ruled by Karl Rove and Dick Cheney makes perfect sense. You know the one: where white, Northern Europeans can travel anywhere in the world, because white, Northern Europeans lead every country, and white, Northern Europeans are the only ones who control weapons, technology, scientific research, education, agriculture, economics, religion (the one with Jesus), public health programs, and the price of a one-day pass to EPCOT. It's a shiny, colorful, plastic world where everyone pays $89.50 to get in, but they get to have a picture taken with Goofy (the CEO of Goldman Sachs) and Daffy Duck (a Ronald Reagan impersonator) after a lunch of deep-fried whateveritis.

Who gets that polluted on a Wednesday?

Looking back, it wasn't a big deal, but I was irritated and mention it here to demonstrate yet again that nothing much changes.

He called that night, because he'd finished half a bottle of bourbon and decided that I needed a couple of parenting lessons.

No laughing!

Okay, go ahead; laugh. It's funny. Getting parenting lessons from my father is like getting dental hygiene tips from a meth addict.

While Dad stayed here, protecting me from my potentially-homicidal ex-husband, he was often the first person in the house to see Homer. I don't sleep late, but it's been a couple of years since I've given a damn to greet the sunrise. Every now and then (okay, every morning) Homer is up before me. It's not surprising: he lives on carbohydrates. He's got all the energy of an Intercontinental Ballistic Missile headed for Moscow. Most mornings he either wanders into my room and climbs on the bed, or he sneaks into Danny's room and turns on the television. I've tried a variety of interventions, but Monmouth County Revised Statutes forbid me from duct taping him into his bed or locking him in a closet.

While Dad was here, Homer carried a blanket and a storybook onto the porch, where my father read to him over donuts and milk. (When Dad's around there are always donuts. They replenish themselves magically, like loaves and fishes.)

Apparently – I wasn't awake for this, so I'm speculating – one morning, Homer stepped onto the porch, and instead of saying, 'Good morning, Grandpa,' he grinned like the pathological, career criminal he is, and asked, 'What the hell are you doing?'

Rather than laughing, my father nearly shot himself in the leg. Thankfully, he didn't start screaming obscenities at my three year old, which would have been his response thirty-five years ago, so we're making progress! Instead, Dad beckoned Homer over, lifted him onto his lap, and said, 'You shouldn't say that word.'

'Hell?'

'Right. That's a bad word.'

'Why, Grandpa?'

I'm sure he groped for an appropriate response here; imagine an uncomfortable pause. 'Because it hurts Mommy's feelings.' And then to hammer the point home, 'and Grandma's feelings.' (Please note: even at his age, my father is not above emotional manipulation to get his way.)

Homer pressed on. 'Why, Grandpa?'

'Well, kiddo, some words are just bad.'

And Homer Watson Teasdale, nefarious leader of an international terror organization determined to take over the Ben & Jerry's factory, looked wonderingly into his grandfather's eyes, and asked, 'You mean like "shit" and "fucking"?'

No gunshots woke me, so I figure Dad survived the conversation without shooting himself. However, I'd bet next week's grocery money that he'd already unloaded the pistol, so the hammer clicked on an empty chamber. I like the idea that Dad contained his rage until three days later. It showed surprising restraint. He knew I was on edge. Rather than blow up on the very day that I expected Richard to shoot me, he somehow compartmentalized his anger at my inability to raise Homer and saved it for a drunk weeknight when he could deliver it like an unexpected present.

When he finally called, he was both drunk and curious:

DAD: 'How could you use such language in front of a little kid like that?'

ME: 'I don't use that language in front of him.' (READ: 'I learned from you, knuckle dragger.')

DAD: 'You must be. Who else is he with?'

ME: 'He heard it in one of Danny's Eminem songs.' (READ: 'You have no idea what I'm talking about.')

DAD: 'M&M? The candy? What are you talking about? The kid said "shit" and "fucking" like he was ordering a pizza.'

ME: 'Eminem, Dad. Not the candy, the singer.' (READ: See? I told you.')

DAD: 'What kind of parent talks that way in front of a two year old?'

ME: 'I don't, Dad. I told you that already. And he's three.' (READ: 'You did, doofus every day.')

DAD: 'Three? What three year old knows the word "fucking"?'

ME: 'I don't know.' (READ: 'I did!')

DAD: 'Get rid of that song. What the hell's the matter with you?'

ME: 'I will, Dad.' (READ: 'Wow, I thought you'd missed the song reference entirely.')

When we hung up, I raved a bit to the boys, noting that their grandfather was, at that moment, tearing a rotator cuff patting himself on the back because he had raised better children than I had. Danny laughed; he's no dummy. 'Mom, does that mean Grandpa's calling us bad kids?'

'Nah,' I said. 'He'd cut off his own head before he said anything negative about you guys. He's just angry with me because Homer swears.'

'Homer swears all the time,' Gerry said. 'You can't stop him. It's kinda funny.'

'It's NOT funny.' I tried reprimanding them without laughing. 'Every time Homer drops an f-bomb, I look like a bad parent. And all the while it's you two felons who are exposing him to foul-mouthed hip-hop artists and Rated-R movies!'

Gerry applied logic and reason, readily defeating me. 'Mom, would you rather we expose him to hip-hop with no swear words?'

'Is there any?'

They answered in unison. 'No.'

'I didn't think so.'

Danny asked, 'Did Grandpa raise you?'

I cocked an eyebrow. Gerry laughed hard enough to snort. I

said, 'A little . . . he taught me how to cut grass, how to mix margaritas, how to catch fish, and how to swear, even worse than Homer!'

And the hands of time clicked off another ten-millionth of an eon. We celebrated with a rousing, kitchen-wide, hip-hop dance party, featuring JayZ and a bowl of peanut M&Ms in Grandpa's honor. Everyone danced, even Homer.

I think Hollywood lies to us, (in case you hadn't noticed). People don't change. Or if they do, it's almost never the vast, soul-cleansing shift that comes from realizing that you've got just one shot at redemption. I think those stories, all of them, should get boxed up and burned in a fascist ceremony protesting all sappy, happy endings. There'd be plenty of brown shirts and goose stepping and burning images of Jennifer Aniston and Kate Hudson.

Has my father changed? Sure. He now prefers Hazelnut coffee creamer to Irish Cream. Is that a big deal? It is if you prefer a sweet, nutty flavor to a Baileys, hey-this-tastes-like-Christmas flavor. Otherwise, that's all we've got. Is he going to stop drinking and enjoy a few sober years with my mother while they're still getting around well? Nope. Is he going to forgive himself for his mother, his sister, my mother, and sixty years of self-destructive behavior? Not a chance. Is he going to admit that he needs help and wants his twilight years to be scarred by fewer hangovers? Nah.

People don't change, not really. I know that's an expensive brand of cynicism, but I've not seen many examples of adults who get their shit together and turn their lives around.

If I'm telling the truth here, though, I'm doomed. Because twenty years ago I grabbed a shovel and helped to dig much of the hole that's currently keeping me prisoner.

I quit drinking. That's a step.

And I've got legal proof that I'm no longer a fifty-percent partner in that purgatorial relationship. That's two.

And I'm still writing to you, over a year later, still telling the truth and missing you and wishing that we'd never met that night in the Ratskeller, August 18, 1992. What the hell were we thinking?

But there's no sense piling on the regrets. I've weathered enough regrets this year to fill a John Irving novel. I'm done regretting. I'm just not done missing you or thinking *what if.*

What if, Billy?

Jennifer

And another thing . . . I spent the past forty years resenting my father because he wouldn't change. I was angry and overlooked the fact that he's *always* been a guy who would spend three nights, armed, on my porch, swatting mosquitoes and waiting for a gunfight. He was *always* the guy who would swim through sharks, crawl through a burning building, wrestle Lawrence Taylor, or climb Mount Everest to bring me a sweater.

Forty years feels like a long time to be angry.

If I'm going to wander through middle age single and raising three boys, I've got to try harder to keep his demons and my demons in different police lineups. If I'm going to be old, Billy, I ought to be fair.

January 12

Billy,

You see . . . I have to forgive my father. I can't forgive Richard, so I forgive Dad. I'm a single woman raising three boys (there's a bit of situational irony for you). If all men are unforgivable twats, what hope is there for me as I try to raise three of them alone?

That's today's dilemma.

Jennifer

February

Cecil B. DeMille, John Ford, Steven Spielberg and Fyodor Dostoyevsky, working together, could scarcely create embarrassment with this depth and breadth.

February 5

Billy –

I saw Myrna today. She told me.

    I don't know what to say. I just hope against lost, buried, and drowned hope that you haven't logged in here and read these notes.

    It'll be a while before I talk with Myrna again. I love her, so I'll probably forgive her some day. Just not yet.

    To be honest, I started these notes – *emails to nowhere*; I guess you can call them – on the advice of my therapist, Dr. Deborah Lane. She's a genius who navigated a couple of sessions with me, realized that I am a verbal animal to my bone marrow, and suggested I put that trait to work as I pushed through my divorce and the scabs it left on my elbows and knees . . . heart, soul, self image, whatever.

    It worked. Writing to you (or pretending to write to you) has been the best therapy I've had in decades. Why wouldn't it be? How often do you get to be perfectly, nakedly honest with someone? That's not rhetorical. I think it's not too often, quite rare. But it's what I needed, and you were . . . *are* . . . the perfect recipient for all of these musings.

    Why?

    Jesus, Billy, don't ask me that.

    Because you're where I want my life to go next. You're the next chapter I'm hoping to live.

    There. Have a handful of warm, sloppy honesty. That's about the best I can do.

    (Awaiting your response.)

    All right then, let's have it. Are you in here with me?

    (Awaiting your response.)

    Fess up.

    (Awaiting your response.)

    Can I come to Albany, buy you an iced tea, and hear your 350 pages worth? I double-dog dare you.

Let me know,

Jennifer

PS: Any time I've ever imagined embarrassment, I was only kidding myself. This is embarrassment on an epic scale. Cecil B. DeMille, John Ford, Steven Spielberg and Fyodor Dostoyevsky, working together, could scarcely create embarrassment with this depth and breadth.

But if you read this, and you're still willing to see me, then we're in pretty good shape, because you could be just about anything short of a mass murdering, plague carrying, truss wearing, middle school gym teacher with a mole on your face, and it'd be an improvement for me. See? I'm finding the joy.

February 17

Dear Billy —

I haven't heard anything from you. I admit I've been hopeful. I don't know what to say, because I'm all upside down on this. If you're half the person I imagine, then you'd never read another's private thoughts. Yet if you're thinking about me like I think about you, well, shit, then you're probably tempted to look this stuff over. And if you're tempted and you give in, then I'm happy. There's nothing wrong with that, even though it looks bad on paper.

I've spent over eighteen months writing these notes to you, and I've never lied.

Granted, this isn't a comprehensive photo album of the past two decades, but it's a hell of an honest start.

So . . . yes, screw it, I hope you're reading every word. Myrna's a bitch for writing to you, a bigger bitch for confessing it, and a tragic inconceivable bitch for being right about me. Once I got over being pissed at her, I loved her for forcing us . . . okay, *me* . . . to deal with this.

But that's not why I'm writing today.

I have another confession.

Richard showed up the other night.

He waited until he knew the boys would be asleep, then he texted from my driveway. I locked the dog up, so he wouldn't bark and wake the kids. My breath came in frightening ragged gasps the whole time I struggled to get him into my bedroom. He's not dumb and knew I was up to something, so I nearly had to drag him down the hall by his collar.

I tried cleaning myself up before opening the front door. I'd started sweating and couldn't stop. It might have been twelve degrees outside, and I'd have been wiping immutable beads of sweat from my hairline. I looked like I'd been dragged behind a cattle drive. In my robe and penny loafers, I tiptoed out front and opened the door.

I didn't unlatch the screen.

Richard Allen Teasdale — the man who convinced me to leave you — stood on my front porch looking like an over-the-hill Abercrombie & Fitch model. Lean, muscular, tan (in February! Who's tan in New Jersey in February?) with cute blonde highlights in his virile mop of sandy-brown hair. He'd let a few days of Matthew

McConaughey scruff sprout along his jaw, and his smile – recently touched up – shone white in my porch light as if he'd not been guzzling coffee and red wine for twenty-five years. In battered cargo khakis and a wash-and-wear sweater, he appeared as comfortably untidy as any perfect, mail-order Adonis I'd ever imagined. Richard could give lessons to aging Hollywood stars. No joke. He was beautiful, sculpted from marble and bronze by some gay Italian master.

I wanted him. He'd been mine for two decades, and I wanted him back. Who wouldn't? I have sex fantasies of Ryan Gosling using my inner thigh as a pillow. Richard looked like Ryan Gosling wishes he could look: the perfect amalgam of effort and laziness, of fitness and wrinkle. Women around the globe would get damp just looking at him. Many did, upwards of thirty that I knew about anyway.

He carried a bottle of *Château Lafite Rothschild*, the 1978 *Pauillac*, and a dozen red roses because he knows I'm a sucker for tradition. We both knew he could have found an equally-impressive wine for $500 less, but that's not Richard's style.

And tied fast to the white ribbon holding his clutch of roses together? A diamond ring, probably a carat-and-a-half, nothing appalling, but enough to catch the porch light and make his point.

I sighed. 'What are you doing here? Are you drunk?'

'Completely sober,' he said through the screen. 'Haven't had a drink in nine days. The boys told me you were off the grape juice, so I figured I'd try it, too.'

'Good for you,' I didn't want to encourage him, but I liked the idea that the boys' father would be sober when they were around. 'It's been a long time. My body needed a break.'

'Looks okay to me,' he glanced at my robe, nothing off-putting or grotesque, but enough to let me know what he had in mind.

'What do you want, Richard?'

'I want you, Jenny. I want us back. I've been awful to you and to the kids, and I can't believe I'm going to grow old and wake up some day in that house by myself.' He gestured down the street with the wine bottle as if *Belle Terre* and his bachelor pad might sit somewhere just offstage. 'Can I . . . can I come in? Can we talk?'

'We're talking fine,' I said.

He caught me looking at the old latch on my rusty screen door. 'Lemme in, Jenny. I brought wine. I mean . . . I know you quit, but this isn't really drinking as much as it's appreciation of art or history.'

'I don't need a drink, Richard.'

'I do.'

'Then have one.' Without thinking, I pulled my robe tighter around the boobs he bought years ago. 'That looks like a very nice wine.'

'It's the best wine within a hundred miles of here. It's all I could find.'

'Only the best,' I said.

'No, no, no . . . wait . . . no. That's not it. I love you. I've loved you since 1992, Jenny. We're meant to be together. We both know it. This is just a . . . was just a screw up, a bad, maybe unforgiveable screw up on my part, but you've got to admit . . . I admit that we're supposed to be together. We have three boys, a history, a future. And I'm sorry. Jesus Christ, I know I can't say that enough, but I'm sorry, Jenny. I'm so, so sorry, and I was wrong, and I want us to try again.' He seemed to remember the flowers, the ring. Holding them up to the screen, he said, 'C'mon, I'll even do this right. I'll get on my knees. I'll swear off women and alcohol, drugs, smokes, anything you need to feel right.' He blinked and tears slid in neat rivulets down his cheeks. Christ, even his tear ducts followed stage directions.

It was his finest performance to date, an award winner from a veteran actor with not one shred, one pinch of self-efficacy. My ex-husband confirmed for me, with his neatly-memorized script, his $15,000 ring, his $1,000 bottle of wine, that I'd been a blind, dough-headed fool for most of my adult life. This bullshit had worked on me again and again and again, and do you know what I felt?

Not pity. If I live long enough to have my life measured in plate-tectonic units by bearded geologists, I'll never pity him. Nope. Rather, I felt embarrassment. Steel barbs of cold humiliation latched on to my heart and began squeezing. This man has no idea that his actions impact those around him. I'll write that again, just because it feels important at this juncture in my evolution from a stupid child to a world-weary woman. (Heh, say *that* 200 times fast!)

This man has no idea that his actions impact those around him. He just plain flat doesn't get it. Sure, I'm having a rough go of things now, but in ten years I'll have the boys and our life together. Dumbass will have nothing.

And you know what saved me, Billy? The old cedar tree in that Hemingway story, 'The Big Two-Hearted River.' Do you remember that tree? You were so fired up about Nick's nap in the pine forest that you missed the cedar tree entirely. It's Nick's gateway, the Garden State

Parkway toll barrier delineating for him all the safe, comfortable, pleasant variables he can control and all the cold, dark, frightening variables he cannot.

My cedar looked a lot like a rusty screen door that slams on its spring like a judge's gavel. It separated me – the new me, the now me, the me who turned down a job because this shithead wouldn't split childcare costs for his own son – from every mistake I tallied as a twenty year old, every dumbass decision I made growing up, every scar I earned crashing headlong through life, half drunk and half horny and half convinced that I had this journey figured out. On my side of the screen I had poverty, but I also had my sea of yellow-green soybeans, my baseball field, my boys, and my hopes for a long life filled with challenges that made sense. On Richard's side I'd have money and security, travel, luxury and opulence, but I'd have to give up every scabbed-over lesson I learned in the past two years. And without demonstrating that he understood or even cared what he asked me to give up, Richard grinned, cried, begged, and expected that I'd roll over and thank God he'd shown up to save me.

I could have killed him. Jesus Christ, I could have broken that bottle of appalling wine over his head and forced him to eat the shards.

But I didn't. Thank God for cedar trees, half fallen across mountain streams. Who knew that a limp-wristed metaphor would pop up twenty years later to save my life?

Pretty ironic actually, to be saved on the porch of my pretend beach house just off my pretend baseball field by Ernest Hemingway, a womanizing alcoholic who loved baseball and the ocean.

Sonofabitch, but this has been one exciting lap around the sun, Billy Klein! How about you come join me for the next one? I sent Richard away, weeping and incoherent. It hurt my chest not to giggle as he backed down the porch steps; I actually got the hiccups from swallowing my need to piss myself laughing. When I turned from the screen door, I caught sight of that dry erase board I'd nailed to the kitchen wall. The words *I CAN* still legible in the upper-left corner. Whatever I'd written on there had been erased, however, to make room for one of Homer's masterpieces, his interpretation of an armadillo barfing up a bean burrito.

Or maybe a giraffe spawning a Prius.

I CAN. Yup.

As I've said before, here we are. I've scrolled through this inbox, and we've covered just about everything from microwaved Mike & Ikes to banana yellow tool boxes to the New York Football Giants' shocking 1981 victory over the Dallas Cowboys. I'm done. Turning Richard away cured me. I don't feel the need to write therapeutic messages to a twenty-year-old apostrophe. If I write to you again, it'll be snail mail with a stamp and a bit of Joan's fancy paper.

Until then, I'll be missing you. So long, Billy Klein.

With love,

Jennifer Cooper

Epilogue

'Or I might decide to just keep going and maybe invade Canada instead. Canada's this way, right?'

April 29

The 3:00 to 11:00 pump jockey at the Bergen County *Exxon* squints pointlessly against the glare as sunlight across new puddles blinds all of North Jersey. The rain has wandered into Connecticut, and cars on the Parkway pass with a wet shush rather than a dry hum. During the busy stretch, from 4:00 to 9:30, the highway's wet whispers will flatten to dry musings. 3 to 11 likes that transformation; although, he's often too busy to hear it happen. One of the morning crew, a slob named Karl, Kyle, maybe Kevin, has left a pair of cheap sunglasses beside the register. 3 to 11 borrows them, just until the sun throttles back or the clouds rally.

A silver Honda Odyssey turns off the highway: *2011 model.* It's a pump jockey Ninja skill.

The redhead is pretty, not sexy, in baggie basketball shorts and a battered Rutgers University sweatshirt. Her hair is stylish: flat, as if it's recently been ironed, and she wears pearls with matching stud earrings. She's too old for loud earrings or dangly hoops and appears to have spent hours on her hair and makeup and then borrowed clothes from her son's floor. When she piles out of the van, 3 to 11 discovers that she's also wearing fatigued Asics running shoes, untied, with no socks. They look as though they've carried her thousands of miles.

She's got Jersey plates; yet she still opens the door when she reaches Pump 5. Handing over her credit card, she asks, 'Can you fill it with Regular, please?'

'Sure, ma'am.' He's learned to be polite. Credit junkies don't tip, but what the hell, polite beats impolite any day. And there's no telling when one of these suburbanites might actually dial in the web address at the bottom of the receipt and say something nice about him. Not that anyone ever had, but it could happen. KarlKlyeKevin, the slob, hadn't yet finished the chapter on *Polite* and felt the manager's sting on his six-month eval. That had been a tense shift, waiting for KarlKyleKevin to return with an assault rifle and take care of business. 3 to 11 remembers the sunglasses and decides to put them back exactly where he found them.

He cranks open the tank, inserts the nozzle, starts the fuel. Through the side window, he sees a cocktail dress dangling from a hanger. Little and black; that's the rule his sisters follow like holy writ. This one's black, but not so little. The redhead's chosen well. She'll look good, but not offensive, wherever she's going. Too many older women try to wear the same style they pulled off at twenty-five. That's a mistake; they end up looking like cartoon characters. It's as if they don't give themselves credit for being attractive at forty or forty five. Do they truly believe men will be so blinded by the dress that they'll subtract twenty years from their date's age? Or maybe they wear those dresses for other women, just a way to shout, *See? I've still got it going on.*

Not that 3 to 11 has many cocktail-dress experiences firsthand. Working in Bergen County, he sees tens of thousands of affluent women roll through the Parkway stop, but he's never dated any. His dates wear flashy T.J. Maxx, off the rack, with noisy red or black patent leather shoes and are the sexiest women on Earth.

Rich guys can't understand that: a poor girl, cobbling together whatever she can to look good, *that's* sexy, no matter whether she's got it just like the magazine.

Through the windshield he watches the redhead scrape at a strangely-shaped splash of bird shit with a wet squeegee. It's impossible to get a sense for her body in that sweatshirt, but he can see that her hips are narrow, her calves shapely. Her boobs are hidden but still sharply enough at attention that they must have cost a small fortune.

That's another pump jockey Ninja skill: assessing silicone implants. What the hell, it's Bergen County.

He checks the pump, then hurries around front where the redhead works the squeegee like a professional. 'Let me help you with that, ma'am.'

'Oh, no, I've got it.' She grimaces and has no idea how absurd she looks. When she slips and nearly breaks a nail, she swears like a Newark sanitation truck driver.

'Ma'am?'

'Nope,' she scrubs with renewed determination. 'I almost got it.'

'He gotcha good, eh?'

Now she does pause, just to appreciate the silliness of her predicament. 'How is it possible that it's raining like the Old Testament for two hours, and within nine seconds of the sun coming out, I drive beneath the one seagull with diarrhea? How does that happen?'

'Just lucky, ma'am.' 3 to 11 offers a final time to scrape the guano off her windshield, but she refuses. He sidles back to the pump, tops off the tank, and returns her credit card. She passes him the squeegee and wipes her hands on her son's shorts. She checks her nails;

they're tipped with white polish, none smudged with seagull shit.

'Thanks,' she says. 'How long to Albany? That stupid woman on my phone says two more hours. Is that right? I hope she's lying. Sometimes she lies. Didja ever notice that?'

3 to 11 shrugs. 'I've never been to Albany. But it's that way, straight ahead.'

The redhead slips past him; she smells good. Poor girls don't smell like that.

'I know, but I always get turned around and backwards up in all those 287-87-Thruway-95-Tappan-Zee coils.' She tilts her head north. 'I've gotta have an extra twenty minutes for all my wrong turns.'

He closes the door when she gets buckled in. 3 to 11 is glad he's got no other customers; the redhead's amusing.

On the passenger seat, she's tossed a hairbrush, deodorant, an iPhone, two pairs of black leather shoes, one dull-colored with thin straps and one shiny with high heels. She's got a small, zip-up bag that must contain cosmetics, hairspray, and a dog-eared paperback the pump jockey doesn't recognize, *In Our Time* by Ernest Hemingway. She looks at him a moment, then grins. 'Wish me luck.'

He frowns, offers it up as a question. 'Good . . . luck?'

She shifts into DRIVE, explains, 'I have a date later.'

'Ah . . . okay . . . that's good,' he returns the smile. 'Good luck.'

'Or I might decide to just keep going and maybe invade Canada instead. Canada's this way, right?'

'Straight ahead, ma'am.' 3 to 11 watches as she merges on to the Parkway and hurries north for the New York line.

Afterword & Acknowledgements

Of the times in my life when I've thought, 'I don't know anything at all about women,' two embarrassing instances shine bright in my memory.

The first took place when I was a graduate student, before my wife and I were married. I remember walking across campus, feeling my chest tighten up, and having a miniature panic attack. Rather than duck into the nearest bar to ride out the storm, I hustled to the library, found one of the research specialists behind the counter, and confessed, 'I'm getting married, and I don't know the first thing about women.'

I swear that I'm not making this up.

The librarian laughed then frowned skeptically when she realized I was serious. Over two decades later I can't recall her name, but within an hour she had me seated in a comfortable chair reading Mary Belenky and Carol Gilligan. I can only imagine the embellishments and hyperbole when she shared my awkward dilemma with her friends. Truth be told, I don't care. There I was, sweaty, breathless, and in a state of utter distress. She steered me through the stacks, dropped books onto her cart, and left me content to read for the weekend, absorbing as much as I could in a basement carrel scrawled all over with misogynistic Guns N' Roses lyrics.

Nope, not kidding.

The next time the Universe slapped me silly was twenty-one weeks into Karen's second pregnancy when I learned that we were having a baby girl. I went to the ultrasound appointment knowing it would be a boy. I wasn't confident; I just knew. We planned to call him Ben, and I already had great seats chosen for the night he pitched his first game against the Yankees at Fenway. I'd been a good dad to my son and felt that I could do it again. A baby girl wasn't an option. I simply didn't fire off any little X sperm, just three hundred million Ys every time.

When the technician said, 'I'm not seeing a penis here,' I demanded that she approach from another angle, get a better view, perhaps from the side, the back, or the roof across the street. All the while I frantically splashed that goopy stuff on Karen's distended belly and waited for confirmation that Ben and I were headed for Fenway

Park.

No penis.

We searched for a long time, humoring me.

Today, my daughter possesses more square footage of my heart and soul than anyone ever possibly could, but that afternoon I almost shoved Karen off the examination gurney to create a soft place for me to pass out. When I could speak, I looked at the technician and said sincerely, 'I can't have a girl. I don't know anything about women.'

It's true. Karen can confirm it for you. Watching me blanch and sway dizzily on my feet was quite a confidence booster for her, with a half-gallon of that smeary glop across her belly.

Not my finest hour, I admit. So I spent the next month tearing through *Vulnerable But Invincible*, *Pregnancy for Dummies*, and my favorite, *The Girlfriend's Guide to Pregnancy*, because Vicki Iovine is honest about all the farting, the peeing, the food cravings, and the mucus plug. Everyone deserves fair warning when awaiting a mucus plug.

So why write it?

For me, the most compelling character in American stories today is the forty-year-old, married, professional, college-educated, mother, friend, athlete, sibling, and daughter, working from dawn to dark at her career, family, marriage, friendships, fitness, and if she can scrape up ten spare minutes, maybe a creative passion as well. She's expected to be thankful for all of the perks of being a woman in the twenty-first century, the realization of powerful ideas generations of hard-fighting women imagined fifty and a hundred years ago.

I couldn't do it all.

I *can't* do it all.

My wife does.

I'm responsible for a list of pretty important things around our house. Karen and I share as many aspects of our lives together as possible. I'm open minded and want to live in a world where my wife's (and my daughter's) dreams can be actualized.

But I'm not kidding myself. I couldn't manage, every day, what she handles without a wrinkle.

Nope. We both know it, but when I ask her to hand over a few of the tedious, wearisome tasks, she nods, smiles, and keeps a tight grip on her entire list. So do my sisters, my female colleagues in education, and most of the women who agreed to be interviewed as I cobbled together Jennifer's story.

That's what makes these women captivating for me and hopefully for you as you read this novel. If I've done my job well, you'll agree with me. If I've tanked, please blame me and not the folks kind enough to point me in the right direction along the way.

A legion of patient women (and a few willing guys) helped me to get this story scribbled. I've spent the past two years chatting with friends, colleagues, family members, even a handful of irritated strangers as I clarified ideas trying to take shape in my imagination or checked interminable details. Granted, this was often boring for my female friends and coworkers. No one wakes up hoping for a barrage of insipid questions about daycare and Pull-Ups.

So for reading, editing, suggesting, rereading, and answering personal questions, thanks to: Mike Hanley, Allie Kieffer, Carla Drew, Lindsey Walton, Artise Gill, Adrienne Phillips, Erika Nichols, Milt Johns, Scott Howard, Sara Brooks, Megan Hostutler, Kathy Smaltz, Cheryl Porter, Dan and Michelle Nemerow, and Deb Lane, who isn't really my therapist but should be. I owe a debt of gratitude to my sisters, Saburnia and Christine, for appointing no topic *Off Limits For Discussion* and to Nancy Schumacher and Laura Senier, who made me work with aspects of Jennifer's personality and background I hadn't considered. I didn't take all of their advice but probably should have.

Thanks to Uncle G and Kyle Pratt for keeping me connected with the rest of the planet, and thanks to June Forte, everyone at Write By the Rails and the Prince William County Arts Council for taking a risk with my poetry. I thank my wife and kids for their patience with me and the hours I spend locked in our basement typing. And thanks to everyone in 1105 for their support and enthusiasm.

Finally, special thanks to Matt Randon, Tom Nichols, Neil Beech, and Kathy Kieffer.